Where the Night Never Ends

A Prohibition Era Novel

By award-winning author of 'Surviving the Fatherland'

ANNETTE OPPENLANDER

First published by Annette Oppenlander, 2019
First Edition
www.annetteoppenlander.com
Text copyright: Annette Oppenlander 2019
ISBN: 978-3-948100-01-8
All rights reserved.
Library of Congress Control Number: 2019901588
Editing: Yellow Bird Editors
Design: http://www.fiverr.com/akira007
© 2019 Annette Oppenlander

ALSO BY ANNETTE OPPENLANDER

A Different Truth *(Historical Mystery – Vietnam War Era)*
Escape from the Past: The Duke's Wrath I *(Time-travel Adventure Trilogy)*
Escape from the Past: The Kid II
Escape from the Past: At Witches' End III
47 Days: How Two Teen Boys Defied the Third Reich
(Historical Novelette)
Surviving the Fatherland: A True Coming-of-age Love Story
Set in WWII
(Historical Biographical Fiction)
Everything We Lose: A Civil War Novel of Hope, Courage and
Redemption *(Historical Fiction).*

QUOTES

"Prohibition only drives drunkenness behind doors and into dark places, and does not cure it or even diminish it." –Mark Twain

"Prohibition has made nothing but trouble." –Al Capone

ACKNOWLEDGMENTS

Had it not been for the many supporting and positive people in my life, writing would've never become by fulltime profession—a profession I love as much, if not more, today.

I want to call out a few of the many friends who have been instrumental in my writer career. Thank you so much to my Bloomington SCBWI writers' group, particularly Teresa, Sherry, Tanya and Keiko. I also thank my writer friends, Dianne, Dave and Susan. I would also like to thank my readers who sent me wonderfully encouraging notes and comments, have left incredible reviews and continue recommending my books to others. Lastly, I thank my husband and best friend, Ben, for always believing in me.

CHAPTER ONE

December 8, 1924
Sam

When I was little, I believed all people lived in families—warm spaces full of laughter and the rich aroma of pasta sauce bubbling on the stove. I thought I'd stay cocooned forever in the knowledge my father, Luca Bruno, would take me every day to the market or the Italian grocer, my hand securely tucked into his as he stopped to chat with shop owners and neighbors.

That was when we lived in a two-room flat overlooking a garden plot, Papa growing tomatoes large as baseballs against the sun-warmed brick walls of our home and Mamma welcoming neighbors to homemade *Apfelstreusel* on Sunday afternoons.

It was a memory I didn't allow myself often because the joy I felt was always snuffed out by the realization I'd never experience such happiness again. These days I preferred to keep my dreams locked up as securely as the rich hide gold coins in a bank vault.

It was easier that way.

The rap on the door was quick and hard—demanding.

Alarmed, I looked at my mother, ignoring the dread rearing up inside my belly. We never had visitors, yet I realized who it was before he spoke.

"Open up. I know you're in there."

Mamma shook her head, her eyes, normally the light blue of an early spring sky, clouded with fear. I knew it well. Lately, my mother was afraid of one thing or another all the time.

"I'm going to kick in the door and you'll pay for it," the voice outside threatened.

I slowly straightened and took a step toward the door. Then another.

"Samantha!" Mamma's voice trembled and she shook her head. My feet stubbornly continued toward the door.

When had things changed?

I didn't remember a day, only Mamma's expression the weeks after my brother, Angelo, didn't return. Her eyes had filled with something less alive—a darkening of features, a weariness that extended to everything she touched.

It was as if Mamma's chest was filled with two animals. One was a fierce lion that roared and fought. It protected. The other was a timid, washed-out mouse, yielding and afraid. Insignificant. In the beginning after Papa was lost, the lion had taken care of Angelo and me. Found smaller quarters we could afford. Visited rich folks to ask for washing jobs. Negotiated. Bought food at the grocer.

I loved Mamma, but I hated the mouse.

I sped up and yanked open the door just as the massive bulk of Mr. Talbott rushed forward. Taken by surprise, he half stumbled, half fell into the room, coming to a stop in front of the ironing board Mamma cowered behind. I bit my lips to hide a smirk. Too bad the landlord hadn't fallen on his face.

"Mrs. Bruno." Talbott, nostrils flared and cheeks reddened, rose to his impressive height once more. "You know why I'm here. Almost three months behind." He gave our shabby room a once over before his deep-set eyes came to rest on me. "I need at least half of the ten dollars you owe or you've got to move out." He extended a palm, each of his fingers the size of a small sausage.

"Mr. Talbott, I'm working on it." Mamma pointed a wash worn forefinger at the mountain of laundry waiting to be ironed. "Two families owe me for several months' washes. Times are hard. Everyone is behind. I will—"

"No more excuses, Mrs. Bruno." Talbott's gaze returned to me.

The fat man gave me the creeps, his skin pasty as lard and his eyes taking my clothes off. It was indecent to say the least. Not even the men lounging in the streets these days stared like that.

"You have until tomorrow." Talbott turned toward the door when he hesitated and, for a man of his size, swiftly stepped to the fireplace. "What do have we here?" Above hung our most prized possession, a Model 12 Winchester shotgun, the only thing left from my father.

Every week Mamma took down the gun and cleaned and polished it like other people polished their family silver. Her softened hands caressed the barrel and stock, her gaze far away as if she could somehow find her husband in the distance of her memories.

Talbott ripped the Winchester off its shelf and nodded approvingly before tucking the gun under his arm. "You'll get it back when you pay." He rushed out the door, leaving behind a scent of stale cigar smoke and bacon grease.

As Mamma sagged on the threadbare sofa that also served as our eating bench, I threw shut the door. "The dirty pig," I yelled.

"Samantha!"

"He stole our gun."

Mamma shook her head and opened her mouth. But no words escaped. She sat slumped over, a beaten down woman of forty who looked sixty. The mouse was back.

Trying to contain the steam building inside me, I folded a bed sheet and draped it across a wicker basket stacked high with neatly pressed linens. I'd blow up if I didn't do something. Who cared about washing when all I wanted was my family back and, of course, to cook again with Papa? Not just any cooking but homemade Italian pastas and rich sauces. You see, I always know what's in a dish. I can tell what spices are used and how things are put together. And sometimes I think I know what's inside a person too—if they are sweet or nasty or angry or plain sad.

I swallowed, my mouth bitter. We didn't even have enough food to make a decent soup.

"I'm taking this to the Winslow's. It's time they pay up." When Mamma remained silent, I tucked the basket under my arm and slipped out the door. The loathsome landlord had disappeared, but the foul cigar still reeked. Three dollars a month rent was a fortune for the one-room apartment. We washed and did dishes and laundry in the enamel sink, while the fireplace either smoldered or sent icy drafts into our midst. Most of the space was taken up by drying laundry because this time of year it was too cold and damp

3

to dry anything on the lines stretched between buildings. I hated it. Hated the smell of damp clothes, the humid walls on the verge of mold, and Mamma's dedication to make every piece perfect.

Taking a deep breath, I descended the grimy stairs and entered the street. The Over-the-Rhine neighborhood of Cincinnati had seen better days. Seventy years ago, mostly German immigrants, including Mamma's parents, had flooded the area, bringing with them the secret of making outstanding beer.

Special strains of yeast produced pilsners, ales and lagers. By the early 1900s, more than forty thousand people crowded in, employed one way or another by the dozens of breweries or those who produced kegs and other equipment, and the bars, restaurants and shops to feed everyone. Houses cramped together, three or four-story brick buildings next to one another, hulking structures that shaded mud-covered roads.

Streets had bustled with horse carriages, people hawking cheap meals, and women and children going about their errands. There were bars at every corner and in-between, a perpetual odor of alcohol, simmering stews, brewer's yeast, and swine manure enveloping it all.

Then World War I hit. And by 1916, being German was a mistake. That was the first time I'd noticed Mamma growing fearful, no matter Papa fought *against* the Germans. People carrying German names were liable to be shunned or attacked. German was dropped from school curriculums. *Bremenstraße* became *Republic Street*. *German Street* turned into *English Street*. Many German immigrants changed their names or moved.

Not three years later, prohibition followed. And Over-the-Rhine grew into a ghost town.

In the blink of an eye, our neighborhood fell apart. Large breweries like Christian Moerlein closed, shops were boarded up, and more families moved away. That is, those who could. What remained were the unfortunate, the weak and the old. Despair set in. Nearly five years of it.

I picked my way across crumbling bricks, broken sidewalks and piled-up waste. The neighborhood smelled different these days. The yeasty aroma of fermenting beer was gone along with the sharp tang of freshly sawn wood and the delicious scent of eateries offering workers lunch and dinner stews. Now it smelled of dung, the stench of pigs living their last minutes on earth. And something else: decay—a rot that began in the abandoned tenements, the empty warehouses and hollowed breweries and extended to the streets where it spread and blanketed all.

I ignored the hoots flying at me from various house entries where men sat idle, playing games or staring into space. Their eyes reflected the emptiness of the streets and the loss of their own purpose, a man's worth working an honest job. When they whistled I often wondered if it was from sheer boredom or if I really looked attractive to them.

Even at barely eighteen, there wasn't much to see. My black hair, courtesy of my Italian father, hung in a single braid between my shoulder blades, and I shaded my face with a battered slouch hat I'd found in an abandoned shop. I wore a pair of second-hand pants of heavy wool, a striped cotton shirt and vest and a coat that had previously belonged to my brother, Angelo.

I let out a sigh. How I missed him.

Three years older, Angelo had taken care of Mamma and me. Until things got really bad two years ago and he'd begun working as a bootlegger.

I looked up in surprise. The Winslow's villa was straight ahead and I hadn't even noticed how I got here. That happened a lot these days. I had to quit the stupid daydreaming.

"May I help you?" The maid curtsied, but when she saw it was me, she extended an arm. "I'll take it from here."

I held tight onto the basket, catching a whiff of Mamma's laundry soap rising up from the neatly pressed stack. "I need to speak with Mrs. Winslow first."

"She is busy."

I stood unmoving, eyeing the maid with her cream puff headdress. "Then I'll return later…*with* the laundry."

The maid's cheeks began to glow. She'd obviously taken liberty to avoid the wrath of her mistress. "Please wait a moment." The door smacked shut an inch from my nose, but I didn't budge.

A minute passed. Another minute. Three.

"You wish to see me?" Mrs. Winslow, a portly woman in a soft brown dress and the fashionable chin-length hairstyle of the twenties, wrinkled her nose in distaste.

"I'm delivering the laundry," I shouted. "And collecting for two *late* months."

I detected the tiniest wince at the word 'late.' Sure enough, after a furtive glance at the passersby, Mrs. Winslow ushered me inside.

In the gloominess of the unlit corridor, I detected a whiff of liquor on the woman's lips. It was rumored that the Winslow's, like most wealthy families, had a well-stocked cellar and threw plenty of parties. Mister Winslow was somehow involved in bootlegging, an activity many able men had resorted to after the shutdown of the breweries.

I fixed my gaze on the woman. "You owe five dollars plus the seventy-five cents for today."

"I'm astounded at your manners." Mrs. Winslow lifted the cigarette she'd been holding to her penciled-in lips and inhaled. "I shall let your mother know next time." She took hold of the basket's rim. "Now if you will excuse me."

Taken by surprise, I yanked hard, dislodging the basket from her hand. Time slowed as finely pressed blouses, table linens and men's shirts sailed through the air and came to rest in a heap on the black and white checkered tile floor, stained with my own muddy footprints.

"What have you done?" Mrs. Winslow's voice was shrill. "My things. Look at this mess. Help."

We're going to lose our home, I wanted to scream. Instead I swept up the laundry, stuffed it back into the basket, and rushed out the door with it while the cries behind me rose into a high-pitched scream that tore at my eardrums. Over my dead body would the rich lady get her *things.* We'd have to rewash and iron everything, remove the spots. It meant extra shifts after dinner and tomorrow, extra coal to heat the room, but I'd not give up this basket until the nasty woman paid up.

One more day until the landlord returned. All I needed was one more day to come up with enough rent money.

The December drizzle had crept beneath my skin by the time I approached my apartment building, the light above a weak gray. In front of it a horde of neighbors swirled like a dark cloud, their tones muted, their heads low.

In no mood to chat, I pushed past, my mind on the task of explaining the dirtied laundry to my mother, not to mention my inability to collect.

"Sam?" A voice cried.

Then another..."Oh, Sam. She's here...her daughter." Voices

mingled and grew quiet as bodies parted like curtains in front of me. Strangers' hands patted me as my gaze fell on the still form lying on the sidewalk. A bloodied rag had been tied around the person's forehead, but I knew instantly that it was Mamma...and that she was gone.

"What...happened?" I managed, taking a step closer. Mamma lay on the side of the road, her legs and shoes coated in muck. Her face remained strangely white and clean, with a trickle of blood running along her temple and from her right ear. She looked straight up, a surprised expression—or was it longing—in her eyes.

"She walked into the street. Right into my carriage." The man who'd spoken kneaded his cap between his fingers. "She never looked."

I sank to my knees and straightened my mother's hair. A wail rose in the back of my throat, so strange, so foreign, it didn't sound like my voice at all. Mamma was dead. Something tugged at my insides, a great rupturing.

Dead.

I didn't remember how I got back into my room...on the sofa with the basket of precious laundry next to me. At some point I shoved it to the floor, clothes tumbling across the worn carpet. Mrs. Winslow could go to hell.

I curled up in the freezing apartment and stared at the peeling walls. I was alone. As alone as I'd never been before. They'd taken Mamma away. Soon some undertaker would demand payment for a coffin and slimy Talbott would return for the rent.

Panic gnawed at my gut like a worm on a rotting apple. What was I going to do? The fire had long gone out. Darkness descended, and with it the cold. Voices crept through crooked walls: assorted neighbors going about their business, children begging for dinner, women welcoming their husbands after work, grandmothers cooing babies to sleep.

It made the silence inside the room...inside me... unbearable. Yet, I couldn't move, couldn't kindle a fire or scrounge for a piece of bread. I sat, knees pulled to my chest, like a frozen statue. I couldn't even muster the energy to cry.

Sometime in the early morning I fell asleep.

A knock awoke me. The door flew open before I could gather myself or find the strength to leave the sofa.

"I just heard." Talbott strode into the room as if he lived

there. "What are you going to do, girl?"

I stared at the fat man with his greedy eyes. That's what I'd been trying to figure out all night. What indeed was I going to do? Mamma was dead. My father gone. I had no money and…

"You can't stay! Got any relatives? Aunts, uncles, cousins? Didn't you have a brother?" Talbott edged closer. "I may be able to find work for you. My son-in-law owns a club. A swell young woman like you, you know…"

"Know what?"

"A gentleman's club." Talbott's expression changed, his gaze raking across my body. "He'd take care of you."

In my vision appeared women in clingy dresses, being groped by wrinkly old men. It took effort to lift my head, my body reluctant to follow. Talbott hovered within a foot of me and licked his lips as a poisonous cloud of cigar stink descended on me.

Alarm bells went off.

I jumped up at the exact moment Talbott's paw aimed for my breast and a whiff of whiskey hit my face.

The alarm bells grew deafening. *Get to the door.*

Stepping back, I pulled out of reach and maneuvered around the ironing board, past the fireplace.

Talbott wheezed like a steam locomotive as he cut off my escape. The ironing board crashed to the floor. I stepped back again, keeping my eyes on the approaching tower of a man whose cheeks flamed like overripe tomatoes. He'd snuff me out like wind a candle.

I feigned a move to the right, then turned abruptly and made for the exit. There in the doorframe leaned Mamma's gun. Talbott probably loved showing it off.

"You little witch," Talbott heaved behind me. "You owe me."

I snatched the shotgun and hurried down the corridor, half flying, half jumping down the stairs.

Outside.

Away.

Before I hurt someone.

CHAPTER TWO

Sam

A feeble sun crept across the sky as I sprinted down the street. I zigzagged through alleys and along deserted roads and came to a stop on Vine Street downtown. I stood, a motionless statue, unable to take a step or even move my head. Shop owners were just opening their doors, sliding aside cast-iron gates. A man with a bowler hat unlocked the portal to the Fifth Third National Bank of Cincinnati.

My nose stung with cold and my stomach churned with hunger. The last meal had been yesterday's lunch with Mamma, a watery soup of cornmeal and onions. What was I going to do?

Terror rose from my stomach like acid. I realized that despite her weakness, Mamma had provided me with a home and place to belong. She'd loved me. My eyes burned with unshed tears. It hadn't even been twenty-four hours and the agony of missing her was like an oozing wound that would never heal. It surprised me. Until last night I'd often loathed the way Mamma did things. That she didn't complain more. Fight harder.

None of that mattered now.

Move. You always think better when you walk. And so with utter slowness that rivaled the speed of an ancient woman, I took a step. Then another. Ignoring the curious stares of street vendors and business people, I crept along the awakening street.

Until my gaze fell on Miller's drugstore and I stopped again. Square bottles with a brown liquid lined the shop window. A sign

9

next to them proclaimed the benefits of herb tonic for your health. Somewhere in the recesses of my mind, something clicked.

Before he left, my brother, Angelo, had worked for George Remus, a wealthy lawyer and bootlegger who was rumored to be making millions with the dispensary of medicinal alcohol. Two years ago, Angelo, frustrated by the lack of job opportunities, had hooked up with a friend who in turn had worked for Remus. Soon after, Angelo had disappeared in the evenings and gone to sleep when I woke up.

Around that time, things had gotten better at home. We'd eaten well, Angelo bringing home flour and eggs, tomatoes and garlic, even red wine to brighten our meals. He'd taught me to make pasta from scratch, mixing the dough, kneading and cutting. After a while I'd created my own shapes and flavors, added thyme and basil from the little patch of yard, spinach and tomatoes, and even bits of cheese. Soon everyone in the neighborhood wanted to taste my dishes, even paid for them.

Mamma hadn't approved of Angelo's new habit of carrying a flask filled with whiskey, apparently a perk he received working for George Remus.

I stared at the bottles and wrappings in the pharmacy's window. It was crazy, but there was only one thing I could do.

The doorbell jingled happily as I entered the gloom. A man with a pointed grayish beard stood behind a counter and looked at me expectantly.

"I need to see Mr. Remus," I blurted. "You know where he lives?" Angelo had told me how Remus 'owned' all the pharmacies, legally supplying whiskey masked as medicine.

The pharmacist wrinkled his nose. "Little miss, he has no time for the likes of you."

I cleared my throat. Stupid man. *I'm no little miss.* Boys never got treated this way. "Please tell me his address."

"Unless you buy something, leave. Or I shall call the police."

Imagining aiming my shotgun at the man, I hurried outside. The smells of freshly baked bread wafted up my nose. Next door a display of breads, rolls and elaborately decorated cakes drew me in. I abruptly turned the other way. My pockets were as empty as my stomach. Next door, an old woman was sweeping the entrance of a hat store.

"Good morning, Ma'am." I did a little curtsy. "I wonder if

you know where George Remus lives. You know, the lawyer."

The old woman blinked a couple of times and rested herself on her broom. "You in trouble, girl?"

I shook my head.

"Mister Remus bought the old Lackman mansion a few years back. West Eighth and Hermosa. Everyone knows that," the woman said.

When I hesitated, she shook her broomstick toward the west. "That way, three miles."

"Thank you," I said, but the woman mumbled to herself and resumed sweeping.

I walked back the way I'd come, past the familiar streets of Over-the-Rhine I'd called home. Twice I snuck into an entry when I thought I saw the hulking figure of Talbott who owned half the tenements in the neighborhood and was no doubt chasing other unfortunates.

The Lackman mansion stood back from the street with a long driveway off to the side. I slowed and then stopped. I had to be crazy. These were rich people. Rich beyond imagination. Angelo had spoken of lavish parties and gifts to guests that included diamond watches and brand-new cars for the ladies.

With my torn and splattered wool pants, blackened fingernails, and oversized coat, I looked like a filthy no-good thug—a nobody.

And yet. What did I have to lose? I'd already lost everything I held dear. There was nothing else. Let them throw me out. Let them laugh.

I sucked in air and straightened my shoulders.

"Yes?" The butler's gaze remained steadfast on my face, a fact I was grateful for.

"I'm here to see Mister Remus."

"You have an appointment?"

"I...no. I'm here about my brother, Angelo Bruno."

The right eyebrow lifted, seemingly independent of the rest of the butler's face. "Wait, please."

To my surprise the door opened seconds later. "This way." The maid's dress was immaculate: black dress, white apron and a tiny headband like a white tiara.

"Angelo Bruno is your brother?" The voice was deep and resonant, used to being heard and obeyed. The speaker sat in a wicker chair, a newspaper folded on his knees. His face was square and fleshy with a pointed chin and penetrating eyes.

I stopped ten feet before the chair. I was in some kind of conservatory. Large ferns and purple orchids lined tall windows. "Yes, Sir. I'm looking for him. My...our mother died yesterday."

"Remus was hoping you could tell *him* where he is."

My mind went blank. Who was this fellow? "But he said he went to Chicago for Mr. Remus."

"That's what Remus thought."

I looked around. "Maybe I should speak to Mr. Remus directly?"

The man's eyes widened. "You're speaking to him."

I did a double take at the rich silky tie, the expensive wool jacket, and the shining black and white wingtips. The man might be rich, but he sure sounded crazy. "He's not been home since...since April," I said aloud.

A frown creased Remus's forehead. Had he thought Angelo was hiding out in our room?

"Remus hasn't heard from your brother since he left. Remus sent him to deliver a message to one of his associates."

The room began to rotate, slowly swinging from side to side—the edges blurred. Angelo was truly missing.

Likely in Chicago.

There were gangsters in Chicago.

Likely he was dead.

Like Mamma.

You're alone.

The floor rushed up at me. Something clattered and splintered. Mosaic-tiled flowers pressed against my cheek, keeping me from melting into the ground. I wanted to close my eyes, yet they remained open—staring.

Far away, a bell rang. Steps approached and I felt myself lifted into a chair.

Though my body refused to move and my gaze was fixed on a pot with a wispy fern, I clearly heard, "Sir, I believe she fainted." It was the butler from earlier. "Not sure what's wrong with her. She does seem quite thin."

I concentrated on my breath as feeling slowly returned to my limbs. How could I be so weak and fall apart in front of this wealthy, powerful man? More voices whispered, nothing I understood, but in the tone swung concern.

At last my mind obeyed, and I was able to move my head. Not six feet away sat George Remus, now buried again in his newspaper. One maid was sweeping up shards of a vase that I had obviously taken to the floor with me. The butler was gone. A second girl was setting out fresh rolls, strawberry jam and butter, the aroma so strong, I sniffed and swallowed with a gurgle. I always knew what was cooking in people's kitchens by my nose. In Over-The-Rhine it was mostly cabbage, potatoes and bits of pork belly. This place smelled like beef roast and steaks, rich buttery sauces, and sugar cakes.

The newspaper slowly sank as Remus's eyes met mine.

"I could go and find him," I said as I forced my attention away from the food spread. "Please, Sir. He's all I've got left."

"Leave business to men," Remus said. "It's dangerous. You have any idea who is running Chicago? Ever hear of Mr. Torrio, Al Capone, and the North Side Gang? It's no place for a lone girl."

"But my brother—"

"No discussion." His gaze turned to my side, where the Winchester leaned against the armrest. "Better get rid of that before you hurt yourself."

Heat crept into my cheeks. I hadn't intended for anyone to see my shotgun. But worse was how dismissive the man sounded. I was tired of being told what I could and couldn't do. With effort I straightened, tucked the gun beneath my coat, and took a step toward the exit. "I'm going then," I mumbled.

At the door, the maid from earlier curtsied and handed me a paper sack of considerable heft. "Miss, I'm supposed to give you this."

I was too numb to say anything. Why hadn't I asked for specifics about my brother's message...who was the associate in Chicago? Had Angelo delivered the message at all? Remus wasn't going to help. I was just a girl. Useless. Weak.

I crept along the sidewalk when an automobile, turning into the Remus villa, honked at me. That's when I remembered my right hand, still holding the paper sack. Whatever it was, it weighed several pounds.

Sinking onto the curb I opened the bag. Inside were two loaves of bread, a hard salami, a piece of hard yellow cheese, a fried chicken breast, a jar of candied peaches and a pint bottle of *Old*

Taylor whiskey. 'For medicinal purposes only' it said on the label. I cried out, tore a piece from the bread and bit into the chicken.

Perfection. In my mouth. Fireworks of flavor. All too soon, I stopped, reminding myself that I'd better ration, that there wouldn't be anymore of this any time soon.

But the strength was returning to my body and my mind was able to think again. Two things were obvious:

George Remus was nicer than he appeared.

And Angelo was truly missing.

CHAPTER THREE

Sam

I awoke in the early morning, my bones chilled as if they could fracture. I stomped back and forth in the abandoned lot until an inkling of warmth returned to my feet and hands. Remembering the sack from yesterday, I pinched my nose and took a drink from the whiskey. I shook myself as the liquid edged a fiery trail down my throat and gathered heat in my middle.

I'd made up my mind to leave.

What about Papa's favorite cooking pot made from cast-iron? And his knife used for cutting ingredients, Mamma's quilt that carried her scent? Should I return and check? Visit my girlfriend, Helen, who lived on the same block? We'd gone to school together, but Helen worked in a canning factory six days a week because her father worked there too.

No, I couldn't risk it. Talbott had no doubt taken over my apartment and everything in it. Or he was lying in wait. There was no telling what he'd do if he caught me.

Straightening my achy knees, I stumbled onto the street and turned south. Frost covered the muddy trail and puddles. I filled my lungs because the air was almost bearable this morning, not yet soiled with manure from the daily herding of pigs to slaughter and the neglected dirty skin of men out of work.

I'd go search for my brother. He was bound to be in Chicago and he had to be alive. I was sure of it. Why else had there been that mysterious *Chicago Tribune* newspaper in the mailbox? It had only happened once—it couldn't be a coincidence. But for some reason Angelo had chosen not to return, not even write. Something big had to have happened, something that had scared Angelo into abandoning mighty George Remus, abandoning Mamma and me. If there was any chance he was still there, I had to find him.

Only when the rail yard came into view did I realize I knew nothing about traveling on trains. In my cluttered brain, I'd figured to catch a free train north. How else was I going to get there without money? Buses required tickets. Walking took weeks and provisions I didn't have.

Hundreds of cargo wagons stretched in every direction, seemingly parked helter-skelter along miles of rails. Where they went was anybody's guess. There was a chill in the air, a frigid wind whistling along the tracks. It carried none of the filthy odor I knew from my neighborhood, but something unfamiliar and hostile. I tucked my coat around me, the shotgun a comfortable weight beneath my armpit. I'd fashioned a loop into the lining, the butt of the gun resting in the inner seam of my coat.

Angelo's blue eyes, so much like my own, appeared in my vision. I angrily wiped a sleeve across my face and climbed over the first rails.

I'd heard of hobos, men crisscrossing the country in search of jobs. Surely one of them knew how to find Chicago. I'd simply ask directions.

"Look what we gots here," a voice snickered.

"Is the girly lost?" another chimed in.

"She needs a fella to help her out," a third voice said as the man attached to it stepped into my way. "Where to, doll?" His grin exposed a graveyard of foul teeth. There was no telling how old the man was, his face hidden behind a jungle of beard and months worth of grime.

I stopped abruptly, hugging the sack with my remaining supplies to my chest. Unless I threw everything down and had space and time to wrestle out my shotgun, I didn't stand a chance.

"What you got in the sack?" Another man dressed in an assortment of shirts and jackets snatched at the bag so quickly, I had no time to react. This time the alarm bells inside me rang up a storm. *Get out now. Run.*

Before I could move back, an arm snaked around my neck.

"What an adorable songbird we gots ourselves."

A horrible stench of rotten bones and unwashed skin assaulted my nose as I watched helplessly how the men tore open the sack. One ripped off a piece of bread, the nourishment I'd so carefully rationed while the other took a whiff of the bottle before gulping down a quarter.

"Hey, hey, share some, will you?" the man holding Sam from behind said. "Always time for that *after* we take care of this here sweetheart. He sniffed. "Hmmm, smells fresh as a newborn babe."

I felt a hand crawl up my thigh, slime its way past my bottom. Any second the man would make contact with the shotgun I kept pressed under my arm.

"Leave me be," I cried. "I'm going to Chicago."

"Hear that, boys," the man with all the shirts cackled. "This dolly is a *world traveler.*"

"We'll give you something to travel with," her attacker said. The other men sniggered. They reminded me of aged vultures with wrinkly necks, hopping around their prey.

Without warning the arm around my throat tightened. The air stopped. My vision blurred…the graveyard teeth wiggled. No telling what they'd do if I passed out. No telling what they'd do with me awake.

"One more sip," the second thug said. As he lifted the pint to his mouth, something crashed on his head and the bottle exploded on the rocks below. The other man who'd had his nose in Sam's bag sank to the ground from a vicious blow to the knees. I was pushed forward as the foul man behind me cried out.

I never heard what he said because my attention was on the fellow with the baseball-like club who swirled between them like a dervish and now motioned me to follow.

"Come on," he panted before turning on his heels and climbing across the coupler connecting two railcars.

By the time I reached the other side, the dervish was already thirty yards ahead. Behind me men swore and spit and …definitely gave chase. Without another thought, I sprinted after the man with the club.

The next moment he was gone from sight. I followed and slid underneath a car. The club carrier was still ahead, but the distance was growing. Grimacing, I straightened and urged on my unwilling legs to race after him. My pursuers were on the other side of the carriage. They wouldn't give up. Not now.

My body was weak from lack of food, the bulky shotgun stiff at my side. What good did it do me if I had no time to stop and aim? I only had a couple of shells anyway, the only two that had been in the gun when I'd stolen it back from Talbott.

The fellow with the club disappeared once again. This time he crawled over a platform. I slid across, but when I climbed down the other side, my coat got stuck on a rusty corner. I pulled hard, swearing at the tough wool.

Behind me the three men scrambled into sight. Graveyard teeth raged.

The dervish reappeared, and with practiced zeal sliced through my coat while mumbling something like "girls." Once again free, I turned just in time to see the first of the brutes approach the platform.

I urged my legs to keep pace, and this time it worked. When the fellow in front slid underneath yet another car, I was right there. We ran twenty more yards before the man crept back beneath the same train and crouched low. As I followed, he placed a forefinger on his lips and shook his head. Not daring to move, I squatted and gave a nod. I finally had a chance to take a closer look. The man's face was half hidden beneath a wide brimmed hat, revealing strong jaws with brownish whiskers. He couldn't be much older than Angelo.

Steps approached to our right. "...little whore...I'll show her...tear her limbs off..."

I shuddered as the footsteps reemerged on the left. My savior motioned me to follow the way we'd come. We crawled beneath another train, then another. Then up the line and across another platform.

My breath grew ragged. I lost track. Stars appeared at the edge of my vision, but the man with the club still ran. He turned for a split second, spitting, "Hurry," before continuing.

That's when I saw it. Just ahead on the right, a cargo train moved out of the yard. Wheels screeched. Somewhere up front, a locomotive chugged. Acrid smoke bit my face and invaded my nostrils.

Ahead, the man with the club vaulted into the open door of one of the moving wagons. The train rolled faster and my lungs bucked. Behind me, steps grew audible. Then shouts. "Get her."

The thugs were back and gaining...

18

Ahead, the dervish's face became visible. "Come on, you can do it."

I sprinted...faster.

I had to.

An arm grabbed me from the open hold. As I toppled into the car and something clattered to the floor next to me, the noise behind me faded. A door was thrown shut and it grew dark.

No, black.

"Girl, you've got to learn to run better," a voice said.

My head whirled. The fellow had some nerve. I'd left half a lung on the tracks.

Something scraped and a yellowish light sprang up to my left. There in the corner sat my savior, affixing a candle stub to the floor. He'd taken off his hat, a roguish smile on his lips.

"Why don't you mind your own business?" I muttered as I slowly, painfully sat up. My knees ached from the fall and my throat was raw from nerves and lack of air. The wagon was empty except for a lone burlap sack and a few blades of straw. Beneath us, the wheels chugged rat-tat, rat-tat.

"Hey, I thought you needed a hand earlier." The man, whoever he was, crept closer. "I'm Paul." As he extended his grimy fingers to shake my hand, green eyes mostly hidden under a mess of darkish hair, met mine. "Hobos help each other."

I shook. Who was I to judge? I had to look pretty rough myself. "I...thought these men were hobos."

"Ha," Paul spit. "Common thugs...bandits is more like it."

I shivered. "You think they're on the train?"

"No worries. No upstanding hobo acts like that. A shame they got your rations. I could use a little refreshment right about now." Then a whistle. "Whew, where did you get that?"

I followed Paul's gaze to the Winchester lying next to me in the dust.

"It's mine," I cried.

Paul held up both palms. "Take it easy. Us 'Bos don't steal from a girl."

I cringed. I was turning into a maniac. "I'm sorry, I mean...thank you. You saved my life."

"Glad I was close. Could've gone the other way. Seen it many a times."

"What?"

"Eh, nothing." Paul scratched his head and squished something between his fingers. "Damn graybacks. Got to boil up when I get the chance?"

I wanted to ask what he was talking about, wanted to know where we were heading, but my body had other plans. I crumpled against the opposite wall, away from the door and passed out.

When I awoke, it was pitch black. Beneath the floor, wheels chugged and I had no idea what time it was or if the man called Paul was still in the carriage. With a pang I remembered the shotgun. As renewed panic gripped me, I patted the area around me. There. My fingers made contact with the wooden stock, still smooth from years of polishing.

A longing came over me then… to sit in the room one more time and watch Mamma rub oil into the wood. Mamma. My eyes filled with tears. What did it hurt? Nobody could even see me. Against my better judgment a sob escaped from my chest. Then another.

"Don't be stupid," I mumbled.

"You never told me your name." Paul's voice was heavy with sleep.

I hesitated. So, he was still here. I smiled through my tears. "I'm Samantha…Sam Bruno."

"Well, Sam, let me give you a piece of advice. If you care to know."

I rolled my eyes. Why did every man I met feel the need to shove me around?

"If you want to avoid what happened earlier, you better turn yourself 'round."

"What do you mean?"

"Go home."

I snorted. "How come—"

Somewhere a whistle blew and the train slowed.

"Shhh," Paul said. He sounded wide-awake, his voice a lot deeper than I remembered. "Got to watch for bulls. Do as I do."

I sensed Paul moving toward the door. Ever so carefully, he slid it open an inch and peeked out.

The pale light of dawn trickled in with it. We'd been on the train all night. Though I trembled from the frozen air tugging at my skin, I moved behind Paul. He shook his head and signaled to be quiet. The wagon shuddered and came to a stop. Paul remained as still as a puppet.

Voices could be heard outside. Two men engaged in an argument... coming closer.

"I knew this would happen..."

"Damn. I never thought—"

Paul shoved me to the left, away from the opening, and pressed himself against the inside wall of the door.

When the men continued down the line, I detected a tremble passing through Paul's shoulders.

The car lurched, wheels screeched. The train was moving again. Paul sagged to the floor, his back on the outer door. The light shaft was enough to illuminate the inside. "That was close. Good thing they argued and didn't pay attention."

"What do you mean?"

"Our door was open and chances are good the bulls check for hobos. Some of them are nice and let us ride along. Others not so much." He paused as if he had to decide whether to continue. "Some of them are bad news."

"Bad news?"

"They arrest hobos, sometimes beat'em up. I've seen it before."

I nodded though I had no idea what Paul was talking about. "Where are we going anyway?" I asked. "I need to get to Chicago."

"Chicago?" Paul looked at me as if I'd said 'the moon.'

"I need to find my brother. He went missing in the spring and—"

"This train travels northwest to Cleveland."

"How do you know? I mean where does it say where the train heads."

"I just know, okay. The tracks lead in certain directions. People talk. There are schedules." When I remained silent he continued. "I've been doing this for seven years."

"How old are you?"

"Twenty-two."

"You've been riding trains since you were fifteen?"

Paul jumped up. "Better that..." the rest of his comment was drowned by a loud whistle as the train disappeared into a tunnel. The train car turned black once more.

When the light returned, Paul sat opposite, watching me intently. "So why would a girl travel by herself to Chicago? You're no 'bo.'"

I explained what had happened, but when I mentioned my visit with George Remus, he shouted, "You crazy? Remus does business with the mob. You can't be serious. You've got any idea who's running Chicago?" Paul clucked his teeth. "And a girl on top."

Heat rose up my throat. "So what I'm a girl," I cried.

"Don't you know anything? The mob is made up of men, dangerous fellows with guns and fists and not afraid to use them. You're talking freaking Capone. Don't you read the paper? He just killed O'Banion, the leader of the North side Gang. Women wear jewels and cook dinner."

"Well, I don't have jewels to wear or dinner to cook. And I can't go home." My cheeks burned with fury. "I need to find my brother." It was true. I'd never go home again. Home. I didn't have one any longer. Papa had stayed in the war. Mamma was gone too. I was on the road like Paul, a feather being carried by the wind this way and that. Saying it out loud made it true, and this new truth stabbed me like a knife.

To my surprise Paul nodded, his eyes unreadable.

The wheels chugged on, uncaring, and I shrugged deeper into my coat. Without a stove, the wagon was as cold as the outside. And here I sat on a train with a stranger, going to some big city without a clue how to find my way.

Chances were I'd travel around for months—if I even made it that long.

CHAPTER FOUR

Paul

The train's rattling comforted me. It was like a hug, a familiar thing, almost a feeling of home. No, better than home because nobody lied and cheated here. 'Bos were honest and supported each other. I was my own boss—free as a bird to fly wherever I wanted to go. *Nobody to tell me things, nobody to make rules.*

What was home anyway? A long time ago I'd belonged. I'd known the feeling of walking into a heated room where delicious smells of a dinner table filled my head. I'd known hugs and smiles, warm clothes, and a comfortable bed. Until Father destroyed it all.

I pushed away the thoughts. I was good at it now, could draw a stuffy airless curtain across my memories at will.

My gaze fell on the strange girl sleeping on her back, hiding that ridiculous shotgun under her huge coat. She reminded me of somebody, but I couldn't put my finger on who. She sure was a pill, that one. She obviously spoke before she thought and then regretted it—kind of naïve in a sweet way. *You don't need that kind of weight right now.* I'd seen some men bind themselves to a woman, and no good ever came of it. Women were burdens, needed things. I had nothing to give, not even to myself.

I'd send her off soon. Get her on a different train north, so I could continue my ways. It was hard enough to take care of one person. Dangerous too. I didn't need some *maeve* messing with my schedule.

The girl mumbled something in her sleep and smacked her

lips as if she were tasting something wonderful. What a strange creature, not like other girls I'd known who craved fancy dresses and giggled all the time. This one had her own head, that much was clear. She was brave to head for Chicago when she knew nothing about traveling on the road.

"You staring at me?" Sam asked, rubbing the sleep from her eyes.

My gaze traveled to the ceiling and back. The girl irritated me. Men never talked like that and the last females I'd been around had been in school a million years ago. "Nothing much else to do." I readjusted my back against the wall. "We 'bos like to talk when we travel together. Pass the time that way, take the mind off, if you know what I mean."

"You like being a hobo?" The girl's eyes, the shade of Lake Michigan on a summer day, watched me.

I shrugged. I'd never allowed myself to contemplate. It was a luxury. "It's a way these days. No honest work around. Families are on the move, people starve. At least I see the country, meet interesting fellows." I swallowed away the unease and continued, "Somehow I always find somebody who needs help with a project. Isn't much, but it keeps me going."

"I always thought hobos were bums."

"Us 'Bos are honest workers. We just travel the trains between jobs."

The girl nodded, watching me intently. "After Papa didn't return, Mamma worked all the time. Rich folks didn't pay what was due."

I tried to imagine small Sam waiting for her father. "What happened to him?"

"Nobody knows. After the Great War ended, he was missing. Government didn't help, so Mamma took on washing."

"And your brother?"

"Once Angelo worked for Remus, he brought us things."

"He's gone too?" I regretted it instantly. Sam's face fell, her eyes glittery. "Sorry, I didn't mean to worry you more." I rummaged in my pockets and produced a pint, filled with water. "How about we cook us a meal?"

One after another, I set up my kitchen near the cargo door. A tin can, cut open on the bottom with holes in the top third, a small pot, and a pocketknife.

"You carry all that with you?"

Wordlessly, I opened my coat. On the inside, I'd fastened a couple oversized pockets, which now hung down empty. "Don't like bindles. Got to be prepared, keep your hands free all the same." I pulled an onion and a carrot from an outer pocket. "Last bit."

I felt the eyes of the girl on me as I poured water, started a fire with a handful of pinecones inside the can, and cut up the vegetables. I didn't mind sharing. It was the hobo way and this girl looked skinny as a spring shoot.

As we took turns sipping the broth, I noticed how a bit of color crept into the girl's cheeks.

"Aren't you lonely?" she asked, her eyes resting on me. Now that the door was almost closed to keep out the wind, they'd lost their color.

"Sure. At times," I said, scraping the pot with dust and restoring it to its proper pocket. "You get used to it. When I was new, I hated the uncertainty. You never know what you find. Where you stop or who you meet. After a while it gets easier. As I said, 'bos are decent. We've got an honor code."

"To rescue girls from bandits?"

"Be a gentleman and respectful. Encourage kids to go home."

"I'm no kid," Sam cried.

I couldn't help but smile. Was there something womanly hidden beneath that huge coat after all?

"I suppose not. But you should go home anyway." To my surprise I continued, telling her about some of the strange fellows I'd met, the wondrous jobs I'd done.

The train chugged and lulled me away, my previous life hazy as a fogged-in river.

CHAPTER FIVE

Sam

"Let me do the talking," Paul said after we arrived in Cleveland and made our way south on Neilston Street. "I've been there before and always gotten work and something to eat."

I kept quiet. Not that I didn't have things to say, but my body was playing tricks. The lack of food filled my ears and mind with cotton, demanding attention on the ache in my belly. A great heaviness was spreading through my limbs, making my knees wobbly and my gait uncertain. We'd stopped along the way, sneaking into a front yard to pump water from a well. My feet were soaked, but at least the burning thirst was gone for the moment.

"Here it is," Paul said at last. The home in front of us was unassuming with white clapboard siding, an open porch with a swing and a variety of empty flowerpots lined up like soldiers along the entrance.

"Yes?" The woman behind the closed storm door wore a frown, her apron coated with what looked like flour dust. Delicious aromas of baking apples and cinnamon wafted past her into my nose, a reminder that Christmas was close. Even when Mamma had had little, she'd managed to fix a cake or cookies, some old German recipe with ginger or almonds. You can't save on the butter, Mamma had insisted, a smile on her worn features. I had basked in that smile for weeks because it was so rare.

"Mrs. Pleasant, it's me, Paul. I was here last year, doing your weeding." Paul spoke faster. "It so happens my friend, Sam, and I are in the area and we're wondering if we could do chores in exchange for a meal."

The woman slowly nodded, her gaze wandering up and down, first Paul's, then my body. "I daresay you've fallen on hard times." She chewed her lower lip. "What's a young couple like you…I don't really have much outdoor work this time of year. The garden is done and I…"

"Anything is fine, Mrs. Pleasant." Paul produced a huge grin. "I promise we'll do a swell job."

"Well, there is one thing." Mrs. Pleasant's smile brightened as she pointed toward a barn fifty yards away. "Neighbor boy is taken ill. Boxes need cleaning. Be careful with the black one, he's a bit mean," she laughed.

Mrs. Pleasant's mirth rang in my ears while I inspected the tools in the barn entrance. I knew nothing of horses, only that they scared me and had killed Mamma. Worse, I felt so faint now that I had trouble lifting my arms, not to mention removing dung-laden straw.

My nose twitched as I took in the roiling stench emanating from the two boxes. Why had I followed Paul into some unknown town?

Because you're a helpless gal without him.

"Come on, hurry up," Paul said as he led one of the horses, a brown mare with a white snip on her forehead, into the long corridor and tied her to a post.

I watched the blackish stallion in the adjacent box. *Come on. Don't be a chicken.*

Wild eyes met mine. The horse's mane was matted, its skin covered with crusted filth. Obviously nobody had been able to get close to clean him.

"I…I can't." I watched in fascination how my arm hung motionless by my side. No amount of willpower made it move.

Paul stormed past me mumbling, "Do I have to do everything?" He deftly opened the chest-high door and grabbed the horse's bridle. "Come on, boy, time to clean house."

To my surprise, the stallion snorted once and followed Paul into the passage. How in the world did Paul know about horses?

With a sigh, I pushed a wheelbarrow inside and began to shovel. It was a disgusting job, the horse's manure ankle deep, the smell overpowering. I coughed and choked, my empty stomach sending bile to my mouth.

If this was hobo life, I didn't want any part of it. About half way through, I could no longer lift the shovel. My shoulders seized up painfully and my breath came in spurts.

Paul, who'd already finished his side, called to me. "You done in there? I'm famished. Can't wait for some real food."

I wanted to scream, but even the effort of speaking was too much. I just stood there as the walls began to wiggle back and forth.

Paul leaned over the partition. "What's wrong?"

"I can't...I..." For the second time in two days my vision blurred.

The next moment Paul was by my side, propping me up. "Take it easy," he said quietly. He led me to a couple of straw bales and helped me lie down. "Wait here. I'll be done in a flash."

When I awoke, the stalls were dark and quiet. An oil lamp burned along the far wall, creating dancing shadows. Somewhere nearby I heard munching. The stench of manure had been replaced with the sweet smells of hay and straw.

I sat up in alarm, noticed a wool blanket covering me. Had Paul left me? I didn't even remember the way to the tracks. With effort, I climbed from the bales and glanced into the stalls. Both horses were sticking their noses into a trough, their coats shiny and their manes untangled. Paul had brushed them.

Remembering my empty stomach, I crept toward the house. My back ached from the cold and my knees didn't want to bend.

Lights blazed ahead, making it easy to see inside. Mrs. Pleasant stood in the doorframe to an enclosed porch and there, in the middle of the room, surrounded by a feast of soup, bread, roasted meat, beans and some kind of streusel cake, sat Paul. He was talking, his hands animated, his voice seeping through the cracks in the door. Had I not known differently, I would've thought he belonged there.

I hurled myself forward and knocked, then yanked open the door. "I can't believe you're eating without me," I blurted. Only to realize that Paul's plate was not yet used, the napkins and silverware next to it clean and shiny.

Paul straightened, the color in his cheeks rising. "Eh, my friend, Sam, has been feeling poorly."

Mrs. Pleasant's expression went from a frown to a careful smile. "You can use the spigot outside the door to wash. I'll bring you soap and a towel."

Only then did I notice the state of my hands and shoes. Both were covered in manure. Mamma had always insisted on me washing and wearing clean things. It was the only way to conduct the business of laundering for rich families. I'd sunk to the status of swine in the matter of three days.

"I...am dreadfully sorry." I took a step back. Then another. *Where in the heck was the door?*

Outside I cooled my burning forehead and scrubbed my hands until the skin throbbed with cold. Leaving my shoes by the door, I returned inside, my head low. I hung my coat on the rack and slinked to the table.

"Let's pray," Mrs. Pleasant said as soon as I took my seat next to Paul.

I only breathed 'amen,' all focus on the spread in front of me. I closed my eyes, playing an old game, guessing the ingredients in the soup: potatoes, carrots, onions, leek, garlic, pepper, salt and some kind of herb. What was it called? Ah, yes, lovage.

"Is there lovage in the soup?" I asked when Paul took a break from talking. He'd been chatting like a market wench. And to my surprise, he discussed the economy as easily as the art of reroofing a house.

Mrs. Pleasant's spoon sank. "Well, yes, how did you know? Not many people grow it around here."

I tried a smile, warmth returning to my limbs. "My mother sometimes used it."

"Sam knows all about cooking," Paul interjected proudly. Why had I told him about my dream of running a restaurant one day? According to his story, I'd been with him for months as we crisscrossed the country via rail.

"You may sleep in the barn, if you like," Mrs. Pleasant said, her eyes on me. "I'll give you breakfast before you leave." She pointed an arthritic forefinger at the pie. "Better take another piece before bed."

Paul

"How did you know?" Sam asked. We were riding another train, heading west toward Indianapolis, chewing leftover sandwiches.

29

"About Mrs. Pleasant."

"We meet people. We've got codes. Did you notice the drawing on her fence?"

"Not really. I was tired."

"A cat symbol means it's a kind woman." I met Sam's gaze.

"I'm sorry for embarrassing you," she said, her cheeks aflame. "I thought you left…forgot me."

"You were out cold in the barn and wouldn't wake. Mrs. Pleasant said to let you sleep."

"I'm an idiot."

I grinned. "What can I say? You're a girl." *Not like other girls though, that's for sure. They'd have fainted long ago.*

As Sam rolled up in her coat, I caught myself wondering what she looked like beneath all those clothes. It had been a long time since Ava. A smile crept across my face in the dark. A million years ago, Ava had been my nanny. She'd also been the one to introduce me to the pleasures of the flesh.

Don't be ridiculous. Time to get rid of the girl. Now that we'd gotten some extra rations, she'd be all right on her own. As soon as we'd reach Indianapolis, I'd put her on a train to Chicago.

I'd be free again.

CHAPTER SIX

Sam

Mamma smiled and handed me a dress with yellow and red flowers. I danced across a meadow in my new outfit, arms raised, the sun in my eyes so blinding, I wanted to turn away.

"Sam, wake up."

I came to, staring into Paul's face. Bluish light trickled in through the opening. The train stood still, and I grew instantly aware of the cold, a chill that went bone deep and made me shiver.

"What happened?" I asked, trying to keep my jaws under control. "Are we in Indianapolis?"

"A few miles east, in Irvington."

A shadow filled the opening. "You, there. Out!"

Silhouetted against the brightness stood a conductor in a long black jacket, bow tie and a formal hat.

"We're leaving," Paul said as I scrambled after him.

"You wait here," the man barked. On closer inspection, he didn't look much older than Paul, but the uniform scared me. Up and down the line, more rail men opened cargo holds, exposing a handful of hobos.

I eyed the adjacent tracks, rusty snakes of metal and not another train in sight. The Winchester felt comforting against my armpit.

Paul threw me a quick glance before addressing the officer. "Sir, my buddy here needs to get to Chicago on urgent business."

"Then tell your buddy, he's trespassing on railroad property."

31

"But sir—"

Ignoring him, the conductor waved at a colleague. "Over here, two more."

"Hold'em," a voice drifted across. I watched as two officers carrying sticks hurried closer, shoving and pushing six hobos in front of them.

"Rotten bulls," Paul said under his breath. He poked me in the side and motioned to follow. I blinked. Paul abruptly shoved the man in the chest. As he stumbled backwards and fell, Paul took off the other way. Down the line, then across the tracks. Behind us, shouts rang out. Then footsteps.

Ahead, an eight-foot wire fence loomed. I followed Paul, who was looking for a way across. The footsteps grew louder. Paul scaled the fence, yelling something from the top. At the same moment, somebody rushed at me from behind and I crashed to the ground.

My head swam as hands pushed me roughly into the mud. The thin layer of ice on a puddle cut against my cheek.

"Damn hooligan. Thought you'd get away, eh?"

I recognized the officer from earlier. When I tried to look up, to tell Paul to get out of here, I couldn't tilt my head. Any moment they'd find the gun and use it on us.

The weight lifted off me in an instant. As I scrambled to my knees, Paul groped beneath my coat, pulled out the shotgun, and smacked the officer with the butt against the side of the head. My Winchester. Uttering a sigh, the man sagged to the ground. Some fifty yards away, two officers whistled. The group of hobos scattered as the two remaining conductors raced toward us.

"Come on," Paul cried. He yanked me to a stand and pushed me up onto the fence. "Hurry."

We'd hardly descended the other side when the two officers reached the fence. "You're *hot* now. We'll keep an eye out," one of them seethed.

I raced after Paul for what seemed like an hour. My legs burned with fatigue, my chest tight from lack of air.

When he finally stopped, we were in the country again, the land barren, corn stalks like brown stubble surrounding us. An icy wind blew freely, crept beneath my coat, and made me shiver anew. My head drooped. Hobo life was nothing but teeth-chattering cold and misery. Without a place to call home, I was a drifter, a nobody.

"Damn," Paul muttered, slumping onto a boulder. "We're marked now."

I sagged next to him. "What do you mean?"

Paul turned to me, his eyes squinty with anger. "That's what I get for traveling with a *maeve*." He jumped back up and began to pace. "Nothing but trouble. I managed for seven years. Two days with *her*, I'm hot."

"What did I do?" Fury rose in me, making it hard to talk. Easy for him to put the blame on me.

Paul stopped in front of me, eyes still blazing. "I tell you what you did. You...we broke the code. I did...to save you... by hitting that railroad man. We're fugitives. These officers will tell everyone to keep a lookout for a fellow and a girl with long black hair. I hit one of them."

"But I never meant—"

"Of course, not." Paul stomped off—only to turn around a minute later. "I've got an idea." He straightened and squatted in front of me. Lifting my chin left, then right, he pulled off my hat.

"What?"

"They're looking for a couple. You're going to become a boy. Will be useful when you get to Chicago anyway."

"Are you daft?"

Paul stepped back, his eyes still appraising. "Think about it. How are we getting to Chicago if the railroad hunts us? We don't have money or food to walk that far. It's winter. Besides, if you want to get anywhere near the men who know your brother, you've got to be one of them. Your father is Italian. Good. Your hair is black. Good. Your eyes, blue. Strange, but I guess that can't be helped."

"Wait, what are you suggesting?"

"We cut off your hair, add some dirt to your face. Work on you using a deeper voice." He drew closer again, staring at my coat. "Looks pretty flat..." His gaze met mine. "You better not have bubs under there."

"What are bubs?"

"Boobs."

Heat rushed to my cheeks. In fact, my entire head turned into a blistering balloon. With the little food I'd had over the past few years, not much was happening in that department. Well, if you looked close, there was something... The womanly changes mostly annoyed me. Who had time for that? I'd never worn a dress, at least not since I'd been a little girl. I had no jewelry, no fancy shoes. I might as well be a boy.

I cleared my throat. How much time had passed? Paul's embarrassing words clung to the air, and I had to say something. Now. "All right."

A grin spread across Paul's face. "Spectacular."

Thirty minutes later, black strands piled around my feet. Paul had produced a pocketknife, assuring me of his expertise in hair cutting.

"Not half bad," he commented, standing back.

I touched my head, my earlobes cold from the unaccustomed exposure to the elements. I would've loved a looking glass, some way to judge if I'd be convincing as a boy.

All through the trim I'd hummed and tried out words in a lower octave. It wasn't easy and I fell back into my usual speech several times, only to be reminded by Paul. He'd also taken a handful of muck and smudged it across my cheeks, upper lip and chin. "Instead of a beard," he joked.

Easy for him to say. The way he acted there was no question he was male.

"Now walk for me," he finally said after slipping his knife between the folds of his coat.

"What?"

"You shouldn't just look the part, you've got to *act* the part." He strode across to me. "You see, a certain swagger. Like a man, with big steps."

I wanted to argue. Except he'd saved me from the railroad officers *and* the thugs.

"No, no, bigger steps, put your hands in your pockets. Stretch your shoulders."

I tried again. And again. Paul found fault with something every time. I squeaked, my steps were dainty, my posture off, my expression girly, and...and.

Finally I'd had enough. "I'm tired. I'm starving," I cried and sank back on the rock. "Now leave me alone."

"You didn't use your boy voice," he said quietly. "Let's find some food. We've got to change trains anyway. Can't go back to Irvington. Got to find the main tracks in Indianapolis."

I looked at the man next to me. He seemed to have grown since we'd met, his green eyes sharp and full of life. For all I knew he could've been my brother. I'd talked to him more in the last days than I had with Angelo for an entire year.

"Are you going to help me?" I asked quietly.

"I'll make a hobo out of you before we get to Chicago."

"What do you mean *we*?"

"You think I'll let a girl get herself into trouble?"

"I thought I was a boy?"

"Ha!"

Somehow that last bit made me smile.

CHAPTER SEVEN

Paul

I had no idea why I didn't just turn away and pick a train to carry me far away from the girl. In fact, the first days I'd often thought of taking off while she slept. It would've been easy and a relief. She'd been nothing but trouble, first getting us caught and then put on the bull's 'wanted list' of criminal hobos.

And yet. She was neither a whiner nor a quitter. Nor was any of this her fault. I had to acknowledge she had grit.

What are you doing?

We were walking though fields powdered with snow. It was as if all color had been sucked away. The ground was gray, the bare tree limbs in the distance blackish bones. A leaden sky hung above. The wind had picked up, a sleety mess hitting our skin. No hat or scarf was tight enough to protect and we both bent low into the storm. It almost hurt to breathe, the air carving a scratchy path down my throat.

"You know where you're going?" Sam asked, her voice muffled behind the collar of her coat.

"I guess."

"You guess," Sam cried. "We'll freeze to death."

"We won't."

"How do you know?"

"I know."

I could hear Sam chewing on my words. Felt her anger grip me like the tentacles of an octopus. Why did I even care what she

36

thought?

"I don't see how." She sounded exasperated. "There are neither markers nor signs. We have no sunlight and this field looks exactly like the last."

"Look," I snapped. "I know." I threw up my arms. "I've got a feel for landscape and direction. Always have."

"You're so *smart*." Sam's voice was full of sarcasm. "Is that why you're a hobo and don't do an honest job?"

I stopped in my tracks. "Don't talk about things you don't understand, little girl. Just leave, then." I marched off at a higher speed, fighting down the urge to turn around and smack her. What did she know about me? Nothing!

You could tell her.

My steps crunched on the icy ground as I rushed forward. I wasn't going to turn around…or wait. Good riddance.

But then I heard footsteps, walking, then running after me.

"Paul, wait," Sam cried. "I'm sorry. It's just so miserable."

She grabbed my arm. Blue eyes met mine. "Please don't be mad. I've got no right to question you. You saved my life."

I almost smiled because she looked so wretched in her bulky coat with the reddened nose. But then I gritted my teeth. "Come on, let's go. We need to keep moving."

Sam nodded and silently retook her position by my side.

Sam

Finding overnight cover in an abandoned hay barn, we made it to Indianapolis the following evening. Below lay the rust-colored rails, dotted here and there with cargo trains.

"Good thing it's getting dark," Paul said. "I bet the bulls are out looking for us."

I inspected the two potatoes in my hand. We'd helped an elderly lady cut and haul a Christmas tree and each received two potatoes as payment. "I'd love to cook this."

Paul sniffed as if he could smell which train would leave for Chicago. "Not now. Need to get on a train—fast."

I bit back a comment. I'd already made Paul's life miserable. He'd done nothing but help me and as a thank you he was now a fugitive. Who knew, we probably had sketches out with our faces. I touched my chin, itchy from the dirt.

"Boys, where to?"

I suppressed a shriek. The man had appeared out of the bushes like an apparition, his face covered under a forest of gray beard and equally long hair. He stepped closer and squinted at Paul. "Li'l P, is that you?"

To my surprise Paul chuckled and hugged the man. "Dr. Mac. Am I glad to see you."

The fellow gave Paul a once over. "Guess you aren't so little anymore. Must've been three years since we rode together." He slapped Paul on the back. "Come on over, got a jungle over there. Bunch of boys cooking dinner."

Paul hesitated. "We're in a rush. My friend is going to Chicago."

"No train heading north tonight. Might as well take a rest."

I gazed back and forth between the two hobos. Secretly, I was glad for the break and the chance to eat. Paul had shared his hobo stove, but I knew it was too small for two, especially with the lack of firewood, leaving both of us hungry. I'd been prepared to chew my potatoes raw.

The camp was a patchwork of canvas, blankets, cardboard, wooden stakes, cook fires, and a mess of men in tattered clothes.

They welcomed me and Paul to join them, and Paul offered his two potatoes for the community mulligan, a joint stew of available foods bubbling above a fire. I gladly moved close to the flames and rubbed my hands.

"Who's your friend?" Dr. Mac asked once we settled.

"This is Sam. Sam, meet the 'Bos," Paul said. "Dr. Mac here is an old friend. They call him the 'Docent.'"

Mumbled greetings joined into a gruff chorus. Unsure about my voice, I nodded hello.

"I'm Flea Trunk." A man, who reeked like a cesspool, handed me a tin cup with a hot liquid. "Here's a tokay blanket. Put some meat on those skinny bones."

"Tha…" I cleared my throat, "Thanks." I had no idea what the man was talking about, so I wrapped my hands around the mug.

Instantly, my throat and belly warmed, and by the time I received a share of the stew, the voices around me had turned to muffles. Hobo speech drifted in and out, words I didn't understand: *cannon balls, bone polishers, the challenges of flipping.* Heat spread across my cheeks and I wanted to take off my hat.

Paul held my arm. "Don't."

How had he gotten next to me? I wanted to mouth off, but something in Paul's eyes held me back.

"You'll freeze...later."

That's when I grew aware of my bladder. The tokay or whatever it was demanded release. "Got to go," I managed.

Paul scanned the group, men sitting quietly talking, one or two sleeping in their makeshift tents. He leaned close and whispered. "To your right. Thirty yards at least."

"Yes, sir, *Li'l P*," I giggled. My first attempt at standing failed and I slumped back down. "Oops." The second time was better and I teetered into the night.

Brush slapped my face as I made my way into the thicket, then past it. I sniggered, imagining Paul glowering at my back. What made him the expert of everything?

When I returned, Dr. Mac chuckled, "Looks like your friend is a lightweight." He turned back to the group, his tone now serious. "Bad road around Irvington, 'bos. Some young couple beat up a bull. No going west right now."

Flea Trunk whistled while some fellow called Upchuck said, "Damn, was going back that way. Now they'll be on the lookout for all of us."

"Didn't *you* come from there?" Dr. Mac asked me.

I was about to answer when Paul chimed in. "We got off in Irvington, but didn't notice anything. You know when it happened? We've been walking a few days looking for work."

"Not exactly," Dr. Mac said, eying us carefully. "You must've missed them."

I shifted my weight and suppressed a groan. A gnawing headache began to encircle my skull.

"Get some sleep and take these California blankets," Paul whispered, stuffing sheets of newspaper into my hand and pointing at a makeshift tarp. "For visitors. Put that paper under your coat before you lie down. I'll be there in a bit."

As soon as Paul said it, I realized how exhausted I was. I mumbled good night and crawled into the tent only to realize that without the fire, the air was unbearably cold. I had no blanket, no pillow, just a piece of cardboard on the ground and some plastic above my head. I stuffed the newspaper beneath my coat, patted the rigid barrel of my gun, and rolled into a fetal position.

Fleetingly I thought of Mamma and how I'd taken our warm room for granted.

The next time I woke, I grew aware of a sleeping form next to me. To my horror I was lying against somebody's chest, my nose an inch from some rough fabric. In the gray light of early dawn I recognized Paul. Beneath his hat, strands of brown hair hung across his forehead. He'd swung an arm around me as if he were drowning and I a lifebuoy.

Annoyed about his forwardness I lifted away his arm and sat up. The icy dampness immediately nipped at my face, sending a tremor through me. Paul had probably saved me from freezing to death. Idiot.

I climbed outside and placed a couple of logs on the fire. Hunger gnawed at me anew and I wondered about the two potatoes still hiding in my pocket. At home I could've fried or roasted them. Here I had no tools. I could eat them raw, now, before somebody stole them from me. Against my will, Paul appeared in my vision, shaking his head. Giving the potatoes a final pat, I straightened and headed for the thicket.

Not two minutes after I returned, shouts rang out. Flea Trunk, the stinky hobo from last night, came running into camp, wiggling his forefinger at me.

"It's them," he shouted. "The couple. I saw her. He's a she…a *maeve*."

Before I had time to rouse Paul, Dr. Mac gripped my arm and tore open my coat. Rough hands patted my chest. So much for my breasts not showing.

"Damn, Li'l P. What you do?"

Paul crept from the shelter, hair standing on end. "T'was an accident. Bulls were mean. I wacked'em once."

"They're hot," Flea Trunk said, giving me the once-over with his eyes. "Got to send 'em off before we all get in trouble."

The Docent nodded gravely and took Paul aside. "Sorry, Li'l P," he whispered. "Look, I get it…about the girl and…" He shook his head and continued loudly, "No room for you here. Cow crate going north this morning. Better take it."

Paul only nodded. Avoiding my gaze, he stalked from camp, me scrambling after him.

We walked in silence until we reached the tracks, stretches of crisscrossing steel dotted with hundreds of rust-colored wagons.

All was quiet.

"Stay here," Paul whispered. "I've got to find the right one."

"I'm sorry I...You can't leave me."

Paul walked off without an answer, so I followed. After twenty yards, Paul turned around. He grabbed my collar and shook me. "I said, stay."

Then he marched down the line, climbed across a coupler and was gone. I stared after him, feeling equally frightened and angry. My heart beat in my neck as I tried to make up my mind. Stay or leave. Run after Paul or wait. He was obviously fuming mad, so what if he didn't come back? According to what I'd heard the bulls were on high alert. Everyone was looking for a girl, and who was I going to kid? It'd taken less than eight hours for the hobos to find me out.

"Great," I said. Only when I heard my own voice, did I realize of how terrified I sounded. *Quit being a mouse, go after him.*

Nothing had ever been as hard. Not even when I'd walked off that morning visiting George Remus. I carefully placed my feet, slid across the same coupler as Paul. On the other side were more tracks and carriages. Hundreds. I looked in each direction. There was no telling where Paul had gone.

I stopped and listened. Footsteps crunched on the far side of the next line of cars. Paul. I ran toward a coupler and slid across as a hand laid itself over my mouth, the other grabbing me around the waist. "Shhh."

I swallowed the scream, the weave of the coat familiar. I'd seen it up close this morning when we'd slept together...like a couple. *Get a grip.*

"Bulls," Paul breathed into my ear.

"Keep an eye out," a voice said. "Chances are that couple will show up sooner or later. Where else are they going to catch a train?"

"Maybe they've gone already."

"Doubt it."

"We have eyes out everywhere and no trains have left since yesterday afternoon."

The footsteps halted. "I'm going back to the office. Will send a replacement."

"Make it quick. I'm freezing my balls off."

I quivered, imagining what would happen if they caught us.

Short hair or not, I felt as vulnerable as ever. I'd go to jail. And Paul? He'd swung the gun and would go away for a long time. It was my fault. I'd brought nothing but trouble and we'd barely made progress toward Chicago. Gratitude flooded me then, a feeling of warmth better than any fire.

Ever so quietly, Paul led me back the way we'd come. "Got to wait here. Train is leaving shortly from the north end."

"What's a cow crate?"

Paul avoided my gaze. "For livestock."

I could tell he kept something to himself. "Meaning?"

He finally faced me, green eyes dark as an evergreen forest. "It means the sides are made of slots for airflow. Empty, the wind makes it freezing hell. Full, you get damn near trampled."

"Can't we wait?"

"No, missy, we can't," Paul snapped. "You're a curse, Sam Bruno." He spit and kicked the dirt, sending a rock flying. "Thanks to you, my days as a hobo are numbered. My reputation...gone." He spit again. "Heck, we may freeze to death before we get to Chicago." He stormed off a few feet, mumbling. "Whatever possessed me to—"

"I'm sorry," I called after him. "I'm sorry for being a burden. I'll walk if I have to. I have no place else to go." I turned and marched the other way until I was yanked to a stop.

Paul's eyes spit green fire. "Don't be stupid. You'll never make it."

"Thanks for your confidence."

His expression moved from anger to contrition. "It's not you. It's this...this lousy rotten life. It's hard enough for a 'bo who knows what he's doing."

When I didn't answer, he grabbed my hand. "Time to go."

I marveled how Paul sniffed out the correct tracks and determined which cars were safe. Now we huddled in the back end of an empty cow crate, the wind whistling freely through the slotted walls. Not even the rat-tat of the wheels was capable of lulling me to sleep.

My fury and gratefulness from earlier had been replaced by something else. What exactly? I wasn't sure if I admired him, but there was that conviction that without him I would've been doomed. Even though I froze like I'd never frozen in my life, my hands were numb, and the raw potato I'd eaten had caused my insides to ice over too, Paul was getting me to the big city. My chances without him would've been zero.

Angelo was somewhere in Chicago, I was sure of it. No matter how long it took, I'd find him. George Remus had sent him to do a job, deliver a message to an associate, maybe Al Capone's men. Something had happened that didn't allow him to come home.

Paul shifted his weight and I nestled back into his embrace. It was no longer strange to sit together. Just this morning I'd been irritated about waking up next to him. Now I was glad he kept me shielded from the incessant draft.

Light was fading when the train slowed. Unable to sit any longer, I peeked through the opening. In the distance, lights flickered—the Chicago skyline.

We had arrived.

CHAPTER EIGHT

Paul

"You sure you want to go through with that?"   I asked as we made our way toward downtown.

"I'm here now, so you can leave."

"No chance."

Sam stopped abruptly and faced me. The way she straightened her shoulders made me smile. "Why?" she said before I could answer. "All you did is blame me for losing your reputation as a hobo. You did your job. You got me to Chicago. Now go back and live your life. Maybe you can explain you fell for the lies of a woman." Without waiting for an answer she charged ahead, getting honked at by a passing automobile.

"You can't even cross the street without putting yourself in danger." I was back by her side. The girl was nothing but a nuisance, but I couldn't just let her loose in Chicago on her own. Just another day and I'd go away. *But this is your home*, the voice in my head murmured. *So what*, I wanted to say. So what if I'd lived here until seven years ago? When things had fallen apart and the life I'd known had evaporated.

Sam shot me a look. "Gosh, thanks for the vote of confidence."

"All right. Tell me what you plan to do."

"I'm going to see Mr. Capone."

I stopped abruptly. "What? You're nuts. He's a mob boss who kills people. He and Torrio run brothels, gambling parlors and

44

saloons. He's a bootlegger. For all I know, he *runs* Chicago."

Sam pushed out her lower lip. "All I want to do is ask him about Angelo."

I was tempted to touch Sam's mouth and tell her how silly she looked when she was pouting. I could tell she was not nearly as certain as when we'd started in Cincinnati. She'd likely expected things would fall into place once she reached Chicago.

Like me.

It was obvious, that now that she was here, the town scared her.

Unlike me.

Cincinnati wasn't tiny, but Chicago was enormous. Skyscrapers towered above streets buzzing with automobiles and trams. Men in fedoras and suits ran this way and that. Women dressed in elegant coats with fur-trimmed collars and matching hats stalked on high heels, carrying wrapped packages. No, the size was fine—the screeching streetcars, the honking automobiles, the grimy air filled with the chatter of people welcomed me home.

But it was different than before. Sam and I looked like a tramps. The girl's coat was encrusted with filth, her shoes scuffed. My pants had holes in the knees and stains on the seat. Nobody would trust us, not even talk to us, certainly not a man like Al Capone who wore fancy suits and surrounded himself with luxury and a horde of guards with tommy guns.

"And you think he'll see you?" I asked.

Sam's eyes were wide with anxiety. Around us, the evening crowd split and melded back together, all of them assured of going home to their families, to comfortable houses, fancy dinners and presents under the tree.

A lump formed in my throat. It felt raw and scratchy as if chafed with a cheese grater. All of a sudden I wanted to pull her close and tell her not to worry. I'd take care of her. Somehow.

You could go home. At least tell her about your past.

Out of the question. She'd get angry and accuse me of leading her on.

When I met her gaze I found her watching me curiously. "You're not listening," she said, new irritation in her voice.

"Sorry, what?"

"I said, not like this. Obviously. I'll have to clean up, get some food. Besides, I've got to find his office."

I clamped my mouth shut. I could've located Al Capone in five minutes if I wanted. In fact, I knew many of the neighborhoods and streets like the back of my hand.

Sam

All evening we searched dumpsters, ate bits of burgers, bread and pizza crusts, even a half-eaten piece of German chocolate cake from a takeout box. It was disgusting, nasty work, competing with rats, roaches and assorted winos.

We drifted toward the South Loop, a seedy area with bars and eateries. At the backdoor of a run-down pub, we pleaded for water and were rewarded with glasses of stale beer.

"You got any work?" Paul asked the barkeep. "My Italian friend and I need a job. We just arrived." The man who wore a greasy towel as an apron looked us up and down. Dusk was falling and the room beyond was filling with thirsty customers. "Look, we'll do anything. Clean, do dishes, run errands. Anything."

"Your friend looks pretty weak." The man scrutinized me. "You say he's Italian?"

"Yes, sir, name of Sam Bruno. Italian father from Palermo."

"Wait here."

Paul punched me in the arm. "Maybe he'll call Capone, eh?"

"Very funny," I said, suppressing the urge to lean against the wall. My legs were ready to dissolve and the constant cold and wind had chafed my hands and cheeks until they burned.

"Voice," Paul whispered.

I cleared my throat. "Sorry, forgot."

The backdoor swung open a second time. "All right, come in," the barkeep said. "So happens dishwasher didn't show. Get yourselves busy and we see about something regular. Call me if you need something. My name is Victor Pazetti."

Paul and I entered the kitchen, a narrow tunnel with a couple of sinks and three thousand dishes and glasses. Flies swarmed and the smell of rotting garbage permeated my skin. A huge pot bubbled on the stove. I resolutely took off my coat and wrapped the shotgun with it, thankful no breasts were apparent under the loose sweater.

"Wonderful," I mumbled. Taking a deep breath, I attacked the sinks where the drags of beer, sour milk, and grease joined into a toxic stew.

As the noise in the saloon swelled, we waded through mountains of dishes. Every time Paul found a glass with a few drops of whiskey or beer, he drained it. As a result he started to whistle, his eyes as shiny as those of the patrons in the other room. Once in a while he squeezed past me, the sleeve of his shirt touching my arm.

"Who would've known?" he mumbled a few times, smiling at me as if he remembered an old joke.

I, on the other hand, grew more and more weary. And annoyed. My fingers had turned to shriveled prunes, and my lower back and legs throbbed. I didn't share Paul's enthusiasm for liquor, and craved a nice glass of fresh water or better yet, a cup of peppermint tea.

We took a fifteen-minute break around ten o'clock to wolf down some of the unidentifiable stew. Even I had trouble determining what was in it, but customers obviously didn't come here for the reputation of the chef.

Ten minutes before midnight, Victor reappeared. "If you want the job, you can sleep upstairs. First door on the right. Bath privileges once a week." He glanced at my mud-stained boots and Paul's grimy pants. "I'm making an exception this once. I'll tell the caretaker to heat the stove and water in the morning. Wash your clothes while you're at it, *capiche*?"

"Thanks," I breathed. Paul followed the man into the barroom and shortly returned with a loaf of stale white bread and a couple of hard-boiled eggs. "Night snack," he commented. "Let's get some sleep."

The room was barely large enough to hold the two cots, but each of us had a couple of sheets, a pillow and two blankets. It reeked of smoke and whiskey—the barroom was somewhere below—but I didn't care. I stored the shotgun beneath my bed, slid off my boots, staring in dismay at the rumpled socks and filthy pants. Not to ruin my somewhat clean bed, I had to remove my clothes. And that presented a problem.

Paul was three feet away. When I looked up, he quickly turned his head. I could've sworn he was watching me.

"No worries, I'll turn my back," he said as if he'd heard my thoughts. To emphasize his point, he turned off the light.

With a sigh, I pulled off sweater and pants and slid beneath the covers. It wasn't exactly warm, but it was luxury compared to cardboard makeshift tents among a mass of hobos and rattling, drafty trains. I was about to drift off when the thought of Angelo pulled me back.

What if he wasn't here any longer? What if he'd returned to Cincinnati looking for me and Mamma? I imagined him knocking on the door, only to find strangers staring him in the face. They'd shake their head exclaiming, "We don't know anyone by that name." Angelo would walk off, asking neighbors and eventually learning about Mamma's death. He'd wonder where I had gone…and never know. While I was in Chicago looking for him, he'd drive himself crazy searching Cincinnati for me.

Why hadn't I thought of leaving a note with one of our neighbors?

After that, sleep refused to come. I finally passed out in the early morning.

"Time to get up." Paul's voice drifted into my consciousness. "Your bath is ready. I'm working on getting a spare outfit, so you can wash your clothes."

I slowly sat up. I should've been excited about the bath. I was excited, but the thought of Angelo combing Cincinnati in search of me made my insides sick with worry.

"You think you could go back to Cincinnati and deliver a note?"

"What?" Paul who'd been chewing on a piece of bread while straightening his bed turned to face me. He'd changed into different clothes, his new pants and shirt clean but only slightly less threadbare than the last.

"What if my brother is in Cincinnati looking for me?"

"What makes you think he's back there?"

I shrugged. "Nothing. I'm just no longer sure he's here."

"He may be dead," Paul said. "Ever thought of that?"

"No!" I jumped from the bed before I remembered my bare legs and draped a blanket around me. "Don't say that. He can't be dead. He's all I have."

"Hey, hey, calm down." Paul glanced at the ceiling, then back at me. "No need to wake the neighborhood. Let's talk, but for right now, you need to get into the bath before the tub ices over."

That got me going. I grabbed my dirty clothes and headed down the hall. The cool air fogged with hot steam as I sank into the water. Paradise had arrived. I scrubbed my skin, washed my hair and extended the time until the water was lukewarm. Half way through, somebody knocked and I almost lost my footing in the tub.

"Your friend, Paul, sends clothes," a girlish voice said. "I set them by the door."

"Thank you," I boomed with my best boy voice.

I inspected the shirt, sweater and pants—two sizes too large—darned wool socks, and a pair of men's underwear. It didn't matter. All were clean. I spent the next half hour washing my old clothes. The water turned beige, then brown. Mamma would be horrified.

My hands halted in midair as my mother's face appeared in my vision. "Oh, Mamma, I miss you so."

I wiped my cheeks and wrung out my washed socks as a small smile crept onto my face. Mamma would have a thing or two to say about the state of my dress. Even when we'd had next to nothing, I'd always been clean.

Our bedroom was empty when I returned. Something pricked my insides, an uncomfortable nudge I got every time I was alone. I draped my wet clothes over the sole chair and the door of the rickety wardrobe. The narrow window revealed an equally narrow street with rows of brick buildings across the way. The sky was a smear of pink and melted snow. For a moment I was transported back to Over-the-Rhine.

I made the bed and found my shoes underneath, still damp with beer spills and covered in muck. I needed new boots. Soon. My stomach rumbled uncomfortably. Hadn't I just eaten dinner and bread in the night?

Time trickled past. The road filled with people. Cars roared below. I couldn't remember when we were supposed to return to work downstairs. With every minute I grew more convinced that Paul had left me. He'd fumed about me destroying his hobo reputation, turning him into a 'hot' fugitive. He'd put me up in a place and said good riddance.

And yet, despite my conviction he'd left, I couldn't move. Couldn't get out of the room. I had to act a boy or bad things would happen. Penniless girls became prostitutes. It was a logical place if you had nothing. A place to work, a room to sleep. Slinky clothes and probing hands.

I shook myself. Not in a thousand years would I go near

strange men. I had trouble baring my legs in front of Paul.

What if you don't have a choice?

I straightened and cleared my throat, doing the humming exercises to lure my voice into a deeper octave. *You can do this.*

With a sigh, I opened the door and headed downstairs.

"About time." Victor eyed the wall clock that showed ten-thirty, keeping his gaze on two men rolling a keg through the backdoor. "Clean the tables and floor in the saloon."

I located a bucket and cleaning supplies and went to work. In the gloominess, I had trouble seeing progress. The benches were covered in cigarette ashes and old grime, the floor muddy. Beer spills formed puddles. The air reeked of whiskey fumes. I kept scrubbing and hauling fresh water until every table and every seat was clean. Obviously, nobody had done anything in months and now Victor was taking advantage of his new help. It didn't matter.

As the day passed, there was no sign of Paul. My mood swung like a pendulum. One minute my blood simmered with anger—the next I felt heavy with sadness, each movement requiring too much effort.

At two o'clock in the afternoon, I took a break, eating two bowls of fresh mystery stew that Victor had made, and washing it down with a glass of ale. The alcohol softened the unease in my chest. As the afternoon crowd thickened in the bar, I went back to the kitchen to clean mountains of glasses and plates. No matter how I hurried, the stacks never shrank.

Yet, I was glad for the solitary task, away from the drunken men and anybody who could find out my secret.

Exhausted and weary to the bone, I crept into bed around midnight. Victor had given me the nod, figuring that thirteen hours were enough. But that wasn't really what bugged me.

Paul remained absent. I hadn't even thanked him for organizing my bath, getting clothes, finding me a job, and the other dozens of kindnesses he'd shown. No wonder he'd been fed up and run off. I curled up on my cot, feeling more alone than I had ever before. Tomorrow was Christmas day and for the first time in my life, I had no one to share it with. Tears squeezed out behind closed lids.

Maybe Mamma had been the lucky one.

CHAPTER NINE

Sam

When I awoke in the early morning, I at first thought there was some racket out in the street, an incessant, annoying rumble. Until I opened my eyes and sat up. And there across from me lay Paul. Well, he didn't just lie there—he sprawled and snored like a logger with his head back and his mouth open.

I jumped from the cot, my initial thought throwing myself on his chest. I wanted to hug him. As relief washed over me, I wanted to strangle him. On closer inspection I hesitated. Paul looked utterly worn, his lids purplish from lack of sleep, his cheekbones angular and his chin covered in brownish stubble. It was easy to imagine how he'd looked as a young boy.

I tiptoed out of the room to use the outhouse and scrounge for breakfast. The saloon was deserted, so I sneaked into the kitchen. Chicken soup simmered on the stove, filling my every fiber with warmth and longing.

"Hello?" I called into the hall.

Nothing.

"Victor?"

Still nothing. We did get room and board, so what could it hurt?

I dunked a spoon into the pot and tasted it. The soup needed things. Salt, pepper, some garlic. I rummaged through the cupboards, added spices, a few herbs and thinly sliced garlic. I tasted it again, nodded to myself and filled a crockpot. Stuffing four slices of bread and two spoons into my pockets, I headed back upstairs.

The form on the bed moved as soon as I opened the door.

"Something smells heavenly," Paul said with one eye open.

I carefully transported the soup to the table and took position in front of Paul's cot, fists stemmed to my hips. "You've got a lot of nerve." Paul's sleep-deprived eyes grew larger, but I was on a roll. "I missed you, I thought something happened... you, you...left." I took a breath. Why couldn't I simply tell him how happy I was to see him?

"You could've asked Victor," Paul groaned as he propped himself on one elbow. "Mmmh, I'm starving." He carefully straightened and walked past me to the table.

I wasn't finished and addressed his back. "Where were you?"

"Working."

"Doing what?"

"You're the nosiest girl, I ever met." Paul slumped down and dipped a spoon. "This is tasty." He smacked his lips. "Real chicken. Much better than that stew."

"Are you going to tell me or what?" I hadn't moved, my heart still beating double speed.

To my annoyance, Paul chuckled. "Soup is getting cold. Come and eat, Miss Nosy."

Still, I couldn't move. The idiot was making fun of me.

In one swift movement Paul towered over me. His eyes flashed and for a moment I thought he'd shout. Instead lips met mine—surprisingly soft and gentle, not to mention warm from the soup. As quickly as it happened, Paul stepped back and retook his seat. A bit of color had crept into his cheeks.

"Now quit being silly and eat."

I was so surprised, I opened my mouth, but nothing came out. I stiffly moved to the table and sat down across from Paul as the rich aroma of the soup hit my nostrils. I began to gobble to distract myself because my head was positively spinning and would've likely flown away, had it not been attached.

After a while I risked a glance across the table. Paul, brown hair dangling across his forehead, was quietly eating: a spoonful of soup, a bite of bread—repeat.

"Here," he said after a while. He placed a five-dollar bill on the table. "Bonus from last night."

Though it was a fortune, I ignored the money. All I wanted was to ask what had just happened. But I couldn't make my tongue form the words. Maybe I'd imagined things…his lips on mine, the hand lightly on the small of my back. I slid a forefinger across my mouth as if I could capture his touch. Paul didn't seem to notice.

Finally I leaned back in my chair and said, "Will you tell me what you did?"

Paul met my gaze, his expression serious. "Victor sent me to help with deliveries. They were short a man."

"What kind of deliveries?"

Paul rolled his eyes. "Booze. What else. There's more bootlegging in Chicago than anywhere else in the country."

"But it's dangerous."

"No worse than being a hobo. And I can earn real money. I'm going to ask Victor to let me work there instead of the saloon."

"Then I want a job there too."

Paul scraped the last of the soup from the pot. "Not a chance. Too dangerous and hard for a girl."

"Listen to you. First it's not dangerous. Then it is. I need money too. Somebody may know about Angelo. Besides, I *am* a boy."

"Fat chance," Paul said. "Just last night I heard the men talking about the Outfit…Torrio's and Capone's gang. They employ thousands." He paused. "And make millions every month."

"How can I find out more, if I scrub dishes all day?"

Paul straightened and searched through his coat. "Sam, it's exhausting work. You've got to carry beer cartons and kegs. I about slept standing up." He fished something from his pocket and placed it in front of me. "It's not much. Merry Christmas."

I starred at the package covered in brown paper, then at Paul who smiled crookedly, his green eyes bright in the low winter light. Inside me, walls crumbled. A tiny earthquake of emotion sent a lump to my throat.

Since I couldn't talk, my shaking fingers unwrapped the bar of Cadbury's milk chocolate. Chocolate! I hadn't had sweets since last Easter and never a real bar like this all to myself. Paul had even gone through the trouble of wrapping it.

Paul had given me a gift. He hadn't run off; he'd worked like a dog to earn money and buy me a gift.

Oh, it was no good. My eyes welled over. "Thank you."

I wanted to say more, wanted to throw my arms around his neck for a hug. Most of all, I wanted to tell him how glad I was he was here with me. Not because of the gift, but because of his presence. Of course, I didn't.

Paul beamed. "Glad you like it." The color was back in his cheeks and he looked wide-awake. "I think that calls for a drink." He produced a pint jar from his other pocket and took a sip. "A Christmas gift from Victor's buddies."

I tasted it, but the strong liquor burned my throat.

When I coughed, Paul laughed.

"You got to toughen up before you can join the men." Then he grew serious again. "I'll see if I can find you a job with me. But you've got to be strong. If they fire you, you'll not get another chance. We may have to split."

I nodded. Right now I wanted nothing more than to rest. It seemed that ever since Mamma's death, I'd forgotten what a good night's sleep was like. And I wanted time to think. Time to figure out what that kiss meant.

"I could use another hour of sleep," Paul said into the silence. "How about we rest and afterwards I'll take you out for a Christmas dinner?"

I climbed onto my cot, a smile on my face.

For sixty cents each, we feasted on beef roast, potatoes, creamed spinach, rolls, butter and apple streusel. I couldn't remember the last time I'd been this full or this content. Paul told more stories about his hobo days, describing some of the characters he'd met, the attacks he'd faced, and narrow getaways.

I hardly spoke, but was happy to listen and watch. Somehow Paul had changed. His eyes were still the same green, but there was something else there, something heavy and watchful. I liked the way his voice resonated, a deep smooth sound that calmed my nerves.

He hadn't attempted to get close again, and I found myself disappointed. Somehow I'd expected him to make a move.

As we drained our ales, he said, "The other day you mentioned I should go to Cincinnati for you?"

I nodded. "What if Angelo is looking for me there?"

"How long has he been missing?"

I opened my mouth and closed it. I'd tried to remember the

exact day he had left, had racked my brain a thousand times, trying to recall what he'd said. But my memory was fuzzy.

Last spring, it had been raining buckets for days, covering the streets in Over-the-Rhine in ankle-deep mud. Everybody was anxious and grumpy, stuck inside cramped quarters. Mamma had tried to dry her laundry in vein, every available surface covered with garments. Angelo had been upset, not having a place to sit, let alone sleep. Words were exchanged.

"He left late April," I finally said. "And he wrote once from Chicago—the letter was dated May 6. After that, nothing."

"And George Remus expected him to return when?"

I shrugged. I hadn't asked and Remus hadn't volunteered any details.

"But you're sure Remus sent him to deliver something to Capone."

"That's what Mr. Remus said. Actually, he said *an associate*. He never mentioned Capone."

"So your brother actually may never have met Al Capone or his men? He may never have talked to anybody important?"

I shrugged. "It's possible."

"But you're not sure."

"No."

"What makes you think something is wrong? It's only been a few months. Maybe Angelo is having a grand time, bootlegging and drinking the proceeds. Maybe he met a girl."

"He never drank much," I said. "It didn't agree with him. And he always stayed in touch. Even when he worked at Death Valley Farm, he never forgot." *And he never missed your birthday, not once.*

A long time ago Papa had been furious with Angelo for arriving late to Mamma's birthday dinner. "Don't ever forget—family is everything," he'd fumed. "Without it, you're nothing!"

"Yes, Papa," Angelo had responded. He'd been nine.

December first—my eighteenth birthday—had come and gone without a sign of Angelo. I'd waited for him all evening, all night because he'd always surprised me somehow. One year he'd managed to find a huge birthday cake with chocolate frosting. Another he'd given me gloves made of kid leather, soft as...

"Sam?" Paul's fingers lay on top of my forearm. They were warm and firm. "What's Death Valley?"

"Remus owns a large tract of land in the country near

Cincinnati. Angelo said they store beer and warehouses are filled with liquor. They call it Death Valley Farm. People are shot for trespassing."

Paul leaned back, looking thoughtful. "I don't know, Sam. Seems like an uphill battle. Your brother could be anywhere."

Or dead. "I know," I said aloud.

We walked back in silence, steps crunching, the air frozen. Snowflakes drifted into my eyes. I didn't mind. Tomorrow I'd begin looking for Angelo.

But the day after Christmas, I was back in the kitchen and Paul disappeared for hours. The day after that was the same and the day after that. I'd secretly taken up fixing the daily stew with spices and herbs and demand had been growing. Now we cooked two huge pots a day.

As New Year approached, I finally had enough and cornered Victor. Not that he had anything to worry about. Six feet tall with solid shoulders and a mostly grouchy expression, he was an intimidating man.

"I wonder if I can get a job like Paul," I addressed his back in my best deep voice. I'd waited for the right moment when Victor was doing inventory and snuck up on him. Since he didn't answer, I continued. "I can work hard."

At last Victor turned. He looked me up and down before shaking his head. "You're pretty skinny, Sam. Not like Paul, he's a strong lad, good for the job. He's quiet. People like him. Besides, I need a dishwasher."

"But—"

"A week ago you arrive all broken up and filthy as a sewer rat and now you want something else?" He spit. "I pay you eight dollars a week plus you get room and board, no?"

"I'm thankful," I said, deflated. "At least let me do the food. I'm a good cook."

Victor stopped counting and faced me. "You been messing with my stew?"

I felt my cheeks burn. "It needed things."

"Like what?"

"Some spices. Garlic, more vegetables." I shrugged. "It was bland...boring."

A low chuckle rose from Victor's chest. "I thought it was

strange how people ordered more." He threw me another glance. "Where you learn to cook?"

I couldn't help smiling. "My brother and father taught me. Mostly Italian."

Victor turned back to his bottles. "Fine then. From now on you in charge of stew. Say, at least two pots. Write me a list and I get you supplies. When we run out, you make more. Capiche?"

I smiled. "Thanks."

"You still do dishes."

At the door I hesitated. "Have you ever heard of Angelo Bruno?"

"Don't ring a bell. Who is he?"

"My brother."

"Sorry, no idea." As Victor returned to his bottles, I made my way into the kitchen. My arms moved mechanically, heating water, scraping plates, stacking and washing glasses.

Despite my excitement about the new assignment, all I saw was me as an old woman, still cleaning Victor's dirty dishes.

CHAPTER TEN

Paul

Initially, I dreaded taking the delivery job. Victor's brother, Vincenzo, who looked like a fatter and squatter version of Victor, had needed a driver, somebody reliable, and after I'd shown some skills behind the wheel—a talent I owed to spending my early teens experimenting with automobiles, Father by my side—I'd soon developed a reputation for being careful and trustworthy.

Every evening I reported to work at Vincenzo's who made coal deliveries during the day. At night his trucks doubled to deliver booze. We drove to Lake Michigan or to some indistinct landmark to pick up whiskey in crates and kegs, which were camouflaged under a thin layer of coal.

To my surprise, I enjoyed seeing the sights, thoughts of family excursions on my mind. I'd spent countless days playing in the sand, Mother watching from a chaise, her jewel-rimmed sunglasses sparkling. Lake Michigan had beaches like a real ocean. I'd seen both by now, the Atlantic and the Pacific. They called to me, the waves calming and mournful. Yet, I'd never stayed more than a day or two, always afraid I'd become hypnotized, my mind dredging up old memories.

Though I always had a partner, or as I suspected, a watchdog so we'd keep each other honest, I hardly talked, which quickly earned me the nickname 'Silo.' That was fine with me. I listened though to all the chatter of the changing passengers who spoke of the piles of cash they'd seen change hands in Capone's offices or the hatred they felt for the North Side gang. Everybody I worked with was Italian or of Italian descent while the North Side gang consisted of mostly Irish.

I tried to avoid taking sides or getting angry. Neither did any good. All I wanted was lie low and make a living for a while until I figured out what to do with my future. With myself...and Sam.

Sam. I'd underestimated her. Watching her work at Victor's, improving the kitchen and keeping up with the mountains of dishes was a wonder. She was toughing it out. I smiled when I thought of her trying so hard acting like a boy. I often wondered how people didn't see right through that.

But then I felt I knew Sam better than anybody I'd ever met. Even some of the hobos I'd lived with, ridden trains with and chased after food and work for months had not been this familiar.

I felt my smile broaden. It was time to call it a night and I looked forward to getting home. Home, what a strange term to use for our tiny space with the two cots. But Sam had made it cozy with a candle in the window, a couple of pillows and two oil paintings of paradisiacal birds she'd picked up along the curb on garbage day.

"Hey, Silo, we need you for another run, *no*." Vincenzo ambled toward me, carrying a lantern. "You got time, right?" he wheezed. "Will's sick."

Disappointment descended like an ashen cloud. "I was hoping to get home, boss. It's three in the morning.

"I know. The others have already left. I appreciate it if you...your discretion. Not something to talk about. Boss knows this rich fella..." The fat man pulled two ten-dollar bills from his pocket and handed them to me. "Need you to pick up a dame."

"Where?"

"*Tooker Alley. Dill Pickle Club.*" Vincenzo squinted, which meant I wasn't supposed to ask questions. "Pick up Miss Sloan."

I swallowed my choice words and nodded.

The streets were deserted, most clubs well hidden behind unassuming doors and darkened windows. The *Dill Pickle Club* was located behind a brick wall. A green lamp illuminated the 'danger' sign above the door, and the words "Step High, Stoop Low and Leave your Dignity Outside" printed in black letters on the orange door.

I'd never been here, but Dr. Mac, my friend and mentor when

I'd first become a hobo, had spoken of the *Dill Pickle Club* in hushed tones. According to him, Ben Reitman, aka the hobo doctor, had been a frequent guest and Dr. Mac had assumed the doctor title in his honor.

The alley was quiet and I wondered if I'd come too late. The woman was likely sleeping in her bed by now. Like I should've been. Mumbling a curse, I parked and approached the door.

Before I could knock, I was face-to-face with a man in a dark suit. Well, it was more like going frontal with a wardrobe. I had to look up a few inches.

"Yes?"

"I'm supposed to pick up Miss Sloan."

Behind the man's massive back voices, laughter and singing mixed in a roar. "Wait here." The door closed.

A minute trickled by. Then another. I was about to return to the automobile when the door opened a second time. In front of the doorman teetered a woman, her hat low above her brows, her hands covered by gloves. Against the massive chest of the man, she appeared birdlike, even feeble.

"1713 Prairie Avenue," the man said as he linked the woman's arm with mine. "You know where t'is?"

I nodded. How could I forget?

That's when I caught a glimpse of the woman's face. I knew her. Colene Sloan was heiress to the largest furniture enterprise in Illinois and had been a beauty in her teens. A million years ago, I'd lived next door. Right now her jaw was slack and her eyes veiled. Premature lines edged her mouth.

"Where's Willi?" she slurred. "You aren't Willi." Her gaze crept up my chest to my face. "Don't I know you?"

I firmly gripped her elbow. "Willi is sick," I said. "Let's get you home."

On the way back, the woman crumpled into the outer corner of the passenger seat and passed out. I was relieved I didn't have to talk or worse, reveal myself. I was sure, she wouldn't remember a thing by morning, the vapors of her breath like the air in Victor's pub.

CHAPTER ELEVEN

Sam

"I've been asking around," Paul said. He'd returned earlier than usual and the noise in the saloon was still intensifying. "Nobody's heard of Angelo."

I continued washing dishes as if I hadn't heard. Off and on I stopped and checked on the soup. We'd run out of stew by four o'clock and I was fixing a new batch of beef soup with carrots, peas and thick homemade noodles. Nobody cared that it was New Years, people as thirsty as any other day.

Victor had raised food prices, but people wanted more anyway. "It doesn't mean much though," Paul continued. "I'm just delivering on the south side. Lots of business going on in Cicero and up north."

"What's Cicero?" I asked.

"A neighborhood west of downtown. Rumor has it, Capone is building up a huge business of saloons, gambling parlors and brothels."

I turned to face Paul. "Then we need to figure out a way to get over there."

"Gosh, Sam. Give it a rest."

"How can I give it a rest when all I think about is what has happened to him?" I cried. But the truth was, it wasn't all I thought about these days. Paul was bringing home good money, so we had an easier time. He was saving most of it in our room beneath a loose floorboard by the window, and I wore a pair of new boots, sturdy wool-lined shoes I loved. More over I wondered about Paul and more specifically his kiss. I was beginning to think I'd imagined the whole thing. In the early morning I often listened to his snoring as a strange heat built in my middle. It was unsettling to say the least.

"We need more time," Paul said.

"What if—"

A crash reverberated through the wall. Whistles trilled. Men shouted.

"Nobody move. You're under arrest," a sharp voice said. It wasn't even that loud, but I could easily make it out among the racket.

"Raid," Paul whispered. He put a finger on his lips, pulled me behind him and peeked around the corner into the hall.

As the saloon exploded with running, screaming and shouting men, trying to get away, some passed us on their way to the back exit. The corridor was thick with panicked drunkards trying to escape. Somewhere beyond, outside in the back alley, whistles trilled.

Paul pointed at the staircase across the corridor, leading to our room. Then he shoved his way through the sweaty mass of drunkards, keeping my hand firmly in his. We climbed the steps two at a time and unlocked the door.

"You think they'll search up here?" I asked as anxiety gripped me by the throat.

"Possibly."

"But we didn't do anything. I don't even drink."

Paul shrugged. "Doesn't matter. You're working in an illegal establishment."

As I made her way to the window, Paul retrieved his hidden money and stuffed it beneath his shirt. Police and unmarked automobiles parked helter-skelter in front of the saloon, where a dozen men in plain clothes were guiding patrons into the backseats of squad vans. Others carried out Victor's whiskey supplies, smashing bottles and pouring contents into the sewers. Beer flowed from kegs like foamy rivers. Alcohol vapors drifted through the cracks of their window.

I tried to keep calm, but the last thing I wanted was to end up in some jail. It wouldn't take long before they'd find out my secret and then...

"What are we going to do?" I whispered, resentful I felt so shaky inside.

By the way Paul looked at me, I realized he didn't know either. His uncertainty scared me more than the raid.

"I'm not going to prison," he finally said.

"But they don't know we work for Victor."

"Likely they scoped us out for weeks. Federal agents are no dummies." He sighed. "Pack your things. We've got to get out of here."

Where to, I wanted to ask. But there was no time. I bundled my few belongings inside a spare shirt, shouldered it, and grabbed my shotgun. With Paul in the lead, we crept out into the hall. The noise downstairs was intensifying as men resisted arrest and screamed insults at the Feds. "Damn cops...don't you have better things to do...find some real criminals, for god's sake...don't tell my wife..." Victor was yelling something in Italian. Though I didn't understand the words, their meaning was clear.

With all the racket, I almost missed the footsteps. Heading up.

"Quickly." Paul pointed to the upward leading staircase. "To the attic."

We climbed to the second floor, then the third. Paul pulled down a ladder from the ceiling and shoved me onto it.

The air grew icy, our breaths white puffs in the gloom. I was glad I'd taken my coat.

"Tread lightly. They're beneath us," Paul whispered. "We'll climb out the window and move across the roofs to another building and then back down." He tucked the ladder back into place.

The attic was long and skinny and filled with an assortment of boxes and cartons. I carefully picked my way to the one narrow window, Paul close behind me. His presence calmed my nerves. He reached over me and opened the latch. The window was chin-high—the roof beyond, covered with clay tiles, sloped sharply lower.

Paul extended a palm. "I'll take your shotgun."

I turned to face him, wishing I could crawl in his arms and bury my face against his chest. Instead I handed over the weapon, wondering how he was going to carry it. "It's too steep," I said. "I'll slide off."

"Hurry. Go."

I felt myself lifted and grabbed hold of the sill, then climbed across. Outside, the shingles were slimy with moss and dampness. My soles found no traction.

Paul's head appeared in the opening. "Look for metal brackets. Make sure you don't loosen any tiles. They'll know we're up here."

I gazed to my right, where the roof ended after thirty feet. There was an alley below so I turned left, my hands and legs spread out like a spider. Ever so slowly, I crawled sideways. The pitch was steep enough to put most of my weight into the legs. I had no time to see what Paul was up to, all my attention on finding the next bracket to set my feet into.

Below, voices grew muted. Or was it my ragged breath clogging my ears? The roof ended with a foot-high wall. Beyond began the next building. I climbed across and continued. When I risked a peek to the other way, I didn't see Paul. The roofline was empty. Why wasn't he following?

I thought of returning to the window, but dismissed it. Maybe he was waiting for the police to leave. The noise downstairs had died down. All I heard were the usual automobiles driving past and blood rushing up my neck.

I edged sideways until the third roof, when I realized that I had no way down. Neither of the next two houses had windows in the attic. It was forty or more feet to the ground. I'd break my neck, if I fell.

The only good thing was that I was now hidden from the area I'd come from. But it also meant I didn't see Paul. Why was he so slow? Surely by now he could follow me.

I pressed my damp forehead against the cool tiles. I sweat and yet my legs quivered. With every passing minute, my muscles grew colder and stiffer. Soon, I'd simply slip off and tumble to the street. Visions of Mamma returned, her eyes staring, blood-soaked cloth crimson on white skin. The pain was back, that twisting and clawing that tore at my insides. Wouldn't it be easy to let go and end this? My eyes blurred. *Stop it! You're becoming like your mother, all fear and exhaustion.*

All of a sudden I knew that Paul wasn't coming. Dusk was setting, a chilly gray gloom. Soon, I wouldn't be able to see.

I grew convinced he'd wanted me out of the way. Take my shotgun and make a run for it. Something slimy climbed up my spine and with it the control of my legs and feet. I leaned forward, flexing my thigh and arm muscles. I'd go back to find him—even if it meant getting caught.

I crawled back the way I'd come, one step at a time, one arm at a time, fingers clinging to the rusty freezing brackets until each muscle seemed to spasm, threatening to let go.

I lost all track of time, trying to concentrate on the next move, the next foot until I reached the attic window. It was closed. I looked back. No, that had to be the one I'd climbed out of. It was hard to tell in the falling darkness.

Peeking through the glass, I saw nothing, just the dull glow of my reflection—a grimy face with eyes that screamed worry. "Come on," I muttered. "What would Paul do?"

With a grim smile, I braced myself and swung an elbow toward the glass. It shattered and covering my hands with the bundle, I'd dragged along, I broke away more shards and opened the lock.

Since no sounds came from below, I climbed inside and moved to the stairs. There was no sign of Paul—nothing but gloomy coldness. My legs grew weak, my ears still on high alert. Nothing. Deciding to wait, I sagged to the floor.

It was dawn when I awoke. The house seemed to hold its breath, an unsettling quiet. I listened intently and hearing nothing, unhooked the staircase. Like a cat, I snuck down step-by-step, third floor to the second. Still quiet. I peeked into our room. Mattresses and sheets lay scattered on the ground, the wardrobe stood open. I remade our beds, the street outside empty. Well, not empty, but a normal scene with the first automobiles driving and people hastening to work. The faint odor of alcohol lingered.

As the sun rose, I decided to investigate the first floor. Afraid to turn on lights, I lit the candle stub Paul had left on the windowsill and descended lower. The saloon was a mess, tables and chairs lying helter-skelter, glasses and bottles broken in-between. I risked the electric light in the kitchen.

A lukewarm stew sat on the stove and I turned it on high to heat it up. Then I rummaged for bread and ate two hard-boiled eggs.

The back exit lock was broken, but when I tried the door, it wouldn't budge. I climbed across tables and upended chairs to unlock the front. Nothing budged. Through a crack in the wooden panel, I noticed that the exterior was secured with a cast-iron gate, now locked from the outside.

I was shuttered in.

Momentarily at a loss, I wandered into the storeroom. I'd never been inside, since Victor always kept a close eye on his stock. Splintered wooden boxes and shards of brown glass littered the floor. The stink of whisky hung heavy in the air.

Aside from a few packages of macaroni, flour, two shriveled heads of white cabbage and five boxes of canned sardines, the shelves were empty. My detailed grocery list hung on the doorframe. Victor had planned to buy food tomorrow. I grabbed a can of sardines and returned to the kitchen. After serving myself a bowl of stew, I ate the sardines and stared into space. Afraid of any light shining through, I turned off the fixtures and lit her candle instead.

On the upside, I was in a building with several days of food supplies. If I stretched things, I could last a few weeks. It was better than the street or trains any day. It was warm and safe and…what?

I was nowhere nearer finding my brother. Paul had either disappeared or been arrested, and my means of earning a living had evaporated along with half a week's pay that Victor owed me. I pulled out the three one-dollar bills and counted them one more time. It was something.

All of a sudden, I jumped up. I turned on the stove and heated water in every pot I could find. Then I went upstairs and took a long bath.

In the light of the single candle, I took stock of my body. All the womanly things were there, my breasts small yet clearly not like a boy's. The fleece beneath had the same color as my hair and there was a strange pulsing between my legs. I muttered something like nonsense to myself and began to wash.

Steam rose as I splashed, enjoying the feel of hot water on skin and the knowledge I was really clean.

"Idiot," I said aloud, the sound echoing in the tiled space. Why hadn't Paul hurried out the window when he had the chance? *Maybe he didn't want to.* Maybe he was hurt. The unease I'd felt earlier was back. What if they sentenced him to years in prison? Nobody knew what these federal agents were capable of. And my shotgun was gone.

The washing didn't change anything. The ache was still there, and after a while I returned to explore. The water was almost too cool now, just a degree above tepid. Yet, my fingers unleashed something I'd never felt before.

After a while, I could no longer stop. It felt too good. My cheeks burned with the knowledge I was doing something forbidden—a horribly secret thing I'd never be able to talk about. When the climax happened, I nearly sank beneath the water. Every nerve in my middle tingled and cried out with pleasure.

What in the world had I done?

Paul

I had no more than helped Sam to the roof when steps grew audible by the attic ladder below. I quietly closed the window, rushed to the back corner and shoved the shotgun into a hollow space between two beams. By the time I returned to the ladder, a man in uniform was climbing up. Panic crept beneath my skin, making me sweat.

I scanned the window, hoping Sam would stay out there and remain quiet. Gripping the handrail, I forced myself to stand still. I'd have to play along and find Sam later. As the officer's face appeared, I raised my arms above my head and called, "I surrender."

The policeman eyed me suspiciously, wielding a billy club. "Stay there," he balked before marching to the end of the attic, around the chimneys and back. Anything larger than a mouse had no place to hide.

"What're you doing up here?" the man asked, returning to me. "Tried to get away, eh?"

I shrugged, but kept my arms raised.

"Off you go," the officer said when it became clear I wasn't going to answer. "No funny business."

I descended the attic stairs and waited for the officer to follow. I could've easily run because the man was slower than a slug, but then there was no place to go. I was trapped like a rabbit in a snare.

The billy stick made contact with my right kidney. "Down. Nice and easy."

Victor's barroom had emptied and several policemen were carrying the last of the alcohol out the front door. Beer foamed in the gutters and mixed with streams of whiskey. The vapors made my eyes water.

A last truck, its benches filled with half drunken men, stood waiting and, with a sigh, I squeezed in-between them. Hopefully, Sam was far away by now. She'd just return later and keep hiding.

That's when I noticed the wooden panels and tools already stacked on the sidewalk. They were boarding up Victors. I had seen other places sealed off before. The police did a thorough job with locks and chains. Sam wouldn't be able to get in.

Sweat trickled down my back as I slumped forward. Not because it was hot, but because I realized Sam was going to be on the street again. Just when I thought we'd had a place to settle, it had been ripped away. Sam wouldn't be going in there and I had no idea where she'd be. We'd never talked about the possibility of being separated or what we would do. Where we would meet in an emergency.

You don't even know when you'll be out again. Who knew how long it took? Would I go to jail? Maybe if I hurried, I'd find her hanging out in the neighborhood. She would wait in front of Victor's.

From that moment on, every hour I spent in custody stretched into infinity. The drive to the police station at Maxwell and Morgan took forever. And the entire time I thought about Sam. How she would return to Victor's only to find it locked up. I felt her uncertainty, her dread. Saw her reddened cheeks, felt her stomach as it ached with hunger. I knew the fear that would creep up inside her, knowing she had no place to go. No food. And no Paul.

One by one, the men were registered, fingerprinted and photographed and marched down a long hallway. Doors slammed. Phones rang. Men hollered drunkenly.

When it was my turn, I announced, "I want to be interviewed. I didn't drink."

"That's what they all say. Now keep your mouth shut," the officer who'd fingerprinted me said. "You'll get your time in court. Like everyone else."

My mouth closed so hard, my back teeth ground together. I welcomed the pain in my jaw. I'd not get out of here any time soon. To my surprise, my vision blurred and I angrily blinked away the wetness. Why couldn't I be drunk and forget everything?

I was handcuffed again and led down the hall. Like the others

before me. There was no telling how long I'd be here.
And Sam would be lost to me.

CHAPTER TWELVE

Sam

I slept better than expected, the house quiet except for the occasional creak in the floor. I was used to that and didn't worry. When the gray outside began to filter into the room, I dressed and fixed myself breakfast of two hard-boiled eggs, toast, leftover stew, and another can of sardines.

What was the use of rationing? Last time I'd lost my bag within a day. Once I'd run out of things to eat, I'd have to leave. Unless…

If I fashioned a rope from one of the upstairs windows, I might be able to climb out and back in after dark. The place was worlds better than anywhere outside. I could find the police station and ask about Paul.

Paul who?

With a pang I realized I had no idea what his last name was. They'd look at me as if I'd lost my mind.

He's tall with brown hair, that hangs across his forehead, a bit roguish, Officer, oh, and I almost forgot, he has green eyes that ignite my insides.

Very funny, Sam.

But I had to do something. What if Paul needed help? At least I could find out what happened to people who got arrested. Were they being tried in court? Did Paul have to go to jail?

I lay on the cot and stared at the empty sheets of Paul's cot. I could still smell him, a whiff of shampoo he'd borrowed from Victor, the Ivory soap he'd washed his clothes with. My heart grew heavy when I realized that my family's shotgun had vanished too. The police had no doubt confiscated it.

A loud crash reverberated through the floor. Paul! He was back.

Without another thought, I raced downstairs. The backdoor stood open a foot, the wind slicing a frozen corridor into the entrance. Nobody was in sight.

Beyond, in the gloom of the barroom, somebody was opening doors. A glass shattered.

"Damn," a voice said. It wasn't Paul's.

I turned quickly and had about reached the staircase when a man came running from the kitchen and collided with me.

"What *yo'* doing here?" The man's gray newsboy hat was pulled low over his narrowed brows.

I twisted sideways, intend on running upstairs and locking the door to my room. But I was too slow. Grimy fingers tore at my wrist with such ferocity, I thought my bones would snap.

"Carl, come take a look."

"Not now," a muffled voice called from the barroom. "Where would he've hidden it?"

"What's *yo'* name?" the man with the newsboy hat asked.

"None of your business," I barked, realizing too late that I hadn't used my deeper voice and that my shirt was thin enough to show my meager breasts.

"Looky, a girl with attitude." The man smiled, the same smile I'd seen on the men in the Cincinnati train yard. "I like it."

"Quit *yo'* mumbling and help me," came the other voice, shrill with irritation.

"Let it go, Carl. I've got something better. Should be worth somethin'."

I felt a pinch in my bottom, then a crude palm made contact with my chest. I sucked in air.

"Like that, eh?" the man chuckled and dragged me into the barroom.

All the cabinet doors stood open and a man was on his knees pounding at the floorboards. "Could be under here."

"How do *yo'* know he kept anything back? The fuzz may have gotten it all."

"I know Victor. He was using this place like a piggy bank." After another two minutes of pounding, during which I searched my mind frantically for an escape without success, the man straightened.

"Who's this?" The man named Carl asked. His eyes widened and he roved across me as if I stood naked.

"That's what I've been trying to tell yo'," Newsboy Hat chuckled. "Found this doll sneaking around in here."

"Who are you?" Carl asked.

"Sam Bruno… the cook."

"I thought they locked this place up."

"They did but—"

"Never mind that now." Newsboy Hat took another pinch of my bottom. "I've got an idea." In the dim light his lids and nose looked purplish. I noticed a strong liquor smell on his breath. In fact, Carl had the same look and smell. They were boozers.

"What?" Carl twisted on his heels, obviously still in search of Victor's hidden stash. "You know where it is?" he cried, his paw grabbing my throat with sudden viciousness.

"Sorry," I croaked realizing I was afraid. It was the same kind of fear that had gripped me in the train yard, except this time there was no Paul wielding a club to save me.

"Don't ruin her. We'll take her to Fizzy's."

"Sell her?"

"*Look* at her. She's got to be worth at least fifty clams. Bet she's a virgin, too," NewsBoy Hat cackled.

"All right. Let's go," Carl said. "We'll come back later and look again."

It was dusk by the time I, framed by the two men, arrived at a building that had seen better days. "*Fizzy's Bar and Club*," it announced in red and white lettering. Lights flashed off and on.

Several times, I'd tried to bolt, but the grip of the men never ceased. Just the opposite. Their fingers clutched me like cuffs, so that my skin felt bruised and sore. Despite my predicament all I could think of was Paul. Christmas morning when he'd been there like a present himself, the gift of chocolate, his kiss.

"Take her upstairs." A woman with wrinkles like an eighty-year old and a voice of a lifelong smoker gave me the once over. Stick thin, she was dressed in a loose fitting, ankle-length dress. The white feather sticking straight up from a gold headband didn't do much to soften her look.

I was shoved into a room and heard the door lock from the outside. Heaving with frustration, I took in my surroundings: a couple of scuffed wooden chairs, a sagging twin bed and a washbowl. The window was barred. I couldn't even open it to allow the stale smoke to escape. I was locked in again.

Tired and dispirited, I sank on a chair and dropped my head into my hands.

ANNETTE OPPENLANDER

CHAPTER THIRTEEN

Paul

The cell I entered was stuffed with men. They occupied every
inch—sat, stood, and leaned. Some slept despite the racket. I
picked my way across the floor and squeezed in-between a burly
man with a full beard and a kid no older than fifteen.

Neither of them spoke, so I lowered my head and pulled up
my legs. I bit down the dread about my arrest, but worse about
Sam and what would happen to her. I envisioned her climbing
across roofs, falling to her death. I thought of her landing on the
street and finding Victor's pub boarded up. There were a thousand
scenarios in which she could get hurt or …

At some point, I looked up. As a hobo, I'd learned to take my
time and study my surroundings, gauge the mood and intention of
a man. One never knew what people did once they were trapped.
Around me, people were arguing, monologueing, coughing, farting,
staring and scratching. As my gaze wandered around the room, I
noticed a man sitting on one of the few benches. He was still as if
asleep, his eyes open, reminding me of somebody frozen.

That's when I began to look closer…and immediately knew
who it was. The likeness was so striking, I felt as if Sam had
returned to be by my side. I carefully straightened and clambered
across the mass of bodies.

"You must be Angelo," I said, feeling my mouth move into a
smile. Those blue eyes and black hair, the shape of the chin
reminded me so much of Sam, I wanted to hug the stranger.

74

Angelo squinted at me suspiciously. "You are?"

"You don't know me, but I know your sister. Sam."

Life moved into Angelo's eyes and the blue flamed brighter. He gripped my arm. "How do you know Sam? Tell me."

"She's fine. At least I think she is. We rode the trains together from Cincinnati. She and I were working at a pub, until the raid today. Sam escaped before the police got to her. I wasn't so lucky."

Angelo massaged a bandaged area on his forearm and made a face. "Why's she in Chicago?"

"To find *you*!" I watched curiously as Angelo shook his head, realizing that the man didn't know about his mother. "Your mom had an accident and died."

Angelo's shoulders slumped forward as if somebody had let the air out of a balloon. He shook his head. "But she wasn't sick. I never..." With a sigh he wiped his eyes.

"I'm so sorry," I said. "Sam was all alone and she knew you'd gone to Chicago. So in her silly wisdom," a chuckle broke from my throat, "she set off to find you...in a city of three million."

A slow smile crept on Angelo's face, followed by the scrunching of eyebrows. "Sam was always impulsive." His gaze met mine. "She does things from the heart. Things that aren't always smart."

"I know."

"So, you have no idea where she is now?"

"Sorry. In fact, I'm not sure how I'll find her again once I get out of this joint."

"What a fucked up world," Angelo said. He spoke quietly and more to himself than to me.

"I'm sorry about your mother." Our eyes met again. "Why are *you* here?"

"Bar brawl. Didn't get out fast enough. I wasn't feeling well." Angelo lifted his arm. The bandage was old and had bled through, the skin around it, bluish and swollen. His gaze returned to me. "So you know my sister. You two an item?"

I stared, not sure how to respond. The kiss came to mind, my gift to her on Christmas morning. Nothing much, really. Almost laughable and yet...

"Not sure, to be honest. I think if we had time I'd like that."

"What's your name again?"

"Paul McKay."

75

"Sit with me for a bit, would you?" With that Angelo shoved his neighbor to make room for me. "Tell me more."

And for the next hour I told Angelo about life as a hobo and how I'd helped Sam get away from the thugs, how we'd run from the police…all the way up to our arrival in Chicago. Only Angelo didn't reciprocate. He remained quiet, asked questions and listened intently. About his own life, he remained mute.

Two days later, I still didn't know anymore about Sam's brother. We'd talked for hours and yet, there was a weight pressing down Angelo's shoulders. He slept in fits or not at all. I requested new dressings and, after a day's wait, rebandaged Angelo's arm. The cut was deep, but seeped less and seemed to heal.

"McKay, out!"

I snapped out of a daze and absentmindedly patted Angelo on the shoulder before squeezing past the men to the door.

Except for a couple of guards, a typist and a man in a cheap business suit, the courtroom was deserted. The judge looked bored and sleepy. "Name?"

"Paul McKay."

"Birth date?"

"March 27, 1902."

The judge's eyes focused for the first time. "McKay…you Regibald McKay's son?"

I was taken aback. In my head I'd prepared a defense, but I hadn't expected a question like that. "Eh, yes, Your Honor."

The judge leaned forward, eyeing me from his high seat. "What are you doing in court, son?"

What kind of a question was that?

"I'm Judge Jonathan Briggs. Regi is an old friend. In fact," here the judge pointed a forefinger at me, "I met you a few times at family gatherings. You were…well, never mind."

I bit my lips. "I don't remember."

Briggs leaned farther forward still, his chest nearly on the bench, his eyes grave. "You realize your father is in a bad way? He doesn't have long. Maybe a week."

What was the man talking about? Father had always had the constitution of a horse, had always recovered from illness quickly. Often up at five and still awake at midnight. He'd hardly slept more than four hours in his life. Surely, there was a mistake. The judge confused him with somebody else.

"I don't think you know my father," I said. But then the judge had called Father 'Regi,' a nickname only his friends used.

"You grew up in the Prairie Avenue District, right?"

I nodded. Stunned.

"I know your house. Your mother...a terrible tragedy."

"Your Honor," the bailiff called from the door, "the next defendant is ready."

"Two minutes." Briggs waved away the bailiff and addressed me. "Now, listen. I'm going to dismiss your case under the condition that you go home. This afternoon. It may be too late already, but..."

I numbly signed a document and staggered toward the door. Visions of home flooded me: Father reading the paper at breakfast, tinkering in his private lab, a place I hadn't been allowed to visit without supervision, my parents welcoming guests at a dinner party...my mother's kind expression when she tucked me into bed.

"He is your *father*," Briggs called after me.

At the door, I almost collided with the next defendant who I'd seen some place in the crowded jail. I briefly thought of Angelo and Sam, but then there was Father who lay dying. A father I hadn't seen in more than seven years.

I hardly noticed the street noise, automobiles bustling, streetcars screeching and ringing their bells. I began to walk. It was drizzling, and a freezing wind dug beneath my clothes. I wasn't dressed for a Chicago winter. Yet, I didn't feel it, the unease of what I'd find squeezing my chest until I gasped for air.

Sam

When the lock turned, I flinched and jumped from my seat, but there was nowhere to go.

"Get up and strip!" The woman from earlier eyed me from the door, now secured by a burly man in a pinstriped suit and fedora. He looked like an oversized closet with fleshy cheeks and a pinkish scar cutting his right brow in half.

I straightened as a horrible feeling of unease gripped me.

The woman took a drag from her cigarette holder. "Hurry up, I don't have all day."

When I didn't move, the woman approached in a flash and impatiently tucked at my coat. At least the men had allowed me to fetch it from my room before entering the icy streets.

"No," I cried. "Let me go."

The woman barked a laugh that turned into spasms of coughing. "Honey. You're mine now. I paid forty five dollars, and you're going to earn each and every one of them."

"Doing what?" I was pretty sure I knew.

"We'll get to that."

I squinted at the wrinkly woman and crossed my arms. "You don't have any right."

"Missy, if you don't strip this minute, I'm going to have Joe here do it for you. He'll love it, I can promise you that."

Joe 'Meathead' grunted. He obviously hadn't received as much attention developing a brain as he had growing a body, I thought. "Can he turn around?" I finally said.

The woman sighed. "Joe, face the door."

I took off my coat, then my new boots, unbuttoned my shirt and dropped my pants until I stood shivering in the boy's shorts und undershirt.

"Take them off."

I shook my head. Tears pricked my eyeballs. *You're NOT going to cry,* I commanded. Biting down hard, I stripped off my underthings, trying in vain to cover myself with my hands.

"Turn around."

I rotated, feeling like one of the pigs taken to the Cincinnati slaughterhouse.

"What's your name?"

"Sam...Samantha Bruno."

Bony fingers gripped my hair. "What happened here?" the woman mumbled. "Too short, much too short." The next moment, a hand groped between my legs. "Virgin, for sure."

My face burned. I wanted to scream at the old hag, slap her disgusting nicotine-stained fingers away, but the words stuck in my throat and my arms hung uselessly.

"Wash and put on these clothes on the bed." The woman gave another cough that sounded like a growl. "Somebody will be back with dinner." She bent low and collected my clothes. "You won't need these anymore."

At the door the woman paused. "I'm Madame Beatrice. Welcome to the club, Samantha."

The door closed, a key turned.

Shivering, I ambled to the washstand. The water was

lukewarm, the towel threadbare and scratchy. I washed slowly from top to bottom and returned to the bed. I grimaced, wanting to cry and laugh at the same time. How lucky could you get? Two washes in one day.

I put on the pair of ivory colored silky drawers, a matching camisole and a slinky maroon dress with a large collar and a row of gold buttons down the front. The mirror showed a stranger. My neckline was so low, it revealed most of my chest bone. But my head was what caught my attention. Paul had done a pretty good job with the hair. Not quite chin-length, it covered my ears and formed a black cap around my skull. Somehow it made my eyes blaze more intensely. Paul.

He'd never find me now…in this place.

I knew where I was. Well, not really, but I had a pretty good idea what was going on here. Sure, I hadn't had any boyfriends, but Angelo had had a girl before and over the years I'd picked up plenty of street talk.

My vision blurred and a gurgle escaped until I sobbed out loud. I'd landed in a brothel, offered to men on the altar of lust until I looked like Beatrice, worn, old and crumpled. I tore off the dress and threw it on the chair. Then I buried my head in the shabby pillow and cried and cried.

I awoke to movement. In the yellowish shine of the ceiling lamp, a girl about my age was placing a tray on the bedside table. She had a round face with a tiny chin, her curls washed out and dull from too much hydrogen peroxide. "Eat your grub."

"I'm not hungry," I whispered.

The girl shrugged. "Have it your way." She was about to close the door when I called after her.

"Please wait. Can you tell me where I am?"

The girl pretended not to hear. The lock turned. I was alone again.

I sat up to inspect the tray: some meat in gravy, a heap of potatoes, green beans and a roll. Taking a sip of water, I pulled up my legs and nibbled the bread.

"Come on. Quit your crying," I said as new tears rolled down my cheeks. *You didn't come all this way to get stopped by some third-class madam. Think!*

But no matter how I racked my brain, I couldn't come up with a way to escape. The window was locked and barred with half-inch metal rods. That left the door. Which was also locked.

Soon, a man would enter, wanting sex. I didn't know all the details, but I knew enough. Mamma had warned me about boys and men. "Stay away from them, especially when they're liquored up. Never follow a man to a room when you're alone."

They'd keep me in here until she no longer cared to leave. However long that took. As new panic gripped me, I slipped beneath the blanket. Only to sit back up.

I needed a weapon. My gaze fell on the fork next to my dinner plate. Stuffing it beneath the pillow, I lay back and smiled grimly.

It was a start.

CHAPTER FOURTEEN

Paul

It took me three hours to reach my old neighborhood, a row of multi-story mansions with sprawling gardens and elaborate wrought-iron fences. There were no tramps, not a speck of refuse on the street. Here, such things ceased to exist. They weren't allowed. Here, men and women paraded in gloves and carried umbrellas. They wore furs, silk, wool and leather, their skin as clean and white as fresh linen.

I realized where I was, not because of the houses or the tree-lined streets and shimmering vehicles, but because of the quiet. All I heard were birds chirping and a lone gardener snipping away at a bush.

At last, my steps slowed and then stopped. I'd driven Colene Sloan home the other night and stopped next door. But standing here, alone, on the street was different. I felt naked and vulnerable, as though I were back in the past, helplessly watching my parents. My strength and resilience of the past seven years had been stripped away the precise moment I'd walked away from the courthouse.

In front of me stood my childhood home, a three-story brick and limestone mansion, its multitude of chimneys sputtering smoke. I was about to reach for the entry gate's knob when I noticed his hand. Well, what I knew was my hand was covered in a grayish layer of dust and filth. My head itched. I hadn't changed clothes in days, the leather of my shoes scuffed and muddy. I was soaked through and through from the steady drizzle of rain. In fact, I was dirtier and smellier than I'd ever been during my hobo days.

What was I doing here? I was a worker now, one man in millions who struggled from day to day. I needed to look for Sam and get a message to Angelo. Then I'd hop another train and be out of here. That old judge would never know if I saw Father.

And if Father is truly dying?

"You, there, the servant's entrance is in back. I'll tell them to feed you." A man in an immaculate suit approached from the other side of the fence, his shoes so shiny, they reflected even the gray light of dusk.

"I'm leaving," I said, my voice so quiet, I hardly recognized it myself.

But the man had heard me. "Wait... Paul, is that you?" The man's voice was no longer reserved, it sounded like a plea.

I had already turned, but then I didn't walk off like I'd intended. I couldn't. My feet and legs were stuck—paralyzed.

"I'm so glad, sir," the man cried as he tore open the gate and rushed to my side. "We thought something happened, we...your father..."

Our eyes met.

"Mercer," I whispered as memories of Oswald Mercer, my father's butler, flooded my mind. The man had been with us as long as I remembered.

"Young Master Paul," Mercer said. "I'm happy to see you even if it is at an awful time. Your father..." he choked as tears shone in his reddened eyes. He struggled for composure and swallowed repeatedly. "I back your pardon. It's...we worried something had happened to you. He missed you terribly." He scanned my filthy coat. "Will you not join us?"

There it was. The decision I'd dreaded. Stupid judge. Why had he ordered me to go home? What were the chances the man knew Father? Now here I stood. It'd been easy when I was away. The longer I'd been gone, the easier it got, the lingering hatred fueling me like a low-heat coal fire. I'd thought of my previous life less and less.

If I left now, I'd never come back. And for all I knew, I would despise myself for the rest of my life. Regret was a terrible waste. It could wreak havoc on a man's soul. Chisel away at it over the years until nothing was left. I had a chance now to make good, to try to come to terms with what Father had done. What *I* had done. Was I really that much better? Had I really understood at fifteen what Father had felt or thought?

Unlikely. Life was complicated. So was love.

Mercer stood patiently, watching me intently. And so I wordlessly turned and entered my childhood home for the first time in seven years.

Sam

I awoke to the sound of a loud crash. Somebody pounded on a door down the hall. A woman screamed once, then again, a lone sound full of terror. Glass splintered, then more pounding. I thought I heard Beatrice's smoke-laced voice.

I got out of bed and turned on the overhead light. No telling what time it was or what was going on.

Somewhere beneath, a piano plinked. The noise nearby had stopped. I put an ear to the door and thought I heard whimpering. Then nothing. I carefully tried the door. No luck.

With a sigh, I returned to my bed, but sleep wouldn't come. The entire place seemed to buzz with alcohol fumes, giggles and singing. Then there were the banging sounds below, a woman's rhythmic cries rising.

When the door lock turned, I quickly laid back and pretended to sleep. A hand grabbed my shoulder.

"Rise and shine, Samantha."

Upon opening my eyes, I was face-to-face with Beatrice, who squinted through the smoke of a fresh cigarette.

"What?"

"We've got a girl out, so we need you earlier than expected." She nodded toward the slinky dress on the chair. "Put that on and come with me."

I let the fabric glide over my head and shook it into place. The fork called to me from under the pillow.

"Don't get any ideas," Beatrice said as we descended the stairs. "Joe doesn't have a sense of humor. Neither does his brother."

On the main floor, I did a double take. There were two Joe Meatheads, the one I'd met and a second huge man with similarly mean eyes, the same vacant expression, but no scar across the brow.

But then I got so distracted that I forgot all about the bodyguards. The parlor, lit with candles and chandeliers, was filled with women in various states of undress. Some showed bare breasts, others wore lacy camisoles that left little to the imagination. All were in close contact with their 'clients,' touching, laughing and chatting away as if the men in front of them were the most interesting people. The visitors wore waistcoats and cravats, drinking whiskey and smoking, unless their hands were too busy fondling the girl in front of them.

"You'll be working with Tina tonight," Beatrice said into my ear, pointing toward the buxom girl who I recognized as the one bringing me dinner. Tina had squeezed herself into a shiny red dress, her blond hair in ringlets around her chin. In the glittering light, Tina looked much older than a few hours ago, her cheeks puffy and her eyelids pink. "Do what she does. Be friendly. Smile." Beatrice coughed a chuckle. "You never know, you may like it." She took me by the arm and guided me toward Tina and her beau.

"Say hello to Samantha. She's new, so show her how it's done."

Tina shot me a look so full of loathing, I recoiled. The next instant Tina smiled sweetly, taking my hand. "Isn't she a doll?" she said to the man in front of her, pinching my wrist.

I swallowed an insult and yanked away my hand.

The man hadn't noticed a thing, his eyes glassy and lewd. "Hey, sweetheart," he breathed as I tried to turn away. Next thing I knew, the man was pulling me close, my nose against his sweat-soaked silk shirt while he patted my bottom. I wrestled out of the embrace and took a step back, only to receive another nasty look from Tina.

"Louis, not so fast," Tina cackled. "You're with me, remember?" She patted his arm and shoved her bosom toward him.

"I want 'er," Louis slurred, his gaze still on me. "Those eyes…I pay extra." Taking an unsteady step toward me, he pulled a wad of cash from his pocket. "Here, sweetie, twenty more should do, right?" He pressed the damp bill into my hand and latched on to my elbow.

Tina huffed something unintelligible as she disappeared into the crowd. I wanted to follow, but the man's grip held me in place.

"Where we going?" Louis said as he ambled forward, dragging me toward the stairs.

"You better stay with Tina," I cried. "She's your girl."

Louis snickered. "But I like you better." His paw made contact with my backside and I felt the heat of his palm through the thin fabric of my dress. Nobody seemed to notice my distress. If anything, the chatter was growing louder.

From the corner of my eye I noticed Tina gesticulate at Beatrice, who shook her head while blowing smoke rings. *Get over to them.*

"This way." I pulled hard to change direction. "I think he's confused," I said as we came to a stop in front of Beatrice. "He wants Tina," I said into Beatrice's ear.

"Hey, sweetie, where's the room?" Louis said at that moment. "I've got quite the present for you." He bent low and planted a wet kiss on my cheek. Suppressing my disgust, I turned my head the other way and wiped my cheek. When I turned back, I caught Tina's glare.

"Number 2, first door on the left." Beatrice hissed in my direction, "Looks like you're mistaken, honey."

Then she smiled at Louis and took his other arm. "Let me show you the way, Mr. Tibbert."

Louis chuckled happily and seized my elbow once more. "Send a bottle, will you? I'm still mighty thirsty." I felt myself being dragged upstairs, my gaze on Beatrice like a lifeline. With every step my heart sank a little lower, until I had trouble catching my breath. I considered running to my room, but one of the meatheads was surely going to drag me back.

"Isn't this the place?" Louis said, letting go of Beatrice's arm and pulling me inside Number 2. I caught a last look at Beatrice, her expression leaving no doubt of what would follow if I didn't obey. I swallowed away the lump in my throat and resolutely turned toward the drunken man.

Compared to my room, this place was decked out all in red: red velvet wallpaper, red satin bedspread, red carpets and curtains.

A knock at the door made me freeze. "Your drink order, sir," a man said on the other side.

I flew to the door. Anything to delay the inevitable. *Don't ever go into a room alone with a man,* Mamma's voice rang through my head. *Oh, Mamma.*

"Put it on the table," Louis slurred.

"Don't lock," the man whispered to me as he left. "Precaution."

I nodded and carefully closed the door. Louis was tearing his tie over his head with his left, wiping sweat from his forehead with his right.

"Pour me a drink, sweetheart."

I measured two inches of the amber liquid and handed it to him as he sank on the bed.

He took a sip, then another. "Sit with me."

"I'd rather stay here."

Louis chuckled, "You a tease, baby?" His eyes raking over my body. "Take off your clothes, then."

I hesitated, my fingers half-heartedly tugging at the seam of my dress. I wanted to move farther from the sweat-soaked lump of a man who reeked of cheap whiskey.

A shadow passed across Louis's face. "Come on. I'm paying good money. Don't waste my time."

"Better drink up," I said. "I'll refill your glass."

Louis drained the whiskey, but when I approached him, he gripped my wrist, suspicion in his eyes. "What you playing at?"

"N...nothing. You're hurting me."

Louis's fingers relaxed slightly though he didn't let go. I poured more whiskey and tried to step back again.

"Oh, no, you're staying here. Put the bottle on the nightstand."

He drained the glass in one gulp and carelessly threw it to the ground, both hands groping for my breast. "Aw, you're a sweet thing."

The next moment I was yanked off my feet onto the bed as Louis pulled up my dress.

No, my insides screamed, not like this.

The man's strength was immense and I was being swallowed. *Don't pay attention, think of something nice.* My mind wandered to the time when my parents had been happy, when life had been simple.

Only to be torn from my daydream by Louis tugging at my drawers. His breath came in spurts, heavy gulps of air as if he'd been running.

"Why don't you lie back and rest a moment while I take off my clothes?" I said. "I'll be punished if you tear them up."

Louis muttered something, but let go. He took off his pants and crawled beneath the cover, his eyes on me like dirty hands.

I slowly removed me dress and hung it across the chair. I was about to place the twenty-dollar bill from the band of my pants and hide it beneath the washbowl when I heard something buzzing.

Louis still lay on his back, his eyes now closed, his mouth open as he snored. I sighed as a chill ran through me. Now that the man was sleeping, I realized how terrified I was. I had to get out of here.

You can't. They'll know. Better pretend you had sex. Let the man think he lay with you.

Remaining in my undergarments, I sat down on the chair and dozed off.

A moan awoke me. In the gray morning light, Louis rolled to his side, rubbing his temples.

Alarmed, I got up from my chair. "Good morning," I said.

"Morning." His eyes focused on me. "You the girl I bought?"

I nodded, forcing my face into a slow smile. "You were good."

"Was I?" He fingered beneath the cover. "Doesn't feel like it. Got a boner the size of Manhattan. Oh, my head is killing me."

I nodded again, faster. "It's the whiskey. I can get you something to make you feel better."

"Oh yeah? Come here, I know exactly what you can do." He moaned again and lay back on his pillow. "On second thought, get me a Bloody Mary."

"I'll see what I can find." I hurried to put on my dress and left the room. The hallway was deserted, the heavy scent of sweat, cold cigar smoke and whiskey in the air. I rushed downstairs in search of the kitchen.

One of the Meatheads was stretched out on an armchair by the front door snoring. I tiptoed through the parlor to the back of the house.

The kitchen was a mess. Dirty glasses piled high, flies swarmed. I wrinkled my nose and opened drawers and cupboards in search of medicines. I found what I was looking for in a separate closet by the pantry. As I was reaching for the aspirin, my eyes fell on a tin of *DeWitt's Laxative Lozenges*.

I smiled grimly. Exactly what I wanted!

Holding my breath, I listened for sounds and when it remained quiet, took ten pills from the box. I crushed them with a knife, collected the dust in a glass and added tomato juice from the icebox. Grabbing a spoon, I headed into the parlor where I'd noticed a half-empty bottle of whiskey.

As I was reaching for the bottle, a shadow fell over me. I'd missed the fact that Meathead no longer occupied the chair. "What have we here?" he said as he twisted my arm to show the glass with the juice.

"My…customer, Mr. Louis," I said, hoping my voice sounded firm. "He needs something for his hangover. I'm getting him a bit of whiskey for the juice."

Joe Meathead looked me up and down and then slowly let go of my arm. "Aw' right. If he wants more action, though, he's got to pay again."

My hand shook as I added a splash of whiskey and swirled the spoon. In the red mess were bits of white, but Meathead didn't seem to notice. "I'll tell him."

Louis sat in his underpants on the corner of the bed, his head in his hands. He didn't look up when I entered.

I approached arm outstretched. "Here's your drink."

Louis took it and downed it in one swallow. He wiped his mouth as his eyes focused on me. "Come here, sweets. Got to go for another round." He pointed at his bulging middle and chuckled.

"Of course," I said, forcing my mouth into a toothy smile. "But first tell me what you do for a living. You must be an important man to have so much money." Louis grumbled something, so I continued. "I really love to know who you are."

A reluctant grin spread on Louis's face, making his bulbous nose spread wider. "You're a curious one, aren't you?" He chuckled smugly. "That Tina never cares."

I carefully sagged on the easy chair, leaning forward in the process. "I'm just so impressed," I cried.

"I'm in the undergarment business," Louis said. "There's a fortune in brassieres. You wouldn't believe the demand." And for the next fifteen minutes Louis lectured me on the fineries of men's and women's drawers, brassieres and other unmentionables.

"So very interesting," I threw in once in a while.

Until Louis stopped mid-sentence, his expression quizzical.

"You wouldn't lead me on?"

"Never," I cried, but moved toward the window to put more space between us. Despite his protruding stomach, Louis got off the bed in a flash. "Oh no, not that game again." He dragged me to the bed and crudely pulled up my dress.

Panic clogged my throat. Not a word came out. Once he found out I was a virgin, he'd realize I'd led him on. Why wasn't the laxative working?

Louis's fat fingers made their way beneath my drawers. I cried out at the roughness. And there was this thing, this humungous piece of flesh digging into my side and now...oh no, I tried to shout, but my mouth filled with Louis's shirt as he shoved me on the bed and struggled on top.

He grunted and then a giant fart filled the air. Despite my disgust, I grinned.

Louis slid off suddenly. "What the..." Then he groaned, but this time it was likely from pain. He half doubled over and hurried to the door.

I rose slowly and straightened my clothes. Louis would be gone for quite some time. Hopefully, he'd consider the alcohol the culprit. No telling what he'd do if he ever found out. I climbed to the third floor and crawled under the covers, the $20 note securely tucked beneath the bedframe.

Sometime mid-morning, I awoke to the door opening. Tina was back with another tray she about threw at me.

"You do that again, you're dead."

I shrugged. "Didn't do anything. He was disgusting."

"Who cares? He always tips well," Tina said, her nostrils flared.

"I don't want to be here."

Tina bent over me, her nose almost touching. "Honey, nobody is asking." Then she straightened and stalked off. The key in the door turned once more.

I leaned back on the pillow. I knew I should eat, but the thought of the fat man trying to stick his thing into me, made my stomach turn. No way I'd be able to do it again. Next time I wouldn't be so lucky. Next time I'd lose my virginity. At least before I'd been my own boss, even if it meant I was hungry and alone.

Not alone. I'd had Paul.

Green eyes moved into my vision: Paul sitting in the cargo train, explaining hobo life. Paul hitting the bull and helping me climb the fence, Paul handing me a bar of chocolate for Christmas…his lips on mine. Fresh tears welled as I realized I'd never see Paul again.

You're here to find Angelo was the last thing I thought of before dozing off.

CHAPTER FIFTEEN

Paul

The curtains in Father's bedroom were drawn, sinking the room in shadowy gloom, my father's features soft.

Last night, I had only washed hands before allowing Mercer to lead me upstairs.

"Sir?" Mercer had said. "This way, please."

I'd swallowed and followed the butler to the second floor and down the hall. I'd told myself I wouldn't cry when I saw Father. Relief swept through me when I learned that he'd been sedated with a heavy dose of morphine.

Every step I recognized something: the burgundy red chair with the ornate carving of lions and giraffes by the fireplace— Father's favorite chair, the painting of Mother as a young girl, her blonde hair long and flowing, the lamps and wall hangings. The smell. For the briefest moment, I closed my eyes. I would've recognized this place by its scent of cigars, furniture polish, even the quality of the dust. Only Mother's perfume was absent.

I slept a few hours cleaning up in my old bathroom. Now I took a seat, watching the still form on the bed. Some of the anger from seven years ago lingered. It was a cloud of something intangible, yet it lay on my chest like a weight and made every breath difficult. The day Father had sent me away was imprinted on my mind as if it had happened yesterday.

That morning, I'd taken breakfast in the parlor as usual. In those days at fifteen, fury ruled me. I was consumed by the need to attack Father for what he'd done. I'd been prepared for another argument, ready to scream insults.

But Father had entered the room that morning and instead of sitting down across the table, had folded his hands—those precise and always clean hands—across his belly and announced: "Paul, this is your last morning. As soon as you're done with breakfast, Mercer will take you to the station and accompany you to West Nottingham Academy, where you'll complete your last three years of school. You can come home on holidays, in fact, I hope that you will. In the meantime," and here he focused his sharp gaze on me, "you will study hard and get along. WNA is a first-class school and offers great preparation for university."

I quit chewing the eggs I'd enjoyed and threw down my fork. "What're you talking about, Father?"

"I think your hearing is just fine. I wish you a pleasant trip." Father had straightened my shoulders and left the room.

I'd jumped up and yelled something. What, I no longer remembered. It didn't matter anyway. Back then I'd left my home for the first time.

Now I was back for the first time, in a room I'd rarely set foot in. Father lay on his rear, mouth open, asleep. His cheekbones stuck out, his mouth caved in. He'd aged twenty years in the space of seven. What was left of his hair white and sparse, his skull bony and dotted with age spots. A woman in a white nurse's outfit hovered nearby, presiding over a table of assorted pill bottles, liniment, bowls, compresses and towels.

My eyes welled over as I realized that the judge had been right. The room was filled with something, I'd encountered before. Death. Father was indeed dying, and maybe I was already too late. All of a sudden, I leaned forward and gripped Father's hands. They were emaciated now, rippled with bluish veins and frail as birds' bones.

"Father, it's me, Paul," I cried. Tears spilled down my cheeks as I fell to my knees. I no longer cared. "Can you hear me?"

The nurse rushed to my side as if she wanted to shove me away.

"Leave him be," Mercer said from somewhere.

The nurse lowered her head and stepped back.

"Father?" I tried again, struggling to recognize the man I'd known. The man I'd held responsible for Mother's death.

Regibald McKay's lids fluttered. Then his eyes opened. I squeezed his hands. "I'm here, Father. It's Paul."

Regibald's gaze focused and for a moment, he was back: the old, super smart inventor who'd taught me riding and shooting, had taken me on fishing trips and later into his factories.

"Paul," he whispered, his formerly green eyes almost colorless. "You are here."

My throat was too thick to let out more than a squeak.

"I thought you were…" Regi said.

"I'm fine, Father."

"Come close."

And so I bent low until my ear was right by my father's mouth.

"About your mother," he began.

I wanted to recoil then, stick two fingers into my ears. Anything not to relive that day.

I still recalled finding Mother. It had been a glorious fall day in 1917, a Sunday when I'd rushed into her room after she'd failed to appear for breakfast. We'd planned a boat ride on Lake Michigan with both parents in attendance.

Most of the time Mother did not participate in excursions. She preferred to stay home or go on trips to town by herself.

After I'd knocked and there was no answer, I'd found her in bed, eyes open and not breathing. She'd taken sleeping pills.

That was the day I'd stopped speaking with my father.

Sam

"Psst," a voice said. "You awake?"

When I opened my eyes, I was face to face with a girl I'd never seen. Brown hair played around her chin—she had a perky nose and a smile, I couldn't help but return.

"I'm Maggie…Margaret," the girl whispered. "I'm not supposed to be here, but…" she slumped on the edge of the bed, a conspirative look in her eyes.

I leaned back and shook my head, my throat tight with tears once more.

"You're going to have to play along…for a while," Maggie said, patting my cheek. "But if you're smart, there's a way." Maggie's eyes turned toward the ceiling.

I sat up and eyed the girl who was as skinny as myself and a head shorter. "How long have you been here?"

"Almost two years."

How can you stand these gross men touching you, I wanted to ask. "What happened?" I asked instead.

"Needed money and...well, I'll tell you some time." She rose and stretched herself, her movements soft and pliant like a kitten.

I produced a smile. "Thank you for talking to me."

"Any time." She giggled. "Oh, I forgot. You're locked in." She grew serious once more. "I'm sure Beatrice will get you working right away."

"Already did. This gross fellow, one of Tina's customers."

"Yikes, Tina is a case." Maggie leaned closer and I caught a whiff of something flowery. "Better be careful around her."

I made a face, Louis's sweat-covered image on my mind. "She can have him."

"There'll be some nasty ones. Just have to be careful."

New tears pressed against my eyes.

Maggie gave me a quick squeeze. "Ah, come on, it'll be all right. Always remember, they can't mess with your mind, unless you let them. Don't give'em that power. Think of something else, play a role. Like an actress."

"What if I never get out of here?"

"You will. Save your money and if you do a good job, you'll get tips. Find men who wear expensive clothes. They smell better and they're often generous."

"You make it sound easy." I thought how awkward I'd been just showing my legs to Paul.

"I'll help you as long as I'm still around." Maggie lowered her voice. "I'm planning to get out of here soon...as soon as the weather breaks."

I propped myself on my elbows and whispered, "How?"

"Working on it. Anyway, you've got to pull yourself together." Maggie poked a forefinger at my chest. "They've got to trust you before they'll allow you freedom, so earn it."

I shook my head. "They have no right."

Maggie nodded. "Life is a bag of garbage, but you'll have to find the treasure within." She straightened. "I've got to go." At the door she turned. "Chin up. Things could be worse."

I crawled out of bed to check the door. Locked again. Somewhere beneath, voices could be heard. Arguing voices too hard to make out.

Inspecting the food on the tray, I went over what Maggie had said. Things could indeed be worse. I could be dead or injured or sick. Or a million other things. At least I was in one piece and they fed me. Pretty well, judging by the beef stew, the rolls and apple. All of a sudden my stomach gurgled with hunger. I carried the tray to the little table by the barred window and wolfed down everything. I'd find a way.

Somehow.

CHAPTER SIXTEEN

Paul

"Tell them to leave us," Father whispered, his voice weak but determined.

"Please give us some privacy," I announced to the room. Mercer nodded at the nurse and they slipped away. "They're gone, Father," I said a moment later.

"I need to tell you something," Regibald McKay said, his gaze glued to my face. "Something I should've told you years ago before you...I never thought." He tried to sit up, but sank back on the pillow.

I stuffed a second cushion behind Father's back, amazed how his chest had shrunk with the rest of him.

Regibald pointed a shaky forefinger at the ornate walnut desk in front of the window. "Open that top drawer. Key's in the pen box."

I found the key and unlocked the desk.

"There's a letter in that brown folder. Bring it to me."

I rifled through a pile of old notes until I found a letter, addressed to my mother, Josephine McKay. "What does it mean?" I asked, handing over the envelope.

Father lifted his forearm, a silent plea for patience that I remembered well. I'd always been much more impulsive than Father, who approached life and its challenges with utmost care and analysis.

Regibald removed a sheet of paper and handed it to me.

"Read it."

I focused on the note though I didn't recognize the handwriting.

"New York, October 20, 1917
Dearest Josephine,
I'm so sorry to bear this news to you. It was almost too much for me to write, but I know how you awaited Jack's return. Last night we got word that Jack fell on October 9 in the Meuse-Argonne battle, fighting the Germans. He had just mentioned in his last letter how he looked forward to returning home and seeing you again. I don't know what else to say. Words fail me. We're all so sad. I must go and prepare funeral arrangements.
Yours,
Debra von Linden

I let the letter sink and refocused on Father who'd closed his eyes. "What is this supposed to be? Who is this woman, this Debra?"

"You should rather ask about Jack." Regibald's lids remained closed, but his voice was cold and sharp.

I remained silent. Somehow the name von Linden rang a bell. As a boy I'd visited a family with that name. As far as I remembered, it was a childhood friend of my mother.

Father's eyes opened. "Your mother was in love with Jack von Linden. Had been since her teens, long before I met her. I thought I could sway her eventually. After all, Jack had only a good name, but no real wealth. I was wrong."

"I don't understand," I said, waving the letter at Father. "You had an affair with that…singer…actress…Mary."

"Yes, I did and I'm not proud of it. But that was later, much later. After your mother and I…Let's just say, we drifted apart after I found out she was meeting Jack on her shopping trips to town." Regibald's bitter laugh turned into a cough. He dabbed his mouth with a linen handkerchief and sighed. "I still loved her, always loved her, despite it all."

I stared. "Mother had an affair with Jack von Linden?" The immensity of this revelation softened my knees and I sank onto the chair by Father's bed.

"And she killed herself after she received this letter. I found it under her pillow." He scoffed. "Actually, the doctor found it and slipped it to me. I think everyone around us knew about your mother and Jack."

"Except me."

"Except you."

"And I thought she killed herself because of you…your affair."

"I know. You were so angry. I tried talking to you. But I didn't want to dirty your mother's name. It was a mistake. You were old enough for the truth. We wasted all this time…"

"Oh, Father," I cried, "what a fool I was. I was angry…blaming you." I rushed forward and lay my head on my father's chest. Sobs clogged my throat and for a while I cried.

"I'm sure you had to grow up fast out there," Regibald said, softly patting me on the back. "I just never expected you to run. I should've known your strength." He dabbed his eyes.

I sat up and wiped my cheeks. "I'm so sorry."

"Never mind that now." Father produced a thin smile and coughed again. "Not much time. Better grab a notebook. We must get busy."

Sam

By early evening I was back in the parlor, sitting with a half dozen girls. Tina glared at me once, but otherwise ignored me. The other girl, Maggie, smiled and winked. It was still early and no patrons had arrived yet.

I couldn't concentrate on what the girls talked about because my head was filled with images of fat lusty men attacking me. I wanted to ask Maggie about details, what I was supposed to do or feel. How things worked exactly. But nobody was paying attention and I would've rather died of embarrassment than ask publicly.

Within the hour three men arrived, got served drinks, and were drawn into conversations. I remained on the sofa as the other girls crowded around the bar, showing off lots of skin.

Only when I saw Maggie quietly signal me to join, did I get up. Just in time because one of the meatheads was about to peel himself off the wall, his deep-set eyes on my chest. I slid on a barstool next to Maggie who was drinking tea masquerading as whiskey. The girls weren't allowed to drink though patrons were urged to buy their chosen ones drinks of 'real' whiskey, which created additional income for Madame Beatrice.

"Relax," Maggie said into my ear. "You look like you're going to your own funeral."

I bit my lip. *Easy for her to say.* "I'm a virgin," I breathed.

Maggie's eyes widened. "Fuck."

Somewhere behind us, the door opened, admitting more men in suits and top hats. Girls chatted, men's laughter boomed. Smoke and alcohol filled the room. "Weren't you with fat Louis last night? I saw him pay Beatrice extra."

I smirked. "He fell asleep...and I gave him laxatives this morning."

Maggie collapsed into a laughing fit until Beatrice swooped up to us. The laughing turned into a cough.

"You working tonight?" Beatrice hissed at Maggie. "Customers are waiting." She glared at me. "Get over there. Both of you."

As Maggie and I wandered into the parlor, a man in his thirties, with a trim moustache and a pinstriped suit was handing over his hat.

As he nodded at me, Tina was making a beeline for him. "So good to see you, Tony," she purred.

The man gave Tina a quick smile before turning to me. "You must be new here?"

I hardly noticed the vein pulsing on Tina's temple or Maggie squeezing my arm and welcoming another arrival. My cheeks blazed as I felt Tony's eyes rove over my deep neckline. *Apparently a regular, but at least not old and fat like Louis.* He smelled a lot better too, a mix of expensive cigars and citrus aftershave.

"Did Beatrice cut out your tongue," he chuckled. As if on cue, Beatrice sashayed closer. "Tony Moretti, how is life treating you?"

Tony pretend-kissed the old dame's cheeks, but his smile never faded. "What's the story with this little bird?" He softly took my forearm and placed it on his.

"That's Samantha," Beatrice trilled. "She joined us yesterday." She leaned closer to his ear. "May I suggest Maggie or Tina? You may prefer a more experienced girl."

Tony's teeth flashed. "Charming, I'm sure. I'll take my chances." He threw a glance at me who still clung to his forearm and nodded at Beatrice. "If you'll excuse me, I'm thirsty."

"Of course, of course." Beatrice's voice was honey, but the look she gave me said otherwise.

Before I could ask myself why Beatrice had had different plans for this Tony, the man led me to the side of the bar.

"What are you going to drink?" he asked. He smiled again and I noticed a tiny gap between his upper front teeth. But instead of making him look ugly, he appeared mischievous. His eyes weren't green like Paul's but the dark brown of hot chocolate. They seemed to notice everything that went on, not just with me, but the entire room.

I shrugged. "Whiskey, I suppose."

"Really?" Tony gave me a once-over, sending fresh heat to my cheeks. I'd never been any good at lying. "I'd take you for a girl who likes champagne, not that watery tea they cheat us with."

Before I could muster a snappy answer, Tony had instructed the bartender to open a bottle of *Rochegré* and I found myself sipping something so light and bubbly, it made me all giggly.

"Where're you from, Sam?" Tony asked once we'd settled on a velvet divan in the corner.

"Cincinnati," I said.

"You Italian?"

"My father was."

"Was?"

"He's gone…since the war. He never returned. We…Mamma only got a letter. He'd been in France."

"I'm sorry." Tony patted my hand. Compared to my travel-roughened skin, his was soft and glowing, his nails immaculate.

Suddenly embarrassed, I pulled away my fingers. "So, what do you do?"

"Business dealings, mostly."

"What kind of business?"

"A club." He took a sip from his whiskey. "It may be forbidden, but people want it. Now more than ever."

From the corner of my eye, I noticed Beatrice approach again. I inwardly cringed. Had she seen me pulling away from my customer?

"The suite is open," Beatrice said.

Tony nodded at me. "Why don't we go up?" And to Beatrice, "Have the bubbly delivered, would you? And a fresh glass of whiskey with ice." His teeth flashed. "Better yet, get me a bottle."

As I followed Tony, my knees wanted to buckle. I had no idea where the suite was, but worse, this time I'd not get away with stalling a drunkard. Despite downing the whiskey, Tony looked alert and way too observant.

"Sit," Tony said once the door closed.

But I stood unmoving because I was too busy taking in the room. One could forget this was a brothel. This is how I imagined an expensive hotel to look. The place was opulent, with a large round bed, a midnight blue and gold brocade bedcover, satin sheets, and matching curtains. The cherry wood of the armoire glowed with polish. Like yesterday, the bartender delivered whiskey, but this time, he also carried a cooler with the remaining Rochegré.

"...be fine," Tony said.

"What?"

"I said the chair will be fine." As I sank into one of the plush loungers, Tony took off his suit jacket, served us drinks and relaxed into the other chair, a sly grin on his face. "You aren't just new, you don't want to be here."

I froze. What was I supposed to say?

The man chuckled. "Hot diggety dog, you look like a spitfire that hasn't been lit." He leaned forward. "Why don't you tell me your story?"

"But aren't we...I mean." My gaze brushed the bed and I took a quick sip from the glass.

"No rush," Tony said. "Tell me how you got here."

I studied the man's expression. He did seem interested. And so I started at the beginning.

Tony leaned back with a hearty laugh. "You mean to tell me you came all the way to Chicago to find your brother?"

"Yes."

"Brave girl. Stupid girl. Look where it got you." He threw back his drink, straightened and walked over to face me. "You have any idea how impossible it is to find people? Especially if they don't *want* to be found? Besides, this is a huge town filled with dangerous men."

I wanted to roll my eyes. Tony sounded like Paul. "Angelo is the only family I have left," I finally said. My mind was playing tricks now because Tony's face turned into Paul's. Worse, I was hot in my dress, the room too stuffy to breathe.

He nodded, his expression serious. "I understand family. Nothing is more important."

"That's what Papa always said."

Tony nodded. "If I hear anything, I'll let you know."

Words danced in my head. Things I should say, smart and witty things, and yet, the room remained quiet. I emptied another glass of bubbly and was no longer sweating, just comfortable, a little like floating in a warm tub. Tony's face shimmered in the dimness.

Tony pointed at the bed. "How about it?"

My breath caught, my legs without feeling. I was sure the door was unlocked, but how far would I get? Still contemplating what I should do, I straightened, amazed my knees kept me upright. How did one go about things as a prostitute? What an ugly word. Mamma would be sick. *She's dead, you moron.*

Before I had time to do more, Tony stepped behind me and unbuttoned my dress. He moved quietly and unhurried, each movement measured. Leaning against my back, his fingertips slid along my cheeks, throat and collarbone, down between my breasts until I shivered. One by one, he slipped off my undershirt, then stockings and drawers until I stood naked.

"You cold?"

I shook my head.

"Why don't you lie down while I'll get out of these things?"

Obediently, I crawled on top of the bed. I wanted to hide beneath the covers, but somehow that didn't seem right. Instead I watched in fascination as the stranger in front of me peeled out of his expensive clothes. His bare chest was wide and almost hairless, his hips narrow. Only when Tony dropped his underpants did I look away.

But somehow my gaze pulled back on its own to inspect the snaky thing in Tony's middle. It was much bigger than I'd imagined, though I wasn't disgusted like last night.

"Lie back, Sam." Tony moved next to me, his palm back on my cheek. "I better show you a few things, so this will be more fun for both of us." He leaned back and grinned. "Though I find it hard to believe that you never had a boyfriend. You *are* new at this."

I croaked something like "yes" and closed my eyes tightly. My insides were swimming, my mind floating. I couldn't think straight. I'd heard about terrible things, pains a woman had to endure. Any second, Tony would force himself...

When nothing happened, I opened my eyes. Tony grinned. A hand was wandering across my throat and back to my breast, the touch light and not at all unpleasant. "A woman's breast is one of her finest possessions." A forefinger found my nipple. "That is an area that women like to have touched."

To my surprise he bent low and flicked his tongue across my skin. The combination of hot breath and dampness was exquisite. I shivered.

Tony moved on to my other breast. Again hot breath, again a shiver.

"There is another place, women like to have kissed." Tony's voice sounded thicker now and to my shock his tongue slid across my sternum, belly and then…lower…between my legs.

I tried moving away. "What are you doing?"

"Close your eyes!"

"But…"

"Close them and be still."

I lay back and obediently closed my eyes. So far it was very different from what I'd expected. After fat Louis, this was almost fun. If I didn't think about the fact that a stranger was looking at my nakedness.

The sensation I felt next made me open my eyes. Warm, soft and oh… how to describe it. My belly filled with vibrations I'd never had before. Currents traveled up and down my legs, along the spine. Against my better judgment I opened my legs wider.

Tony continued. Feathery light, quick…slow.

A moan escaped me. Another.

And then the most wonderful sensation flooded my being, making me cry out. It'd felt exactly like that time in the tub…

Tony's face appeared in my vision. He grinned again, yet at the same time, his cheeks were flushed, his eyes glassy. "My turn," he breathed and before I had time to ask what he was up to, he unwrapped a paper and tugged something rubbery over his…. The thing, I'd watched on Louis, looked less threatening and was now finding its way into me. Tony began to move.

"Lift your legs. Push your hips against me," he instructed. "The pain will go away soon." He halted for a moment, his dark eyes melting into mine. "Do you trust me?"

I nodded. No matter what or who this man was, at least he was kind and patient. I lifted my hips toward Tony's body and soon got the hang of it. Only when Tony grunted and stopped did I grow still.

Without another word, Tony got up and busied himself at the washstand. The penis I'd so feared earlier looked like a soft lump now and much smaller.

"You think you'll live?" he asked, returning to the bed. He pulled back the cover and slid beneath, leaning his head on one elbow.

"It wasn't horrible," I admitted.

Tony chuckled. "You didn't seem to mind earlier."

My cheeks burned. "I…yes. It was good. Why did you…"

"It is much more fun when we both enjoy it." He tucked the sheet around me and closed his eyes. "You're too cute, Sam Bruno. I shall see you again."

To my surprise I smiled. I wasn't going to mind.

CHAPTER SEVENTEEN

Paul

Regibald McKay passed away that evening. I remained by his side until the moment when he simply forgot to breathe. My eyes were dry by then, but my mind continued to rake over the events and the promise I'd given. Father had asked for a favor. How could I refuse after wrongly accusing him for years?

Now that I knew the truth, I wondered how I couldn't have seen it earlier. I remembered how reluctant Mother had been to take me to town. I'd thought she dreaded me getting tired or bored of looking at women's clothing. The few times I'd come along, she'd seemed distracted, even irritable. She'd not wanted me because she'd had other plans...with another man. Jack.

After Dr. Brenner left and the nurse packed up her things, I entered my old room on the second floor, a sprawling space with double doors to a balcony and a private bath. Deep in thought, I opened my closet where the clothes from 1917 still hung. I rifled through them and closed the doors again. Nothing was going to fit. I could've rung for Mercer, but I preferred to go downstairs instead and ask. A little bit of the hobo was still around.

That's when my body refused to move on and I sank onto the bench by the foot of the bed. I'd wasted seven years being angry. Seven years of resentment, accusing Father of adultery and killing my mother. Guilt flooded me. Guilt so overwhelming, I was paralyzed. Sitting next to my dying father had distracted me from this new truth. I'd used my last shreds of energy to pay attention to the man, promise him to continue the company, promise him to take care of...

My thoughts wandered to the little woman I'd picked up at the Dill Pickle Club. Colene Sloan, the girl I'd admired when I was twelve. Back then, Regibald McKay had made a pact with Colene's father, Henry Sloan, his best friend. One day, there would be a wedding between Colene and me. We were perfect for each other.

Apparently, the old Sloan had visited Regi many times and expressed his disappointment that I was gone...missing, which had driven his daughter into despair.

Right. I shook my head. We'd not even kissed. How could the woman have such expectations of a teenager she hadn't seen since I was fourteen? Was that how her old man excused Colene's drinking? But then there was Father who I owed...for eternity.

A knock drew me from my stupor. "Sir, Mercer here, I've got clothes."

With a sigh, I straightened. "Come in. You can take all the old things away. Donate them to a shelter."

Mercer nodded. "Sir, may I draw you a bath?"

"I'll do it." I forced my body to move into the bath, wishing Mercer would quit calling me 'Sir.' But Mercer would never agree. You would never get the butler out of him.

While I scrubbed away my hobo past, Mercer moved some of Father's clothes into my closet. I'd have to go shopping, a task I dreaded. I was the same height as Father, though my shoulders were broader and my waist skinnier.

Lying in that tub, my thoughts wandered back to Sam. Not long ago, I'd shared a bathroom with her, and every time I'd been in there, I'd found myself aroused thinking about Sam spending time in that same tub.

Sure, I'd had Ava and a few women along the way. Even hobo life had its perks when it came to the opposite sex. There was the occasional female hobo and once in a while, a lonely housewife who needed work done also had other needs.

But Sam was different. Now that I had time to think, I knew that what I felt for the willful girl from Cincinnati was something new and precious. I smiled to myself, remembering our Christmas meal, her excitement over the chocolate I'd brought. The girls I'd known while living in this house were all spoiled, strutting in fancy dresses and wrinkling their noses at anybody and anything different from themselves.

Not Sam. She was down to earth—a real human being with inner strength and such love, a love that made her brave the terrible hardship of hobo life to find her brother.

But even if I did find her, I had promised Father... A harsh sound broke from my lips. A kind of laugh that hurt like a sob. "You're a complete idiot, Paul McKay," I cried. "Now that you figured it out, you lost the woman you love and get to marry the one you don't care about." My eyes blurred once more, but this time I didn't mourn the loss of my father, but the woman I'd never see again.

Unless.

But you promised Father!

A small smile crept on my face. I could at least help Sam get settled and maybe find her brother. Resolutely wiping my eyes, I jumped up, sending a tidal wave of water onto the tiled floor. I dressed in one of Father's suits and headed to the garage. I'd not driven a fancy automobile since I'd left at fifteen and mumbled as I tried out the gears.

The Chrysler B-70 was shiny black as the waxed wings of a beetle, its leather interior immaculate. Father had probably driven it a few dozen times. My father....

I hadn't thought about him in years. At least, not officially. Because I now realized that deep down I'd always acted as if Father were looking over my shoulder. I'd wanted to please him even in his absence.

Shoulders slumped forward, I put the vehicle in motion. In the end, Father's intelligence and wit hadn't saved him. According to Dr. Brenner he had died of complications from malaria.

Regibald McKay had grown up on the east coast and contracted the disease as a young man. I remembered a few bouts when Father had been in bed with chills switching to high fever and terrible cramps. In those years, it had been a matter of a few days before Regi, driven by his inquisitive mind, had returned to his work.

You did this, at least partially. Chances were, he may still be alive if he hadn't worried himself sick about you.

"Hurry up," I mumbled as I maneuvered down Michigan Avenue. I needed a distraction. Quick. After ten o'clock the south loop was still reasonably busy. I parked along the curb and slowly strolled toward the corner.

Victor's pub had been boarded up with care, the glass front covered, entry door and gate locked with heavy chains. I rattled the padlock and knew immediately that nobody had gone through since I'd been arrested. Sam wouldn't have been able to get back.

Why hadn't I thought of a way to hide her in the building? But then she'd been stuck inside. I decided to wait, but none of the passersby looked vaguely familiar. A few stopped briefly to study the chains and then strolled off—likely former patrons. I headed down the alley to the backdoor. It was also barred with heavy-duty chains except.... I bent lower and found that the chain was loose and only appeared to be locked. Somebody had cut one of the links. Sam.

My heart thumped as I untangled the chain and crept into the gloomy corridor. I was thankful, Father kept a flashlight in the automobile. The beam illuminated the torn-apart pub room, the kitchen. I touched the stew pot, Sam's favorite cooking vessel. Cold. The food beneath the lid was spoiled. Sam wouldn't let food go to waste. A shred of doubt tugged on me. I pushed it away, all thoughts concentrated on finding her sleeping upstairs...waiting for me.

I quietly ascended the stairs and knew something was wrong when I saw the open door. Our beds had been made, but she wasn't there.

So she had returned. *She's gone some place and will be back.*

I sank onto the cot and curled up beneath the blanket, my mind full of memories of Sam fixing soup, lighting a candle by the window...attempting to cover her bare legs. I smiled about her modesty as hope filled my insides with the most glorious lightness. She'd return to find me here and we'd figure a way... *You promised your father.*

I awoke to the first light of dawn. The room was freezing. Abandonment lay in the air, a desolation that gripped my heart. Right then I knew she wouldn't return. Not here. Not ever. Something had happened.

Head low, I returned to the Chrysler, yet couldn't stop myself from studying the people rushing to and fro, their shape and gait. None of them was Sam.

I returned to my new home for breakfast, bleary eyed and exhausted. I had a funeral to arrange.

In the confusion of the morning I briefly thought of Angelo sitting in that jail, but then Mercer entered the room with a notepad. Father had been a well-known man.

I owed him a good-bye. Owed him so much more, a debt I could never repay.

Sam

When I awoke late morning, I stared into the frowning face of Beatrice. "You think you're so smart," she huffed. "We'll see about that. Get your skinny ass to your own room."

The old dame looked worse in daylight. Not even her fancy jewels could detract from the fact that her skin sagged around her eyes and that the corners of her mouth drooped.

I rubbed my face as the experience of last night came flooding back. I scrambled to collect my clothes and climbed to the third floor. To my relief, nobody was in the hallway. My room was stuffy and ugly. I closed the door, washed with cold water, and brushed out my hair. The memory of Tony sliding his tongue across my skin sent tingles down my spine. Wasn't I supposed to feel ashamed? And yes, there was that tiny voice of criticism. Green eyes squinting in anger. Paul wouldn't have approved.

Paul is gone. You better get used to it. And so far, I hadn't done very well with Tina and Beatrice. I needed to find Maggie, ask her for advice.

Not wanting to ruin my only dress, I put on the threadbare housecoat, hanging on a hook. The door was still unlocked and I made my way to the first floor. A couple of girls sat at the dining table. I contemplated stepping out the front door. That is until I saw one of the meatheads sitting in the nearby alcove. No doubt, he was keeping watch. A look out the window made me chuckle. I wouldn't have gotten very far in the sleety mess of the Chicago winter.

Maggie walked in from the kitchen, an apple in her hand. "How was your night?"

"Okay."

"Just okay? I heard Tony is pretty fun."

My cheeks began to glow. "He was...nice."

Maggie leaned close and whispered. "You lucked out, kiddo."

"I know." I scanned the room. Nobody was paying attention, so I pulled Maggie into a corner by the large wardrobe. "Why is

Beatrice so mean?" I asked.

Maggie shrugged. "She's running a business, I suppose. Try to see it from her side. Unless you do what's asked, you're costing her. Besides, she reports to some fella who reports to the big boss."

"Capone?"

Maggie's pug nose wrinkled. "Not that one, the old thug, the one Capone works with. I read someplace in the paper…what was his name…Johnny Torrio, yes, that's it."

"Does he ever come here?"

"Who?"

"Capone or Torrio?"

Maggie giggled. "Not that I know of. These guys have better places to visit."

"Like what?"

"Oh, Sam, you're such a baby." Maggie took a bite from her apple.

"Then teach me." I wrapped my housecoat tighter around my waist. "I sure feel like an idiot."

"I've heard of fancy ballrooms and speakeasy clubs." Maggie's eyes grew dreamy. "Crystal chandeliers, white tablecloths, women flappers in beautiful evening gowns and rivers of whiskey and champagne. They dance through the night to live music."

"I thought drinking alcohol was against the law."

Maggie giggled. "Honey, people drink more now than they did before prohibition."

"But how can they—"

Tina swooped in and positioned herself in front of me. "Your turn to clean the kitchen. Don't think you can play the queen around here." Her tone was cold.

"Why don't you leave her alone? She just got here," said Maggie. "Remember your first week or has it been too long?" She sounded playful, but somehow Tina backed off. She huffed and walked back to a couple of girls who made pouty faces and whispered to each other.

"Just ignore them," Maggie said. "They'll straighten out after a while. It's always hard for them when a younger and prettier girl arrives."

I stared. What was Maggie talking about?

As if Maggie had heard my thoughts, she said, "Yes, you, Sam. You'll be a knockout one day." She abruptly leaned close. "Promise me to get away. Don't let them use you up."

I nodded. Maggie was going to leave soon. *How soon*, I wanted to ask. *How are you going to do it?* I loved Maggie's strength, her easy friendship. She was so different from my friend, Helen, in Cincinnati who'd dutifully done everything her father demanded.

"I'd love to see those beautiful places one day," I said aloud.

"Fat chance," Maggie scoffed. "The likes of us take care of the Louis's of this world. You must leave Chicago. It's a cesspool."

I bit my lip. Tony had been from that other world. I was sure of it. But who knew when he'd be back. If he ever returned. Not after meeting such a simpleton like myself.

I glanced around the room to make sure nobody was listening. "When will you leave?"

"Soon. I've got almost a hundred dollars saved."

"But what will you do? Go home to your family?"

"Mother's boyfriend would love that. He's the reason I took off." Maggie gazed out the window. By the way her eyes shone, I knew not to ask. "I'll go west to California. Open a café or at least work in a nice department store," Maggie continued.

Her eyes met mine. They said *soon*.

When I returned to my room I knew somebody had been there. It wasn't obvious, but there was that weird feeling of another presence, my dress draped differently across the chair, the pillow leaning against the headboard.

I raced to my bed and lifted the mattress. The money was gone, all twenty-three dollars. What a gullible idiot I was. The faces of Tina and Beatrice swam into my mind. It had been one of them. I was sure of it. Probably Tina because she'd claimed Louis as her customer and was angry.

I wanted to spit. Stupid Tina. She could have him—all of those foul-smelling sweaty men who wanted nothing but to stick their thing into women. At this rate, I'd be used up and old before I got away. How had Maggie managed to set aside her money?

I sank on the bed, my vision blurry. Sounds drifted through the walls: a door slammed, a girl sang 'All Alone,' laughter bubbled and somewhere on the sidewalk two men argued. I thought of my father's shotgun. Somehow I now understood Mamma's obsession with keeping it oiled. At least she'd had her gun. For myself there was nothing. The shotgun had disappeared along with Paul, my home gone and my brother vanished. I was alone.

Pull yourself together, Sam Bruno.

Easier said than done. All I wanted to do was curl up beneath the blankets and forget about life. I'd managed to lose what little I had and now I didn't even have freedom any longer. If I were honest, things had gone from worse to horrific ever since Mamma died.

"What would you do, Mamma?" I whispered.

Of course, there was no answer—only giggles from the floor below.

Beatrice showed up at dusk, her face freshly powdered, her cheeks dark with rouge.

"Get ready, quick," she said, yanking the blankets away. She clapped her hands. "It's Wednesday night and we expect a full house."

I didn't answer, but dragged myself to the washbasin.

"Five minutes," Beatrice said. "And put on a smile or there'll be consequences."

I pulled on the dress, took a last sip from the tea Tina had brought, and clambered downstairs. The parlor was already half filled with men. Thin, bald, fat, in striped suits and white scarves, they'd all come for one purpose.

"Sam, over here," Maggie called from the bar. She was sitting with a dark-haired fella with a crooked nose and full lips. The man was downing whiskey as if it were water while his left paw lay possessively on Maggie's shoulder.

"Mario Russo, meet Sam Bruno," Maggie said. By the way she slurred her words, I knew she'd been drinking the real thing. The man was a brute, but Maggie didn't seem to notice. Or maybe he tipped well and Maggie was desperate to leave.

I managed a nod while maintaining a safe margin between the thug and myself. All I wanted was to pull Maggie aside and tell her to be careful.

"Time for some quiet," Russo said, half lifting Maggie from the barstool. It looked like he could break her in two with one arm, but Maggie giggled.

Something icy crept up my back as I watched my friend disappear into the staircase. Her neck shone pale beneath the upswept hair.

The next moment I was face-to-face with a skinny man in a fedora and pale blue eyes. Obediently, I ordered whiskey for my customer and sat down next to him. Only to feel bile enter my mouth. The wave of nausea was so powerful, the features of the skinny man blurred. His nose moved up, then to the side. I wanted to laugh, but then I clamped a palm across my mouth and burst from the room.

The outhouse was out of reach, so I vomited onto the small grass patch next to the backdoor. My insides wanted to turn themselves over in one giant cramp. When I felt empty, I crept back inside. Every time I straightened, my stomach screamed, so I walked bent over, holding my belly as if to keep my intestines in check.

Just the smell of the parlor caused new waves of nausea. I swallowed hard, trying to focus on the bar, trying to find my customer. Other couples ringed the counter and then I saw Tina shoving her cleavage into the skinny man's face. Over his nearly bald head, she met my eyes and smirked, her gaze as cold as the ice in the man's glass.

"What is going on *now*?" Beatrice, dressed in a robin-egg blue tunic and an assortment of peacock feathers on her head, materialized in front of me. One bony forefinger, its nail a blood-red claw, poked me under the chin and forced my head upward.

"Had to upchuck," I said. "My stomach hurts." I threw another glance at Tina who cackled like a market wench, before bending low once more. Cramps traveled from the bottom of my belly to the top and I groaned.

"Did you drink?"

"No. Had to be something I ate." How could I explain Tina's vendetta? I'd never prove a thing.

Beatrice's wrinkles lengthened. "Tsk, Sam. Had I only known what a terrible investment you'd be." She shook her head. "Go upstairs. Quick. Before you retch on our customers."

I lowered my head—it was too heavy to keep straight anyway—and crept to my room and beneath the threadbare covers. Curling into a ball, I wanted to sleep forever.

Early in the morning, I woke. It was barely dawn, the pale light as frigid as my room. Shivering, I put on the robe and climbed downstairs. The pain in my middle had subsided, replaced by a gyrating headache. What had Tina done to make me so sick?

113

Reluctantly I opened the cabinets in the kitchen. From across the hall came the sonorous buzz of one of the meatheads who lay sprawled on a chaise near the entry door. Cans of stew, bags of rice, beans and pasta lined shelves. A few spices stood above the stove that had seen better days. Splatters of hundreds of meals caked the top.

"Nothing fresh," I mumbled. Underneath the sink I found soap pieces, dishwashing liquid and worn out pads and dishcloths. The sink itself ran over with glasses and dishes.

Remembering my time at the bar, I heated water and went to work, washing and drying. The tedious work calmed my nerves and distracted me from the sour emptiness of my stomach. By the time the first girl slinked into the kitchen, everything sparkled. Well, as much as an old place like that could sparkle. I had found a few leftover leaves of peppermint and made tea.

"You do all that?" The girl who'd addressed me was dressed in a fancy ankle-length housecoat with embroidered pink and white lilies. She lit a cigarette between her full lips and sank onto a chair.

"Couldn't sleep," I said. Was this one of the girls Tina hung out with?

"Beatrice will be speechless," the girl said with a smirk. "Doesn't happen very often. She sucked on the cigarette, a puff of smoke rising between them.

A scream rang out. Somewhere above, doors opened and footsteps ran back and forth. The girl and I exchanged a glance before bolting into the hallway. Upstairs more screams. The second floor or the 'client' floor was abuzz with running and shouting girls. Beatrice appeared, her hair in rollers.

"Stop that shouting at once," she ordered.

"Come quick," Tina cried. Her round face showed traces of tears, her blonde hair in disarray.

When I saw which door Tina entered, my mouth went dry with alarm. I hurried after Beatrice and Tina who were shoeing other girls back into the hallway. I ignored them and used my elbows to gain entry.

On the bed lay Maggie, her brown eyes open and wondrous. Bruises spread across her throat around the sides of her neck.

Beatrice bent low, but I knew. Just as I'd known with Mamma. Maggie was dead. All her dreams of getting away and starting a new life had vanished along with her soul.

I remembered the brute from last night, his lustful eyes, the way he'd shoved Maggie out of the room.

"Who found her?" Beatrice's voice cut through the chatter.

"I did," Tina said. "I...the door wasn't closed and it seemed strange..."

Beatrice let out a sigh and straightened. "Never mind that now. I want all of you out." Her gaze fell on me as she locked the door. "Call the police, Samantha. I'll review our visitors from last night."

I carefully eyed the wall telephone and my shaking fingers. I'd never made a call in my life. My mind reeled with what I'd seen. Maggie, so full of life, was gone. She'd been the only one to approach me, encourage me. Now she was dead. Killed by some animal.

"Hello," I cried into the receiver.

"Operator. Who are you looking for?"

"I need the police. Hurry."

The line clicked, then a new voice. "40th precinct, may I help you?"

"I, this is Sam Bruno, a girl is dead at Fizzy's. Could you please come quick?"

"The brothel?"

"Yes."

"Don't touch anything."

"Madame Beatrice—"

The line clicked. Silence. I hung up the receiver. My legs wanted to collapse under the weight of this new truth. By the looks of it, Maggie had died of strangulation. I thought of Maggie's dreams of freedom, the money, she'd saved. Was it still in her room or had somebody stolen it like they'd stolen my twenty-three dollars?

Beatrice stood by the sink, drinking coffee, staring out the window.

"They're coming. We're not supposed to touch anything," I said to her back.

"Joe's keeping watch."

I sank on a chair. Most of the girls were downstairs now, their chatter muted. I thought of Paul, his green eyes, and the way his mouth had felt on mine when he kissed me. Maybe I could get away while the police were here. In the commotion, doors tended to open and close.

But then, where would I go?

To the police station to inquire about the raid? Even if I knew which station had been in charge, they'd surely want to know why I was interested. Which in turn meant, I would have to admit I had been with Paul *inside* the bar. I didn't know his last name and if he'd been sentenced and sent to jail, I didn't gain anything either. Worse was that I didn't have decent clothes. Beyond the windows, Chicago was in the midst of winter. With every patron, an icy swell entered. All I possessed was a thin dress and uncomfortable shoes—no coat, no hat and certainly not the boots, Paul had bought me.

I was stuck. And alone. As alone as I'd been after Mamma died. I might as well hang around. At least I had food and shelter. Even if it meant meeting disgusting men. *Who might kill you!* No, I couldn't stay either. It was gross and dangerous.

With utmost slowness I straightened and went to my room. The threadbare bed didn't look quite as appalling, the washstand almost familiar. I rinsed my face and crept under the covers.

Maggie would save me.

CHAPTER EIGHTEEN

Paul

I spent all day organizing Father's funeral. The undertaker came to pick up the body—there were flowers, the headstone, the plot next to Mother, the church, sermon, memorial speeches, and the feast afterwards.

I knew my father wouldn't have cared if we'd thrown him into a hole, but for me nothing was good enough. The flowers, white lilies and carnations, had to be brought in special from California. I spent hours on an obituary and a short speech I wanted to give during the service. Nothing seemed right. I wrote and rewrote, the floor covered in wadded paper. The phone rang incessantly and Mercer had strict instructions to only allow the most important calls through.

That is, until the butler knocked and announced a visitor.

I looked up from my scribbles. "Send him away. I don't have time as it is."

Mercer bowed in his usual way. "Sir, it is a she…Miss Sloan."

I felt heat rise beneath my collar. I wasn't ready to see the woman, hadn't made up my mind on anything. Even if I had promised Father, I…

"Where is he? Paul?" Colene Sloan rushed past Mercer and came to a sudden stop in front of my desk. "So, it is true," she cried, her eyes blue orbs. But where Sam's eyes reminded me of the Caribbean sea, Colene's were arctic as the blue sky of an Alaskan winter. Her rosy cheeks didn't match the deep-red lipstick, but her outfit of black wool with a fox collar was immaculate. I'd forgotten how alluring Colene could be, yet I couldn't help wonder what the person beneath the veneer of her makeup looked like.

"Hello Colene," I said. I had to admit she looked worlds better than the woman I'd picked up drunk from the Dill Pickle Club. But the ravages of too much alcohol were showing in the slack skin around her jaw and the fine capillaries on her nose. She stood firmly, but I thought I caught a whiff of gin. She was a year younger than I, but appeared much older.

I nodded at Mercer, who quietly disappeared while Colene slumped into the leather chair in front of me. "You sure are a surprise," she said brightly. "We all thought you were dead." She threw me a glance I couldn't interpret and went on. "Dead as a fish in the desert. I always told Father I thought you were alive. I would've known otherwise." She patted her furry collar. "I knew it all along. Told Regi as much, but he was convinced—"

"I'm sorry," I said simply. What else could I say? I wasn't about to share the last moments with Father. Or the hurt squeezing my insides every waking minute. Both were inextricably linked and locked up in my heart like others protected diamonds in safes.

Obviously, it wasn't enough for Colene. She leaned forward. "What? That's it? You were gone all these years and I get no explanation. We were promised to each other. Promised!"

I cringed inwardly, wishing I could run from the room and leave Colene there in her self-fabricated agitation.

"That was a long time ago," I said, keeping my expression neutral. "We were kids."

"What does that mean?" Colene's voice was shrill. "Father just saw Regi two days ago and they talked about us."

"Two days ago Regi didn't know I was alive." I studied the little woman in front of me. She'd torn the hat with the matching fox fur from her head, her chin-length hair a blonde cap.

"But you *are*...here." Colene's large eyes filled with tears. "You don't love me anymore."

I wanted to throw up my hands. She couldn't be serious. I'd been a boy when we'd held hands and walked through the park. We'd talked about Colene's clothes and toys and travels. She'd chatted incessantly while I focused on the feeling of her fingers against my palm. The touch of skin was exciting, but it hadn't even occurred to me to kiss her.

"Well, say something," Colene said, pulling me back to present day. "I saved myself for you...waited."

Don't be ridiculous, I wanted to shout. Everything in me recoiled to take this woman seriously. But there was the promise to Father, his last wish.

"Please take care of Colene," he'd said. "Her father and I...I know it isn't fair. After all this time, but the old Sloan made me promise if you ever returned..."

I had nodded and squeezed Father's hand, my mind heavy with the knowledge I'd accused him, hated him unjustly. All that emotion...and time wasted.

Sam is gone, the voice in my head reminded me. What were the chances I would ever see her again? Slim to none.

I forced a smile and refocused on Colene. "Why don't we take it slow. Have dinner with me tomorrow night? We'll go some place quiet? I'll pick you up around seven."

Colene's expression turned angelic, her eyes brimming with tears once again. "Yes, my love. Of course."

"I better finish these obituaries." I reached for the bell when I'd rather have fled the room.

Colene's arm shot forward and stopped me. "No need. I'll see myself out."

After Colene closed the door, my attention returned to the task at hand, but the pen in my hand sank uselessly to the paper. My mind reeled, a confused muddle of thoughts and images.

Two days ago I'd been poor and destitute—heading to jail. Now I was rich once more, had a huge estate, a company and...Colene. The life I'd led for years had been built on lies and deceit.

But I'd been happier as a hobo. My world had been simple. I'd spent my days fighting for survival, seeking food and shelter, forging friendships. Yet, I'd lived in a fantasy world, my decisions baseless.

Anger gripped me suddenly—anger so hot that I tore the stiff collar from my throat and tossed it across the room. I knew I couldn't go back to my old life. It was gone just like Father...and Sam. I had money now. Status. All the things people dreamed of.

Happiness was another matter.

Sam

In the afternoon, the police interviewed all girls. I didn't know anything and said as much. Nobody else did either. Rumor had it, Beatrice mentioned the brute by name. He'd disappeared sometime during the night, a normal occurrence in the business, but nobody could remember seeing him leave. Unless they were too drunk to leave, few men stayed overnight. The meatheads weren't any help either.

Now suspicious of my food, I ate little while warily observing Tina from across the table. Before dinner was over, she hurried upstairs. The hallway was empty, the two Meatheads in the middle of annihilating huge piles of potatoes and cabbage.

I knocked on Maggie's door. Nothing.

The doorknob turned and I slipped inside. The bedside lamp had been left on as if Maggie would return any moment. But her bed had been stripped, her personal belongings removed from the nightstand. Earlier in the day, several men had taken Maggie away.

My eyes blurred. Maggie had been full of life. She'd been kind when nobody cared to speak to me. Now she was gone and there was nothing left of her, not even her scent. It was as if she hadn't existed.

I stood, unable to move, all energy evaporated. Somewhere below, Beatrice coughed her deep bark. There was nothing for me to do here. At last, I walked to the window. Outside snow swirled and a frigid draft crept through the ill-fitting frame and hit my bare forearms. It was time to dress for work.

Yet, I couldn't leave. The room seemed to call to me.

No, Maggie did.

Come on, Sam, what are you going to do? I angrily wiped my face and grinned, imagining Maggie watching from the bed. *Don't be a chicken, take the money and run.*

My gaze returned to the bed. It looked abandoned, the air around it still. Where would Maggie have hidden her stash? She had to have known about the thieves in this house. I eyed the dresser, opened each drawer. All empty. I slid a hand along the back. Nothing. The mirror didn't butch.

The mattress lifted easily—just as flimsy as mine. I ambled around the bed. Nothing beneath, the seams of the mattress tight with no holes.

I was about to kick one of the bedposts, when I noticed the

floor. One of the boards appeared different from the rest. I only saw it when standing near the nightstand with the lamplight falling at an angle. The seams around one board were clean. I dropped to my knees and stuck a fingernail into the joint. Too tight. I needed a knife or something pointy to pry open the wood.

Chatter erupted in the hallway. Dinner was finished. I ducked low, though why would anybody come in here? Something creaked outside. I held my breath. The door slid open just a crack, then wider. Somebody slipped inside. I crawled beneath the bed, thankfully, surrounded by a ruffled skirt. Footsteps. Dresser drawers opened and closed. Steps to the bed. Lying on my back, I lifted the fabric an inch. I knew those slippers. Pink with tussles, heels scuffed. Tina.

Was she looking for Maggie's money? Like she had stolen mine? Now I was sure it had been Tina. Getting even for losing Louis's favor. Worse, Louis hadn't been back. I grinned, wishing I could teach all those men a lesson. Beatrice would have to close shop due to diarrhea. A gurgle wanted to break from my chest and I clamped a palm on my mouth.

"Where is it?" Tina mumbled to herself. She walked back and forth, then stopped somewhere near the door. The room sank into stillness. On the floor above, somebody walked to the window, then back.

My nose tickled. Dust bunnies cradled my cheek. Another minute. Then the door opened and closed and Tina was gone.

Slowly, I crawled back to the strange floorboard. I'd think about Tina later. On the windowsill lay one of Maggie's hairpins. I shoved it into the groove and lifted.

Just as I'd thought, the wood came loose. Beneath rested a cigar box—and a stack of letters. I felt funny fingering the papers. These were private—Maggie's correspondence, maybe with her lover. Maybe this person needed to know about Maggie's death. With shaky fingers, I pocketed the letters and lifted the cigar box from the hold. Without looking inside, I hurried to the door, listened, and slipped out.

Meathead no longer watched my door. They'd probably figured I had no place to go. If they also kept each of us penniless, we were as good as slaves. Maybe it wasn't Tina after all. Maybe it was Beatrice or one of her thug bodyguards.

I sank on the bed and slowly opened Maggie's cigar box.

Inside laid photos of a young man in a fine suit and elegant hat and that of a little girl, no older than two, on the steps of a narrow two-story brick-sided house. The back of it carried the initials P. C.

But then my gaze was drawn to the roll of bills tied in a rubber band. I counted nineteen ten-dollar bills and two fives...a fortune. I'd finally be able to get away. A slow smile spread across my face. Surely, Maggie wouldn't mind. Not now.

Tucking the bills inside my waistband, I unfolded the first letter. After reading a few sentences, my fingers began to shake until the letter sailed to the floor. For a moment I saw nothing.

Taking a deep breath I picked up the paper once more.

May 3rd, 1924
Maggie,
Poppi is doing fine. She's saying a few words now. The other day she called Tim 'Daddy,' can you believe it? I'm sorry, I know she's yours, which brings me to the other subject. Tim still hasn't found a job. It's getting awfully tight here. You remember we agreed on taking Poppi for a while. But, Maggie, you must get her soon. Things are not well around here and I'm pregnant again myself. Sorry, I've got no better news.
Your sister, Mary-Rose

So Maggie had a little girl. Probably by that fancy dude in the photo. I snorted with anger. The asshole got her pregnant and then...

I pulled out the money a second time. Little Poppi would never see her mom again, but this was her inheritance. Taking it now was as good as stealing. Poppi was innocent. She hadn't asked to be born.

I scrambled through the letters until I found an envelope with a return address. Mary-Rose Dickins, 59 Lacross Street, West Garfield Park, Chicago, Illinois. So Maggie's daughter wasn't far away at all. Maybe that's what Maggie had planned. Run off, take Poppi and disappear toward the west coast.

My hand sank to my lap. I didn't know where West Garfield Park was, but I had to get the money to the little girl. One way or another. Taking the fork from under my pillow, I crawled beneath my bed and starting wiggling at the floorboards.

CHAPTER NINETEEN

Paul

I had thrown on Father's leisure jacket, a green and brown tweed that was a bit too wide, a checkered scarf that didn't exactly match and a black felt hat.

Mercer tsked once and exclaimed, "Sir, if I may, can I ring the tailor?"

Shaking my head, I strode to the door. I couldn't care less what I wore or how I looked. I drove the Chrysler into the street and down a hundred fifty yards before turning left into the Sloan driveway.

The maid threw me a curious glance before curtsying and stepping back.

"Ah, if it isn't Paul McKay?" Sloan Senior marched toward me with outstretched arms and a broad smile. Compared to Father, time had been kind to him. Where Regi had worked nearly around the clock and forged his wealth from nothing, the old Sloan had inherited a large furniture factory. His jovial attitude did little to soften the slyness of his eyes.

"Nice to see you again, Mister Sloan," I said.

"Nah, nah, call me Henry," he chuckled and patted me on the back. "We're practically family. Your father and I...ah, where are my manners. Come in. You have a moment, right? I think Colene will be ready soon. You know these girls take their time, but then, it's worth it." He stopped to come up for air.

I forced a smile. "We have a reservation...Henry." I'd never understand what Father had seen in Henry Sloan. Except that they'd known each other since they'd been choir boys at Old St. Patrick's Catholic Church, they had little in common.

"Tomorrow is the day," Sloan boomed. His expression grew momentarily serious, showing the same instant chameleon-like change that his daughter had displayed.

I nodded.

"He was a good man, that one." Sloan produced a tear, but I couldn't help think that the man wasn't nearly as sad as he pretended. "If I can do anything…anything at all."

"I've got it," I said, wishing myself far away once again.

"Why don't you leave Paul alone?" Colene swept into the room in a floor-length burgundy dress covered in sequins and fringes. More baubles sparkled around her neck and the four fingers of her right hand. She seized my arm and pulled me toward the door.

"Have fun," Henry Sloan shouted after us.

In the automobile, Colene leaned toward me. "I'm so happy to see you. I was getting ready all day. Shall we go to a club? How about the Dill Pickle Club? It's so much fun. Last time—"

"I thought we'd go some place quiet. To talk…"

"Oh, Paul, darling." Colene's forefinger traced along my jawline. "Be a good sport. I got all dressed up to sit in a dark stuffy restaurant?"

I swallowed my comment. Maybe it was better to live a little…forget. Tomorrow Father would be buried and I sure could use a drink. "Let's go, then," I said, quietly wondering if Colene had any recollection of the man who'd picked her up from the Dill Pickle Club just days ago.

When I awoke, I didn't know where I was. A hammer was chiseling at my forehead with such ferocity I hardly could tolerate the dim light from the window. Squinting, I sat up with a groan. My throat ached as if I'd swallowed a cheese grater, my stomach gurgled and burned. What time was it anyway? Where was the damn clock?

That's when I noticed I was naked. In a strange bed. I carefully turned my head and there, next to me, laid Colene. Like me, she was naked, at least the exposed breast was, and snored like a drunken sailor. Her makeup had deteriorated all over her cheeks, the corners of her mouth smeared with remnants of lipstick.

I rubbed my temples, but that movement nauseated me further. Ever so slowly, I crawled out of bed and tiptoed toward the bathroom. My drawers lay strewn on the carpet along with the tweed jacket, shirt and pants. Holding my head with one hand, I picked up my clothes. The movement sent a fresh wave of nausea up my throat. I gagged and rushed to the toilet.

Afterwards, I near drowned myself in the sink, rinsed my mouth to lessen the dead animal taste on my tongue, and brushed my hair.

The man staring back at me from the mirror had red-rimmed eyes, flushed cheeks and a huge frown between his brows. I couldn't remember the last time I'd actually looked at myself, but there were lines around my mouth, I didn't remember.

"What have you done, Paul?" I addressed the image. "You lost your mind."

That's when I remembered Father's funeral. "Shit."

I dug for my pocket watch, courtesy of my dead father, and tried to focus. It was after nine o'clock. In less than an hour, I was expected at church. As quickly as my throbbing temples allowed, I dressed and slinked to the door. Colene hadn't moved. Maybe she'd forgotten everything. What exactly? I hesitated for a moment, trying to think back. I'd been drinking whiskey at the Dill Pickle Club, then another. In fact, I was sure I'd left the Chrysler some place along the way. Just where…

Get going. Ignoring the curious stares of the maid, I marched out the front door into a snowstorm. Icy flakes hit me, crawled beneath the collar of my coat and up my sleeves. The freezing wind cooled my sweaty forehead in record time…and then some. Thankfully, I only had a few minutes walk.

Mercer didn't say a word when he opened the door, but I read disapproval in his features. "Sir, will you have breakfast before you go?"

I wiped myself down before the word breakfast registered and triggered a new wave of nausea. "Perhaps an aspirin?" I managed before rushing upstairs.

Mercer waited for me in the dining room, offering two aspirin on a platter and a cup of peppermint tea. I had changed into Father's black wool suit and vest and long underpants. None fit particularly well, the waist too large and my chest a bit squeezed, but what did it matter.

"Should I drive?" Mercer asked nonchalantly. "Perhaps a safer choice this morning?"

I would've laughed had I not felt so miserable. My neck and torso had begun to itch and my throat was raw. I'd almost forgotten the notes for the speech and was already late and now the snow was making things difficult. "Good idea, Mercer. Thank you." I downed the pills with the tea and headed for the door, when Mercer called after me. "Your hat and gloves, sir?"

I returned to retrieve the top hat, I'd borrowed from Father and tugged on gloves. It was no more than fitting to wear what Father had cherished.

"We'll need to take the Mercedes," I said as we headed out the door. How was I going to find the missing Chrysler?

It'd be a very long day.

CHAPTER TWENTY

Sam

"Sam, come down immediately." Tina's voice sounded foggy as I awoke from a dream. I'd been having dinner with Mamma and Angelo, eating piles of homemade pasta and Italian meatballs. The aroma was still in my nose and now mixed with Tina's body powder.

Judging by the gloomy light, it had to be early afternoon. Not yet time to work.

When I reached for my housecoat, Tina commented, "Beatrice says you're supposed to wear your dress and shoes."

"Why?" I mumbled. "What could possibly be this important?"

But Tina had already left. I threw a last glance at the dull mirror above the washstand. My eyes looked dark blue in the low light, a bit mysterious. I ran a palm across my face as if to snuff out the image and hurried downstairs.

A man I didn't know, dressed in a black calf-length winter coat, hat and gloves leaned at the bar, an untouched drink in front of him.

"Ah, here she is." Beatrice swooped to my side like an eagle looking for pray, her left fake eyelash threatening to take off in flight. "Maybe now you'll tell us what this is about?" she said, addressing the visitor.

The man ignored the woman and focused on me. "Sorry, miss, Mr. Moretti sends his regards. I'm supposed to give you a lift." He finally turned to Beatrice. "Mr. Moretti will provide compensation, of course."

Where to, I wanted to ask. What does Tony want?

Instead I stood openmouthed, taking in the well-dressed man. "Who are you?" I finally managed.

"Mr. Moretti's associate." He turned to Beatrice again. "Does the girl have a coat and hat? This weather is a bear." I followed his gaze out the window, where snow was falling in thick sheets. More than a foot had accumulated since this morning.

"I'll get something," Beatrice mumbled. She returned with a flimsy cape and misshapen beige hat. "Looks like you got yourself a daddy," she hissed. I frowned and wished for my old coat and winter boots. Obviously, Beatrice didn't expect any of her girls to set foot outside ever again. My thoughts traveled to the box beneath the floorboards. Poppi lived in West Garfield Park and she needed the money.

"I forgot something," I mumbled.

"What could you have possibly forgotten?" Beatrix mocked. "You came with nothing."

"Let's be quick," the man added. "More snow is on the way." He gripped my elbow and guided me to the door.

The *Rolls Royce Phantom I* wore a layer of fresh snow by the time we stepped outside. The wind howled around me as if it wanted to tear the clothes off my skin. Icy crystals hit my cheeks and made breathing difficult.

The vehicle's heater blew on full, yet my feet were numb. Somewhere a streetcar shrieked. The little passenger area grew a bit warmer. The man didn't speak, apparently intent on keeping the automobile on the road. All I saw was snow sleeting in the headlights. If we got stuck, I'd freeze to death in an hour. *You're in Chicago. Quit being afraid.* Still, I couldn't keep myself from trembling.

It seemed hours had passed by the time we arrived in front of a narrow two-story brick home. The driver sighed. "Sorry miss, I was worried about the weather."

He rushed around the vehicle and helped me to my feet. Immediately, I sank ankle-deep into a drift. Snow trickled into my shoes, crept up my calves, and attacked my ears.

A girl in white and black opened the door. The scene was so eerily similar to the time at George Remus's place, I smiled.

"Please follow me," the maid said with a curtsy.

She led the way up the staircase. The driver had disappeared. A thick wool carpet with some tropical birds in the weave swallowed my steps. After the gray and white of outside, it almost hurt my eyes to see so much color.

The maid opened one of a four identical looking doors.

"I have prepared a bath," she said with flushed cheeks. "Your clothes are on the bed."

I tried to take it all in. What in the world was happening? The last time I'd taken a bath was in the old pub after Paul had disappeared which had only been...I shook my head. Only five days had passed since I'd been taken by those men and enslaved by Beatrice.

The bathroom, tiled in white and black, was larger than my old bedroom. A tub was filling with sudsy steaming water.

"Please ring the bell, if you need anything." The maid pointed at a lever next to the door, curtsied again, and disappeared.

I sucked in the fragrant air, something flowery and fresh that reminded me of Maggie. On a shelf, glass vials held red, pink and blue bath salts. Thick towels were stacked next to the tub.

I stripped and leaned back in the tub. I'd gone to heaven. The tub was so large, I could stretch my legs all the way and still not reach the end. My limbs thawed.

Wrapped in a towel, I inspected the bed: fine flesh-colored stockings, garter belt, silky underwear and a long black dress. The front was high-necked, but the back plunged to the waist.

When I walked to the mirror I stared in shock. The black of the dress matched my hair, and my eyes sparkled like blue crystals.

I tried a smile, but the jitters were too great. *Quit your gallivanting. Nothing good comes of it.* Resolutely, I rang the bell.

The maid seemed to have waited nearby, because the knock came almost instantly.

I opened the door. "I'm ready."

"Please follow me." The maid curtsied again. I wanted to tell her to quit the nonsense.

We descended the same stairs and entered a double glass door. Beyond lay the most sparkling room I had ever seen. Everything appeared to shine—the mahogany table and matching chairs, the sideboards, the glasses and carafes.

The room was empty.

I stepped to the floor-to-ceiling bookshelf, eyed the hundreds of tomes. Who had time to read like this?

"Do you have a favorite author?"

I flinched and turned on my heels. Citrus aftershave tickled my nose. Tony Moretti, lounging in an armchair, a book on his lap and a snifter by this side, grinned at me.

I immediately felt self-conscious, but also annoyed. Despite the gorgeous surroundings, I was still a piece of meat being shoved one way and then another.

"What a face," Tony chuckled. "Cat got your tongue again?"

"I'm sorry, Mr. Moretti, what am I doing here?"

Tony's eyes grew serious. "I think you know me well enough to say Tony?"

My cheeks blazed as visions of our encounter returned. I'd thought about it every day since.

"Honestly, I'm not sure myself." He kept staring at me, his gaze never leaving my face. I opened my mouth. Closed it. What the heck was that supposed to mean?

"I guess I couldn't get your story out of my mind. A single girl traveling to Chicago in search of her missing brother." He clicked his tongue. "It's a recipe for disaster, Sam."

I shrugged defiantly. "I couldn't sit in Cincinnati and wait either." Without a home, I wanted to say.

"How about we have dinner and you'll tell me what you know?"

I nodded.

Dinner had been simple but delicious. Tomato bisque, cheese toast, followed by pork tenderloins, potatoes and leek casserole.

Ignoring the increasing pressure in my stomach, I devoured three huge portions.

Now I sat almost miserable on a sofa in the same room with the books. A four-foot fire crackled in the corner and the room was comfortably warm. Too comfortable. I felt sleepy and awkward at the same time. I'd told Tony all I knew about Angelo which was precious little. I didn't even know who he'd come to see, what day he'd arrived or if he'd arrived. Still, Tony had refrained from comments and made a few notes.

"Time to go, baby," he said without preamble.

I straightened slowly. "Where to?"

"I want to show you my club." He waved at the maid, who

carried an ankle-length wool cape with a sable fur hood. The weight of it was reassuring.

"Will you bring me back afterwards?" I asked.

Tony slipped into a navy coat and chuckled. "Where to? Oh, you mean Beatrice's." He rubbed his nose between thumb and forefinger as if you contemplate his answer. "Sam, you're not going back there."

I wanted to shout, *but I have to.* I said nothing, hardly noticed being led to the automobile, the snowstorm still in full force. The seats inside were red leather, the automobile even more luxurious than the last one. What was I going to do? Maggie's money for her daughter rested beneath my bed—next to the photos and the letters from Maggie's sister. The little girl had to get her mother's money.

"Where are we?" I asked finally as the vehicle slowed in front of a brightly lit entrance.

"This is *Tony's.*" There was that chuckle again. "Couldn't think of anything fancy."

"I mean where in Chicago are we?"

"Westside. Why?"

I shrugged. "Just wondering. You happened to know where West Garfield Park is?" But my last words drowned in the buzz of hundreds of voices laughing, singing, talking and clinking glasses.

The light was blinding after the darkness on the street. A theater style open room with upstairs semi-private boxes overlooked the main floor. Dancers swirled to the sound of a jazz orchestra, a crowd pressed against the thirty-foot bar. The rest sat at tables, stood or lounged. The women glittered in lacy dresses with fringes and sequined headbands. Most men wore dark suits or tailcoats.

Every person we passed nodded or bowed as Tony shook hands and called out greetings. I wanted to disappear, especially because all the eyes jumped from Tony to me and I could feel their curiosity as clearly as a touch. By the time we sat down at a corner table I was dizzy.

A glass of champagne appeared in front of me, just as the lights dimmed and the orchestra stopped.

"Ladies and gentleman, let's welcome Annabelle," a man in tails and a top hat announced.

A woman in her thirties, with wispy blonde chin-length hair

and a dress that seemed entirely made of sparkling stones, stepped next to the piano. Her voice was smoky and much deeper than I expected.

"What'll I do…when you are far away…" she sang. My thoughts returned to Paul and the way he'd looked at me—with that expression of watchfulness and honesty. The image morphed into Angelo's dancing eyes when he told us about his upcoming trip to Chicago. My heart ached and I wasn't sure who I missed more.

The lights brightened. I hadn't heard another word from the singer. Sweat dripped between my breasts. I realized I'd been happier at Beatrice's rundown bordello than here amidst the glamor. At least there I'd known what was expected of me. Here I didn't know how to act or what to think.

"I need to powder my nose," I said quietly.

Tony, a frown wrinkling his forehead, was in conversation with another man in a suit who seemed to manage the bar. "Whiskey is running low. Last two deliveries from Cinci didn't make it," he just said, his caterpillar eyebrows jerking upwards. "We'll be out in a couple days."

I straightened and made my way to the front. My eyes burned from the cigarettes and cigars rose in such clouds, it was hard to see the floor. *Stupid drinking business.* The floor wiggled with dancing and swaying couples. To my left, a woman shrieked and teetered before collapsing onto a chair laughing. Who needed alcohol when I had enough trouble just walking in heels?

I stopped at the front door and stared longingly into the night. Snowflakes danced in the overhead lamp. Nobody appeared to watch. But how could I leave? The weather was forbidding and I had no place to go.

I was still a prisoner. Despite the fancy dress.

When I returned to our table, Tony was nowhere to be seen.

I awoke to grayish light. The maid from last night was opening curtains. A cup of coffee steamed on the nightstand.

Fragments of the evening returned: the elegant dress, the dinner and club. We'd gone home in the early hours when I almost dozed off at the table. Tony's distracted embrace in the hall and then his grip tightening on my wrist, pulling me to the living room, yanking up my dress, his mouth a flask of whiskey, hard and unforgiving on my neck.

He lifted me upward against the wall. The pain as he shoved into me…afterwards hushed steps as he disappeared to some other part of the house.

"I laid out a dress, miss." The maid curtsied. "Would you like help with your bath?"

"I'll manage," I said.

Last night I'd dragged myself upstairs and bathed, but the feeling of dirtiness remained along with a dull throb between my legs. Tony's attack had been so different from his visit at Beatrice's. It confused me.

Outside, the snow had stopped, the street covered in white. Here and there a lone person fought through the drifts.

Once the maid had left, I dressed and slipped downstairs. The dining room was empty, one of the two plates full of crumbs. Tony had already left. I pulled my legs under me and nibbled on a piece of toast. Despite the spread of jams, cheeses, scrambled eggs and sausage, I wasn't hungry. All I wanted was to get Maggie's money to her daughter, Poppi.

A giggle rose in my throat and burst into the stillness. Instead of searching for Angelo, I'd added another problem—to find a girl. *And Paul?* My mouth felt dry.

"Concentrate," I said aloud. "You need money…a map of Chicago. One thing at a time."

"Talking to yourself?" Tony said. "That's something my mother used to do."

I forced a smile. How much had he heard? His lids were puffy. Obviously, he hadn't slept well.

"Maybe I figured out what happened to your brother," Tony said, pouring himself a cup of coffee.

I wanted to jump from my seat—one part ready to flee, the other to force Tony to speak faster.

"Does the name Jake Guzik ring a bell? Also called *Greasy Thumb?*"

I smirked. "Not really."

"He's a friend of Capone's, does his dirty money business." Tony took a sip of coffee. "Last year, in early May, he got insulted by some thug in a bar, name of Joe Howard."

"What does that have to do—"

Tony raised an arm to cut me off. "They say Capone walked in there later and killed Howard. Shot him six times.

133

"But didn't somebody see it?"

"Sure. There were witnesses. But by the time police arrived, Capone had disappeared. A month later he turned himself in. Meanwhile the witnesses either vanished or changed their minds. Capone walked."

Tony bent forward and patted my hand. "What if your brother was involved, watched the whole thing? Thought he had to split to protect himself…and your family."

I tried to imagine the scene. Angelo drinking a beer in the back of a pub. Capone walking in, words being exchanged. Gun shots. Blood splattering…Angelo being interviewed by police, getting scared and running off. I shook my head. He would've sent a note, some sign he was alive.

Which confirmed my worst fear. Heat raced to my cheeks. "You think he's dead. That's why you're telling me this. Capone killed my brother." My voice grew shrill. "Because Angelo watched him murder Howard?"

"No—"

I jumped up and began to pace. "He would've sent word," I cried. "You don't know him." The room was much larger than the dinky room, I'd shared with Mamma, so I took huge steps. Eleven one way, eleven back. "He's gone." I crumpled on the sofa by the window, my mind clinging to the Chicago newspaper we'd received last September. Who else would've sent it to our mailbox if not Angelo?

"Let me ask around," Tony said. "It was just a guess. For all I know he could've worked for the North Side Gang."

I raised my head, Tony's face blurry. Somehow I didn't believe Tony. "I need some money. Left my savings at Beatrice's." Paul had said I was a terrible liar, but Tony didn't notice or care. Wordlessly he pulled out a money clip and threw a twenty on the table.

I slowly straightened and came near. It wasn't enough to repay the little girl, but it would allow for a down payment. "What am I doing here, Tony?"

He absentmindedly rubbed his chin and stood. "Not sure, Sam," he said without meeting my eyes. "Right now, I've got to straighten out these shipments or we'll be as good as finished."

That night, Tony didn't come home. I waited after dinner, having spent all day trying to decide what to do. I was obviously not being watched, because the maid who also cooked went about her business and nobody else was in the house.

After exploring the various rooms, opening a few drawers and gazing out the window, I returned to the living area with its walls of books. I pulled out tomes, first by color, then by size or the way the titles sounded.

When Tony wasn't there the next morning, I tracked down the maid in the kitchen. "Do you know where Mr. Moretti went?"

The maid curtsied. "I'm sorry, miss. He didn't send notice." She hesitated. "He may be at his club."

"Does he usually stay out all night?"

"I don't think so, but then…I go home at night."

"I think you can clean the table now. I'll be reading for a while."

I returned to the living room, but not to read. What I planned was none of the maid's business and I hoped to remain unobserved.

I rushed through the backdoor into the hall, up the stairs into the outer part of the house where Tony had his quarters. I hadn't been here before and hesitated, then resolutely opened the door.

Tony's bed was huge with a blue and white cover. The matching curtains were open, allowing enough light to see without lamps. I scanned the room. No wardrobes, just a dresser. Beyond one door lay a gray-marbled bath with a tub and separate shower. I stepped backwards and opened a second door near the corner of the room.

Inside hung Tony's suits, arranged by color, shirts and ties. Separate compartments held sweaters, socks and underwear. I scanned the offerings. I had to be crazy, but this was the only way to get some answers. I abruptly kicked away my shoes, slipped off my dress and stockings. In my underwear, I grabbed a dark-blue flannel shirt, socks, a pair of moss-green corduroys and a wool pullover. Everything was huge on me, so I affixed suspenders to keep the pants in place and rolled up the sleeves of the shirt and pullover.

In the entrance to the cellar I'd discovered a pair of rubberized boots—for a moment my heart squeezed as I remembered Paul buying me winter boots—and an old overcoat and hat, maybe the gardener's.

I picked up my discarded clothes and returned them to my room before tiptoeing downstairs. The maid rummaged around in the kitchen, singing a little tune, the same as I had heard in the club the night before last.

When I reached the cellar entry, the doorbell rang. Tony was home. But then why would he not unlock the door himself? Had he lost his keys? *He better not see you now.*

Just as a gust of icy wind hit me, I quietly closed the basement door behind me. The dark was immediate. I groped along the wall for a light, found it. Voices traveled along the corridor.

"May I help you?" the maid could be heard.

"Officer Delany, I'm looking for Samantha Bruno."

"One moment, sir."

"No need. I'll have a look myself."

Footsteps marched off and by the sound of it, there were several men. I cringed. Why were they looking for me? Had Tony gotten into trouble? But then, what did that have to do with me? Had they found Angelo?

Beyond the door, steps bounded upstairs. "She isn't here," somebody said.

"What do you want with her, anyway?" the maid cried.

"Wanted for murder at Fizzy's." Officer Delany's voice was cold.

I clamped a hand on my mouth. Maggie. *No time,* my mind screamed. *Get out of here.*

In the gloom I scanned the wall hooks, yanked a coat and hat down. Stuffing the boots under my arm I slipped downstairs.

A long hall led away from me, several doors on each side. A barred one by two window allowed a bit of light. Beyond lay darkness—a dungeon. With a shiver I pulled on coat and boots. The coat almost reached to the floor, but that couldn't be helped. Upstairs footsteps.

Hurry! I rushed to the first door: wine cellar, then laundry, furniture storage, food pantry, coal storage. Somehow I'd expected a backdoor to the outside like the houses in Over-the-Rhine. But this place had no other door, just tiny barred windows. I was stuck.

The door to the cellar opened.

"She wouldn't be down there," the maid could be heard.

"Oh, yeah?" Delaney said. "You wouldn't believe what criminals are capable of when they're cornered."

"But she seemed so nice."

I stopped. Something scraped at my memory. No time.

Retracing my steps, I threw another glance at the coal partition. Half hidden by the pile was a trap door—the coal chute. Footfalls descended the stairs.

I was out of time.

Scrambling across the piles of coal, I yanked at the square cover opened when coals were delivered. My heart hammered. Now they'd think I was guilty because I'd run.

Icy air hit me as I slipped through a gap into the narrow angled tunnel filled with snow. Then I closed the door and waited.

Even crouched in the chute, the freezing wind hit me like a wall. What had looked beautiful and white from the inside was actually a horrific winter storm. The sweat on my forehead turned to frost. Why did the police think I'd murdered Maggie? The scene in the girl's bedroom repeated. Maggie's staring eyes, the bruises on her neck.

I began to shake, and it wasn't just from the icy air creeping down my neck.

Somewhere in front, doors slammed and engines started. They were leaving. The initial relief was replaced with dread. I was a fugitive. Surely, they were watching the house now. Had it not been freezing, I would've simply crumpled into a heap, my limbs heavy as a pile of rocks. Somebody had framed me for Maggie's murder. A grunt escaped me as fury fired up my insides. I needed to talk to Beatrice and find out what happened.

I couldn't stay, couldn't explain it, but something wasn't right with Tony.

Taking hold of my hat, I crept through the backyard and lowered myself into the wind.

CHAPTER TWENTY-ONE

Paul

Even before I made it home, I knew something was wrong. Despite the Mercedes' heater on full blast, I shivered uncontrollably. The ache in my temples was back and extended to squeeze my skull. My neck was stiff, and every little movement sent darts of pain down my spine. Worst was my throat, which felt like it was closing up all together.

The funeral had been successful—if you could call laying your father to rest a success. The church had brimmed with mourners: neighbors, friends of the family, a distant cousin, dignitaries, politicians, businessmen and a few curious onlookers. Most had come to say good-bye, but an equal or greater number had been there to study the long lost son.

I had kept calm, shaken hundreds of hands, smiled and nodded, endured hugs and pats on the back. "Good to have you here," they said. "It's a relief. So sad, he had to go so soon..." And so on. Only when we'd carried Father to the graveside and it was my turn to add a shovel of sand, had I begun to cry. It was still snowing and few people had come along, so I was glad for the shrunken audience.

In the church, Colene and her father had been by my side, acting like family. Colene's arm stuck to my sleeve as if it were glued in place. She repeatedly dabbed her eyes and whispered sweet nothings into my ear. I would've preferred to shake her off like a pesky fly, but I was too tired and miserable to afford the energy.

Relief swept through me when Colene feigned a backache, which didn't allow her to accompany me to the burial site. I knew she wasn't about to stand in two feet of snow when she could sit by a roaring fire sipping gin tonics.

It didn't matter. This was better. I could be alone with my thoughts and speak a few words, even if I had no recollection of them.

I'd lost a father I'd hated. I hadn't just lost seven years; all the horrible feelings I'd harbored had been wrong. *I* had been wrong. Not only had I wasted my heart on hateful thoughts for Father, but I'd wasted time I could've had being near him. In fact, I'd probably *caused* Father's death. Everyone had mentioned how worried he'd been and how they'd thought me dead.

The guilt seemed to pull me over, making it near impossible to move my limbs. I parked and dragged myself inside.

Sure, I'd learned a lot from being on the streets. I was, as they say, 'street smart.' But what about business matters? Accounting? Dealing with suppliers and vendors? Hiring and firing employees? In these matters I was clueless and over my head.

At that moment, I vowed to study all I could about Father's company. If only my throat didn't ache so badly.

"Sir, a nightcap perhaps," Mercer said when he opened the door, his eyelids still pink from the church service. "Sir, are you all right?"

I stumbled past Mercer into the entry. "I'm afraid I—" the ground rushed up to me and everything grew quiet.

Sam

Within minutes, I knew I'd made a mistake. Though no more snow fell, the wind cut through me and my toes grew numb in the thin rubber boots. I hardly made any progress, each step laborious. Either the snow was high or had been cleaned, leaving a slippery, rock-hard surface. My lungs ached from cold. Every few steps I turned my head this way and that. With the neighborhood unfamiliar, I'd get lost. I'd never make it to Fizzy's. Not like this. *You're stupid, Sam. You could die out here.*

Since Mamma's passing, I'd made nothing but bad decisions. Maybe I should've stayed put and waited for Angelo. Worked out a deal with the lecherous landlord.

"Oh, Mamma, what should I do?"

139

The air remained quiet, every sound muffled from the snow. It was as if I walked in a vacuum. Mamma wasn't going to answer. She was dead. Neither Paul nor Angelo would help. I couldn't return to Fizzy's. Not to get the money or even to find out the truth. Someone had found Maggie's letters and pictures, the two hundred dollars in cash. They probably thought I'd killed Maggie for the money...framed me. Either Beatrice would turn me in or enslave me anew. Good thing Tony had gotten me away. That had to count for something even if his behavior was kind of odd.

Defeated, I turned around and walked back in my own footsteps. Tony's house stood back from the street, the backyard deserted. Still, I couldn't risk being seen. Bushes and trees framed the borders—places for me to hide. Inside was a warm bed, and even if I had to tolerate Tony's moods, it was a world better than living with the likes of Tina and sleeping with disgusting men. Or going to prison for murder.

I crept into the bushes near the back fence and waited.

After dark, I straightened and almost screamed from the pain in my frozen bones. Lights shone in the kitchen as I turned the knob. The door was locked. Damn, I'd hoped to slip inside and somehow weasel my way back to my room. Then I'd come out and play surprised.

"Sam?" Tony stood in the door in shirtsleeves. His cheeks glowed and he reeked of whiskey.

"I'm sorry." I wanted to step inside, but Tony's arm in the doorway cut me off.

"Where did you go?"

I shrugged and to my frustration, tears stung. "My friend Maggie died and I found out she has a little girl. I wanted to see if she was all right. Maggie left money behind. I mean to take it to her daughter...Poppi. I didn't get very far...the snow."

Tony's expression remained cool. "Why didn't you talk to me? Act like an adult? You're wanted for murder? Maybe I should leave you outside."

I looked down. "I'm grateful...an idiot. I didn't kill anyone. Maggie was my friend."

When I lifted my gaze, the arm was gone from the doorframe and a smirk played around Tony's lips. "Nice outfit. You look like a stray."

He stepped back and pulled me inside. "Now get out of these

clothes and come back down. "We've got to have a talk."

"You asked me what I want," Tony said a few minutes later. He sat in his usual chair by the fire, watching me. I'd changed into a plain brown velvet dress and was thawing my hands. "What do *you* want? I mean other than to find your brother."

My eyes grew large. Nobody had ever asked me that. I'd survived as best I could, done what I thought was right.

A whiff of something frying hit my nose. Papa's smiling face appeared, his forefinger pointing at a green tomato growing on a vine.

"I want to cook," I blurted.

"Cook?" The astonishment on Tony's face made me smile.

"Italian food. Tasty things, cannelloni and sauces, and bread—"

"You're full of surprises, Sam Bruno. Here I thought you wanted jewels and champagne." He straightened and tossed another log to the fire.

Somewhere in the ensuing silence, a phone rang. The maid appeared shortly after. "Sir, an urgent call."

When Tony returned, he looked pale. "There were more raids. I've got to go."

At the door, he turned. "Don't run off again. If you do, you're not coming back in."

I slumped into a chair, resigned to spend a boring evening waiting. At some point I returned to the bookshelves, where my eyes lodged on a brown linen cover: *The Cook's Decameron: A Study in Taste, containing over 200 Recipes for Italian Dishes.*

The remainder of the evening, I spent reading and studying the book. I mumbled to myself, shook my head or cried a loud emphatic, "yes."

At some point I got up to look for paper and returned with a pad from Tony's desk. I began making notes—first there were lists, random comments. I again stood next to Papa fixing pasta from scratch, mixing flour, eggs, olive oil and salt. I smelled the dough, saw the pot on the stove as Papa carefully lowered his creations into the boiling water.

When I grew tired of reading, I got up and headed into the kitchen. On a shelf by the icebox, I found *Good Housekeeping's Book of Menus, recipes, and Household Discoveries.* By the stains it was clear the maid used it. Luckily, the girl hadn't seen me return.

I began opening cupboards and drawers. An idea was forming in my head.

I awoke from a sound in the hall. A door closed. A cough. I scrambled from the couch where I'd fallen asleep, reading about *Cooking with Fruit by Harriet Schuyler Nelson.*

Tony stuck his head in the door, his hair shiny from melting snow. "You still up?"

I took a wobbly step toward him. "I cooked dinner." I could tell he was exhausted. Shadows beneath his eyes made him look gaunt. "I didn't know when you'd get here."

I expected him to turn me down, but he patted my arm before pouring himself a whiskey. "I better see what it is," he said before sinking into a chair.

"It'll be a bit. Need to warm things up first." And from the doorway, "just stay there. I'll bring it to you."

By the time I returned with two plates, he was sleeping. I removed the half-empty glass from his fingers and got a blanket— all that work wasted.

But when I covered him, he opened his eyes.

"Done already?" He sniffed. "Smells delicious."

I placed one plate on his lap, the other on the arm of the chair. I'd only half-cooked the pasta and finished it now. There hadn't been fresh tomatoes, but I'd discovered a can, pureed it, added onion, thinly sliced garlic, basil, and a few other spices, I'd found.

Tony ate with gusto. "This is delicious," he said twice, half to himself. By the time he was done he took a deep breath. "Well done."

Wordlessly, I handed him the other plate. On it laid pale egg-shaped cookies. "*Amaretti legieri…*almond cakes."

Tony selected one, then another. Between bites he continued to mumble. "So good."

At last I smiled. "It was fun. I could use more ingredients though."

A shadow ran across Tony's features. "Not sure how to tell you this. I had to close the club tonight. My supply line got compromised. Trucks broke down; there were raids. I'm sorry."

I collected Tony's dishes. "I don't understand. What does it mean?"

142

"Unless I find a new supplier tomorrow and a way to bribe the police," Tony said, "I'm ruined."

To my surprise, I found myself back at his side. I placed a palm on his head, trying to imagine what it felt like to have so much to lose.

Tony leaned back in his chair and took my hand. By now I understood what reflected in his eyes. It was the same with all men I'd met. Lust.

He caressed the inside of my forearm and pulled me on his lap. This time I knew what to do. I pulled off my drawers and straddled him. His hand now on my legs, he pushed up my dress. Each movement was unhurried, yet purposeful. And for the first time, I found interest in the act. I unbuttoned his pants and fitted myself to him.

His lips found mine and together we rocked back and forth. Slowly. Tony's hands pulled down the sleeve of my dress and began to lick my breast the way he'd done the first time.

Inside me, things began to change. The nerves along my spine tingled, spread to the front, up and down my belly. Tony pulled down the remaining dress and exposed my breasts. His tongue flicked. The rocking continued. I felt myself tightening, the intensity spreading to my limbs…up my back. Tony moaned, his forehead damp now against my skin. The climax surprised me nearly as much as the time at Beatrice's. I pushed against him as a tiny gurgle escaped my lips.

Our eyes met, a slight grin on Tony's face. "That was delicious," he said, straightening his clothes. "Now we need to rest."

Upstairs, he led me to his room where we undressed at opposite ends of the bed. The sheets were soft, the bed large, but I had trouble falling asleep. The man next to me was still a stranger and yet, here I'd made love to him and enjoyed it. How was that possible? Was I a whore now? Such an ugly word, one Mamma had taught me. "Don't ever lie with men, Sam," she'd said. "Only when they marry you, is it proper."

Oh Mamma, I'm long gone from proper. All I do is survive.

Tony was gone when I awoke. The maid had stared suspiciously as she laid out breakfast. I ate alone. Unable to relax, I kept my ears peeled to the help's activities and approaching cars on the street. What if the maid called the police and turned me in?

Tony didn't appear for lunch or dinner. He didn't even return by the next morning. Around ten o'clock, the doorbell rang. I hovered in the living room, cookbooks and papers strewn around.

"The police are here," the maid announced before being shoved aside.

My stomach clenched painfully. They'd come to get me. Before I could think of what to do, a tall man in an ankle-length wool coat rushed up to me. Beneath, he wore a gray suit, a matching hat clutched under one arm. His hair was parted in the middle.

"Captain Morgan Collins. Who are you?" the man said unsmiling, his eyes squinty behind the round glasses.

"Sa...ra Brown, I'm...a friend." I straightened as several books clattered to the floor. Any second he'd call my bluff and whip out handcuffs to take me away.

The man stood uncomfortably close, yet he made no attempt to seize me. "When did you last see Tony Moretti?"

A puff escaped my throat. "The night before yesterday he came home late. The next morning when I got up he was gone. He hasn't been home since."

The man continued to squint while I spoke as if he didn't believe me. "He didn't call or stop by?"

I shook my head and swallowed. Obviously this plain-clothed cop worked for a different division. "What's going on?" I asked, hoping my voice sounded strong. "Is he in trouble?"

The corners of the man's mouth drooped further. "I'd appreciate if you called me, if he returns." He handed me a card. "Don't do anything stupid, Miss Brown. We'll be watching."

The maid ran off shortly after, telling me she hadn't been paid for two weeks and could no longer afford to wait.

I spent all evening searching the house for valuables. I found two men's watches, a gold necklace and a ring with a square blue stone—but no money. After placing my findings on the table, I hesitated. Taking them meant I was a common thief. No better than those thugs out there. With a sigh, I put them in my pocket— survival was more important. Since reading and sleeping were impossible, I fixed another Italian dish. Tortellini with leftover herbs I'd found on the windowsill and fresh white cheese.

After eating a lone meal, I cleaned the kitchen from top to bottom. Not only because I'd left a huge mess with flour dust on every surface, but I wanted to leave things in good condition. Tony had been nice, had rescued me from Beatrice's hellhole. Without him I might sit in prison already.

Sometime in the night I, awoke. Had I heard footsteps? Or was that from my dream in which I'd seen Paul dance with another girl in Tony's club? It made me stinking mad because the girl laughed and turned into the woman who'd sung at the piano.

There. A creak. From the kitchen. A cool draft crept up my legs. It had to have come from the kitchen door. I about jumped when a shadow emerged and rushed toward the hall. Remaining quiet on the sofa I listened as the steps moved upstairs. Floorboards groaned. Back and forth they went. Then quiet.

I sat for a bit, but then curiosity got the better of me. I snuck into the hall and grabbed an umbrella. No sounds came from upstairs. On the second-floor landing I listened again. Nothing.

But wait.

A low grumble emanated from the room to my right. Tony's room. I moved to the door, glad the carpet swallowed my steps. The grumble grew. Somebody snored.

I turned the knob and tiptoed to the bed. Then backed up. It was too dark to see, so I fumbled for the light switch.

Tony lay on his back, his mouth open, a blackish shadow of beard on his chin. He looked drawn and didn't wake even when I moved closer. He'd thrown his coat and hat on a chair and tossed his shoes in the corner.

With a sigh, I turned off the light and snuggled next to the man. He still didn't wake, just put an arm around me and mumbled something. I was wide-awake. I was supposed to call that grey-haired policeman with the part in the middle. But if they knew he was here, they would've kicked in the door already. And chances were, the other police would show up to look for me. I dozed off.

At dawn I awoke to movement. Tony came out of the bathroom with a kit in his hand. "I thought you'd left," he said simply. He'd changed into clean shirt and pants, but the easy smile from last week was missing.

I got on one elbow. "What happened?"

Tony sank on a chair. "My club was raided, guests arrested or scared off. The last reserves of whiskey and gin are gone." His voice grew heavy. "I'm finished."

"You ran off before they got you?"

"Had a secret door in the office. A few of my staff got away."
With a grimace, he straightened. "I'm afraid I need to hide for a bit.
Going to Cicero."

He rushed to my side and took my hands. "Look, Sam, I'm
sorry. Can't keep you here. The police will be back and look for
you too. Even if you didn't kill your friend. And that Collins is
unrelenting. I heard Torrio is trying to grease him. No chance." He
straightened and began throwing clothes into a suitcase.

"I want to go with you," I heard myself say.

Tony hesitated, then shook his head and resumed opening
drawers and throwing the contents into a second bag. "I've got a
room. Maybe when I get back on my feet." He pulled out his wallet
and handed me a twenty. "Rent a small place and do laundry."

"That's what Mamma did," I cried. "She worked herself to
death. I've got no place to go. I'm not returning to Beatrice—they
all think I killed my friend." I climbed out of bed and moved into
his way. "Please. I'll cook for you. Do your laundry. Anything."

Tony's mouth twitched. At last he pulled me close and spoke
into the crown of my head. "All right. For now. No promises,
though."

I bit my lip because I hated the sound of my own desperation.

Paul

A blinding light drilled into my skull. I wanted to scream and push
away the brightness, but I couldn't move my limbs, not even an
inch. My skin itched as if thousands of tiny feathers tickled me, my
throat so dry that my tongue seemed to be glued to the roof of my
mouth. Yet, I couldn't utter a word.

Voices filled my ears. Mother called to me, smiling and
waving, but when I approached, her face turned into that of an old
woman, wrinkles carving themselves through her face, her hair
turning white. Her smile turned into a grimace, then morphed again
into ash until she crumpled into a heap. I fell on my knees, but all
my hands grasped were bits of gray dust. I screamed, my throat
scorching.

The next time I awoke, I noticed movement nearby. A cool
hand rested on my forehead. I wanted to crawl into it, because I
was burning up. Heat spread across my chest and belly, up to my
head and down to my fingertips.

"Nobody can visit," a voice whispered nearby. Then I was

asleep again. In my fever dreams I met Father anew. Regi was much younger and looked like the morning he'd sent me away to school. Except this time, he gestured for me to come along. He never spoke, just smiled as he waved me upstairs and into Mother's bedroom. Mother was lying on her bed, her eyes open. Next to her laid a man in a brown uniform and domed helmet, watching me. Father marched to the man and yanked away the helmet, revealing pinkish flesh where the skull had been torn away.

I screamed again, but the heat held me prisoner.

When I awoke, the light had faded. I carefully opened my eyes. The soft yellow of a wall sconce illuminated Mercer napping on a chair.

I cleared my throat, the pain tolerable. I swallowed carefully.

Mercer's eyes opened, our gaze meeting in the dimness. "Sir, you're awake," he cried, stumbling toward the bed.

"Water, please," I whispered. Mercer held a glass to my lips as coolness extinguished the fire in my throat. "What happened?"

"You were gravely ill, sir," Mercer said. "Scarlet fever, very contagious."

"But *you* are here," I said. I wouldn't have known if a hundred people had visited. Or none.

"I had the disease as a young man."

I tried to imagine what the old butler had been like in his youth. It was hard to imagine. Had he dreamed of becoming famous...or rich? Or doing some important job?

"Thank you for your kindness," I said quietly. "I'm very much in your debt." I lay back, secure in the knowledge of knowing a man I could trust.

"Not at all, sir. I think the worst is past." Mercer straightened and assumed his butler stance, hands behind his back. "May I bring you something to eat? Perhaps some chicken soup?"

Sam

Tony hadn't lied. It was a hole of a room behind a bar in Cicero. Laundry lines crisscrossed the backyard and the only window looked out on a brick wall.

While Tony took off to find 'business' opportunities, I straightened up our chamber, washed laundry in the sink and cooked on a hot plate. Strangely, I didn't mind because it reminded me of living with Mamma. Except here I was bored. Sure, I shopped for groceries and thought up menus in my head. Along with the notes, I'd taken the two cookbooks with me. But the single plate and pot didn't allow for anything creative. Besides, Tony had little budget for food and seemed to drink more than he ate.

He was gentle most of the time except when he returned drunk. It seemed he forgot who I was and took what he wanted. Afterwards, he passed out and snored so loud that I spent the night in the only chair. It was uncomfortable, but at least my eardrums didn't burst.

Tony had taught me awareness of my body. The way it felt when aroused, my insides all pliable and warm. The orgasms that overwhelmed me still. It was something to be thankful for, even if Tony seemed more and more preoccupied.

One night he returned early. He'd been driving a truck delivering beer and wine while making new contacts and trying to decide what he should do next.

"Torrio got shot," he said storming into the room. "Looks like he may die."

I'd been mending my favorite shirt, formerly Tony's, that I wore whenever I left the house. I dressed like a boy not only because it was safer and I was less likely to be found out, but because the long pants and layered tops kept me warmer. I'd perfected a gangly walk, practicing in the room, posing in front of the half-blind mirror. Paul would've been proud.

"Who did it?"

Tony shrugged. "They say it was the North Side Gang, Hymie Weiss and two others. If he goes, Capone will be in charge of the Outfit."

"You think I could talk to him?" I asked.

Tony's eyes widened. "You must be crazy. He doesn't talk to *girls*."

"But he may know what happened to Angelo."

"I'm not going to help you with that," Tony said. "I'm trying to get on his good side so I can open another shop."

"So you met him?"

"Once. Delivering hooch. He walked in while I was stacking boxes in the kitchen. I talked to him about losing my club."

"Will you at least tell me where I find him?"

"You *are* crackers, Sam Bruno." Tony at last took off his coat.

"You realize he has guards. You won't get within fifty feet of him. He runs the Hawthorne Hotel and Smoke Shop on West 22nd."

I'll find a way, I thought.

CHAPTER TWENTY-TWO

Paul

Colene resumed her daily visits. Like a glittering butterfly she descended on the house, chattering and smiling.

I still tried to piece together what had happened after visiting the Dill Pickle Club before the funeral, but I was too embarrassed to ask Colene. And the more she tried to impress me with her scooping necklines and bare arms, the jewels and elaborate make-up, the more I resorted to wearing Father's oldest outfits. Not that Father owned anything I would've worn as a hobo. But there was the occasional slouchy sweater with patched elbows. And though she never mentioned it, I could tell it bothered her. It made me smile inwardly.

And yet, hadn't I promised Father I'd take care of her and fulfill what had been discussed so many years ago? *You owe it to him.*

Over and over, I lived through the scenes of finding Mother, of shouting insults at my father and giving him the silent treatment. Mother's funeral had been torture. Me standing near Father, but never making eye contact, my loathing so great, I wanted to push Regi into the hole.

Oh, why hadn't I understood? Why had they spared my feelings, not told me about Mother's infidelities? It wasn't just Father who'd remained silent. The house staff, family, and friends had remained equally muted and allowed me to whip myself into a frenzy of hate against Father.

"Why the secrecy, Father?" I mumbled as I listlessly shuffled through a pile of papers on my desk. I began to understand that nothing was ever as it seemed. Well, at least not in this world. Hobo life had been straightforward. You looked for work, food and shelter. You shared with other 'bos and told stories. The simple code worked.

My thoughts returned to Sam in the hobo camp, the night we'd slept close together under the tarp. I'd never told her how I'd found her shivering in her sleep and fitted myself to her backside to keep her warm. The feeling of her body against mine had calmed me. But it had also stirred up things I hadn't felt since Ada, the maid, my first teenage love.

"Where are you, Sam?" I said aloud.

"Who is Sam?" Colene threw me a suspicious glance. I'd forgotten she was in the room.

"Nobody." My focus returned to the papers on my desk. "I should review these."

"Father thinks you should take a vacation…take time away."

I've already taken seven years, I wanted to say. Instead I kept my head low.

"We could visit Hawaii. I've never been. They have marvelous beaches. We could take a boat. One of those pleasure boats with private suites, wine and jazz every night."

"I'll think about it."

Colene blew a puff of air. "You're such a bluenose."

As if on cue, Mercer appeared in the doorway. "Sir, Mr. Sloan is here to see you."

"Father." Colene leaped off the sofa as if she hadn't seen him in years.

"Now, now," he said, brushing her off. "Be a good girl. I've got to talk with Paul here." He addressed me with a chuckle. "Paul, you still look pale."

"Hello, Henry." I straightened and reluctantly left the safety of my desk.

"Fine then, leave men to their *boring* business," Colene pouted. "Honey, promise me to call, will you? I'd love to try this new club." I nodded, my eyes still on the elder Sloan.

"What can I do for you, Henry?"

"Colene says you're working already."

I nodded, wondering what else Colene told her father. "I'm going to join the board."

151

"Son, you've only been back a few weeks. Give it a rest." Sloan drew a leather cigar case from his pocket and offered it to me.

I'm not your son. "No, thanks," I said, returning to my desk. Sloan cut the end off a Cuban and lit a match. In the ensuing silence, cigar smoke rose between us. Henry returned his attention to me.

"You didn't get much exposure to the business world." Sloan drew on the cigar as puffing sounds emanated from his lips. "Not to mention, you were gravely ill. I gave Regi my word I'd look out for you. I can manage and explain to the board—"

"I'm quite capable of learning," I said, trying not to cough in the increasing smoke. "Of course, I appreciate your help."

"Naturally." Sloan smiled, dropping ashes into a tray by his seat. "Ask me anything, son. That's what I'm there for."

I smiled back. "Maybe another time."

Sam

Over the next weeks, I perfected my disguise, placing a hat in such a way that it covered my growing hair and most of my forehead, leaving my eyes shadowed. However, ideas on how to get to Capone were impossible to find.

Worse was that I couldn't get the scene of Maggie's murder out of my head. Every time I closed my lids, I saw Maggie lying on that bed with her eyes staring. Who had a motive to accuse me? Tina? Beatrice? Some other unknown person?

I contemplated stopping at Fizzy's and finding out for myself. But I never did. Once I walked all the way there and paced back and forth across the street. I hadn't expected to feel fearful, but just seeing the 'open' sign made my knees shaky. I remembered the moment I'd been dragged inside—the meatheads and their empty stares. The horror of feeling utterly helpless. What if Beatrice imprisoned me anew? Tony was no longer protecting. He had neither money nor much interest in me.

Most nights I lay awake, unable to relax. Rings appeared beneath my eyes and my movements grew wary and slow. *You're turning into your mother*, the voice in my head proclaimed any time I looked at the spotted mirror above the sink.

Spring arrived and the mountains of snow finally melted. Torrio had survived, but was now in jail. The papers were full of notices about shootings, raids and arrests. A clock with the 'hands of death' appeared in the newspaper, showing murders by guns, moonshine and automobiles.

"We're going out tonight," Tony announced one afternoon. I feigned excitement. This was the third time this week, and I dreaded the boozy speakeasies, the gambling halls, and clubs Tony dragged me to. It seemed that the money he made flowed more and more into drink. I felt the darkness growing inside him like a thundercloud gathering during a storm.

"Why don't we go to the waterfront instead?" I asked. "I'd love to see the lake."

Tony's cheeks flushed red, but then he seemed to catch himself. "Maybe on Sunday. Tonight I want to celebrate. I got word. We'll open a new establishment." He paced back and forth in front of me. "You wait, I'll come back from this."

By drinking again, I wanted to ask. Instead I pulled out the black dress. The crushed velvet was getting shiny in spots and there was a small stain on the skirt. But it was the best I had.

"You look smashing," Tony said as we headed toward 22nd Street. A freezing wind, so typical for Chicago, whipped around the buildings. I shivered in my thin dress and wished for my wool pants.

Eyes followed my every move when we approached The Green Mill. From the street it appeared smallish with a round window in the green painted door. Inside, a jazz band played a slow song though nobody seemed to listen. The half-moon shaped bar was packed, and so were booths and tables. Tony pulled me through the racket and tracked down a waiter. He stuffed a ten-dollar bill into the man's pocket and winked. "Keep it coming. Whiskey please. My lady friend likes champagne."

I nipped on my glass, watching the mayhem. The noise was deafening. Everyone either talked, shouted or laughed shrilly. Tony was in conversation with a big burly fellow who kept one fat paw on the waist of a blonde girl.

I had gotten in the habit of watching people. It was the only thing I was comfortable doing. A waiter squeezed past and approached a table near the bar. He was skinny with a bony Adams apple. Surprisingly, he carried a huge tray of drinks as well as three full bottles. That's when I saw it. Al Capone sat, one arm around the shoulders of a woman in a red glitzy dress, the other hand gripping a glass. Four fellows sat around them. Two additional men stood near Capone's back, eyes circling the room. My heart hammered. He looked fatter than the picture I'd seen in the paper at Tony's house, his round face shinier.

I'd never get through to the man here, and Tony would explode if I tried. I kept watching, positioning myself against Tony's side. Capone didn't wear a hat, and his hairline was receded, his face round. He laughed and talked though I couldn't understand a word he said. Even from a distance, an aura of power surrounded the man.

"I'm going to the lady's room," I said into Tony's ear. I needed time to think, to somehow figure out how to approach the mob boss. *Tony is right. You're nuts.*

Deep in thought, I exited the bathroom and collided with a man rushing toward the men's room.

"Pardon me, miss," he said. At least back here, the noise was bearable.

I'd had a few choice words on my lips. Instead I froze. The man had already passed, but I swiveled to watch him come to a sudden stop.

"Paul?" My voice was thin and didn't carry, but somehow the man had heard me. He slowly turned on his heels. Green eyes met mine.

"Sam?" Disbelief and joy showed on his features. In a flash he stood in front of me. "I can't believe it. Sam Bruno. What happened to you?" He looked me up and down. "I searched for you. Went to Victor's."

I took in his tweed coat and mismatched cravat, the familiar features of his face. There was a new brooding quality about him, a weight on his shoulders, I'd never noticed before. Despite the strenuousness of the rails, Paul had seemed relaxed. Now he was tense as he glanced past me toward the bar.

My legs had turned to mush, my stomach knotted and jumpy. He'd grown since we'd last met. Or was it my faulty memory?

"Say something," Paul continued. He gripped my hands, their warmth familiar and reassuring. "What are the chances? I'm so glad to see you."

You were right, I wanted to scream. *I got into trouble the minute you left me. Now I'm a prostitute and wanted for murder.* "You're talking for two already," I said aloud, my throat dry. "You're still in Chicago.

I—"

"Sam, what is going on?" Tony's arm clamped around my shoulder. I felt him swerve against me, his breath like a bottle of whiskey.

"Nothing. Just met an old friend," I managed, my eyes still on Paul. Even in the gloom I noticed Paul's face falling. "Paul, meet Tony Moretti. Eh," I laughed nervously. "I never got your last name."

Paul bowed politely and held out a hand. "Paul McKay. Pleasure."

Tony gave a sloppy handshake. "Yeah, same here." He gave my shoulder a twist. "Come on, babe, time to hustle. Martin and Nina are waiting. There's a new club on Wabash."

The last thing I remembered was Paul's expression of surprise. Then I was back in the crowd, outside, in a cab. The new club was like the last, just larger and more brightly lit. I didn't pay attention to the conversation, nor did I talk to the blond woman.

All I thought of was Paul. His clothes were different, but he was all right. Probably working. And he'd searched for me. A small smile played around my lips.

"Something funny, darling?" Tony's face and his thick breath were close. For the first time I felt sick.

"Nothing," I said.

"Didn't look like nothing to me." He squeezed my forearm. It hurt. "Who was that fella?"

I shrugged, trying to appear indifferent. But my cheeks blazed with sudden fervor as if my body wanted to defy my attempt of lying. "Nobody."

"What did you talk about?"

"Nothing," I said again. "He was just surprised to see me."

I took a sip from the champagne glass. I craved some nice fresh water or tea, but that appeared to be an impossible drink in these places.

"So you *did* know him."

"From my travels." Somehow I didn't want to share anything about Paul. The thought of his presence was like a warm blanket cuddling my heart. Tony had no part of it.

Tony chuckled and addressed his companion. "And here I thought she was an innocent girl." They laughed like it was a great joke.

I bit my lip. "Can we go soon?"

"Not yet," Tony said. He clinked glasses for the hundredth time, his voice a loud drone. I wanted to lie down and think about tonight. Seeing Al Capone in the club…and Paul. What were the odds?

It was early morning before we arrived home. I had quit drinking hours ago and helped Tony stay on the road. When it was apparent he couldn't go on, I hailed a taxi with part of my grocery money.

His clothes still on, Tony collapsed on the bed and fell into stupored sleep. I moved onto the chair, half sitting, half hanging over one armrest. I was cold, my legs heavy as boulders. Yet, I couldn't sleep because every time I closed my eyes, I saw Paul's face when he'd realized that Tony was with me. Had I only imagined it or had he been genuinely upset.

A horrible anger began to brew inside me. It was Tony's fault I'd not even gotten Paul's address. Why had he shown up? I could've explained things to Paul, told him about my troubles. Something had to happen before Tony destroyed my life like he'd destroyed his own. I could taste his darkness like over salted soup. The universe was telling me something or I wouldn't have seen Paul and Al Capone in the same spot.

There was only one thing I wanted to do.

CHAPTER TWENTY-THREE

Paul

"You're such a Flat Tire." Colene cried. "It's not even eleven."

"I'm beat," I said calmly as I dropped her off at home. Inside me raged a storm. Sam was still in Chicago and she had a boyfriend. My insides twisted as I relived the encounter. Maybe the man held her hostage, had forced her somehow. Her brilliant eyes were even more sparkly than I remembered. Except she'd looked tired, almost harrowed. Something was bothering her.

Ignoring Colene's sullen expression, I clipped "good night" and swung back on the street.

I felt empty, sort of hollow. Sam was gone once more and I'd been unable to do anything about it. Ahead my family's mansion loomed. Lights shone in the entrance and on the second and third floor. *It's your home.*

Warmth and comfort.

Coldness and shadows was more like it. A shiver ran up my spine as I unlocked the door.

Mercer appeared from the hallway. "Sir, you had a visitor."

I only half listened. All I wanted was to go to bed and sleep for a week. Maybe recall Sam's features and daydream about another encounter.

"A man named Angelo?"

I swung around, taking in Mercer's immaculate suit. Even at this hour, the butler was perfect. "Angelo Bruno?"

The eyebrow shot up. "He didn't give his last name."

"Where did he go?"

"I don't know, Sir, but he did leave a note." Mercer handed me a scrap of paper with a few scribbled lines. "He didn't want to wait, so I suggested the paper."

"Good thinking," I said, but my eyes were already on the note.

Sorry, I didn't know...you're rich. Looking for Sam. Please send word. I'll be at Larry's Diner tomorrow from noon to two o'clock.
A.

My mind raced. Angelo had gotten my letter, the one I had written a couple of days after returning home. And he was out of jail. Now all I needed to do was get in touch and somehow convince Angelo to stay around.

And wait for Sam to find us. Maybe Angelo could help find Sam. After all, didn't he know her best?

I scoffed, the sound echoing through the empty hall. Very funny.

What were the chances?

Sam

I awoke from something crashing, a mismatched sound of glass breaking and doors banging. Tony was pacing back and forth, dishes, spices and food supplies tumbling to the floor, my careful organization destroyed in seconds.

I rubbed the back of my sore neck and straightened. "What're you looking for?"

"Need my damned wallet." Tony's eyes were bloodshot, hair plastered across his damp forehead. His expression changed to a squint. "You took it." Fury showed in his features, his shoulders hunched forward as if he wanted to strike me.

I shook my head, my outward calm betraying my racing heart. "It was already gone last night. I paid the cab fare from my grocery money."

"But it had my whole week's wages," Tony whined. Eyes squinting, he moved to the bundle I'd kept under the bed, tore it apart. A ring with a blue stone, the necklace and watches spilled onto the floor.

"What's that?" Tony said quietly. Ever so slowly, he bent low and picked up the jewelry. "So you stole from me. When I shared my home...got you away from that brothel."

Dread crept through me and my legs wobbled as I moved toward the door. "I kept it for an emergency. For *us*."

With sudden viciousness he spun around and grabbed my wrist. "I don't believe you."

I tugged, but Tony's grip held. "Let me go. I have never taken a dime from you. I should've told you, but I was afraid. The way you act sometimes, it scares me."

Tony swiped a palm across his face and let go. "Oh, Sam, I'm sorry. I don't know what's gotten into me." He looked truly regretful, but I carefully put a couple of steps between us. Not that it'd do much good if he decided to attack me again.

"I'm going to get bread," I said. "At least we'll have something to eat."

As Tony sank back on the bed, a burst of air broke from my throat. At least he still let me run errands. I yanked on my coat and hurried outside.

Breathe! I needed to be outside. Now.

It was time to admit that Tony was getting worse. It had to be the booze...or maybe our situation, losing the club. It was getting to him. And now he was losing even the few possessions he'd kept. The ring and assorted jewelry would be gone by tonight.

If I couldn't help him, I needed to leave. But where to? Paul had entered my life like a miracle and then left it again. Tears stung with sudden ferocity. I stopped in front of a storefront with pharmaceutical supplies. Five months ago, I'd been in front of a store like this in Cincinnati. Before I visited George Remus. It seemed like a lifetime ago. My face blurred in the glass. A sob rose.

On a whim, I began to walk. Gray clouds let out a drizzle, not enough to soak, but plenty to chill. The Chicago skyline loomed ahead, a bulky mess of stone and cement, hard and unyielding. Around me, people went about their work, rushing along, heads bent against the wind. Street vendors, selling hot dogs and potato soup, called out to me. I passed speakeasies and clubs. Even at the late morning hour, men gambled and drank. The prohibition was achieving just the opposite of what it intended. It was human nature to desire what you weren't supposed to have. Especially, when the government tried to control you. From some doors, whistles and catcalls followed me.

"In here, sweets. Have a taste."

I could just imagine what sort of activities were going on inside. If there was one thing I'd never do again, it was work in prostitution. *Ha, you're a prostitute now. If Mamma knew, she'd skin you alive.*

I continued, trying to ignore the turmoil in my belly. It felt good to move after being stuck in the little room that filled with fear every time Tony was in it. Yet every step away from that room made me question my idea.

I missed regular work, a real purpose. Even when Mamma was alive, I'd helped take care of the laundry business. Now…what was I now? A kept woman. Kept by a drunkard, a man fallen down on his luck who blamed me for his actions.

I picked chunks of bread from the loaf in my bag, my throat dry. I craved a cup of tea, but couldn't afford any. Nothing had changed since I'd first arrived. I still didn't know about Angelo and I'd lost Paul.

Again.

On the street, blue handbills were taped to columns: "*The Woman's World Fair, Chicago,*" they announced. How grand that sounded. Smart women doing important things.

Unlike me. I stopped.

Why couldn't *I* do something that mattered?

Anything. At that moment, I realized I had to get away. *Tony won't let you.* But I could at least start making plans and… investigating. A tiny smile played on my lips as I resumed my walk.

When the Green Mill came into view, I slowed. I had to be crazy. What was I doing here? Neither Paul nor Al Capone would be here at this hour. Still, I had to try. It was my only hope at finding a glimmer of a chance to change my life.

The green door was unlocked, but the inside semi-dark and deserted.

"Hello?" I called. Now, without people, the air saturated with stale smoke and alcohol vapors, the place didn't look nearly as interesting. A huge swirly sign, showing the club's name, dominated the stage. Along the curved bar, hundreds of glass bottles sparkled and reflected in the mirror behind them.

When nothing moved, I hurried to the hallway in back where I'd seen Paul last night.

A door flew open and almost hit me in the chest. The man

charging at me wore a dark suit and matching hat, his face as red as Papa's best tomato sauce. He huffed something I didn't understand and disappeared.

I took another step and hovered in the doorframe. Inside sat a huge fellow in rolled-up shirtsleeves, a cigar between his lips and stacks of dollar bills on the table in front of him.

"Who are you?" The man's voice was deep and threatening.

"Sorry, sir." I tried not to stare at the wealth on the table. "I'm looking for a man who was here last night. His name is Paul McKay."

"First of all, we're closed and you're trespassing," the man boomed as he puffed a cloud of stinky smoke in my direction. "Second, I'm not in the business of providing free information." He lowered his eyes to scan my chest all the way down to my feet in the worn-out heels. "If you want a job as a hostess, you can fill out an application. Other than that, scoot before I lose my temper."

I turned and stumbled out of the club. I didn't know how I got back home, but when I opened the door, Tony charged at me, eyes blazing.

"You got any idea what time it is? I'm worried sick." Then came that horrible transformation again. His eyes squinted, his lips pressed. "You meet that fella from last night?" He coughed and wiped his mouth with the back of his hand. Sweat pearled on his temples. He seized my upper arm and yanked away my coat. His hand slit between my legs. "Let me see if you're wet."

My cheeks burned with shame. "Let me be," I cried. "You have no right."

"You're mine," Tony said with an evil grin. His gaze fell on my bag. He tore it from my shoulder and inspected it. "So you did get bread." He broke off a piece and chewed. "Phew, dry as my grandmother's bones." He seized my shoulders, his nose inches from mine. "For the last time, where were you?"

"You wouldn't believe me anyway," I said. "I just walked around." I tried to pull away, but Tony's fingers clamped down. "I'm tired of being in this room. I'm bored, I—"

"Tired of me," Tony said. This time he was quiet. Too quiet. Anger brewed inside and tried to find release.

"No, just…I need something to do." There, it was out.

"I'll find you a job. Nice club, good tips."

"Please Tony, not that."

"You think you can make demands? Choose?" He pushed me away and sagged onto the bed. "If you haven't noticed, we aren't exactly swimming in cash."

"You want me to be a prostitute again?"

"Just working to entertain." Tony grinned. "You still come home to me."

"I'll find something else, something honorable."

"Like what?"

"Maybe work in a bakery or a clothing shop."

Tony didn't seem to hear. "I've got to find out when the club opens. Should be soon. You can work with me there. We'll manage it together. You wear pretty things, make the fellas thirsty." There was the laugh again. "I run everything else."

I watched Tony sitting there in the squalor of this room that seemed to shrink every day. Light was fading outside and hiding the ugliness of the dirty walls, the grime of previous tenants. How could I have ever thought following Tony was a way to better things?

When Tony returned in the early morning hours, he didn't even pretend to be considerate. Groping in the dark, he yanked up my shirt. Afterwards he fell asleep, his snores echoing from the walls.

"Slight change of plans," he said the following morning when he discovered me on the chair mending a sock.

"What do you mean?" I asked, keeping my gaze on my hands.

"Talked to Jimmy Emery. He wants you to hustle."

"No!" My sock dropped to the floor and I jumped up. "I'm not doing that anymore.

"You've got no choice." Tony's dark eyes reminded me of coals and there was that strange quiet in his voice again. "We need the clams."

I shuddered. For the first time, I was truly afraid of Tony. He'd scared me before, especially the first time he'd taken what he wanted. I'd dismissed it because he'd been nice afterwards. But now the alcohol and the pressure to dig himself out of the hole made him mean. And there was something else that worried me. In the beginning, Tony had used a condom. He no longer did. Probably didn't want to spend the money. Chances were I'd get pregnant. Mamma's voice reverberated through my mind: *Never lie with a man. He will make you a baby and you will become destitute.* I jumped because a rough sound like laughter rose from my throat. I already *was* destitute.

"Come on, get dressed. That black thing you wear," Tony said. "I told Emery I'd bring you around."

"I won't do that again."

In a flash Tony was by my side. He towered over me, one arm raised. "Don't make me do this," he seethed.

"I thought you liked me," I whispered.

Tony laughed. Not the light-hearted laugh I remembered from the first time we'd met, but a cold chuckle that hit me like an icy fist.

"Of course, I do. Now get a wiggle on, I don't want to be late."

Shakily, I walked to the rickety closet and selected the dress I'd worn the first night at Tony's house. I put on garters and hose and slipped on the dress. At least it wasn't as cold now because the flimsy overcoat did little to keep out the wind.

Inside I was cold too. A frozenness overtook me like the moment I'd seen Mamma lying motionless in the street. It had been my fault. I'd offered to go with Tony, no, begged him to come along. Now he thought he owned me. *I'm my own person.*

Jim Emery was a good-looking chap with a mop of black hair. He looked me up and down, the way it always happened, the way one looks at a piece of meat at market. While Tony and Jim spoke, I was expected to remain quiet. So I watched.

The club we had entered was small with a long narrow bar and yellowish light. It wasn't exactly like the pubs in Over-the-Rhine, but it was nothing upscale either. I could just imagine what sort of men came in here. The drinking and groping and then…

"Excuse me," I said. "May I powder my nose?"

Emery, who relaxed against a plush chair, waved me toward the back. Tony hardly seemed to notice, his attention hanging on every word Emery produced.

I hurried through a swinging door where a narrow corridor led to the facilities. The door at the back was barred but stood open. Two men lifted boxes from a flatbed truck. Glass clinked. Whiskey.

I opened the door to the lady's room as they hastened past me toward the bar. I hesitated. Took a deep breath. And hurried quickly out the back.

I found myself in an alley and walked on, cursing my heeled shoes. If Tony noticed me gone, he'd find me in a second. I strode faster. Around a corner, then another. The streets were filled with rushing people. I pulled down my hat and joined them. Inside me, a voice called *where to, where to?*

I don't know, I wanted to shout. Just away. Away from Tony, away from another brothel. I hurried past shops and pubs until the streets grew quieter. Yet I couldn't stop, and I had to resist the urge to look over my shoulder. In my mind, Tony dashed up to me from behind and grabbed me in a chokehold.

I passed single and two-story homes with tiny front yards. Zigzagged down one street, then another. A few dirty-faced children played outside. Laundry stretched between buildings. A terrible longing overcame me. Over-the-Rhine hadn't been much, but it had been home—the place I'd had happy memories.

Some.

If I were honest, those memories lay far in the past, before the news came of Papa. I remember returning from an errand, finding Mamma sitting on a chair in the kitchen. She didn't cry, just stared blankly at the wall. For hours. That was the day, my world had crumbled like a slow-moving earthquake. You didn't see the cracks in the floor, not at first, but by the time they broke, it was too late. The ground beneath you was gone and your home with it.

I kept walking, trying to decide on what to do. Go back to Cincinnati? Nothing waited there for me. And taking more harrowing train rides was out of the question. There wouldn't be another Paul. My gaze fell on a grassy area. Across the street, oak trees shaded a park. Maybe I could just sit in there and rest for a while. My heels hurt.

I noticed a sign: *Garfield Park*.

I knew that name. Poppi, Maggie's little girl lived in West Garfield Park. I relived the moment I'd opened the hiding place in Maggie's room. The letters. They had to have heard by now that Maggie was dead. Or had they? Did Maggie's sister even know what Maggie had done for a living? Hardly? Maggie had lied to me. Well, not really lied, but kept things to herself. Many things. Who could blame her?

My feet forgotten, I rushed through the park. There was one thing I could do.

CHAPTER TWENTY-FOUR

Paul

I parked the automobile around the corner from *Larry's Diner*.

It was a hole-in-the-wall place with grease on the tables and cheap coffee pervading my pores.

A blondish waitress in a pink dress and tired ruffles was listlessly wiping the counter and didn't look up.

In the very back, hidden by walls of booths, sat Angelo. The cut on his arm had healed, but his appearance was as downtrodden as during our meeting in jail, his jacket torn at the elbow, his shirt threadbare and stained.

I slid in across from him, once again breathless at the likeness of brother and sister.

"Thanks for coming," Angelo said. "Food is tolerable if you care." He pointed at a plate with the remnants of a pork bone.

"What can I get ye?" The waitress held a pad at the ready.

"Coffee and apple pie," I said.

"Ice cream?"

"Sure."

My gaze returned to Angelo, who still wore the haunted look. "You could've waited for me at the house."

"Nah, too fancy. I'd spoil your sofa with my pants."

I scoffed. "Nonsense. Remember, I was a hobo once. Would've gladly spent time indoors."

"I've got a place," Angelo said. "It's just…"

"You're looking for Sam."

165

"Yes."

I cringed. Now I had to tell Sam's brother about the Green Mill. "I saw her a couple of days ago."

The transformation was immediate. Angelo's eyes grew animated, even sparkled. "Where is she?"

My face fell and I hardly brought out the next words. "Don't know."

Angelo's hand clamped down on my forearm. "You said you saw her."

"A chance encounter. She...we were at a club...the Green Mill. She was with a fellow, Tony Moretti."

"Don't know him." Angelo's eyes blazed. "How did she look?"

"Well," I lied. "Very pretty."

"Why didn't you ask where she lives? I mean you hadn't seen her since you both worked at that club, Victor's, right?"

I couldn't look away. "I've been beating myself up about it. As I said, it was a surprise and then the fellow showed...I lost my..."

"Mind?" A smile played around Angelo's strained mouth.

Did that the first time I saw her. "Train of thought, I meant." I wanted to make it sound funny, but thinking about Tony Moretti's possessive expression, I couldn't even produce a smirk. I leaned back as the waitress placed coffee and pie in front of me and retreated with a hasty "enjoy."

"Now what?" Angelo asked. He picked up the pork bone and tossed it back on the plate.

"I could hang out at the Green Mill," I offered, taking in the gelatinous pie and the coffee that looked like sludge. I picked up a spoon and tried the ice cream. "She may return."

"At least leave a note with the bartender?"

"A bribe?"

"Why not?" Angelo's gaze wandered across my tweed jacket and mismatched shawl. "Can't fool me. I saw your mansion."

"I'll do it." I pushed away the plate and leaned forward again. "And I want to help you."

"I don't need your help." Angelo abruptly straightened and slipped from the booth. "Just find her."

"Wait," I called after him. "How will I tell you?"

"I'll find you."

Sam

I recognized the skinny brick-sided house from the photo, but the real building at *59 Lacross Street* looked much worse. Bricks were missing, and the front yard was littered with refuse. Windows and doors were gray from lack of paint. A smell of decay and disillusion hung over the home.

Taking a deep breath, I climbed the stairs. Despite my aging black dress, I felt overdressed. It didn't matter. I'd come for a reason.

The bell didn't work, so I banged on the door with my fist.

Sounds grew louder from the inside, then the door was torn open. A snot-nosed boy of perhaps five with a three-wheeled wooden toy truck under his right arm stared at me.

"Richard, didn't I ask you not to open?" A woman in a stained apron with a baby on her hip approached from the murky living room.

"Hello, you must be Mary Rose," I said, hoping my smile appeared genuine. A horrible stench of soiled diapers and cooked cabbage stung my nose.

Suspicion edged across the woman's face. She looked decades older than Maggie and yet, I recognized the same upturned nose and squared forehead.

"And you are?" Mary Rose said.

"I'm Sam Bruno, a friend of Maggie...your sister."

"I know who my sister is." Mary Rose half closed the door. "Dinner is burning."

Indeed a scorched smell now joined the stench.

I took a deep breath. "Would it be all right if I came in for a minute? I'm not asking for money. Just the opposite." I bit my lip. *Shut up, Sam Bruno.* Why had I come here? Maggie's money was surely gone.

"What are you saying?" The woman seemed to waffle, uncertainty in her voice.

"Something happened," I said. "And I could use a glass of water." I coughed for emphasis.

"All right." Mary Rose stepped aside and as I closed the door, the woman raced to the back of the house. Dishes clattered, a curse. A minute later, she reappeared with a glass of water in her hand.

She waved me to sit. The boy, Richard, stared at me and then

167

resumed playing with his truck. The couch was covered in mutilated toys and assorted dirty clothes. I cleared a spot and sagged down. My calves throbbed from the long walk in the unaccustomed heels. I took a sip of the water.

"I'm sorry, Maggie is… passed away."

"You think I don't know that?" A strange transformation occurred on Mary Rose's drawn face. She placed the baby on a blanket on the floor and pointed a forefinger at my chest.

"They were talking about you. Now I remember. Sam Bruno, they said to call them if you showed. You killed my sister," she shrieked.

"No, no, Maggie was my friend," I cried. Panic flooded me, taking my air. "I found your letters and the photo of Poppi," I panted. "I hid them in my room along with…Maggie's money. To give to you…for Poppi."

"I don't believe you."

I jumped from the couch. I didn't think Mary Rose had a phone, but I wasn't about to take any chances. "Maggie helped me when nobody would."

"At that…brothel," Mary Rose spit. From her lips it sounded like hell.

I realized that nothing I said made a difference. Except…

"Look, I don't know. Maggie's money may still be there. Did the police tell you—

Mary Rose's eyes fixated on me. "Maggie was always broke. You sure…" She licked her lips as if she were hungry.

"Maggie wanted to move away and take Poppi with her. She knew you had too much work. She wanted to—"

"We could really use the money." Mary Rose licked her lips again.

"Well, I think Maggie wanted it for Poppi."

"Of course, it's for her." Mary Rose straightened. "I wouldn't take it, just help manage it until… How much is it, anyway?"

"Not sure." *You don't even know if you can get it. Or if it's still there.* "Maybe I could see Poppi and come back later?" I said. I gripped her hand. "I swear on my life, I didn't kill Maggie. She was good to me."

A vein pulsed beneath Mary Rose's eye. I took it as a good sign.

"As I said, she's next door with my neighbor." I wondered

why Mary Rose's tone was defensive.

Time to go. I headed for the door. "How about I'll see her for a minute and come back with the money in a few days?"

Mary Rose nodded enthusiastically and produced a thin smile. "Yes, sure." She walked to the door and pointed at the house across the street. "That one with the white awnings."

White was an overstatement. At least Mary Rose's house was brick. This place had wood siding with paint peeling in most places, exposing bare wood. The front yard was littered with broken pieces of furniture, assorted toys, mud, and sticks.

And there among the junk moved something. I had to look twice because the few remaining bushes had been left to grow wild.

"Hello?" I called.

An oval face above a soiled sweater dress much too thin for the weather appeared amidst the filth. The skin was dirty, but I immediately recognized Maggie's daughter.

"You must be Poppi," I said.

The little girl skillfully climbed across the debris and faced me across the wire fence. "Hi." Unlike Maggie's brown eyes, the girl's were the dark blue of a mountain lake. She smiled at me. "You want to play?" she asked.

I scanned the windows on the first floor. When nothing moved, I quickly slipped through the gate. "What are you playing?"

Poppi took my hand and pulled me to the side of the house. She'd built a shelter from bits of wood, leaves and rocks. Beneath lay a tiny feathered bird.

"It's sleeping," Poppi said. "I made it a house."

"Good girl," I said. My throat closed up, seeing the girl in her dirty dress whose little face showed signs of malnutrition. Judging by the earlier photo and her size, she had to be about three. I got to my knees and took one of Poppi's hands. "Say, would you like to go on an adventure?"

Poppi's eyes appeared older than her years. "Will we go and see Mami? Aunt Mary says, Mami has gone away."

I swallowed a sigh. "I will tell you all about your Mami." Straightening, I held out a palm.

Poppi's hand disappeared in mine. We left the front yard as I fought the urge to turn and watch the windows again. Any second, somebody would call and challenge me. I was prepared to run. But nothing moved, nobody appeared or called. Not from that house

169

nor from Mary Rose's.

I set my jaw and walked on. We were slow and after a while I lifted Poppi on my arm. The little girl leaned her head on my neck and fell asleep. Who knew how much sleep she got? My arms heavy, I returned to Garfield Park and sank on a bench.

That's when it hit me.

I was out of my mind. Crazy as a lunatic. I had left Tony, had no home, no place to go and no money. And yet…how could I leave the little girl with people who didn't even notice me walking off? Who let her live in filth and without enough to eat?

Poppi awoke and crawled off my lap. Her blond hair was curly and stood in all directions. Heaven knew when it had last seen a comb, let alone been washed. The girl's eyes grew large as she realized she was nowhere near the street she knew.

"Are we going home now?" she asked. "I'm hungry and I need to pee."

I quickly scanned the girl's bottom. At least she didn't wear diapers. "How about you go behind this bush to pee? I'll help you." I straightened and led Poppi into the brush.

"Now, we'll better find something to eat. I'm hungry too."

I nodded earnestly.

The sun was fading as we entered the commercial area east of Garfield Park. My feet ached with every step, my heels a burning mess. For the last mile I had carried Poppi again. The girl's shoes were worse than my own and she had to be exhausted, not to mention starving. Still, she hardly cried, just whimpered a bit once in a while. We'd drunk from a hose somebody had left lying outside, but I had no idea where to find food.

As dusk descended on Chicago, I stopped in front of a small Italian grocery store. Tomatoes, cucumbers, onions, and potatoes filled baskets. Loaves of bread beckoned behind the window next to bottles of olive oil and stacked spices. I thought of my cooking experiments at Tony's place, how happy I'd been creating delicious meals.

Despite my misery, I realized that Tony had made me understand that I wanted something more than survive and find my brother. I wanted to do something meaningful, have a purpose. Maybe become a cook one day.

Laughable, the voice in my head sneered. *You can't even get your hands on a chunk of bread.*

"I'm hungry," Poppi cried as soon as I sat her down and cleaned her nose.

"I know, sweetie, I'm hungry too."

Streetlights had long come on when I snuck into an alley behind a restaurant. Last winter Paul had crawled into the dumpsters to scavenge for food scraps. Paul. Tears blurred my vision.

I resolutely wiped a sleeve across my face before setting Poppi on the ground. "Wait here. I'm going to find something to eat."

A disgusting smell of rot hit me. Last winter when we'd first arrived, it'd been too cold, but now the sun brewed everything into a horrific stinking stew. Gagging, I quickly pulled a couple of bags from the top of the heap and threw the lid shut.

My hands had long forgotten clean, my fingernails black and my skin gray with who knew what. I rubbed my palms a few more times on my coat and offered Poppi a piece of burger bread and some lettuce leaves. Poppi smiled and bit into the bread as if it were a wonderful meal. New tears threatened. *Quit being a wimp*, I scolded. *You got yourself and this little girl into this mess. Now dig out of it.*

But it was easier said than done. After swallowing a few crusts and a handful overcooked beans, I carried Poppi into the far corner of the alley. A deserted doorway offered some shelter, but little else. I folded Poppi into my arms and dozed off.

Paul stood in front of me in a suit, offering a hand to pull me up. Then he led me to a shiny black automobile. Inside a table was set for four: crystal glasses, white porcelain plates. "It's for Angelo," Paul said smiling. He snapped his fingers and bowls of pasta, rich red and white sauce, salami and bread appeared on the table.

"Miss, you can't stay here," a voice said.

I tore away from the dream and opened my eyes. A light blinded me and behind it a figure hovered in the doorway. "You hear me. You've got to go. What are you doing to that little girl?"

I lifted Poppi into my arms and wandered off. The voice behind me kept talking... "Shame, shouldn't be allowed to be a mother..."

It was hard to tell what time it was. The streets had thinned, but out of some pubs filtered shouts and laughter. In fact, behind every second or third door seemed to be a saloon or gambling parlor. A man staggered from an open door and almost collided with me. Worried about being attacked, I hurried on, clutching Poppi to my chest.

Where to, where to, rang in my ears. Beatrice would either kick me out, turn me into the police or enslave me anew. And what about Poppi? She couldn't live with a bunch of prostitutes.

I finally leaned against a wall. Above me, a narrow sign announced *Marina's Restaurant*. The windows were dark, but next to it was another alley. I dragged myself into it and slid to the ground.

Tomorrow I'd find a solution.

CHAPTER TWENTY-FIVE

Sam

I awoke to the aroma of fresh bread and coffee. My stomach lurched. How much worse did it have to be for Poppi? I carefully smoothed the girl's locks and straightened. My bladder demanded release. I reentered the street when I noticed a small sign in the window of the restaurant. *Kitchen help needed. Cook preferred.*

Lights were on inside, an older man with wisps of gray plastered to his skull behind the counter, drying cups and plates. Without a thought, I knocked on the glass. The man looked up. Our eyes met.

I pointed to the sign and nodded.

The man slowly came to the door. "Yes?" he grumbled.

"I'm looking for a job. I'm a cook. You—"

"Miss, the way you look, you can't even enter my place. Not to mention touch my food." He closed the door and turned toward his kitchen.

"Wait," I screamed. I still held Poppi who suddenly squirmed and awoke.

"I want to go home," the girl cried.

But I didn't pay attention. My focus was still on the old man. "Please, sir. I can clean up. I had to rescue this little girl yesterday. I had no choice. She was being neglected."

The man didn't turn around, but he also didn't move.

"I'm a great cook," I continued. "Just give me thirty minutes. I promise, you won't regret it. I can do great things like…like

173

ravioli with herbs, Italian sauces…anything."

The man still hadn't turned, but I was on a roll. "What if I were your daughter needing help? I'm willing to work really hard."

At last the man faced me from behind the glass. His eyebrows were thick as brush and as gray as the sparse hair on his head. A touch of curiosity swept across his eyes. They were dark like Papa's had been.

"Why don't you go home to your family?"

"Mamma is dead, so is Papa. My brother is missing. I have nobody else and I need to give this little girl a home. She deserves it."

Poppi's dark blue eyes swam wetly as if to emphasize my words.

Keys rattled anew and the man opened the door. "I will give you one day to prove yourself," he sighed. "Upstairs is a bathroom. Clean up and make yourself presentable. Then you help me with the breakfast crowd. If your little girl makes any trouble, you'll have to go."

I smiled. I wanted to kiss the guy on his grizzly cheeks. "Thank you." Patting Poppi on the back, we disappeared in the staircase.

Despite the girl's squirms, I wiped Poppi down from head to toe. There were no other clothes, but I brushed off the worst. Then I took stock of my own appearance. The man hadn't exaggerated. I looked like I'd slept in a dumpster.

I went to work scrubbing myself, rinsed my hair and dusted off my dress. My stockings were ripped, so I took them off and washed them. I cleaned my shoes and scrubbed my fingernails until they were white again.

Exactly thirty minutes after I'd entered the diner, I plopped Poppi on a chair next to the backroom and reported to work. My stomach gurgled as I scanned the supplies stocked for this morning's breakfast rush.

"Better eat before you cook. No use on an empty stomach." The man waved toward a tiny alcove where a table for two was set with bread, butter, jam, sliced cheese and scrambled eggs. I scanned the feast, the two glasses of milk and pitcher of water. A knot closed my throat.

"Come on, what're you waiting for? Customers will be here in twenty minutes." He handed me a red apron. "I'm Arthur, by the way."

"Thank you," I croaked. "Sam Bruno, and this here is Poppi, the daughter of a friend of mine." *Dead friend*, I'd wanted to say. How could I mention Maggie when I hadn't told Poppi that her mother would never return? I grabbed the little girl and placed her at the table. Oh, what glorious feeling to chew and let buttery bread fill your belly. I ate fast, too fast and my stomach began to ache.

"You eat as much as you want," I said to Poppi. "I'll get busy cooking now." I wiped a drop of milk from the corner of her mouth. "Promise me to be a good girl and be quiet when people arrive?"

Poppi nodded, her eyes earnest.

I had never cooked much breakfast. When Papa had been around, Mamma had prepared most meals except when Papa taught me Italian dishes. Then later, we'd mostly eaten oatmeal and two-day old bread.

Now I looked at the piles of fresh eggs, the mixing bowls for omelets and pancake batter, the stacks of bacon, the pots stewing with hot cocoa and grits. What was I going to do with all that food? It was one thing to prepare pasta and sauce, another to manage orders from dozens of people.

The door opened and a couple of workers in blue coveralls entered. They sat down at the counter while Arthur swept over and filled their mugs with coffee. I heard something like "the usual" and "you know what I get."

Before I had time to ask Arthur, the door opened again and four more people entered. Arthur hurried over to me with a couple of written orders. Eggs, bacon…toasted bread, stacks of pancakes, more eggs, omelets…

By eight o'clock my head swam. I was throwing things on the griddle, my yolks runny and my plates messy. It didn't matter. Despite the never-ending orders, Arthur's grumbles and the chatter of the morning crowd, I smiled. Once in a while I threw an anxious glance at Poppi who sat on the floor in front of the storeroom and played with a couple of mugs and a set of straws.

By ten, my arms were ready to fall off. I'd burned my fingers a dozen times and my shoes were covered in bits of dried egg white and pancake batter.

Arthur shuffled over. "You ever cook breakfast before?"

I slowly shook my head. "Not like that."

"Obviously." He gave me an intense look, his eyes unreadable. Then he nodded and began wiping down tables. "Better take a break before the lunch crowd. Today's menu is chicken soup, Italian pasta and homemade burgers. You think you can handle that?"

"I'll do it." I fixed a blanket in the storeroom and placed a sleepy Poppi on it. Then I took off my shoes and curled onto a wooden box. Just a few minutes of sleep.

"Break is over." Arthur stood above me, ladle in one hand.

I rubbed my eyes. It took me a second to remember where I was before I rushed to the bathroom to wash my hands.

After tasting the soup Arthur had started, I added more pepper and a handful of herbs. "What are we using for pasta?" I asked.

"That." Arthur nodded at the boxes of noodles stacked on the shelf above the griddles. They looked pale and not too appetizing.

"I could make some pasta." I eyed Arthur. "Papa taught me. He was Italian."

Arthur threw a glance at the wall clock. "Hurry then, lunch crowd arrives in less than an hour."

I hurried off to collect ingredients, measured and mixed, kneaded and rolled. During the rest period I cleaned. Ten balls of pasta dough lay ready. I cut long thin strips and hung them to dry. Soon every available surface was covered.

In the heat of the stove, everything dried quickly. Arthur had made the sauce, but when I tasted it, I tried to hide my disgust.

"What? You don't like it?" Arthur said as he was writing today's menu choices on a black board by the door.

I swallowed and decided to speak my mind. "Tastes like tomatoes from a can. It needs things."

Arthur's chalk hovered in midair. "What things?"

"Basil and salt, pepper, garlic, maybe parmesan."

Arthur straightened with effort, his expression grave. "My wife always cooked and I took care of the shop." His upper lip trembled and he waved a dismissive arm. "Quick. Do what you can with it."

I got busy at the stove, but when I turned to look for the hard cheese, I noticed Arthur hadn't moved. He still stood by the door, chalk in hand, his gaze far away.

I cleared my throat. "Was Marina your wife?"

Arthur's watery eyes focused on me. "She was from Naples. Arrived here as a young thing, barely out of school. I married her six weeks after we met." He abruptly wiped a sleeve across his face and turned toward the counter. "She died last month."

"I'm so sorry," I said, though I wasn't at all sure he'd heard me.

The lunch crowd began storming in around noon. I fixed pasta dishes and ladled soup, cut bread and fried burgers. Upon leaving, an older worker commented on the pasta. "Really good, Arthur. Just like Marina used to make." He patted Arthur on the back before placing a ten-cent tip on my palm.

Poppi awoke and came toddling in after two. I put her at the little table and fed her bits of pasta and garlic bread.

"You did good," Arthur said behind my back.

I nodded, too tired to speak. I wanted to lie down, hide under a blanket and never emerge.

"Let me show you something."

Despite my fatigue, I placed Poppi on my right hip and followed Arthur upstairs. He opened the door to a bedroom darkened by heavy curtains. Along the back wall stood a massive wardrobe with ornamental flower carvings.

He pulled open one side. "They're probably too large, but you can't possibly go on in that rag you wear."

My eyes widened. "Your wife's…"

"Marina liked pretty things."

In wonder I let my fingers slide across the fabrics: cotton, silk, velvet, elegant gowns next to frumpy housedresses.

"You can try them on in here. I'll close the door." Arthur's eyes were shiny. "Marina would've wanted a pretty thing to wear her outfits." He hesitated. "Over there, that basket has sewing tools. You may need to make adjustments."

Before I could muster a response, the door closed. With a sigh I placed Poppi on the bed. "Look at all the nice clothes."

Poppi giggled and pointed a stubby arm at the closet.

"This one?" I asked.

Poppi nodded eagerly. "It's pretty."

"You're absolutely right." Smiling at her, I removed a burgundy velvet dress with inset lace from the hanger and held it in front of me. The mirror on the wall reflected a young woman whose cheekbones stood high beneath bright blue eyes.

I hardly recognized myself. Had I only been gone from Cincinnati for six months? It couldn't be.

In the end, I decided on a brown cotton shift with a broad silky belt. It was too wide, but fine for work, especially when I wore an apron over the top and could cinch the waist.

"I guess this means we have a job," I said before picking up Poppi who'd busied herself with bits of ribbon.

The knock on the door startled me. "Come in."

Arthur stuck his head through and after a moment's pause gave a satisfied nod. "Marina loved that dress. She said it was one of the most comfortable."

"I thought it'd suit for work."

"Fine."

"Thank you," I said. "I don't know what to say."

Arthur seemed embarrassed, his ears red. "You look a lot like Marina when she was a young girl." The color intensified and crept into his cheeks. "It was tough back then."

"I'll help you in the restaurant as long as you need," I said.

"I don't suppose you have a place to sleep?" Arthur asked. "Or are you using a shelter?"

Tony's angry eyes loomed in front of me. "I had to leave a man," I said simply. How could I describe losing Paul, searching for Angelo and Tony's disastrous fall, my seemingly endless flight from disaster?

"You don't have to explain," Arthur said. "I have a spare bedroom. My daughter used to sleep there. She's been gone a long time."

"What happened to her?"

"She had an accident." He abruptly waved me on. "I'll show you her room."

"But I can't pay."

"We'll work it out."

The space was narrow with two twin beds and a wooden chest along the wall. "I forgot to mention, there're some children's clothes in the box….For the girl. Marina kept some things." Arthur glanced at his watch. "We start prepping for dinner in an hour."

A feeling of warmth gripped me. Tears threatened. "I'll be there," I managed, a smile on my lips. What were the odds? I'd been finished and yet, here I'd found the one person who was willing and able to help us.

"Look," Poppi squeaked. She pointed at a shelf with a doll and two stuffed bears and immediately began talking to the doll and carried her to the bed.

I dug through the trunk. A dark blue hanger dress with a white collar caught my eye. It was a bit too long, but I'd take in the hem until Poppi had grown. While the girl played with her newfound baby, I went to work adjusting our clothes. A small smile played on my lips as I selected matching thread from the sewing kit. I hadn't made any progress finding my brother, but at least I was safe and Poppi was off the street. Tonight I'd tell Poppi about her Mami.

The evening crowd was small, hardly enough to bring in a few dollars. Secretly, I was glad. I was exhausted, my thumb and forefinger covered in blisters from multiple encounters with the griddle. I'd created plain fresh pasta and we'd sold out of it and the accompanying white sauce. Still, I knew Arthur wasn't happy.

"Why aren't more people eating dinner?" I'd sorted napkins and now wiped down salt- and peppershakers on each table. "Are you charging too much?"

"Damn laws," Arthur grumbled. "It's the prohibition. What's an Italian restaurant without decent wine?"

I turned around. "But there are clubs and speakeasies all over the place." I wasn't about to tell Arthur about Beatrice and my own visits to the clubs.

"No kidding." Arthur counted out the money for the morning and hid it in a box beneath the stove. "Capone is getting rich selling booze. I heard he's bringing in whiskey from New York. And I can't even sell bottles of Chianti."

I washed out the rag and threw a glance at the sleeping form in the backroom. "You have any? I heard it's not illegal to own the stuff."

Arthur smiled grimly. "Got a basement full. Marine bought up a truckload early on. It is probably turning to vinegar as we speak."

"Why not do it anyway?" It was out before I had time to think.

Arthur's eyes were on mine. "You know it killed Marina...our restaurant doing poorly. We had to let our help go. She worried herself sick." He rubbed a sleeve across his eyes.

I rushed up to him. "No really, why couldn't we sell wine?"

"It's a crime. They could close what little is left. I promised Marina…"

"Couldn't you call it Italian red tea?" I said.

Arthur gave a throaty chuckle. "Funny, but you can't sell alcohol."

"What if we don't sell it? What if it's part of a meal?" I said. "Without a separate price, not even mentioned. Like a menu thing."

"How would that work?"

I shrugged. "Don't know, buy the dinner, get a free drink? If it's free, it's not being sold."

A transformation happened on Arthur's face. Hope competed with doubt, but when he began to smile I knew that hope had won. "You may be on to something."

He rushed off and within two minutes reappeared with a glass bottle, its roundish bottom wrapped in a straw apron. He handily pulled the cork and filled two small water glasses.

"Let's have a look."

I sniffed and took a sip. The Chianti had a dark burgundy color and fruity aroma. It didn't burn like whiskey. I kind of liked it. "Tastes good."

Arthur drained his glass and poured another. "Not bad at all." A smile played around his lips. "If I didn't know better, I'd say, this is prime stuff."

I smacked my lips. "How much do you have?"

Arthur chuckled and slowly got out of his chair. "Come on, I'll show you."

My gaze wandered to Poppi's still form.

Arthur went to adjust the girl's blanket. "She'll be fine."

I followed Arthur down a narrow flight of stairs into the gloom, the air markedly cooler. Ahead lay a long narrow room with a curved ceiling, but that wasn't what I was looking at. Barrels were stacked along the wall, barrels as far as I could see. Across sat wooden boxes filled with the types of bottles, we'd sampled earlier.

"Arthur, this is a fortune."

"That was Marina's idea. She hadn't thought it through, though." A heavy sigh escaped Arthur.

I smiled. "We'll charge a dollar instead of 40 cents and offer a free drink."

CHAPTER TWENTY-SIX

Paul

Much to the delight of Colene, I spent the next three evenings at the Green Mill. While she tossed gin fizzes, I nursed a single whiskey on ice and sat watching the crowd. Neither Tony Moretti nor Sam showed, and with every hour my heart sank a bit more.

Around midnight on the third day, I took Colene home. Earlier, I'd excused myself and approached the bartender with a fifty and a note, doing my best to describe Sam and Tony. The bartender had shaken his head. No, they weren't regulars or he would've recognized them.

Still, the fifty left an impression and I hoped to hear back.

When I came to a stop in front of Old Sloan's estate, Colene turned to face me. "I wish I knew what's eating you," she said. In the semi-darkness her large eyes glowed.

When I shrugged, she went on. "I think I'm pregnant."

"What?" It was out before I could stop myself.

"You and I...we..."

"I know," I cried impatiently. Memories of that night had stubbornly remained fuzzy and I didn't remember having sex. "You sure?"

Colene began to cry. "I thought you'd be happy. What will I tell Father?"

I patted her arm. "It's just...I wasn't prepared. Not yet, at least. Give me some time to think."

After Colene entered her home, I sat unmoving and stared out the window. I was going to be a father. Where was the joy, the excitement?

I felt nothing but dread.

The next morning when I sat brooding at my desk, I was no wiser. My life had left its certain path. As a hobo, I'd traveled on this train and that, the rails taking me to a particular city, a new job and adventure. Ever since I'd arrived at home, I'd felt off the rails—out of control. Father's revelation about my mother had put in question everything I had believed in.

"Sir, Mr. Sloan is here to see you." Mercer took his usual bow. Before I could answer, Henry Sloan pushed into the room, waving Mercer away like an irritating fly.

"When are you going to make things right?" he boomed as he came to a stop in front of my desk. "I must say, I'd thought better of you, son."

"What—"

"Colene told me. You two were…" Sloan cleared his throat. "She's expecting and her reputation…our reputation… How could you?"

"She just told me last night," I said. "I needed time to think about it."

Henry produced a smile. "And I don't understand why you need time. This is a joyous occasion. I thought the two of you were a pair. Regi, your father, wanted—"

I jumped up. "I know." *I'm not ready,* my insides screamed as I began to pace.

The old Sloan adopted a tone of fatherly understanding. "It's a big step, son. But you're an honorable chap. Like your father…Regi would be proud." The smile was back.

Ever so slowly, I nodded. Father had loved a woman who'd loved another. "It's just a bit sudden," I said quietly.

Sloan headed for the door, "So you'll visit us later and ask Colene? Make it official?"

Sam

By the end of the week, evening traffic had doubled. By the third week, we took reservations and a line formed outside thirty minutes before opening. It wasn't just the wine that had somehow managed to mature into a beautiful vintage. It was also my contribution of authentic Italian dishes. The first days, I'd made fresh pasta and shaped it differently every day. Then I ventured into fillings, creating cannelloni, tortellini and ravioli filled with cheese, herbs, mushrooms, meat, and more cheese. We sold out every night and for the first time, Arthur whistled a little tune when he greeted me in the morning.

Despite our success, a worry cloud followed me though the day. On the one hand, I'd found a new home for Poppi and myself. Poppi was clean…most of the time. Two afternoons ago, she'd decided to make pasta too and covered herself and everything in sight in flour. I'd been angry, but seeing the little girl's earnest eyes as she explained her plans of helping, made me smile.

But thoughts of Angelo had returned with a vengeance. I could stay here and cook until the end of time and never learn what had happened to him. Probably wouldn't anyway. I worked six days a week and on the seventh we sorted and cleaned and planned new menus. Outside, the Chicago sky sparkled blue and in the little remaining time, I took Poppi outside to one of the small parks or to the beaches of Lake Michigan.

I was deep in thought, plating spaghetti and meatballs for a table of six, when a man impatiently knocked on the counter in front of my kitchen. It happened sometimes that people wanted to order directly from me because lately we also offered take out.

"Sir, please ask Arthur to take your order," I said over my shoulder, sprinkling Parmesan over the tomato sauce.

"Boss wants to try your tortellini, mushroom if possible," the man said with a heavy Italian accent. His voice was deep and throaty, so I looked up from my pots. Something about the man seemed familiar, but I couldn't remember. He wore a charcoal-colored fedora and an impeccable suit with a white shirt. In the plainness of the aged restaurant, he was clearly overdressed.

"I don't have any right now," I said. "It's on the menu for tomorrow evening."

"I can come back later, say six o'clock," said the man as if he hadn't heard. "Order is for Mr. Ross. Make it big."

I opened my mouth to protest, but the man had already disappeared. *Arrogant jerk to order something that wasn't even offered.*

"Did I hear that right?" Arthur appeared at my side and grabbed four of the six plates. "Did the man say, Mr. Ross?"

"Something like that."

A shudder went through Arthur's massive shoulders. He bent lower and whispered. "You know the Metropole Hotel?"

"That huge place around the corner?"

"Yes, that one. Mr. Ross stays there."

"So he is rich," I said. What difference did it make? Rich or poor, they all had to eat. With the tip of my apron, I wiped a splatter from my stove.

"That's Capone." Arthur swept away with his dishes and left me standing open-mouthed.

All of a sudden my fingers shook. The man who was running Chicago, who they rumored to be wealthy beyond belief, but also equally ruthless, wanted my pasta.

"I guess he's going to shoot me, if he doesn't like it," I mumbled to myself. "Nonsense," I chided just as Arthur returned for the remaining plates.

"What's nonsense?"

"Nothing, just talking to myself."

That afternoon, as I prepared the fresh pasta for Mr. Ross, I wondered how on Earth Capone had heard about my food. Had he been in here? Unlikely. I would've noticed a well-dressed man, and I sure would've noticed Capone whose picture was in the paper every second day and who I'd seen in person at the *Green Mill.*

So somebody had told him or…What difference did it make? I knew I'd better fix a knockout meal.

"What are you making?" Poppi asked a little later. She cradled a small doll in a well-handled dress we'd found in a box upstairs.

"Tasty dinner for an important man," I said. I hesitated and looked at the little girl. "How about you help me?"

Poppi's face lit up, and with it my heart.

Over the past weeks I'd thought about Poppi all the time. The girl had filled out, her cheeks dimpled and her arms and legs stronger. She no longer asked for Maggie nor did she mention Mary Rose. I had told her about meeting Maggie and how Maggie had helped me feel at home. "Your Momi was very sweet."

I fashioned a dishtowel around Poppi's waist and showed her how to knead dough. Poppi's clumsy fingers crunched bits of flour and oil, and she laughed with delight.

I was taken back to Cincinnati where Papa had shown me how to cook. It seemed like a hundred years ago.

"Well done, Poppi." I took her tiny portion, quickly kneaded it through and wrapped it in plastic. "Now we let it rest and later you can make little shapes."

The meal I packaged for Mr. Ross was enormous. I'd taken several takeout boxes and filled them with a variety of dishes, mushroom tortellini gooey with cheese, fragrant tomato sauce and meatballs.

The man with the fancy fedora appeared at six on the dot, dropped a twenty on the counter and hurried off.

Already all tables were filled, and more people waited outside. We'd added a couple of benches in front of the store window and the assembling crowd was drawing even more people.

That night we cleared more than three hundred dollars, a fortune. Arthur hid some of the newfound wealth, took some to the bank and handed me a twenty, more than a week's worth of pay. "Bonus," he said, wiping his brow with a dusty handkerchief. "You deserve more, but I need to pay back the loans first."

"It's fine," I said, stuffing the bill in my apron pocket. "You gave me a chance when nobody would. I'll always be grateful." I stretched tall and placed a kiss on his cheek. "Thank you."

Arthur turned pink and cleared his throat. "I think we're good for each other." He eyed Poppi sleeping on the bench in back. "Tomorrow after breakfast you'll buy her some new dresses. My gift. I'll handle the lunch prep."

"But—"

"No buts. Now you two better head for bed."

I smiled. Poppi looked like a doll in the little red-checkered hanger dress and black shoes. We were running behind and rushing along State Street. Arthur would be swamped with the prep by himself.

I would've much preferred to carry Poppi, but my arms were loaded with assorted bags and two shoeboxes. I'd bought three dresses for Poppi, underwear and socks for us both, and splurged on a new pair of flats perfect for every day work and one with heels for going out—whenever that would be. I'd found two blouses for ninety-five cents at Sears, a matching skirt and hat. The hat, narrow brimmed with a small bow in front, wasn't really necessary, but every decent young woman wore one. I was still drunk from the feeling of being able to shop, spend money, and choose between different designs and fabrics like a normal woman with a normal life.

A shrill scream rang out. Somebody shoved me from behind. The pavement rushed up to me, packages and bags flew, boxes opened and my new hat landed in the dust. A sharp pain tore through my right knee.

Before I could collect my thoughts or inspect the damage to my leg, I heard another scream. This time it was Poppi's.

Mary Rose stood red-faced over me, one dirt-stained forefinger pointed at my nose, the other arm clamping down on a squirming Poppi. "You thief. Thought you could run with my daughter. Keep the money for yourself." A glob of spittle landed on my cheek. "I should've gone to the police and turned you in when you showed up at my door." With that, she gave my new hat a kick, so it flew into the street and got flattened by a passing truck. "First you kill Maggie and then you steal her daughter," she cried. "If you ask me, you did it to get the girl." She yanked Poppi on top of her right hip and hurried away.

People stopped and I felt curious eyes on me. A young man helped me up. A woman with kind eyes collected my bags and when I didn't grab them, placed them at my feet. I stood, my mind numb. "Poppi," I said quietly. It wasn't really my voice, but that of a stranger.

Mary Rose had disappeared down the street, Poppi's cries growing quiet until one could only hear the street noise. Vehicles driving, a honking horn, a woman whispering to another…deep throaty laughter across the street.

"Miss, where do you need to go?" The young man was still by my side. He was no older than fifteen and his green eyes reminded me of Paul.

"I'm fine," I heard myself say. With utmost slowness, I picked up my bags and wobbled on. My right knee throbbed and I could hardly put any weight on it.

Poppi was gone. Back to that dirty place where nobody loved her and they let her play unsupervised on the street.

I knew that the only reason Mary Rose had been so angry was because of the money. Because she'd thought I was keeping Maggie's money for myself. *You're not her mother. But neither is Mary Rose.*

I halted because all of a sudden I couldn't move. The pain in my chest was so great, I doubled over. I loved that little girl. And I'd lost her. Why hadn't I paid better attention? Looked around, recognized Mary Rose. I'd walked into disaster like a blind idiot.

It was after eleven thirty when I returned to the restaurant. Arthur's face was almost as red as the tomato sauce he was stirring. "Where've you been? Customers are lining up," he hissed. But then he stopped and took in my bloodied dress, the torn stockings.

"Poppi." It was all I could muster before collapsing on a chair and beginning to cry.

Despite the growing crowd outside, Arthur hurried to my side. "What happened? Did she have an accident? Is she in the hospital?"

"She's with her aunt," I cried. "I'd taken her because she was so dirty and unloved. I owed it to Maggie."

"Wait, Maggie is her mom, right?"

"Yes," I said. "She was killed in the brothel where we worked."

"You worked in a brothel?"

"I...they think I murdered her."

"Who?"

"Somebody told the police that I murdered Maggie. But she was my friend, the only person who was nice to me." My eyes met Arthur's. "I'll pack my things. I'll be out of here in a few minutes."

A heavy hand pushed me back on the chair. "I don't care what you did. All I know is that you have a kind heart and took real good care of that little girl. And you're a hell of a cook."

He gently lifted my chin. "Why don't you get washed up and we'll feed these folks? Afterwards we'll sit down and make a plan. I promise you, I'll do everything I can to help you get Poppi back."

Lunch dragged for hours. I messed up orders and burned my palm absentmindedly putting a hand on the stovetop. My prep counter was a mess. Every few minutes the scene on the street repeated itself. I heard Poppi's screams and saw Mary Rose's dirty poking finger. My knee throbbed with dull persistence. I almost welcomed it, because I wanted to feel the punishment I deserved for being so stupid.

Somehow I hadn't ever thought about Mary Rose. I'd supposed the woman was glad about getting rid of Poppi.

"Now tell me what happened," Arthur said once we sat down in one of the booths." He hadn't mentioned my terrible performance and instead filled two bowls with ice cream. As I retold the morning's events and the ice cream melted, Arthur's face grew longer.

"You just took the girl?" he asked at some point.

"I had to," I said. "You should've seen the garbage she played in. Nobody was watching. Anybody could've taken her."

"So you did, thinking to replace her mother...Maggie?"

I nodded. "Not in the beginning. But I..." my voice faltered and fresh tears dripped.

Arthur awkwardly patted my hand. "Now, now. I understand. Children have a way of gripping your heart."

"If I can get the money, I'm sure she'll let her go."

"Poppi is her niece."

"Mary Rose said so. In her letters she said she wanted to get rid of Poppi." I dunked a spoon into the melted ice cream and licked it off. "I could go back to Beatrice and see if the money is still there. I hid it beneath the floorboards."

Arthur's forehead turned into wrinkles. "You think they'll let you waltz in there and search your room? They think you killed Poppi's mother. Besides, it's likely the police took those letters and the money." Arthur sighed. "How much does she want?"

"I didn't tell her. Maggie had two hundred dollars saved."

Arthur whistled. Then his gaze focused on me again. "I don't think it's a good idea for you to return to Beatrice's brothel, no matter what."

"Will you go with me?"

"Oh no," Arthur cried. "I'm not setting foot in a place like that. Marina...she'd turn in her grave."

"But you're not going there to...you know."

Arthur shook his head. Then he straightened with effort and walked to the cash register. "I'll give you a hundred dollars. The woman doesn't know how much Maggie had saved. She'll be happy."

"No, Arthur," I cried. "You need to pay back your loans."

"I'm almost paid up," Arthur said. "Another week or two and we'll be in the black." A smile played around his lips. "Thanks to you."

"I'll pay you back." The lump in my throat was back. "I swear it."

Arthur put five twenty-dollar bills on the table. "Here."

"Will you go with me?" I asked.

"I could on Sunday."

"But that's five days from now."

Arthur shrugged. "I'm sorry. No time. We can't close the restaurant. Garfield Park is a ways." He looked at me and then sighed. "You go tomorrow after breakfast. I'll manage."

With every step, I grew more nervous. I'd taken the streetcar for part of the way west and walked the remaining mile. The street looked even shabbier than the first time. I recognized the brick house immediately. Nobody had bothered to cut the grass or pick up sticks and refuge.

My fingers trembled as I banged on the door. Cries and shouts reverberated through the cracked window. Maybe Poppi would open.

"Coming." Even from a distance and through the walls I heard Mary Rose's irritation.

"You!" Mary Rose stood in the entrance, a snot-nosed child stuck to her right hip. "What do you want?"

"I'm here to get Poppi," I said.

"You've got a lot of nerve. I should call the cops."

"I'm sorry," I said, trying in vain to look past Mary Rose's frame. Somewhere inside was Poppi and I wanted the little girl to see me. I could've sworn the screaming from earlier had been Poppi. But now it was eerily quiet.

"I think we got off on the wrong foot," I hurried. "May I come in? I brought money and I wanted to help…"

"How much?" Mary Rose's eyes scanned my clothes as if to determine where I had hidden the bills.

"A hundred dollars."

An internal fight mirrored in Mary Rose's eyes. Greed and anger competed.

"Show it to me," she said.

I bit my lip. That's not what I'd wanted, but what choice did I have? Slowly, I opened my waistband and pulled out the small wad.

"Thank you." Mary Rose snatched the money so fast, it was amazing she could move like that carrying a toddler. Oily fingers counted the bills. "That's not enough. Poppi is worth more than that." Her eyes squinted almost shut. "I saw all those shopping bags. You're rich, and you want my sister's girl for nothing."

She's your niece. My hands balled into fists, the fury so great I couldn't get a word out. I just stood there, staring at the woman

189

with the mop of dark hair, so like Maggie's. But that seemed to be the only thing they had in common. For a brief moment I thought of smacking the woman and forcing my way inside. But then I heard a man's cough from somewhere. Mary Rose's husband was home.

"I cook at Marina's. I work from six in the morning until ten at night," I said. "Poppi needed clothes."

"She can wear hand-me-downs." Mary Rose clipped. "And you're lying."

"How much do you want?" I asked finally.

Again Mary Rose's features reflected the internal fight of hunger and fury.

"Four hundred more."

"What?" I screamed. "Maggie didn't have that much saved."

"I don't care." Mary Rose shrugged and began to shut the door. "Then she stays."

"Wait." I pushed against the doorknob. "You mean the police never gave you Maggie's money?"

"No money, just my letters and photo."

I swallowed. So somebody had found my hiding spot and taken the cash. "I'll get it," I heard myself say. "It'll take some time."

Mary Rose's mouth twitched with contempt. "I knew it."

I gripped Mary Rose's forearm. "Promise me. If I bring the money, I'll get Poppi." The woman nodded slowly and shook free her arm. "Please make sure she gets her afternoon nap," I continued. "Tell her I'll be coming back."

But the door had already closed—the apartment behind it silent.

I didn't remember much of the return trip. Where was I going to get four hundred more dollars?

Arthur's face was puffy, his forehead damp when I entered. Pots and bowls covered every surface. With a sigh, I put away my bag, changed, and went to work. By the time the door opened, my kitchen was clear again, each pot where it belonged, bowls with salad ingredients sorted, sauces hot and ready to serve.

I'd shaken my head when Arthur asked about Poppi, afraid tears would begin to roll and never stop again. The only solace I found was my work and the understanding that cooking food was healthy for my soul.

"Mr. Ross would like the same as last time."

I recognized the burly man in the fedora who looked like he'd slit your throat if you served him the wrong meal.

"Six o'clock?"

He nodded and turned, but before he got to the door, he called to me: "Mr. Ross wants you to deliver. Metropole Hotel, don't be late."

CHAPTER TWENTY-SEVEN

Sam

All afternoon I argued with Arthur.

"Too dangerous. I'll go."

"He asked for me, so *I'll* go," I said though my insides twisted with anxiety. I rushed toward Arthur, who sat at the little table in the kitchen. "You need to run Marina's. I'll be fine."

With a helpless shrug, Arthur returned to prep, throwing a weary look at the window. A waiting line was beginning to form. Recently, it reached down the street and we'd hired a serving girl. Takeout orders had also increased, which put more pressure on the cook—me.

"Hurry," he called after me.

Despite the summer heat it was cool and a bit gloomy in the hotel. I took in the cushy seats, the tiled floors and gleaming counters. That's when I saw a man in a striped burgundy suit leaning against one of the columns. His head was half hidden behind a newspaper, but I'd have known that brutish face anywhere.

Don't look. He might recognize you too. I tugged my hat lower and rushed to the reception where I asked for directions. The fifth floor appeared deserted but then I noticed two men in suits who stood like marble statues and now came to life.

"I'm delivering food for Mr. Ross," I called.

One of the men waved me over and inspected the contents of my basket. "All right. Third door on the left.

After I knocked, the scene repeated itself. Another man checked me from head to toe and then opened an inner door.

At first I saw almost nothing because the curtains were closed and only a strip of light sliced through the room. Well, it wasn't just a room. The place was larger than the entire Marina's restaurant with groupings of sofas and chairs, a giant dining table and a bar in the corner.

"So, you're Sam Bruno." The man's voice was gravely.

As my eyes adjusted I noticed a bulky man sitting at the desk. Despite the gloom I immediately recognized Al 'Scarface' Capone. Another man stood guard by the door to another room.

"I've got your dinner, Mr. Ross," I said, hoping my voice didn't sound as puny as I felt in front of the mighty crime boss.

"Put it on the table." As I rushed to set up my dishes, he asked, "Where did you learn to cook?"

"Papa taught me."

"You Italian."

I nodded. "Half German too."

Capone laughed. "Just keep that to yourself." Then he moved my way and sat down. "You're pretty thing. Ever want to work in my clubs, let me know."

My cheeks flared. "Thank you, I'd rather cook."

Capone laughed again. "Money would be better." He began opening boxes.

"Sir, I'm sorry. I've got to go and help my boss with the restaurant. Five dollars is your total."

Capone gave me a once over. Prematurely balding, he was pretty unattractive. He looked overweight in a bulging suit and pasty as if he hardly saw the sun. Probably didn't with all the night trade he ran.

"All business, little miss," he said, put down his fork and pulled a wad of cash from his vest pocket. Then he counted off two tens and a twenty and tossed them on the table. "Here, keep the change."

I had heard about the incredible wealth Capone's dealings brought in from running bootlegged whiskey, bars, brothels and gambling halls. Still, the unexpected bills awed me.

The man standing guard indicated in no uncertain terms that it was time to leave. But as Capone dug into his dinner, I hesitated. This was my chance.

"Do you know my brother, Angelo Bruno?" I hurried. "He worked for George Remus and came here a year ago in April."

Capone stopped chewing. He dabbed his mouth with a white linen napkin and eyed me curiously. "Remus went to prison. What's wrong with your brother?"

"He's missing," I said. "Since last spring when he went to Chicago." I watched Capone for some clue, some reaction that indicated he knew Angelo, but there was none. Mr. Ross appeared to genuinely think about my question.

"Don't think I know him." Capone turned back to his food.

"Time to go, Miss," the guard said before I could reply.

At the door I stopped. "I've got one more question," I said as Maggie's lifeless body appeared in my mind. "There's a man downstairs. Mario Russo. I think he may have killed my friend." The last words grew quieter because I had no air left in my lungs.

Capone looked up from his meal. "How do you know?"

"My friend, Maggie, was found strangled to death at Fizzy's. The same night, Mario Russo was her client."

The fork in Mr. Ross's hand sank. "So, you *did* work in the establishment."

"It's not my thing," I said. "And Maggie, my friend, paid for it with her life."

I turned on my heels and rushed from the room, afraid I'd keel over or Mr. Ross would whisk me into one of his clubs.

Wiping tables after the breakfast crowd, I folded up a wrinkled copy of *The Chicago Daily News* somebody had left. I was about to toss it in the garbage when my gaze fell on a photo. The man in the picture wore a suit and hat, his expression somber. It was Paul. Next to him stood a young woman with a strand of pearls around her neck, blonde hair framing her face.

I forgot about cleaning and sagged into one of the booths. It couldn't be Paul, the hobo I'd met on the train. Paul was poor and destitute just like I'd been.

My eyes skimmed the lines beneath the picture.

Paul McKay, the only son of recently deceased Irish millionaire and inventor Regibald McKay, has returned to the family business and is to marry Miss Colene Sloan, the heiress of the Sloan furniture corporation. The wedding will take place next Saturday, September 12, 1925 at Old St. Patrick's

Catholic Church. Wedding guests will include many luminaries and figures of Chicago's finest.

My focus returned to Paul's face. In my mind, the black and white print turned to color, Paul walking up and down in the carriage, his arms gesticulating, his voice animated as he explained the best way to catch a train, where to find schedules and get on the good side of conductors. How often had I thought about those green eyes, the way they flashed when he was excited or angry? Or how he'd looked at me the last time we met at the Green Mill when Tony had interrupted us. I couldn't help but wonder how my life would be if Tony hadn't shown himself. If we'd had time to talk and maybe…

Don't be daft. He's rich and is going to marry another rich woman.

But when I rose to throw away the paper, my bones filled with lead. The joy I'd felt earlier—the feeling of belonging to Marina's restaurant—faded. All I saw were worn seats and scuffed floors, the grease stained stove and my own burn-marked hands.

It had been easier to imagine Paul out there making runs delivering whiskey. He no longer belonged to my world. My throat grew tight until I could no longer hold the tears because I realized that Paul was as good as dead. I tried to tell myself that I was happy for him. He didn't have to struggle to survive anymore. But it was no good. I wiped a sleeve across my face and resumed cleaning tables.

"We'll find a way," Arthur said a moment later, patting me on the back.

I looked at him through a haze. No use to explain, so I went along and nodded, because Arthur was thinking my sadness came from losing Poppi.

"I know," I said sniffing. After lunch I fished the paper back out of the garbage and carried it to my room. Smoothing the picture, I thought of Christmas morning when he'd presented me with a bar of chocolate. The surprising kiss.

Why was it that I could still smell his skin, and the chicken soup in the bowl we'd shared? How was it possible that I could still feel the softness of his lips, the way his body had pressed against mine in that instant? Paul's kiss, however brief, had lifted me out of that dreary room into another world. Something had happened back then, something I just now realized. I loved Paul. Loved him from afar and across worlds and yet. This feeling was different from loving Poppi. Deeper and more painful. Aggravating and maddening.

I curled up on the bed and let myself think back to the time Paul had saved my life from the thugs, when he'd taught me to walk like a boy. The impeccable table manners he'd shown at the good woman's table. The way he'd handled the horses. Neither had registered as odd at the time.

Why hadn't I understood then that he came from a wealthy background? I didn't pick up on it because like me he'd been hungry and cold, had worn old clothes and straggly hair. Still, something had been off, even then.

I regretted not asking him more about his family. Not that he'd volunteered. In fact, he'd been tight-lipped about where he came from, talking only about his years as a hobo. The longer I thought about it the more questions I had. How could he be rich? Why had he run away?

A deeply brewing fury took my breath. He'd lied to me. Not in so many words, but he'd purposefully kept things from me. I wanted to strangle him, pound his chest with my fists, until he fell to the ground. Kick him in the side and then...

Kiss him. A strangled sound escaped my throat. Damn stinking love.

That's when I remembered something: the Winchester—my shotgun...no, Mamma's shotgun, the most prized possession of our family. Paul had kept it when we ran from the raid in the pub. What if he still had it?

"He owes it to me!" I jumped from my own voice, wishing I'd remembered to ask when we'd met in the club. He didn't need my gun. He needed to give it back. It was all I had left of my family.

I scanned the paper one more time. Paul would get married on Saturday.

And I'd go and see him.

CHAPTER TWENTY-EIGHT

Paul

A ray of sun crept through a slit of the heavy curtains when I awoke. For a moment I lay there. Quiet. Exhausted despite the eight hours of sleep I'd gotten.

I preferred to sleep in my old room, a place I'd intended never to set foot in again. The walls still held my memories. Pictures of airplanes hung next to drawings and a pencil of Mother I'd attempted when I was ten.

The desk still stood in the same place with schoolbooks, adventure books, and an atlas loaded the top. Beatrix Potter's *Tale of a Tittlemouse* lay on top of Edith Nesbit's *The Magic City* as if I'd simply stepped away from my childhood, ready to resume enjoying my favorite stories.

There was no dust in the room, no odor, just a faint lack of air. I was unable to move. I lay there on that large four-poster bed, my limbs frozen in time. A faint echo of laughter reverberated through my mind. I was running across the room, careless and happy. For a moment, I allowed myself to stay there in that memory and a smile crossed my face.

A knock on the door brought me back.

"Master Paul, nine o'clock." Mercer strode into the room, every inch of him the perfect butler. White gloves, gleaming shoes and a black striped suit with white shirt.

"I'm awake, Mercer," I said.

"And not a moment too soon." Mercer placed a glass of water

on the bed stand. Then he rushed over to draw open the curtains.

"The windows, too," I said as I sat up to take a drink. The blinding light made me squint.

"Sir, allow me," Mercer said. "It is a bit windy this morning and we don't want a draft."

"Open them. I like it that way." I stepped next to Mercer who silently and—by the way he held his shoulders—disdainfully opened all windowpanes. Nobody understood that I didn't sleep well in a soft bed, surrounded by luxuries I hadn't seen in years. Despite my memories I felt like a stranger, an impostor.

"May I draw your bath, sir?" Mercer resumed his deference, his upper body in a slight bow, one hand behind his back.

"It's all right, Mercer," I said. "I'll be down in a bit."

As the butler turned to leave, Mercer's expression remained neutral though I knew the man did not approve of my refusal to be served.

How had I ever lived like this? Had found it normal, even fun?

Deep in thought, I washed and dressed, once in a while eyeing the formal charcoal gray suit and matching hat hanging from a coatrack.

I nodded at the mirror. "You ready, 'bo?"

The fellow in the reflection frowned and turned away.

Sam

I put on my new dress, the one I'd bought the day I'd lost Poppi. So far my savings had reached one hundred sixty dollars, mostly courtesy of Mr. Ross's generous tips. I'd offered them to Arthur, but he'd waved me away. 'You earned them,' he'd said.

Thankfully, somebody picked up Capone's meals and I hadn't needed to return. Yet, the money wasn't growing fast enough and with every passing week, I worried more about Poppi's wellbeing. I didn't dare go and check though I often felt a strong draw to watch the house in West Garfield Park. But I never did. Not only because I didn't have time, but because I was afraid of what I'd see.

Yesterday, between shifts, I'd run to telephone the church and found out the address. I'd pretended to be a guest who'd misplaced her invitation.

The ceremony was scheduled for two o'clock in the afternoon, and my nerves were frayed by ten in the morning. I'd told Arthur I needed to meet somebody and leave during lunch. Arthur had grumbled a little, but said nothing, his doleful eyes on me. I'd be back in time for Saturday evening prep.

I had studied the map to find Old St. Patrick's on Adams Street, taken a streetcar part of the way. My heels ached in the unaccustomed shoes and I nervously checked my hair and dress in the shop windows along the way.

A crowd mingled in front of the church and covered the steps ascending to the triple doors—men dressed in formal suits, women in embroidered and lacy dresses. Gold and pearls sparkled. I felt out of place and kept to the side where a few curious onlookers were watching the spectacle.

Bells began to chime overhead, their melodious sound reaching into my soul. Why was I even here? I turned to leave when an open carriage stopped in front. The bride was dressed in white and held a small bouquet of pink and white roses. An older man in a black top hat with a white moustache led her toward the church. A veil, fastened by a diamond tiara, cascaded down her back. The woman was even more beautiful than in the photograph. Her blonde hair sparkled, though I was drawn to her eyes that were large and appeared a bit surprised. She was tiny, her shoulders narrow and her arms small, almost frail.

Shouting erupted from the watchers surrounding me, while the fancy people in front of the church formed a path. My heart hammered against my ribs, my mouth was dry. Time to go. But my feet didn't obey. Paul wasn't there and for a moment I allowed myself to think it had all been a mistake. This woman was here to marry a different man. Not Paul.

The stairs of the church emptied and organ music was rising from the door. When a late couple hastened up the stairs toward the church, I hurried after them. Behind me the doors closed with a bang.

Incense tickled my nose as I tried to get my bearings. Flower arrangements of white and pink roses and carnations decorated each pew. Rose pedals covered the carpet in the middle where the bride was now approaching the front. I clamped a hand to my mouth to stop from crying out because there to the right of the altar stood Paul. A Paul so fancy and distant, I hardly recognized him. But it was him. He gazed at the woman who stopped beside him.

A whisper reached my ear. An usher pointed at an empty spot in the last row. I clambered across the feet of two elderly ladies and turned to face the front, glad to be far in the back.

I watched in curious detachment as the priest began the ceremony. This wasn't really me sitting here. I floated in the space above, unable to connect my mind with my body. The entire time my eyes were on Paul, searching for the man I'd known riding the train and sharing a room above Victor's pub.

Obviously, I didn't know much about anything. Or had I been too self-occupied to ask a lot of questions?

"Will you, Paul Ian McKay, take this woman to have and to hold…" the priest droned. When Paul answered I did not hear his voice, only saw his mouth move 'I do.' At that moment I wanted to scream. No! You can't. I love you. Instead a sob rose from my chest. Deep and raw and so full of agony, I wanted to curl up on the bench.

Had it not been for Mamma's shotgun, I would've fled from the church right then. I never watched the bride's side nor their kiss as instructed by the priest in a booming proud voice.

Organ music started anew as everyone stood to watch the freshly married couple walk down the aisle. I straightened too. Paul was approaching, his expression serious, almost severe, the little woman hanging on his arm.

When he was almost past, his gaze met mine. It was brief, no more than a split second. As recognition mirrored on his features, his back stiffened, a hesitation in his step as if he wanted to stop. His bride looked up at him questioningly and… they were gone.

I was one of the last people to leave the church. I dreaded the bright light, the cheers and laughter outside. Thankfully, nobody paid attention and I slipped to the side and down the steps to the street. Paul and Colene stood surrounded by well-wishers who all seemed to speak at once. Rice and flower petals rained.

Now was the time to approach and ask for my gun. But I stood unmoving.

"A beautiful couple, isn't it?" A roundish woman in a butter-yellow dress with ruffles beamed at me. "You with the bride or groom?"

Neither, I wanted to say.

"The groom."

I flinched. Paul stood in front of me, ignoring the pink

woman. "What are you doing here?" he asked. "Where's Tony?"

Squeezing the handle of my purse, I risked a peek at Paul's face because I wasn't at all sure what my body would do. "I'm here to get my gun," I said.

"Your gun?" Paul looked incredulous.

"Remember," I said, hoping my voice remained steady. "When we had the raid in Victor's pub and I climbed on the roof? You kept Mamma's shotgun. I thought you'd follow and—"

"Honey, time to go." Colene's high voice drifted across.

Paul's focus remained on me. "The police got me, I couldn't go with you. And when I did search for you a few days later, you were gone."

I crossed my arms. "Well, then where's my gun?"

"I hid it in the rafters. For all I know it's still there."

I turned without another word and was face-to-face with the bride who only reached to my collarbone. Mumbling "congratulations" I scrambled past.

"Sam, wait," Paul called after me.

"Honey, we have to go." To me, Colene sounded like a petulant girl not getting her treat. "They're waiting."

The entire way up the street, I fought not to turn around. I wanted to have one last look at the man who'd awoken my heart and then shattered it. But I didn't. I marched forward with my head held high. One step, then another. *Walk*, I ordered.

Again, there hadn't been time to talk. About what, anyway? *Idiot. He is married now.* At least I could search Victor's pub. If it was open. If I could get into the back. Upstairs...to the attic.

That had to be enough.

CHAPTER TWENTY-NINE

Sam

A week later, I made my way to Victor's. I'd wanted to go the day after Paul's wedding, but when I awoke that Sunday morning, I couldn't move. Just getting dressed was a chore and despite the sunny weather, I remained in my room most of the day.

Arthur had been sweet. He hadn't asked or commented, just brought me soup and tea and left me alone. He probably thought I was upset about Poppi. Which I was. Not an hour went by without me thinking of Poppi. But this was deeper, rawer. And the feeling refused to go away.

I breathed a sigh of relief when I recognized Victor's pub. There was no board in front of the door. I knew it wasn't unusual. Pubs, clubs, gaming dens and brothels were often shuttered and then reopened a day, a week or a month later.

When I stepped inside, the familiar fog of whiskey hit my nostrils. Victor hadn't changed and still wore the stained apron.

"What can I get you?" he asked, wiping his hands.

Our eyes met, recognition hit. "Sam?" Then he chuckled. "You sure changed."

I tried a smile and patted my hair which I now wore chin length. "I guess I wasn't a boy after all." I took a deep breath. "Listen I forgot something—"

"Actually, Paul already told me…. That you might stop by." Victor rummaged beneath the counter, mumbling, "Where is it?"

"What do you mean?"

202

"He came by last week. Said he'd left something upstairs. He didn't stay long. Just left a note."

Fury bubbled up my throat, I wanted to spit. "Did he carry something?"

Victor stopped his search and looked at me. "No idea. It was busy, one of my waiters quit." His gaze wandered down to my cleavage. "Hey, you wouldn't want a job, do you?"

I wanted to jump across the counter. "Victor, listen. What did Paul give you?"

"Oh, wait." He abruptly turned and searched between a couple of accounting books. "I put it in a safe place."

My fingers seemed to burn as I gripped the paper, some thick embossed material with a faint citrus smell.

Without another word I hurried out of the bar, ignoring the catcalls along the way. I made it exactly twenty yards before I gave in and opened the note.

Sam, I'm sorry, we had no time to talk. I've got your gun. It was where I left it. Will you please telephone me at Prairie Avenue District 3412? I want to explain.
Paul

Cryptic as usual. Why hadn't Paul left the gun and let me collect it? Idiot! Now I had to take more steps in my already busy life. At the same time I rejoiced that the shotgun was safe.

Hurrying as fast as my legs could walk, I headed for the telephone booth at the drugstore near Marina's.

My fingers trembled as I inserted the nickel. "Come on. Get it over with," I mumbled. "He is probably away on some honeymoon anyway."

"Operator." The voice was cool and bored.

I gripped the earpiece tighter. "Prairie Avenue District 3412, please."

"Hold the line."

"Hello, may I help you," came a man's nasal voice.

"Yes, eh, I'd like to speak with Paul... Mister McKay." My armpits were suddenly damp.

"M'am, may I ask who is calling?"

"Sam...antha Bruno, please."

"One moment."

The line went dead.

"Sam?" Paul was breathless. "I'm glad you called."

"Why didn't you leave my Winchester where it was?" The accusation burst from my lips. "Now I have to make another trip. My life isn't as swell as yours."

"I'm sorry. I'll make it up to you, I swear."

"So you're going to give me my gun?"

"Of course." Paul sounded exasperated. "I never meant to…I'd forgotten about it…and I didn't know where you were. I thought you were with that Tony."

Is that why you married the little woman, I wanted to ask. Instead I bit my lip until I tasted blood.

"Sam?"

"Yes."

"How do I find you?"

"I work at Marina's Restaurant." The line clicked and at first I thought, Paul had hung up.

"I'll find you," Paul said, his voice now almost too low to hear. "I've got to go."

The line clicked again. Paul was gone.

I was in the middle of plating three orders of tortellini with herb cheese filling when Arthur swept over.

"Man wants to talk to you." He immediately ran off to hand out menus to arriving customers.

When I looked up, Paul was standing in front of the counter. He didn't look as fancy as on his wedding day, but the contrast to his hobo days was stark. He wore a white shirt and no tie. The muted greenish tweed of his suit reflected the color of his eyes.

"You can't be here," I said, wishing I weren't so hot and sweaty, wishing my apron weren't full of splatters. "Only staff is allowed," I barked.

"Sorry, I'll order something." Paul picked up a menu. Across his shoulder I noticed a fancy leather strap and a longish bag.

"I'm busy." I turned back to my food. Why couldn't I at least be civil? But why did he have to look so good?

For the next hour I peeked ever so carefully in the direction of the table on the back wall where Paul sat. He'd ordered salad and baked pasta, plum cake and coffee. Now he sat watching the restaurant and often, when I was busy at the stove, I imagined his eyes burning a hole into my back.

When Arthur locked the door, Paul was still sitting in his spot. He was reading the paper and drinking another cup of coffee.

I wiped down my workstation and nodded to Arthur who was carrying a cryptic smile. Reluctantly, I walked toward Paul's table. Time to get it over with.

"Nobody miss you at home?" I asked.

Paul let the newspaper sink. "Why don't you sit?"

"Some people have to work for a living."

"Fair enough. Sit down, Sam."

I don't want any of your stupid stories. But I slumped on the chair anyway and out of nowhere a cup of coffee materialized in front of me. Arthur slinked off immediately and we were alone.

"First of all, I did not intend for you to feel betrayed," Paul said. "But before you judge me, I'd like to tell you what happened." His eyes were even greener than usual, a forest color I wanted to get lost in. I caught myself and took a sip of coffee.

"When I was fourteen, my father had an affair," Paul began. "He fell for some twenty-year old club singer and didn't hide it very well. Mother was distraught." Paul paused and swallowed. "She killed herself."

"Oh, no," slipped from my mouth.

"I was furious with Father, so he sent me to a boarding school. I hated it and ran. I met you seven years later after I'd been a 'bo for a while. During the raid at Victor's I was arrested. But the judge knew Father. He said he'd let me go if I went home…to see my dying father."

Paul rubbed his chin, his gaze far away. "I went home. Father died the next day. He made me promise I'd marry Colene. Our families had made a deal when I was eleven. I hadn't seen her in eight years. And you…" A shadow passed over his eyes.

What about me? I wanted to ask. When I remained silent, Paul went on.

"How did you get here?"

I leaned back as scenes of sweaty Louis and Tony's harsh hands played in my mind. How indeed? No way, I'd tell Paul about being a prostitute. Just the idea…

"Sam?"

Heat rose from the collar of my dress and spread to my cheeks. "What?"

Paul's gaze was on me, reflecting worry and curiosity. "There's something else I need to tell you. Unless you already know…"

"What?"

"Have you heard from your brother?"

"No."

Paul's eyes bored into mine. "When I was arrested and thrown in jail, I met Angelo."

My hand slammed on Paul's arm. "How? Tell me. What happened? Where is he?"

"You know he looks a lot like you," Paul said. "Black hair and those blue eyes. He was sitting by himself and I went over. At first, he didn't want to talk, but when I asked him if his name was Angelo, he perked up. He'd been arrested during a brawl."

"Was he all right?"

"He had a nasty cut on his arm, but was fine otherwise. I told him I'd met you…about your mother. He didn't know."

"Why didn't he write or come home to Cincinnati?" I cried.

"I had the feeling he didn't want to talk. Didn't even want his name mentioned. I was let go soon after. Cops didn't really have much and with the jails over full…"

My eyes sparkled with tears. "But where is he now?"

Paul shrugged. "I wish I could tell you. We were at W. Maxwell and S. Morgan…22nd district." He produced a smile. "At least he knows you're in Chicago."

"You never saw him again?"

"Once. I'd sent a note to the jail and he came to my home. Asked about you? That was right after the Green Mill." Paul gave a helpless shrug. "I didn't have a chance to ask."

"So you know where he is?"

"He said he'd find me again."

"And?"

"Nothing, so far."

My head sank to my chest, too heavy to carry any longer.

Paul's hand lifted my chin. Our eyes met. I smelled the soap on it, something lemony. How I longed to preserve his touch. "When he shows, I'll tell him about Marina's. You'll see him soon." He glanced around the restaurant. "I'm glad you've found a place to cook. Your pasta is wonderful."

"Thanks," I said. "Arthur has been very kind." I stopped. Nothing else came to mind. It was as if a strong wind had blown away my thoughts.

"Oh, I almost forgot." Paul lifted the leather bag from the back of his chair. "Here is your Winchester. I cleaned and oiled it. Should be good as new." This time the grin he produced was like those I remembered from the trains. "I'm sorry I'd forgotten about it."

"Thanks," I said again. "I hope you'll be happy."

Paul shrugged. "Happiness is a fleeting thing. Are *you*...happy?"

"I've got a place to stay. Work." *Get a grip!* I forced a smile and straightened. "Much better than riding in train cars."

Paul took my cue and stood up. "How much do I owe?"

"It's on the house," Arthur yelled from the other side of the room, but Paul shook his head and placed a ten-dollar note on the table.

As I unlocked the door, Paul turned to me. "Take care of yourself."

"You too."

By the time I had locked the door a new lump clogged my throat. Luckily, Arthur kept to himself, so I slipped upstairs and rolled up on the bed.

Paul

I didn't head home after meeting with Sam. I couldn't. My mind was in turmoil, and so was my body. Despite the cool September wind, I sweat. And yet inside I was cold as if it were the middle of winter.

What had I done?

Ever since I'd said good-bye to Father, things had gotten worse. A laugh bubbled up and burst free. Two fellows carrying a box into a house entrance curiously stared.

Here I'd considered hobo life and bootlegging hard. Sure, they were dangerous and scary. People got shot or arrested. I'd been cold and hungry, worked nights.

So what?

Sam's face swam into view. Her black hair was longer again, more feminine. I chuckled as I remembered cutting it on a snow-covered field, teaching her to speak with a deeper voice. She was a terrible actress. Everything showed on her face. Well, at least to me it was clear.

You lie a lot better. It wasn't so much lying but omitting, I thought. Semantics. Again! But how could I have told Sam that her long lost brother had looked like he'd fall over any moment. He'd had dark rings under his eyes and seemed unhappy.

I returned to the present, wondering where Angelo had gone and what had happened to him to make him so wary.

And that other thing? Mother's deceit, the lie you'd based your decisions on?

A small part of me rejoiced knowing I'd dropped off Sam's shotgun and returned something she loved. Seeing her working and doing what she enjoyed.

Knowing where she was.

I huffed. *Like it's any of your business.*

But she seemed so sad...no, hurt. And my entire body screamed with the desire to make it better, to make whatever pained her go away.

A sigh escaped me with such force, the man at the street corner jumped. I ignored him and hurried on. Then stopped.

I was at a turning point. Either I could let others like Colene and Henry Sloan walk all over me or...

I smiled grimly. I might be married to the wrong woman, but Regi McKay had left a legacy. I might as well make myself useful, concentrate on Father's business, and assure it continued so his accomplishments weren't forgotten.

Find a purpose.

CHAPTER THIRTY

Sam

The news that Angelo was in Chicago calmed me, even if I didn't know his whereabouts. At least it confirmed he'd arrived and stayed, whatever his reasons.

Like Paul, he'd worked in the trade. And like Paul, he'd been arrested. Chances were he still worked some place. It was known that the North Side Gang didn't like Italians and often attacked bars and shops in Italian neighborhoods. So it was unlikely Angelo worked for them. Since Capone didn't know him either, he had to be in some smaller organization, maybe somewhere on the outskirts of town.

But first things first.

The next free time arrived two days later when the lunch crowd had been unusually light and Arthur agreed to clean up by himself.

I hesitated when the police station at Maxwell and Morgan, a large squat two-story brick building with a curved limestone-ringed entrance, came into view. I had to be crazy. They were looking for me. At least somebody had months ago. Would they find me out? But I had to take the risk, had to know what happened to Angelo.

I took a deep breath and pushed open the door.

The man behind the counter was writing something and didn't look up until I cleared my throat.

"Yes, miss?"

"I'm looking for a man who was arrested here in January," I

said.

"Why is that?" The man reluctantly straightened and stepped to the counter. He was short, his thick nose out of place with deep pores and weather beaten skin, his cheeks a spider web of blue veins. But his mouth drew the most attention, a parallel of deep vertical lines creasing their way to the chin. They spoke of permanent bitterness as if he'd been on a diet of lemons.

"I'm looking for my brother, Angelo Bruno."

"That his name, eh?"

I suppressed rolling my eyes. "Yes, and I'd appreciate if you could tell me when he was released."

"Did he get sentenced?"

"Don't know."

"What was he in for?"

"I think he was arrested during a brawl."

"Where?"

"Don't know."

"You don't know much, do you?"

I wanted to jump across the counter and grab the stupid man by the throat. Instead I forced a smile. "Look, sir." My eyes searched the man's uniform for a name, but didn't find one. "Officer. I've been searching for my brother for a long time. You'd really help me if you could look up his record."

The man's cheeks grew redder. "Detective Tom Miles." He turned his back to me and sat back down. "Don't have time to hunt for some lowlife."

I wanted to scream, but then I remembered something...someone. The man who'd looked for Tony. "Maybe I should ask for Captain Morgan Collins. He told me to contact him if I needed help." I sent up an inner prayer. Sorry, Mamma. I've got to find Angelo.

Miles head snapped up, his watery eyes appraising. "How do you know Captain Collins?"

None of your business. I smiled. "I met him in the spring, a very nice man."

An inner struggle reflected on Detective Miles's face. He straightened again and handed me a piece of paper. "Write down your name, address, place of work and your brother's name and birthday. I'll see what I can do."

I scanned the exit. So far Detective Miles hadn't realized I was wanted for Maggie's murder. It was a gamble, but what choice did I have? I'd needed to give my name to prove I was Angelo's relation. But what if they connected the dots. Somebody searched the files…come across my description.

Something cold trickled down my back. The unease made me swoon and I gripped the counter. *Go now*, my mind urged. Yet, I remained standing, the eyes of the detective on me like burning coals.

Half an hour later, I left the station with a printed copy of a discharge document, stating that Angelo Bruno had been released from jail on January 27, 1925.

That wasn't what excited me as much as what was written beneath Angelo's name: his home address. A terrible urge spread through me. I wanted to go there. Now.

A look at the nearby church tower stopped me. Almost four o'clock. I had to rush back and help Arthur with the evening crowd. Our wine cellar was one third empty as the number of evening patrons continued to increase. Some nights we had to turn people away because we couldn't seat anymore and customers wanted to enjoy their 'meal.'

Arthur never offered refills, nor was wine mentioned on the menu. So far nothing had happened. Arthur had paid off his loans and was steadily building a nest egg. Worried about break-ins, he'd opened an account at Union State Bank.

"I've got an address," I announced as soon as I was back, having trouble keeping a straight face.

Arthur clapped his flour-covered hands. "Good girl." As usual he was behind and over his head, counters covered in spills, so I changed and jumped into action. These days prepping was routine, cutting up ingredients for tomato sauces and salads, shredding cheeses and rolling out dough. We'd added yeast bread with garlic butter as an appetizer, which Arthur was in charge of kneading and baking.

A second serving girl helped fix drinks and clear plates while Arthur took orders and collected payments—cash only.

"Sam." Arthur's voice was urgent. "Turn around slowly. Don't look at the door."

"What is it?" I said as I placed two platters of the 'evening special' for pickup. Then I saw. Rather I saw *them*. Two policemen in uniform had ignored the line outside and now stood by the 'please wait to be seated' sign.

"Just act normal," I said between my teeth. "Don't let them see you're worried." I nodded encouragingly. "Smile."

Arthur sucked in air and headed to the front door. But I recognized the quiver in his massive shoulders as fear. Only when Arthur led them to the table in back we kept open for surprise guests, did I recognize one of the men. It was Detective Tom Miles from the 22nd district.

The same dread I'd felt at the police station returned, a premonition of doom. "Don't be silly," I mumbled. "He's checking up on you. Or maybe he has news about Angelo."

But neither of the two men approached me. Just once in a while I felt their eyes on me. Not in a warm and comfortable way like with Paul, more like a creepy hand sliding across my back.

They ordered the special and Arthur served it himself. Other tables had long turned over, the second rush almost finished. Yet, the men still sat and watched. I couldn't tell what they thought or talked about.

Only when the restaurant cleared, did the men get up and approach Arthur at the cash register.

"A fine meal," Miles said, nodding over to me, the spidery veins in his cheeks glowing.

"It's on the house," Arthur said with a smile. "We're glad you're protecting us."

"That's mighty generous," Miles said. "What you take in tonight?"

Arthur shrugged. "Don't know, haven't done the count."

"Guess then you won't mind if we cover our travel expenses to come here." Miles stretched out an arm and I watched in horror as the officer dipped into the till and pulled out four ten-dollar bills."

"Sir, I protest," Arthur said weakly. "I have to buy supplies and we're not making that much."

"Would you rather I turn you in for illegally supplying alcohol to your customers?" Miles mocked. "Surely, you have heard of the Volstead Act." He turned toward me. "And you're on the lam for murdering a prostitute." His dark eyes shrank into slits. "I thought I'd seen your name some place."

"But you…" Arthur said, his gaze on me.

"We what?" said the other officer, his voice like a freshly

sharpened blade.

"Nothing." Arthur closed his mouth as his arms fell to his side.

"Have a nice evening," Miles said and tipped his hat. "We'll be back. Food is mighty good."

Arthur locked the door and leaned his forehead against it. "Marina always warned me. I should've listened." He shook his head. "What did they mean with travel expenses?"

Watching the whole thing from the kitchen, I rushed to him. "Oh, Arthur. It's my fault. I met that man with the red face, Miles, this morning. He didn't want to help me, so I said I'd tell this captain I'd met a while back. Miles didn't like it, but he finally gave me Angelo's address. I was so happy, I never thought…" I threw myself into Arthur's arms. "I'm so sorry. He's getting even. I had to leave my address. They came all the way from Maxwell and Morgan."

Arthur patted me on the back and let go. "And found us doing something illegal, so they can blackmail us."

"Or arrest me." I took a deep breath. "Maybe they won't be back. It's a long way."

"Maybe."

But I knew Arthur doubted it. And if I were honest, I doubted it, too. I'd led those thugs straight to Arthur… who'd done nothing but help me.

How was I going to stop the thief? He was police after all—and he held all the cards.

CHAPTER THIRTY-ONE

Paul

I spent the next weeks familiarizing myself with the family business. Father had owned rental properties, entire blocks of apartments in the Lake View neighborhood, a moving company, several tracts of land west of Chicago, a summerhouse on Lake Michigan, and then there was his company, of course.

McKay Industries specialized in gadgets. All sorts of useful parts other companies used to manufacture products. The latest had been parts for the Ford Model T.

I rose before six o'clock and was out the door by six-thirty. I visited factories, combed through the books and met with employees. There was no need to fool myself. I had neither Father's talent for invention, nor his engineering background. But I understood business and people, something my hobo days had taught me.

And I knew immediately that something was rotten in Father's business. So I buried myself in the company, spent every waking hour there and often slept on a divan in the corner of Father's office.

I waded through the accounting books, but soon found that my knowledge was limited. The firm's financial officer, Mr. Tott, watched me guardedly across the desk, the man's eyes flittering this way and that as if he were looking for an escape route. I had summoned him a second time this morning.

"How long have you worked for my father, Mr. Tott?"

"Going on twenty years, Sir." Tott bowed in his seat and shook his head. "What a terrible loss."

I decided to keep my suspicions secret for now and continued, "Who helps you with the books?"

"Eh, I've got a team, the accounting department and of course, the board oversees everything."

"I see."

"Who's been running things while my father was ill?"

"Not sure what you mean, sir."

"Who has been in charge in my father's absence?"

"Well, your wife's father, Mr. Sloan. I thought you knew that."

I stared. I'd known, Sloan was somehow involved in Father's company. But I hadn't expected Sloan to be in charge.

"Your father felt it was best to nominate Sloan. That was probably two years ago. After all, they'd been longtime friends and you...."

"I know I was absent. Wonder why Sloan never mentioned anything," I said quietly. "Why don't you get me all the books from the last two years?"

"Very well, sir. I'll have my assistant collect them for you."

By evening, I was up to my neck in numbers. I'd never spent time studying accounting, so I wasn't sure what a lot of the accounts were for. I'd also asked for the order and production books, which now lay spread across the floor. I made notes, wrote down questions and often mumbled.

At some point I fell asleep on the sofa, only to be awakened by my secretary in the morning. After half drowning myself in the sink and drinking a pot of coffee, I was back at it.

"Sir, Mr. Sloan is here to see you." The secretary, a youngish thing in an old-fashioned gray dress stood in the door.

"Young McKay," Sloan laughed, pushing his way past the secretary, "Tott tells me that you asked for the books. What in the world did you get yourself into?" Sloan scanned the room and waved away the secretary.

I squinted with irritation, but decided to let it go. "Nothing much," I said, noting how Sloan rubbed his sideburns nervously. "Just getting familiar."

"I see. Would be happy to give you a tour. Just ask me anything. Your father had full trust in my abilities. After all, I've been a business man all my life." There was the chuckle again. He waved a forefinger across the stacks of books. "No need to confuse yourself with these."

I forced a smile. "I've already looked at the factories." I straightened. "Now, if you'll excuse me…"

Sloan wrinkled his forehead. "Sure thing, young chap. I'll be in my office, if you need me."

When Sloan was at the door, I called after him, "Say, when did you take over for my father?"

Sloan turned. "Maybe a year ago, not sure. Your father wasn't doing so well and he approached me."

Hadn't Tott said Sloan joined us two years ago?

Maybe I'd misunderstood.

Sam

When Miles didn't appear the next day or the day after that, I breathed a little easier. I hadn't dared leave Arthur, though I burned to find Angelo's place. The map said it was somewhere near Garfield Park. Not as far west as Poppi's home. Poppi.

Oh, the poor girl. The longer it took to save the four hundred dollars, the angrier I felt about Mary Rose's extortion. Everyone wanted something for nothing. It was the way of the world. Thugs and bootleggers ruled. Al Capone was getting mightier, and the police who were supposed to protect the people had succumbed to corruption.

Thursday evening, when I was fixing the last plates of spaghetti and meatballs for a handful of late arrivals, Detective Miles pushed through the door in plain clothes. Without his uniform he looked more like a thug—short and mean.

Miles immediately went to the closest table and sat down. Arthur had already noticed and hurried to his side.

"Sir, I'm sorry, the kitchen is closed."

I cringed, but was equally proud of Arthur for standing up to the man.

"Look." Miles's pigly eyes wandered to me. I stood unmoving, staring at him defiantly. "She can fix me some leftovers, capiche? I take that menu special you offer."

Arthur's mouth clamped shut. He stood a moment, obviously thinking on what to do, but at last he moved toward me. "You heard him," he whispered, the worry frown on his forehead deepening. As I scraped together the last of the spaghetti and a crust from the lasagna and slopped sauce on top, the last guests paid and left. I marched to the detective, who was already sucking down his wine, and smacked down the plate. "Closing in five minutes." To emphasize the point, I locked the door.

Searing pain shot through my wrist. Detective Miles's sinewy fingers squeezed me so hard that my skin turned white. *Arthur*, I thought. But Arthur had gone to prepare his cleaning buckets.

"You better be nice to me, Missy," Miles hissed. "I checked your story, you lying bitch. Collins questioned you once."

Despite my pain, I cried, "That doesn't mean I can't tell him about you." By the way the man reeked, he'd been drinking whiskey.

"Try it," Miles said, hurling alcohol vapors into my face. "I've got friends."

"Something the matter?" Arthur asked from the backdoor.

Miles dropped my arm and returned to his meal. "Just having a friendly chat."

I returned to my station, secretly rubbing my wrist. As I began cleaning, my mind whirled. Miles knew I'd bluffed. But worse, the sudden violence brought back memories and the conviction that no place was ever going to be safe for me. For a while, I'd allowed myself to believe I'd found a new home. Arthur was like a father to me, providing a place to belong—a place to earn an honest living. Ha! Honesty didn't pay these days. Why did I even try to hold on to an ideal when the world was crumbling?

"Bring me another wine." Miles's voice was thick.

Arthur stopped his broom and approached the table. "Sorry, sir, we are now closed. And we don't sell wine."

Miles chuckled, an ugly sound like a hyena. "Get me some wine. Now!"

Again, Arthur hesitated. I noticed how his hands twitched. He could've easily grabbed Miles's scrawny neck and snuffed him out. But that wasn't Arthur. He was kind to a fault—too kind for the likes of Miles. Fury clogged my throat and I wished once again I had the strength.

When Arthur looked at me, his gaze searching my face for help, I nodded. What difference did it make? The detective was a criminal. Kind of worse because he hid behind his uniform, pretending to protect Chicago's citizens.

Without a word, Arthur marched off to fetch more wine.

While Miles got even drunker, Arthur and I finished cleaning and prepped for breakfast. My feet ached terribly and I longed for bed. Arthur had to feel worse. He'd gained more weight, probably from my cooking and often wheezed these days when he climbed the stairs to the apartment.

Now staggering, Miles got up. "Where's yo' till?"

Arthur pretended not to hear and continued rolling silverware into napkins. "Where's your fucking till?" Miles hollered. He teetered toward the door and caught hold on the little table where Arthur usually collected payment.

Arthur slowly turned. There was turmoil in his eyes—and loathing. I wanted Arthur to attack the mean snake. But he didn't. He bowed his head and pulled the cash drawer from its hiding place.

He slowly opened it, coins and small bills ready for breakfast. He counted out four five-dollar notes and extended a palm. "Here."

An evil chuckle broke from Miles's chest. "You kidding? I'm collecting for three days, not one."

"But that's—"

"What?" Miles stepped closer, his head at Arthur's chest. Obviously, the alcohol and the meanness made him fearless. "You saying something? Because I can be back tomorrow with a few colleagues and close your joint down."

You will anyway, I thought. Just steal it all first. All our hard work lost.

Arthur had returned with a wad of bills and smacked them on the counter.

Miles suspiciously eyed the money. But then he counted before stuffing the bills into his pocket. He wordlessly moved to the door and yanked. The door didn't budge. I hurried over and unlocked, forcing myself not to kick the crook in the ass.

By the time I'd relocked, Arthur had dropped into a booth. "He's going to close us down. One way or another."

I put a hand on his shoulder. "It's all my fault," I cried. "I made him mad, asking for Angelo's information."

Arthur wiped his eyes and looked up at me. "Nonsense. That's his job. The fellow is meaner than the devil. And he knows he has us pinned. He's enjoying it too." A heavy sigh rose from his chest.

"All the profit from the week is gone and I've got to go to the bank tomorrow, so we can buy supplies."

"What do we do?" I said.

With a groan Arthur straightened and shuffled to the backdoor. "I wish I knew, Sam. I wish I knew."

CHAPTER THIRTY-TWO

Paul

I spent days and nights in my office. Well, it wasn't really mine yet. Everywhere I looked there were memories of Father: the cigar box with inlaid wood in the shape of a lion, a gift of my mother years ago, the painting of a sailboat I'd been on as a boy, a lump of pottery I'd made in first grade that held pennies, Father's collection of whiskeys and bourbon in the glass cabinet, and…

The only thing different so far was my new chair. I'd requested a replacement because I was much taller and the old leather chair hurt my back.

My new work schedule wasn't just because I suspected foul play. I knew being here made me feel closer to Father and the loss I still felt burning a hole into my chest.

For the tenth time, I went over the accounts, acquisitions and sales, and the profit and loss statements. Something wasn't right, but I was still no farther along. Maybe I was imagining things. After all, wasn't Sloan rich from his furniture empire?

I sat back and stared into space. Or was he?

On a whim, I grabbed my coat and headed home. When Mercer opened the door, I carefully peeked around the entry before beckoning the butler into the pantry.

"My wife out?"

"Sir, she went to see her father."

"Good, I'd prefer if what I said would remain confidential."

Mercer's lids closed and opened in silent agreement.

"You've known Father for forty some years," Paul said quietly. "You've also known Sloan for a while."

Mercer nodded. "Nearly as long, sir. Your father and Mr. Sloan were friends for decades."

"What do you know about Sloan's company?"

Mercer's eyebrows rose. "Only what one reads in the paper. Mr. Sloan's furniture business produces everything a modern home needs."

"Yes, right," I said, wishing Mercer wouldn't sound like an advertisement. "Could Sloan have run into trouble? I mean financial difficulties?

Mercer remained quiet for a moment and I appreciated that the man took his time to think before he answered.

"I do remember that Mr. Sloan visited a while ago. Words were exchanged, though I regret that I didn't hear the argument. And when he left he was quite upset."

"Two years ago?"

Mercer nodded. "Shortly after, Mr. Sloan joined Mr. Regibald in the company. First as an advisor and later as an officer of the board. I read it in the paper."

I sighed. "I'm afraid that won't help us much. Thank you. I'll have a bite to eat now."

"Sir, if I may," Mercer said. "Miss Lola, the Sloan's housekeeper, is a friend."

My turn to raise an eyebrow.

"Well, I've known Lola for a long time and we...shall we say...have an arrangement."

What arrangement is that, I thought, trying to keep a straight face. So Mercer was having a romantic relationship after all. I'd often wondered if Mercer had ever had a girlfriend.

"I shall ask, quietly of course."

I gripped Mercer's right hand. "I don't want this to be obvious."

Sam

Detective Miles returned. Not every night, but several times a week. He always collected for his 'missed' evenings, sometimes bringing a friend. By October, Arthur's new savings account was exhausted. No matter how hard we worked, we couldn't get ahead. Even raising menu prices by fifty cents, didn't change anything because supplies also became more expensive. And the wine cellar was shrinking at an alarming rate.

At some point we'd have to organize more, but that took money. Deliveries had to be prepaid and would require a substantial amount. Arthur no longer had it.

One evening, after Detective Miles left drunk and eighty dollars richer, Arthur told me that we wouldn't be able to open because he had no more money to buy eggs and flour, bacon and bread. With a heavy heart I went upstairs and returned with eighty dollars.

"No, Sam. I can't." Arthur pushed away my hands. "It's for Poppi."

"Without the restaurant we have nothing," I said. Tears pressed as I stuffed the bills into his apron pocket. It was all my fault. Arthur had been nothing but good to me. And I'd mishandled everything. Lost Poppi, led Miles here. It had been my idea to serve wine. I was the one wanted for murder, giving Miles ammunition to blackmail us. I sank into the booth, my head too heavy to carry.

Arthur said, "It's no good. Just prolongs the suffering and—"

As I looked up, he gripped his chest. His eyes stretched wide, sort of surprised. He gasped as if he couldn't get any air. Then, in slow motion, he crumpled to the linoleum.

I flew to his side. "Arthur!"

Arthur struggled for breath, a gurgle rising from his throat. Sweat droplets appeared on his forehead and upper lip. He tried to speak. The wheezing grew louder.

"Can't… breathe…"

"NO!" I bent low, my fingers shakily loosening Arthur's collar. Deep down I knew that something terrible was happening and my insides screamed *too late*. "I've got to get help," I cried though I couldn't tell if he heard me. "Lie still, I'll be right back."

I raced from the restaurant, down the street to the drugstore where I'd called Paul from one of the new phone booths. I had no air, my rip cage wanting to burst. Ripping the earpiece from the machine I yelled, "Help! My friend is sick. I think it's his heart. Quick, send a doctor. Marina's restaurant, South Indiana Ave."

The operator's voice seemed cool and detached, like a ghost. "I'm calling the fire department."

"Please hurry." I slammed the earpiece down and raced back.

Arthur lay in the same spot, and even before I closed the door, I knew that he was gone. It was the same stillness that had surrounded Mamma.

I threw myself on Arthur's chest and pounded my fists until they bruised. "No, Arthur. Don't leave me like this. Not like this." I sobbed, a wailing foreign sound that rose and filled Marina's, crept onto the benches and covered the tables until it occupied every inch. I gasped for air.

A door flew open and several men in uniform stormed in. They pushed me aside and began to work on Arthur, opened his shirt, listened with a stethoscope, felt his neck for a pulse. At first one, then two more shook their heads.

One of the men approached me. "He's gone."

"I know."

"Are you his daughter?"

I shook my head when I realized I might as well have been his daughter. He had saved my life. "I help him with the restaurant," I whispered as fresh tears rolled down my cheeks.

"Will you need help with the arrangements?" the man asked, his eyes kind.

"I'll manage." I needed time. Alone. To think.

The men helped me bar Arthur on two of the tables. Heads low, they filed out, mumbling condolences.

A sigh rose from my middle as I gazed around the space. My home...once again lost. The restaurant was done...and I out of a job and a place to live. And a family. Tomorrow was the last day of October and the landlord would soon come to collect November rent.

All night I kept watch by the light of a candle. At some point a doctor arrived to officially confirm Arthur's death. Angina, the paper said.

The feeling of doom returned. I'd have to hurry. Miles would be back, no doubt. In the morning I would go to the undertaker and arrange Arthur's pickup. Then I'd head to see Angelo. Together we'd find a way to make a life. I dozed off.

In my dream, Paul and I walked down a meadow. He was holding my hand, laughing and talking. It wasn't anything important or memorable, just the feeling he understood me, our laughter soaring, souls adjoined.

Paul's steps began to echo and as I was searching for the

source of the terrible noise, I awoke.

Fists banged on the glass door. "Hello, anybody in there?" Several faces were pressed against the windows. My eyes raced to the clock. After seven. I'd overslept. People were coming for breakfast.

I clambered to the door and unlocked, my body stiff and sore, my mind numb. "I'm sorry, Arthur is dead," I said, my voice trembling again.

"What happened?" one of the regulars asked. "He wasn't sick, was he?"

"His heart," I choked.

Murmurs erupted. People shook their heads and slowly the crowd disbursed. I drew a sign and fastened it in the window.

Closed due to death in the family.

Arthur had been my family. And now he was gone too. Like Mamma and Papa. And Angelo. A sigh escaped me as I washed, put on my best dress and headed to the casket maker who promised to stop by later and take Arthur with him. He'd wanted to know whether Arthur went to church, what faith he prescribed to, where his wife was buried, but I couldn't answer any of the questions. Why had I never asked?

Finally, we agreed on burying Arthur at a nondenominational plot and I would order a headstone from Sears and Roebuck. I'd seen a catalog with pages of headstones for sale.

Relieved to finish Arthur's burial plans, I headed into the morning. It was cool, the trees carrying a first layer of frost like sugary icing. My steps crunched on the mishmash of leaves and twigs, announcing that winter was on its way. I wasn't really dressed warm enough, having waited to buy a heavier coat. What did it matter?

Maybe Angelo would help. I checked the map several times, crossed Madison Street, dodged streetcars and hoped my heels wouldn't get stuck in the tracks.

The house on West Adams Street had three stories and looked a lot better than Mary Rose's place. But when I studied the doorbells, I did not find one for Angelo Bruno. In my mind I imagined Angelo giving a fake address to the police.

Disheartened, I pressed one on the first floor and heard the ringing inside through the door. A man in his seventies opened, his chin grizzled, his shirt stained with food spills.

He eyed me suspiciously, his bushy brows drawing together. "Yes?"

"I'm looking for my brother, Angelo Bruno. Does he live here?"

"Never heard of him."

My face fell. "Are you sure?"

As the man stroked his chin, it crackled. "Jenkins upstairs had a guest a while back. Didn't know his name. Dark fella, blue eyes."

"Is Mr. Jenkins home?" I asked, nervously scratching my throat.

"You can try. I'm not keeping schedules."

I breathed thank you and rushed past the smelly man.

"Third floor," he called after me.

I climbed the stairs. Inside, the house was run down with mud and dust on the steps. So much for appearances.

Arriving on the third floor landing, I sucked in air and eyed the three doors. Where are you, Mr. Jenkins?

I knocked on the first door. When nothing happened, I moved to the second. Another knock.

A woman in a housecoat opened the door. "You lost, girl." The woman wore makeup and though she had to be in her forties, reminded me of Beatrice.

"I'm looking for Mr. Jenkins," I said, trying to ignore the deep neckline and the half uncovered breasts.

A hoarse laugh broke from the uncovered chest. "Mr. Jenkins has been dead for five years." She focused on me. "I'm *Mrs.* Jenkins."

I tried to hide my shock. What had Angelo been doing with this woman? But then, maybe it hadn't been him. "I'm looking for my brother, Angelo Bruno."

Mrs. Jenkins's eyes traveled from my face across my dress down to the stockings and shoes and back up. "Angelo isn't here."

"Do you know where he is?" I said. "Please, I've been looking for him for almost a year."

"Honey, he didn't tell me his plans." She hesitated. "He did leave something, though. Figured I'd keep it, but now…you look a lot like him." Another hoarse chuckle. "Wait."

A part of me rejoiced, knowing Angelo had been here.

"Here, sweetie," Mrs. Jenkins said, a cigarette dangling between her lips. She handed me a two-inch wooden cross on a leather strap. Mamma had given it to him years ago and Angelo had never taken it off.

"When did he leave?" I asked.

"Nine months ago, maybe."

"Do you know where he worked?"

The woman shrugged, her half exposed breasts jiggling. "Honey, he didn't talk much. Just needed a place." When she saw my disappointed face, she leaned forward and patted my forearm. In a lowered voice, she said, "He worked on the lake. Was often wet and cold when he got home. That's all I know."

"Why did he leave?"

"I think it was too far from his job. He was tired a lot. Said something about too many stairs."

Only when I was back on the street walking toward Marina's did I realize how much I'd hoped to find my brother. Somehow I'd figured we would plan our lives together. Help each other get settled. But there was no future—I could see that now. Not with him, nor Arthur.

My future had dissolved. There was nothing left of the place I'd called home. I was out of work with two hundred and five dollars—Poppi's money—and I'd now need it to survive. Find a new place to live.

I locked the door behind me and let my fingers slide along the worn counter, the tables and benches. A feeble sun shone through the windows, dust flecks hovered in midair. Any moment Arthur would bustle in, his arms loaded with assorted groceries from the market. Instead there was silence.

Somewhere outside a horn blew, people chattered. Life continued out there. In here, it had stopped.

I walked down the aisle to the back, into the kitchen… the storeroom. I looked at everything as if for the first time—the neatly folded towels, the stacked napkins, vegetables sorted in their bins. Arthur had been a mess in the kitchen, but he'd kept order. Provided structure.

Arthur was dead.

And Miles would return to extoll more money. And if he couldn't get that, he'd demand something else…blackmail me. I needed to leave. Fast.

Instead, I sank onto a bench and buried my head in my arms. A wail rose in the stillness as I mourned my big friend with the bigger heart. Out of the corner of my eyes I saw people stopping to enter, then read the sign, peek inside, shake their heads and leave.

Loud banging startled me and I staggered to the door. Some fellow obviously couldn't read. But when I unlocked the door, I was face to face with the man in the fedora and fine suit—Mr. Ross's assistant.

"What is going on?" he demanded. "Why aren't you cooking?"

I suppressed a nasty comment. "Arthur died last night. We're closed."

"That won't do, miss…Sam. Mr. Ross would like his usual, plus he has three guests."

"Sir, I can't run the place by myself." My voice grew thinner with every word. "He is dead."

"I'll tell Mr. Ross. He won't be happy."

Tears burst as I yelled, "Tell Mr. Ross, I've got bigger problems than to fix a meal. I can't pay the bills because a corrupt policeman has been robbing us blind. Now Arthur is dead from all the worry and I have to find a new place to live."

I slammed shut the door, leaving an open-mouthed fedora man on the street. New sobs broke from my throat as I ran upstairs.

It was over. All those little hopes and wants I'd allowed myself to nourish since moving in with Arthur had vanished. Angelo remained lost and I no longer had a way to get Poppi. Maybe never. I'd lost the home I'd hoped to build with Poppi, and with it, the hope that Arthur would be like a grandfather to her.

Out of nowhere I remembered Paul. Not only was there no more home, no child to love, I'd lost Paul too. *You never had him in the first place*, my mind mocked. *He's rich and doesn't care about a former prostitute cook from Cincinnati.*

I lay on my back on the bed that Arthur's daughter had once occupied. The room was so still. A long time ago, Arthur's daughter had been up here, listening to the bustle of the kitchen, the doors opening and closing, people eating and laughing and sometimes singing. Arthur had told me that his daughter had passed away more than ten years ago. Now there was nothing, just emptiness, a dark hole that swallowed all memories.

At last I climbed off the bed, collected the money stash and items from the bathroom. I was about to pack a battered suitcase

I'd found in Arthur's room, when I heard loud knocking. It about sounded as if somebody wanted to kick in the front door, so I rushed back downstairs, ready to take somebody's head off.

Outside paced the man with the fedora. When he noticed me, he waved frantically. "Open up," he yelled through the glass.

"What?" I shouted. "I already told you I've—"

"Mr. Ross wants to see you," the fedora man said. He was chewing on a cigar and spitting bits of tobacco on the street.

"I'm about to leave," I said. But I knew it wasn't wise to put off Al Capone. With a sigh, I unlocked the door. "I'll be ready in five minutes."

Mr. Ross had not changed. For a man in his twenties, not that much older than Paul, he seemed old. Maybe that was the price to pay or maybe it was because he was overweight and prematurely losing his hair. His face appeared rounder and, in the glow of the yellow ceiling lights, the scars on his right cheek shone pale and a bit otherworldly. Like Fedora man, he was smoking a cigar, but the smell was much more pleasant.

"If you were a man, I'd offer you a cigar," he said without preamble. He was leaning back in his chair, eyeing me with renewed interest. "You're closing Marina's. Why's that?"

I threw an irritated glance at Fedora man. Hadn't he told Capone anything?

Swallowing my annoyance, I began anew, telling Capone about our secret wine menu and Detective Miles visiting to extoll our hard-earned cash, Arthur's worries, his sudden death.

Mr. Ross threw up a hand. "You telling me that copper crook grabbed all your cabbage?"

What was Capone talking about? "He came all the time and took more and more money. We basically would've closed anyway because we could no longer afford to buy supplies."

Something dark crept across Capone's features. "You say his name is Miles?"

I nodded. "Detective in the 22nd district. I asked him about my brother, Angelo, and he got mad. He later followed me home and that's when it all started. It's all my fault," I cried.

Ignoring me, Capone waved over the guard and began to whisper. Then the man disappeared, being replaced by another man.

Capone's gaze focused on me again. "Listen, Sam Bruno. I want you to go back to Marina's. Hire some help, a couple girls or something, you know...waitresses. Then you buy supplies and tomorrow, you open up Marina's."

"But—"

Capone's arm shot up. "I'm going to take care of your landlord and your start-up dough. I'll get you more wine." He chuckled. "Can't have a decent meal without vino rosso."

"What about Mr. Miles. He'll come and...."

Mr. Ross puffed a great big cloud into the air. "Detective Miles won't be back." His dark eyes focused on me. "Mr. Russo no longer works for me either."

My eyes widened, but before I could comment, the guard at the door waved me through. I found myself back on the street with a wad of twenties with which I was supposed to buy food. We'd agreed I'd keep the money as long as I kept the doors open for a year. Otherwise, I'd owe Mr. Ross, and likely there'd be hell to pay.

I knew the address of one of the serving girls I'd dismissed this morning and planned to send a runner to invite her back. I'd hang a 'help wanted' sign out and announce Marina's new opening tomorrow.

But first I had to make a shopping list.

CHAPTER THIRTY-THREE

Paul

I couldn't quite get used to Father's employees smiling at me, their deferential bows and shy greetings. As a hobo I'd been poor and every man had been the same, on one level. Now I was the boss, a rich man, yet I felt most at home on the factory floor. Except I was no longer one of them. I was part of the wealthy crowd, most of them arrogant pricks who took their riches for granted. I despised them because they had no respect for the little people and their daily struggles.

What a difference good clothes and full stomachs made. As a hobo I'd worked for most meals, often starved, had survived because of the support of others as well as my willingness to do what it took. Rich people never questioned why they had so much. They took it for granted, considered it a god given right.

What fools! For the first time since I'd returned and learned about my horrible mistake, I felt that my hobo days had not been wasted entirely.

I wondered how life would've been with Father running things. Sometimes I imagined walking the halls with Regi by my side. *You could've had all that.* That's when I took in a deep breath and erase the memory of my dying father from my mind because the darkness that followed otherwise snuffed me out like a black fiery cloud.

The shrill whine of the phone yanked me from my daydreams. "Sir, your wife is here. Shall I—"

The door flew open and Colene, dressed in an ankle-length mink coat and matching hat, swept in. "Is that where you spend all your time," she said, wearing a sweet smile. "I asked Mercer. He doesn't want to talk to me," she pouted. "I had to ask around where I can find you."

"I work, Colene," I said. "That's what men do."

"But Papa says you should spend more time with me." She patted her lower abdomen, which was flat as ever. "He's worried about your hours. Frankly, I am too. I hardly ever see you."

I fought to keep a neutral expression. "I've got a lot of catching up to do. Which you should know."

"But we could travel. I want to go to the Carolinas. It's so frightfully cold this time of year, just boring. And I need a change. Father says I'm too pale and the sea air will do me good."

"Why don't you go?" I said. "Take your maid with you."

"But I want you by my side. We'll visit friends, go to winter balls."

I shook my head. "Sorry, I can't. The company doesn't run itself and I—"

"Papa will keep an eye on it."

Is that what he told you, I wanted to ask. *Get me safely out of the way.* I swallowed my thoughts and produced a smile. "I appreciate your father's help, but this is something I've got to do myself." I hesitated. "Isn't Henry occupied with your family's business?"

Colene wrinkled her nose. "Not that busy. He's got lots of help."

"A general manager, right?" I said innocently.

"Papa doesn't talk much about work," she said.

Because you don't care. Except to spend his money and now mine... I scanned the paper stacks on my desk. "I've got to finish these reports..."

Sam

Life was tough without Arthur—much tougher than I had expected. It wasn't just that I missed him terribly. In the beginning I'd been elated to save the restaurant and honor Arthur and his wife. But I quickly realized I'd done my big friend a great disservice, overlooking or plain ignoring the many things he'd done.

Now that I was on my own, everything I couldn't delegate had to be done by me. I still helped with prep, but while customers ate, I was out front, greeting and seating, taking orders and collecting money. I'd hired a young cook, Dino, from Naples. He'd come over on one of the ships landing in New York to seek his fortune and over time had moved westward. In his late twenties, he was a redhead, quite talented and fast, but not too keen on cooking my Italian recipes. We spent several weekends cooking together and reviewing my dishes. Even Dino had to admit that it wasn't advisable to provoke the legendary Mr. Ross.

Mr. Ross ordered regularly and left substantial tips and I was soon able to pay back what I owed and begin saving again. Detective Miles did not return. A few weeks later, a note in the newspaper spoke of an unnamed policeman being indicted for corruption. I wondered if it was Miles or if Mr. Ross had fitted him with cement shoes and sent him on a swim in Lake Michigan. Like Mario Russo, Maggie's murderer.

I smiled grimly.

In earlier times, I would've been upset, but I didn't care anymore about the men's destinies. They'd probably destroyed other businesses and with them peoples' lives. Likely, they'd killed innocent folks. Like Maggie. And Arthur. Good riddance. Question was, did the police know that Mario Russo had killed Maggie? More likely, the next honest policeman would arrest me. I took a deep breath and had to trust that nobody cared about the unsolved murder of a prostitute, and hope nobody found me.

As Marina's flourished, I often wished that Arthur could've been there to see it. I updated the interior décor, asked our waiters to help paint. We redressed benches and tables with red pillows and red and white-checkered tablecloths. All staff wore red aprons and black shirts.

At night we sat together and discussed issues and devised improvements over a glass of red. Mr. Ross had come through with kegs of wine from Sicily, a new favorite among regulars.

As December approached, I decided to visit Mary Rose, secretly hoping to see Poppi. I'd wanted to go for months, but ever since Arthur's death, I'd been too busy to even get away for a few hours. My savings had grown to $350 and I'd soon be able to get the rest. My goal was to have everything ready at Christmas time and have Poppi move back in with me. We'd take turns watching her in the restaurant.

In hindsight, I wished I'd told Paul about Poppi. He would've probably offered to pay, but I realized I didn't want that. I wanted this to be my own money, produced with my own sweat and tears because Poppi was going to be mine alone.

Earned.

I carried an early Christmas gift, a baby doll I'd bought for $1.99 at Sears during a quick shopping trip. It was way too much money, but I hoped Poppi would remember me by it.

Guilt crept up in me as I walked toward Garfield Park. I hadn't had any time to inquire about Angelo, and with every month gone by, I was less convinced I'd ever find him.

Mary Rose's house looked even more dilapidated than during my last visit. The refuse in the front yard piled higher, gutters leaned or were missing altogether. My insides cringed with worry.

Since the doorbell was broken, I knocked. Nothing happened at first though I heard movement inside.

"Hello," I called and knocked again.

At last the front door was yanked open. A man in a grayish undershirt and a three-day beard glared at me. He was tall with powerful upper arms and wide shoulders and my worry and irritation turned to instant fear. Something in the man's reddened eyes looked unhinged like some evil force within was ready to erupt. I took a step back.

"What do you want?" he said.

"I'm Sam Bruno… here to see Poppi."

"You that girl who stole our daughter, murdered Maggie?"

She isn't your daughter and by the looks of it, you don't care anyway. But I forced a smile, knowing that arguing would only make things worse.

"You know good and well that I didn't kill Maggie. I just want to help," I said simply. "Make it a bit easier for you. Get you some money." *And take Poppi as far as away as I can.*

At the word 'money,' the man's pupils contracted and his lips parted. He leaned forward. By now I recognized it from a mile away: greed.

"Can I see her for a minute?" I patted my bag. "I've got a gift."

The man lingered uncomfortably close. "I thought you brought money."

"I did…I'll soon be ready. It's been very hard…my boss." I

233

closed my mouth. The drunkard didn't care a lick what I went through or that I'd lost Arthur. All he wanted was cash.

For a moment I was tempted to ask Mr. Ross for help. I was sure he'd support me and teach Mary Rose's husband a lesson. But what good did that do other than get even in a nasty way. Al Capone was a killer, but I was not. I would not stoop so low. I wanted to be a role model for Poppi. Teach her about goodness and… love.

The man turned abruptly and hollered, "Poppi, come here, on the double."

I almost cried out when I saw the little girl. Instead of growing an inch, she appeared smaller, her skin almost translucent. Except the area around her right eye bloomed bluish-green. Somebody had smacked her in the face. I let out a puff, bent low and opened my arms. *Not now, not here.*

"Poppi," I cried. "I brought you something."

The little girl appeared confused, even scared as her eyes darted between the big man and me. She took a tentative step, then another as if she expected punishment for her forwardness. I called her with my eyes, though I watched through a haze of tears.

"You remember me?" I whispered, ignoring the brute.

Poppi nodded. "Where is Arthur?" she said quietly and not at all like a three-year old.

"Arthur has gone to heaven," I said. I still held out my arms and finally the little girl pressed herself to my chest. I almost buckled from the force of feeling Poppi in my arms. Sweetness poured through me, a terrible yearning. I kept very still, so still I thought I felt the little girl's heart beat against my own ribcage.

"Will he come back soon?" said Poppi into my ear.

"I'm afraid he'll be gone for a while," I said, unsure how to explain the finality of death. Fresh anger brewed in my belly because I noticed the terrible smell emanating from Poppi. It was obvious she hadn't had a bath in a long time.

"You giving her the gift or not?" The drunkard stared down at us and I could've sworn he leered at my neckline.

Ignoring him, I leaned back to pat Poppi's chin, careful not to touch the swollen part of her cheek. "Look what I brought you," I said, allowing Poppi to pull the brightly wrapped package from my bag.

Poppi held the parcel as if she couldn't decide what to do with it. I had never given her presents so maybe Poppi simply didn't know.

"You can unwrap it," I said. "Here, I'll help you." I gently guided Poppi's hands to tear away the paper. "Do you know what it is?"

Poppi's eyes widened. "A dolly," she cried, pressing the baby doll to her chest. She looked at the brute who still towered near us. In her eyes stood fear. I wanted to cry then and carry Poppi away from the filth and cruelty of this place.

Instead I straightened. "I will be back on Christmas Day. I will have the money for Poppi." Despite my disgust I stepped toward the big man and his assaulting stench. My dread turned to rage. "I expect Poppi will bathe today and get clean clothes," I said. "We had an agreement that I expect you to honor. If anything happens to Poppi, I will not give you a dime and I *will* call the police for neglect."

The man didn't answer, but he nodded ever so slightly.

"Hey, darling girl," I said, bending low once more. Poppi was carrying the doll in her arms, patting its head. "I'll return very soon, you hear." I enfolded the girl in my arms and then tore away. More tears threatened, but I swallowed them away. I threw another warning glance at the man and waved at Poppi who waved back with her left, pressing the doll to her chest.

That picture imprinted itself on my mind like one of those photographs and from then on whenever I thought of Poppi. I saw her standing there on the doorsill of the ramshackle house, waving, with the tiniest smile in her eyes and what I preferred to think of as hope.

The weeks before the holidays were filled with ordering and prepping food, menu tweaking, crowd pleasing, serving, cashiering and keeping the peace. And as Christmas approached I had just one wish. Actually, three. But finding Angelo was close to impossible and the other thing, the thing I hadn't allowed to let myself think of, was absolutely impossible. Paul was married and gone out of my life. Once in a while I found him mentioned in the papers and each time I cut out the accompanying photograph to stick it in the little box behind my bed. Paul never smiled, but he looked regal and out of this world. My world.

And in the quiet hours early in the morning when I lay awake thinking about life and how I was going to raise Poppi, I couldn't help but think of Paul. The scene in the little room above Victor's pub repeated itself in unending loops. Sometimes, I imagined him touching me, removing my clothes and making love. I always scolded myself for being stupid…and I felt drained.

Only one thing helped, and that was hard work. So I jumped out of bed and raced into the day as if I could outrun the longing and the memories that scraped my insides. Most days, at least, I was able to find distraction.

CHAPTER THIRTY-FOUR

Paul

The morning of Christmas Eve I was back in the office. Colene had returned from North Carolina, laden with boxes and bags. She giggled and proclaimed that Santa had been busy.

I mumbled something about urgent business and left in a rush. I had to think about Mercer's information. Last night the old butler had served me a late dinner and then fidgeted uncharacteristically.

"What is it?" I had asked.

Mercer bowed. "Sir, I got word from my lady friend, the Sloan's housekeeper."

I forgot to chew, the bite of bread stuck to the roof of my mouth.

"Turns out that about two years ago Lola almost left because she'd not received pay for three months. Groceries were tight and they only bought the bare minimum. Old Sloan made a bunch of excuses, money tied up, misunderstandings with the bank, etc. Then overnight, the problems went away and everything returned to normal."

"You think that's when Sloan went to see my father?"

Mercer shrugged. "Possible."

"What if old Sloan borrowed money from Father? Or Father gave him a gift." I drew circles on the tablecloth with my spoon. "I didn't find any sign of a loan or a gift in the books."

"Miss Lola thinks there's something amiss with Sloan's

company, though."

"Oh, yeah?"

"Old Sloan used to leave for the factory every morning. He no longer does that. At least not regularly. And he's nervous, paces and sighs. Throws doors. Lola says, he used to be jovial and now he complains and yells at people."

I leaned back from my desk. Something had definitely happened. Was that why Sloan had pushed me to marry Colene? So he could get his hands on my family's money? I thought about Colene's return, the loose-fitting dress that showed no sign of a baby growing. How many months had passed since that night I still couldn't remember? Five at least. If Colene was pregnant, I was the Prince of England.

But Colene had only access to a household account and received a monthly shopping allowance.

I began to pace around the room. "I could really use your help, Father," I mumbled, coming to a stop in front of a framed photo. Before the doors of the Chicago Hospital, Father was shaking hands with a smiling man.

The generous donation of $250,000 by one of Chicago's most prominent inventors, Regibald McKay, will support the opening of a children's wing. Furthermore, Mr. McKay has pledged his support for years to come. Chicago Hospital and its small patients will be forever grateful.

The newspaper clip was dated February 1921, more than four years ago. I eyed Father who appeared to wink at me from the past. "What are you telling me?" I said aloud. The silence was absolute.

With a sigh, I returned to my desk.

The shrill whine of the phone awoke me and I almost toppled from the chair when I picked up the earpiece.

"Hello, Paul McKay here." Even before I finished my name, Colene's voice drilled into my ears.

"Honey, you didn't tell me we'll have guests tonight. You should've told me. I've got nothing to wear, and when are you coming home. You know it's Christmas Eve and—"

"I'll be home this afternoon," I said, throwing a glance at the grandfather clock in the corner: a couple more hours of peace.

"I don't think we've got any gifts," Colene continued as if I hadn't spoken. "You invite people, you've got to have things for them."

Something stirred in my mind, a memory, a list of accounts...Father's photo donating to the hospital. All of a sudden it clicked. "Thank you, Colene," I said before replacing the receiver.

In a flurry of activity I began rifling through the ledgers until I got to the page named '*charities*.' I reviewed this year's accounting pages. Credits had been entered every month, typically $20,000 to $30,000. Just a month ago, a debit for the entire year, amounting to $275,000 had been debited. Next to the entry it said donation Chicago Hospital.

I returned to the pile of accounting books to look for the previous year, 1924. The same had happened. Every month, payments had been credited, and twice during the year, the account had been brought to zero. Each time Chicago Hospital was the recipient of the donation, each time totaling $125,000. Father had really believed in the good the hospital did for its young patients.

I scratched my chin. I needed to shave, probably take a bath. I'd invited a few people from the company, some neighbors and clients. On a whim, I picked up the phone.

When the voice of Mr. Tatts came on, I asked, "I'm sorry to bug you on your day off, but who's in charge of donations...you know charitable giving? I don't think I've ever been asked."

"Yes, sir," Tatt said, "that would be Mr. Sloan. When your father was doing poorly, Mr. Sloan offered to help. I believe he's been good to his word."

"Has he then?"

"Sir?"

"Nothing, Tatts, we'll see you tonight."

My arm hovered over the phone. One more call. With a sigh I said, "Operator, Chicago Hospital, please."

Sam

On Christmas Eve I celebrated with my staff. Dino had decorated the restaurant with greenery and red bows and had baked delicate almond crest cookies and a cream-filled *torta*, his grandmother's recipe he'd carried in his jacket pocket all the way from Italy. We feasted on roast and homemade tagliatelle, enjoyed pudding, and gave each other small gifts.

On Christmas morning, I was in good spirits because Marina's was closed and in an hour I'd go and collect Poppi.

I poured a second cup of coffee, counted the money for Poppi…four hundred dollars in tens and twenties. As I bound the notes into a tight roll and turned to write a shopping list for the New Year, the door jangled open.

"We're closed," I called. Irritated about forgetting to lock after hanging up a new sign, announcing a New Year's eve special, I rushed to the door. I was proud of coming up with the idea, a four-course meal with three glasses of red wine included, some confetti, music, and the cook's special midnight dessert of German buttercream cake. One of my customers played accordion and had agreed to perform.

"If it isn't my girl!" Tony Moretti, dressed in a battered calf-length coat, filled the doorframe. "You sure were hard to find."

I froze and almost missed the second person standing behind him. The man had been my first lover and once been nice to me, but the girl….

Tina had aged, the skin around her mouth and neck saggy, her lips covered in gaudy red.

"So this is the hole you fell into," she chirped, gripping Tony's forearm.

I was so surprised that I couldn't think of anything to say. All I heard were warning bells. Tony's eyes were bloodshot, though he seemed alert, his gaze on me appraising…waiting…a lion stalking a gazelle. Tina's expression was cold and yet, there was that downturned mouth that spoke of envy. How had they found me?

"You lose your tongue again?" Tony chuckled, throwing the door shut and taking a step toward me.

Tony stood in the aisle to the entry and back stairs. The main dining area of the restaurant had no other exits. Realizing I was trapped, I cleared my throat. "What do you want?"

"Not sure." He waved an arm and moved closer. "Looks like you're doing well for yourself."

I shrugged, realizing that most of Tony's problems stemmed from being unable to decide on things and of course, a terrible drinking habit. "It's hard work, mostly."

Tony chuckled again. "You wouldn't happen to have some leftovers. Haven't eaten much yet. It's Christmas after all."

"Yeah, I'm starving," Tina chimed in. She marched to the counter and back, one hand trailing the tops of the booths. I wanted to kick her in her sagging behind.

"I've got a bit of almond cake left. Kitchen is closed today."

Something unhinged flitted across Tony's expression and I knew I'd made a mistake.

"You sure didn't mind cooking when it was on *my* dime," Tony said quietly. In a flash he grabbed my wrists and pulled me so close I smelled the alcohol. "If you aren't cooking, then you'll at least play nice." He squeezed my bottom. "You didn't mind before. Without me you'd still be a cheap prostitute at Fizzy's. The least you can do is thank me."

I forced a smile, my gut heavy with fear and a glimmer of fury. I wouldn't let him see either. "No need to get upset. I'll fix something and we'll talk." *Anything to buy time.* The streets were nearly empty today. None of my staff would be back till tomorrow, everyone celebrating the holiday one way or another.

Tony seemed to back off and slumped on a seat. "All right then. Just don't think you can play me."

"Life isn't treating you too shabby," Tina cried. That's when I remembered the roll of bills on the table…Poppi's money. Helplessly, I watched Tina stuff the cash into her cleavage. "I guess you owe me for stealing my customers."

"That isn't yours," I cried, reaching for Tina's arm. My cheek exploded as Tina slapped me—hard. Tears stung. A terrible fury ignited my insides, paired with the feeling of helplessness. If I attacked Tina, Tony would come to her aid.

Tina wandered over to Tony. "Aw, poor baby," she mocked. "Isn't she a sore one?"

"It's not mine." I carefully touched my aching skin, my gaze on the clock. Already eleven.

"Why should *we* care?" Tony said. "Now make us some food…and fetch wine."

He opened his coat and tossed his hat on a chair while Tina slumped across from him, her bleached curls jiggling. "Just be glad I don't call the police. After all you murdered Maggie."

Already on my way to the kitchen, I turned abruptly. "*You* told the police."

Tina's laugh was full of mirth. "It was easy. Just took a bit to find your stash under the floorboards. Police found your letters and the thirty dollars."

"You stole Maggie's money and accused me?"

Tina shrugged. "Maggie was getting on my nerve. Taking my

customers, just like you."

My eyes grew large and I whispered, "You killed her."

Tina rushed from the booth and gripped my throat, a movement surprisingly quick for her bulk. "Just be glad, it wasn't you," she hissed.

"Tina, sit down," Tony said, annoyance in his voice. Tina gave me a shove while letting go. Wordlessly, I stumbled behind the counter, pulled on an apron, my mind ablaze, my head throbbing. Tina had framed me, stolen Maggie's money. I'd been wrong about Mario Russo. My throat ached from the sudden attack as I set up my workstation. Had I had a gun at that moment, I'd have blown the stupid woman away. But my shotgun rested upstairs under the bed.

First things first. I tried to remember where Tina had stuck the money—Poppi's money. I needed it. Needed it now.

I'd told Poppi's stepfather I'd be back today. "I'll be there at noon," I'd said. "If you want the money, have Poppi ready to go."

I hardly knew what I was doing, throwing tomatoes, onions and garlic into a pan. I had leftover gnocchi from last night, I'd planned to eat for dinner. My mind whirled…maybe I could exterminate them. Where was the rat poison? They'd know if I left the kitchen, would guess my intention. I had to act naturally. My gaze casually wandered upward into the room and my eyes met Tony's. He was watching every move.

"Don't try anything stupid. I'll know." He got up and passing by the front door, turned the key and pocketed it. Ever so slowly he sauntered near. "Smells delish."

I ignored him and continued my meal. In the kitchen were no poisons, nothing to even put them to sleep. I'd kept a few sleeping powders, I'd found in Arthur's room, but Tony would never let me go upstairs. The feeling of entrapment returned, my throat tight as if the collar of my dress were choking me.

After my previous escape, Tony surely wouldn't even let me go to the bathroom alone.

I clunked the plates on the counter. "Done."

Tony grabbed the food and said, "And here I thought you were cooking with love."

I remained mute, cleaning up my workstation and washing pots. The familiar tasks usually calmed me, but today my fingers shook with nerves. I scrubbed and polished, but my mind refused to offer a solution. Not only had I lost Poppi's money. Who knew what Tony and Tina would do. Kill me? Would Tony force me to have sex? Unlikely with Tina here.

Tony and Tina were wolfing down their meals as if they hadn't eaten in days. They demanded wine and I served a cup, forcing me to leave the bottle on the table. My heart broke thinking about Poppi, who was waiting for me in vain. I had promised to be there. Promised to pick her up at noon. Now Tina had my money...held all the cards. My vision blurred as I dried the pan. I turned toward the wall and swallowed a sob.

Come on, Sam, think!

But there was nothing, just emptiness, a sort of giving into fate. Soon, Tony would—

The knock on the door was frantic and I flinched.

"Who's that?" Tony cried. He hurried to the door and suspiciously peeked through the glass. "We're closed," he yelled.

"I'm looking for Sam." The knocking resumed. "Please open, it's an emergency."

I nearly dropped the pan. I knew that voice. Rushing around the counter, I joined Tony. "Open the door," I said, trying to take in the figure on the other side of the glass.

"Please hurry." Mary-Rose's muffled voice was heavy with anxiety.

Tony awkwardly fumbled with the key and turned the lock, just as I pushed past him. I found myself face-to-face with Mary-Rose who was carrying Poppi.

"What's wrong?" I cried because Poppi lay unmoving against Mary-Rose's shoulder.

"Don't know for sure," Mary Rose said, not meeting my eyes. "Found her like this today. I want my money."

"Don't have it." I took in the woman's worn coat and dirty fingernails, felt her desperation. And for the tiniest moment I felt sorry for her. That's when I took a closer look at Poppi. The girl's eyes were closed and her cheeks glowed with fever. Something was terribly wrong.

"But you promised. I should take her back," Mary Rose cried, her eyes defiant.

"You came all this way," I stepped closer as fury rose inside me, "To sell Maggie's daughter...your niece. You didn't take care of her. And now...now" My voice cracked.

For a moment, Mary Rose stood as remorse replaced the greed in her eyes. She held out her arms. "Here, take her."

I cradled Poppi in my arms, sensing the instant heat, emanating from the small body. "It will take a while."

"Never mind," Mary Rose said, her gaze on Tina. "She's going to get us all sick. I wish I'd never said yes to Maggie." With that she hurried off, her head low.

"Why's Mary Rose bringing you a kid?" Tina asked. I could tell she wasn't pleased.

"Her name is Poppi," I whispered, though I wasn't really listening, my attention on the girl who just hung limply in my arms.

I didn't know much about illnesses, but it was clear that the fever was high. Too high. "Get me a cold cloth," I barked at Tony. Surprised at my attitude, Tony obeyed, returning with a dripping towel.

Gently, I bedded Poppi on a bench and wrung out the towel on the floor. Poppi's lips were chapped and her hands ice cold. She didn't really wake, not even when I placed the cool cloth on her forehead. My heart cramped in the knowledge that Poppi was very ill. She needed a doctor. Now.

But Tina had all my money. And it was Christmas.

"What's she doing here? She yours?" Tony asked.

"She is now."

"I don't understand—"

I don't care, I wanted to shout, but I had no energy for this drunkard and the murderess lunatic by this side. That's when I had an idea.

"Listen," I said, locking eyes with Tony, "I think Poppi may have Polio. You know, the disease that leaves you paralyzed…or dead."

"You sure," Tina cried, throwing a glance at the little girl.

"Not sure, no, but if I were you, I wouldn't risk it."

"She's your daughter." Tony made a face as if I held onto a giant cockroach.

"She's Maggie's daughter, the girl Tina killed." That's when I realized Tina had mentioned Mary Rose by name. Tina knew Maggie's sister, had read her letters when she found my hideaway under the floorboards. Mary Rose had told Tina about me and that's how Tony had found out about my whereabouts.

"That broad I mentioned." Tina's smug expression carried a

touch of doubt.

Comprehension registered on Tony's face. "So she belongs in an orphanage."

"No," I shouted. "*She belongs with me.*" I rushed up to Tony and though I was easily a foot shorter, I was no longer afraid. "I suggest you two leave before she makes you sick. You've got my money. Go."

Tony wordlessly turned and pulled on his coat and hat. He yanked Tina with him as she shouted, "Crazy bitch, good riddance!" The door slammed shut.

"What have they done to you?" I mumbled as I rinsed the cloth and got two more, just the way Mamma had done when Angelo had been sick with fever years ago. I wrapped one around each of Poppi's calves and reapplied the first on her forehead. Then I fetched a glass of water, and ever so slowly, placed a wet spoon on Poppi's lips. At first, the girl remained still, but after a while, she began to lick her lips. Encouraged, I kept reapplying the cloths and trickling a drop or two of water into Poppi's mouth. Dusk settled and I turned on a light in the kitchen.

I ran back and forth, but couldn't really tell a difference in Poppi's fever. In fact, it seemed to go higher. Poppi's face blazed as she whimpered weakly. Cold fear gripped me. A fear I'd never known.

Poppi could die. Right here. Tonight.

Panic settled in my bones and made thinking difficult. I knew I had to get help.

But who? I didn't know any doctors. Had no real friends. No money to go to the hospital.

But you know a phone number! A person who would help. He said so.

No, you can't. He's married. He'll resent you disturbing him.

But he said he'd help.

I wanted to shout with frustration, trying to calm the voices in my head. "You're going crazy," I said aloud. "Quit being a chicken." Who cared what Paul thought of me? All that mattered was Poppi.

With a last look at the girl, I rushed upstairs, pulled on coat and hat, and grabbed my warmest blanket, a felted thing I'd kept from Arthur's bed.

I wrapped Poppi into it, smoothed down her curls and placed my own wool hat on Poppi's head, until only her nose and eyes showed and hurried out the door. The phone was down the street at the pharmacist's. Not much of a walk normally, but with Poppi and my anxiety, every step seemed to drag into oblivion.

"*Prairie Avenue District 3412,*" I shouted into the receiver after depositing 5 cents.

"McKay residence," a nasal voice answered.

"Sir, I…need…Mr. McKay, please."

"M'am, Mr. McKay is currently entertaining. May I take a message?"

"Yes, it's Sam. I need help. It's life and death. Can he please call? I'll wait by the phone."

"You wait where?"

"Johnson's drugstore." I eyed the number on the apparatus. "1509…something. I don't know."

The other side was silent for a moment. Then the nasal voice returned. "I will ask Mr. McKay right now. Please hold."

Seconds passed. A minute. Then Paul's breathless voice: "Sam, what's wrong? What happened?"

To my surprise, I didn't get a word out. Hearing Paul brought back all the buried emotions, I'd tried so hard to forget.

"Sam? Where are you?"

A voice in the background mumbled… "Johnson's drugstore."

"Listen," Paul said. "Stay where you are. I'm coming to get you. Right now." And after a pause. "No, wait. Go to the restaurant… Marina's. You're still living there, right?"

"Yes."

"It's warmer, wait there."

My hand shook as I replaced the receiver. I kept Poppi pressed to my chest. Even through the blanket, her little body burned. Maybe Poppi was too hot and I was killing her right now with the blanket. Unsure, what to do, I pulled the hat off Poppi's head. In the shine of the street lantern, her little face glowed otherworldly.

As if she were already dead.

No! I cradled Poppi and hurried back to Marina's. The girl wasn't heavy, but I felt weak, almost faint by the time I stumbled into the restaurant.

I placed Poppi on the bench and began to pace. How much time had passed? The street was deserted, people celebrating with feasts and candles. They were merry and laughed.

When two headlights appeared outside, I tore open the door.

"Sam?" Paul's tall figure raced around the automobile.

In the dark I couldn't tell what he looked like, but I smelled his expensive cologne, the remnants of a fancy cigar.

"What happened?"

"It's Poppi, my little girl," I croaked, waving him inside.

"Who?"

"Maggie's daughter…a friend who died. She's sick, I mean, Poppi is sick and I'm worried…"

"Shhh," he said, gripping my forearms. Green eyes met mine and I felt the overwhelming urge to lean against him. Instead, I nodded toward the bench. Poppi, cheeks aglow, had not moved. Only her lips trembled a bit once in a while.

Without a word, Paul picked up Poppi, tucked the blanket around her and headed for the Chrysler.

"Lock the door. Let's go," he called over his shoulder. I rushed after him and crawled into the backseat, where Paul bedded Poppi beside me.

Only then did I notice that another man at the wheel. "On the quick, Mercer."

"Yes, sir," the driver said.

I didn't remember much of the trip, one palm on Poppi's chest, the other clamped across my own mouth.

"Dr. Brenner will be here shortly. I'll send our guests home after I show you your room," Paul said as we headed toward an expanse of lit windows.

All I could do was nod.

CHAPTER THIRTY-FIVE

Paul

I hurried this way and that, glad to be busy, glad to distract myself. I'd not had a chance to question Sloan, a nasty task I didn't look forward to. But worse, I needed time to digest the shock I'd felt, seeing Sam. I'd expected to have this chapter of my former life behind me. Somehow talked myself into forgetting. What hogwash. I'd been lying all this time. Colene would never work, even if she stopped drinking and became a human being. Neither could be expected—not really.

If I were honest, I'd loved Sam from the first moment I'd laid eyes on her in the train yard in Cincinnati. In her oversized coat, the silly shotgun by her side, she'd stolen my heart and tucked it securely away. And now that I knew, I'd do whatever I could for her. If she didn't care for me, at least I'd help the little girl.

"What do you think, it is?" I asked Mercer, who shrugged in response. Both of us were waiting in front of the room where Poppi and Sam were being seen by Dr. Brenner. I paced from one end of the landing to the other while Mercer sat in a chair, nursing a glass of water. I had turned down any drink. After the party I needed my wits. Although just seeing Sam in the restaurant, her eyes so full of worry, would've made me stone sober.

How long had the doctor been in there? The huge wooden clock ticked so slowly, I wanted to choke it to move faster.

When at last the door opened, I rushed to Dr. Brenner's side. "What? Tell me," I cried.

"The little girl...Poppi has pneumonia." Brenner took off his glasses and polished them with an embroidered handkerchief, his expression somber. "It's serious, an infection of the lungs that..." He cleared his throat and replaced his glasses. "The girl is small und undernourished. I'm afraid that bloodletting is not an option."

The door opened and Sam slipped out, her eyes huge pools of worry. "What is it, doctor?"

Dr. Brenner turned toward Sam. "I'm afraid, it's serious. She should be in the hospital."

"No," Sam cried as I imagined cold sterile rooms void of color.

"There's got to be something you can do," I said. "No matter the cost."

Brenner shook his head, his oversized white moustache wiggling. "There's a treatment, a pneumococcus vaccine. Mostly effective in the beginning stages." He looked at Sam. "When did she show symptoms?"

Sam hung her head. "I just got her tonight."

Dr. Brenner picked up his bag. "I'll check the hospital and will be back soon." He turned toward Sam. "You did the right thing. Make sure you continue the cool wraps to manage the fever."

With a nod Sam opened the bedroom door once more.

"Sam," I said quietly. Our eyes met and I wanted nothing more than to hold her close. But Sam's motionless gait and maybe Mercer's presence kept me from moving. Sam gave me a quick smile and disappeared, leaving me staring at the door.

"What's that woman doing here?" Colene, still dressed in a black sparkly gown, teetered toward me.

"She's an old friend who needed help."

Colene's eyes narrowed. "I remember that face. She was at our wedding. You spoke to her and..."

I forced myself to grip her forearms. A whiff of gin hit me. "Nothing happened between us. Her daughter is sick and we're going to try to save her."

A cackle rose from Colene's throat. "You always loved saving people. As long as they're poor and worthless."

I let go and sagged onto a chair opposite Mercer. *Poor is not worthless.* The woman in front of me was a stranger. Much more so than Sam, who I hadn't seen in months. But I had no energy to argue. I needed time to think, time away from everybody. I hardly noticed when Colene left in a huff and the hall sank into quiet.

"Sir, maybe you should rest? I can keep watch until Dr. Brenner returns." Mercer's voice was soft.

I shook my head. I'd forgotten Father's butler was there. "It's all right, Mercer. You go and lie down. I'll ring if I need anything."

I leaned back in the seat. I was dead tired, my legs full of rocks, yet my mind refused to rest. I thought of joining Sam inside, but then I felt guilty for wanting to be near her. *The little girl may die and you're pining? Lecherous fool!*

I closed my eyes, reliving my hobo days with Sam.

Sam

Though my body screamed for sleep, it was impossible to close my eyes. Poppi's breathing had gotten louder and the doctor had stuffed a second pillow under her back to raise her head.

At some point I heard arguing outside. There was Paul's calm voice and the shrill one of his wife, Colene. I couldn't understand what they said, but I knew for a fact, that the woman was angry. Likely at me.

Ordinarily, I would've fled. But Poppi was more important than some fight between husband and wife. I'd do anything to save Poppi. If it meant that Paul had a spat with his wife, I was willing to accept it. I wouldn't have cared if Colene wanted me dead.

Dr. Brenner had explained there was fluid in Poppi's lungs that made breathing difficult. A little while ago he'd returned, placed an oxygen tent over Poppi's bed and stuck a syringe in her arm. According to the doctor, we had to wait and see if Poppi was strong enough to fight the infection. The girl's limbs were so thin, they appeared almost translucent.

I returned to the washbasin for a cool cloth, I placed on Poppi's forehead.

"Hey, sweetie, it's Sam. You're safe now. I'll take care of you," I whispered. "I'll buy you a new dollie…and a stuffed bear." Tears blurred as I caressed Poppi's cheek. "And a new dress. Just get better now, you hear."

Poppi mumbled something and her eyelids fluttered.

"I'm right here," I said, crawling onto the huge bed next to Poppi. I placed myself next to the little tent, one hand on the plastic cover.

At dawn, I heard Paul enter the room. I had my back to him,

but I knew it was him. He stopped half way into the room and stood quietly. I felt his eyes on me, heard his uneven breath. Oh, how I wanted him close. But not now, not this. He was married. For the briefest moment, I wondered what Paul had told his wife about his new guests.

The next time I awoke, it was morning. A gray misty light filtered into the room. Outside, snowflakes twirled. The day after Christmas. Oh, so quiet.

Poppi. My gaze turned to the still form by my side. Poppi was dead.

I hastily leaned over the little girl, who still lay on her back. Her eyes were closed as before, but the torment of earlier had left. She looked peaceful.

"Oh no," I cried. That's when I noticed Poppi's chest rising and falling. She was sleeping. Carefully, I opened the tent and touched Poppi's forehead. Cooler. Not normal, but definitely not burning.

A sob escaped me.

"What?" came Paul's sleepy voice from the corner where he half lay, half sat in an armchair. I scrambled from the bed and stumbled into his arms just as he straightened. "Poppi's sleeping," I cried. "She's better."

Quivers ran through me in waves as Paul held me steady.

Our eyes met and I noticed his were as damp as mine. No words were spoken. I felt Paul's arms support me, felt his warm body.

To my disappointment, Paul led me back to the bed. "You need to rest," he said. "I'll get Dr. Brenner. He may have additional ideas."

I only nodded, my throat clogged with unspoken words. There were so many, they choked me. Paul didn't seem to notice. He covered me with the blanket and leaned over Poppi before tiptoeing from the room.

My every bone ached, yet I could not close my eyes again. Could not. Nor could I think about Paul. Not now when I had to concentrate on Poppi.

I rolled to my side and watched the girl sleep.

CHAPTER THIRTY-SIX

Paul

The following day, I moseyed around the house. One part of me felt relief. Poppi was out of danger and Sam's face had relaxed a bit. It was time to confront Sloan. Yet, I felt sluggish and tired this morning, couldn't really make my limbs obey. Just smelling the fried sausages sent bile to my mouth.

Was it a relapse from the illness I'd had a few months earlier? Had I contracted pneumonia from Poppi?

"What's wrong?" Sam watched me from across the lunch table, her eyes dim with concern and lack of sleep.

"Got to see somebody today and not looking forward to the meeting."

"Before you go...I want to thank you for—"

I raised an arm, the movement sending a fresh wave of nausea through me. "No need...excuse me." I raced to the bathroom and vomited. My stomach was on fire, the skin inside my mouth pricked with a thousand needles. Wiping my face, I vowed to ask Dr. Brenner's advice when he returned this evening.

When I returned to the dining room, Sam was gone and the table cleared. The thought of getting dressed and seeing Sloan seemed too much. With a groan I sank back into a chair by the window.

Strange that I hadn't seen Colene yet. She was surely up by now. I thought I should call for Mercer, but my mind seemed to go in circles. Words grew slippery, nothing to hold on to. I should get

up and ring the bell, yet I remained seated. My forehead was damp
with sweat and my throat parched. I needed water.

Even after returning to Father's home, I still preferred plain
water to drink. It was a reminder of my hobo days when fresh
water was a delicacy. I intended to remind myself how precious it
was, no matter how many types of fancy drinks Colene ordered for
our home.

The carafe of water stood on a sideboard, laughing at me.

Only a few steps, yet I couldn't make my legs move. Not even
a bit. Somewhere in the background I heard the front door and
Colene's laughter. Then her father's. The old Sloan was here. I
needed to...

"Paul?" Colene's face swam above me. "What's wrong,
honey?"

I babbled something, I couldn't make out. I was parched, just
dry as the desert, my throat so sore.

"I think he said he wants water." Sloan Senior was watching
over Colene's shoulder.

"What's wrong?"

Was that Sam's voice? Her features were all wrong, sort of
unfocused and blurry like an aquarelle painting.

"I think you should leave," Colene said in a cold tone. "Don't
you see he's sick? Probably got it from your daughter."

A cool palm landed on my forehead. So cool and soft. It was
the last thing I felt before sliding off the chair.

Sam

Alarm bells went off in me. Paul was sick, terribly sick and
something was bothering me about the woman and her father.
Why didn't they run to the phone to get Dr. Brenner?

Instead they were trying to force water into Paul who sat on
the ground, his back against the chair, his head lolling.

"Here, sweetie, drink," Colene said, supporting Paul's head.
"Just a sip. It'll make you feel better."

The man stood over them both, just watching. Waiting.

For what, I wanted to scream. That's when I knew. They were
as foul inside as an old apple.

They wanted Paul out of the way—gone. Wanted his money.
Why hadn't I seen it before?

Quietly I turned and once in the hall bounded upstairs, all the while hoping that Paul kept his lips closed.

Mercer was still with Poppi.

"Mercer, quick. Colene and her father, I think they're...Paul is really sick. Please stop them, they..."

Mercer jumped from his chair and put a calming hand on my shoulder. "What is wrong with Paul?"

"He's unconscious, just fell off his chair and I don't think his wife is helping..."

Mercer was already at the door, calling over his shoulder. "Call Dr. Brenner, quick."

I made the call and raced after the butler.

In the hall, I met Mercer. He was carrying Paul in his arms, the old Sloan by his side. On a whim I peeked around the corner into the dining room.

Colene was heading toward the kitchen, the carafe and water glass in her hand.

"Could I have some of that before you take it away?" I called, noticing the slight hesitation in Colene's shoulders.

"Let me get you a fresh one," Colene said, turning her back.

I sped up, glad I was fit from months of restaurant work. I caught Colene at the entrance to the kitchen and took hold of the carafe. "I'll help myself, thank you." In her surprise, Colene let go.

I quickly turned and walked down the hall and up the stairs. Let Colene try to wrestle the thing from me. There was no doubt in my mind that this water was as poisonous as the bite of a rattlesnake.

But Colene didn't follow. She probably figured that she'd get rid of me just as quickly. I headed for Poppi's room because there was an identical carafe on her nightstand. Throwing an anxious glance at the bed where the girl slept peacefully, I carefully opened the carafe's lid and took a whiff. Nothing. I held the bottle against the light. Nothing.

Was I wrong? What did I know about poisons? Not much. I hid the decanter in a sideboard, took Poppi's carafe, grabbed a glass and carried it to Paul's room. Colene was already there.

"Just needed a glass," I said as I poured water, one anxious glance at Paul on the bed. Mercer had covered him with a wool blanket and wiped his forehead with a damp cloth. He muttered something, I didn't understand, his eyes glistening.

Colene held out a pitcher. "I've got a fresh one for you."

A minute ago you wanted me out of your house and now you're hurrying to get me fresh water? "Thank you." I smiled at Colene over the rim of my glass and drank. There was the tiny flinch again.

"I guess you won't need this one any longer." Colene gripped my carafe and hurried out of the room. She hadn't looked at Paul once.

"What happened?" Dr. Brenner cried as he rushed to Paul's bed moments later, Colene entering behind him. "Who found him?"

"I did," Colene and I cried simultaneously. Colene glared at me before continuing, "I don't know what happened. He probably has the flu."

"Will you please leave the room?" Brenner's words were clipped. "All of you. Have Mercer wait outside, so I can call on him."

I dragged my feet. I needed to tell the doctor about my suspicion, needed to do it without the others knowing.

Out in the hall, Colene turned on me. "I thought you were packing."

Sloan senior chimed in. "And get that little rat out of the house before I call the police."

Panic rose in me. Paul could die. It was up to me to protect him. My gaze met the butler's who quietly nodded. I slowly walked toward Poppi's room, unable to think past Paul's still form on the bed.

"Miss Colene, the Hoffman's called earlier," Mercer said. "They wondered if you could ring them back. They mentioned a horse…"

"Oh," Colene cried. "They finally want to sell him." She raced off, having seemingly forgotten her husband and Sam. On the stairs, she hesitated. "Father, I'll need your help with the price. They'll surely want too much."

Old Sloan nodded and followed his daughter downstairs.

I turned on my heels and raced back to Mercer. "They poisoned him. I need to tell Dr. Brenner."

The old doctor was listening to Paul's chest when I entered, Mercer on my heels.

"Sir, I believe the water was poisoned."

Brenner's gaze turned to me. "You're sure?"

"The water," I said. "He was throwing up and very weak.

Collapsed and fell from his chair."

"When?"

"Less than an hour ago. I called right away."

"*You* called?" Brenner shook his head and turned back to the bed. "Colorless and odorless," he mumbled as he sniffed Paul's mouth and nose, "not arsenic." For a moment he hovered. Then he almost jumped off the bed, smacking a palm against his forehead. "Idiot. Of course. Get me a bucket, quick," he ordered, already rummaging in his bag.

"You stay," Mercer said to me. "I'll fetch a bucket."

I had lost feeling in my toes and feet as I watched Dr. Brenner lubricate a rubber hose. Paul couldn't die. I wouldn't allow it.

"Help me lift him. The pillow over there."

Paul half sat, half leaned as Mercer rushed in with the pail. Already Brenner was inserting the hose into Paul's mouth. "Nice and easy." He lifted the hose to his own mouth and sucked before hanging the end into the bucket. Paul choked and coughed as liquid ran from his stomach.

"Get me fresh water," Brenner barked, keeping his eyes on Paul.

Mercer again ran to Paul's bathroom and returned with a glass. Paul groaned as Brenner removed the hose and mopped his own face.

"Sam, see if you can wake him. We need to get water into him. Fresh water."

I leaned across the bed, gently cupping Paul's cheek. My eyes were wet, blurring. "Paul, it's Sam. Wake up."

Somewhere inside Paul a groan rose and his eyelids fluttered.

"Come on, 'Bo, I need you to get up," I cried. "We've got things to do."

Paul mumbled something and licked his lips.

"You're thirsty, I know," I said, pushing the cup against his mouth. "Drink, slowly."

Paul's lips opened a bit and he began to swallow.

"That's right. A little more, come on."

In my haze I noticed Dr. Brenner speaking with Mercer just as voices rose outside. "Where's that damn butler?" old Sloan growled. "Embarrassing to disrupt the Hoffman's the day after Christmas. I don't know what got into Mercer, he was always reliable."

"I want that woman out of the house. Now," Colene could be heard.

As Dr. Brenner turned toward Paul, he whispered over his shoulder, "Quick, Mercer, lock the door, call the police…"

Mercer rushed over to throw the lock before taking giant steps to the phone.

My focus never left Paul's face. He seemed to have regained a bit of color though his lids were still closed.

"I love you, you big 'Bo," I whispered. "Now drink some more."

Paul's mouth moved into the tiniest smile. "I knew it," he muttered. He opened one eye the smallest bit. "Hey."

"You're not going to get away that easy," I said, new tears pressing. "Not again."

Steps approached from the hall, followed by banging. "Dr. Brenner?" Sloan's voice was forceful. "You in there? Open at once."

Dr. Brenner, who'd returned to Paul's bed and was watching as I trickled more water into Paul, put a forefinger on his lips. "I'm very busy right now," he called loudly. Mercer had gripped a poker and stood arms raised by the door. "I'm afraid, I've got bad news…"

I couldn't keep myself from touching Paul's face. I wiped his forehead and brows and stroked his hair. A faint smell of soap reached me and at that moment my heart opened fully. I wanted to crawl into Paul's arms and never leave again.

He was awake now, the green of his eyes as dark as an evergreen forest. "What's happening?"

"Colene poisoned you," I whispered as the banging outside repeated.

"Mercury Bichloride." Dr. Brenner scratched his chin thoughtfully.

"I don't care what you do. Open this door," Sloan shouted.

"Or maybe her father," Paul said.

"They must believe you're dead," Dr. Brenner whispered. "The police will be here any moment." He turned toward the door. "It'll be just a few minutes. Ugly in here. Let me clean up so Paul is presentable."

"All right," Sloan said outside. "But hurry up."

"Father, that sick little girl is still in her bed." Colene's voice was loud and clear. "Where's that woman?"

"I'll take care of it," Sloan said. "Let's throw the girl out. The mother will follow."

CHAPTER THIRTY-SEVEN

Paul

I watched helplessly as Sam cried "Poppi!" and rushed to the door, only to be held back by Mercer.

"I'll go," he said. "Lock behind me."

"What're you going to do?" she whispered.

"Take her to my friend for now. Until this is sorted."

"Sloan's housekeeper?" I asked.

Mercer nodded. "Sloan won't know. Miss Lola will hide Poppi in her room upstairs. Only staff goes there." He rushed off and Sam relocked the door.

I wondered how Mercer knew these things, but I had to admit, I knew little about Mercer's private life. I'd always assumed the man had none. *You're an asshole,* I scolded, vowing to sit down with the old butler to learn his story.

The terrible burning inside had lessened, my throat almost bearable. Sam had retaken her seat by my side when terrible shouting erupted. Sloan's voice boomed through the walls, "Mercer, you're fired. Pack your things and get out of my sight."

Mercer's answer was too quiet to understand, but there were footsteps down and then a door slammed. How easy it was for Sloan to dismiss a man who he didn't even know. Who'd served the McKays for decades. A terrible fury brewed in me as I realized they thought I was dead. Out of the way, an easy naïve target. Now Sloan assumed himself in full reach of the company's money. With Colene's help they'd gut everything and Regibald McKay's legacy would wane.

An ugly chuckle escaped me as I tried to remember the first time I'd had symptoms, the slight nausea, the diarrhea and fuzzy headaches. I'd assumed it was another bout of the flu, making me tired and restless. Oh, how I wanted to jump out of bed and strangle Sloan and his daughter. All I did was fidget keeping my eyes on Sam by the door, her shiny black hair distracting me from my pathetic body.

The doorbell rang.

"That must be the police." Dr. Brenner stepped next to Sam, listened intently and then opened the door to hear better.

Sloan's voice drifted up from the entrance. "No sir, I think that has to be a mistake. Everything is fine. My daughter, Mrs. McKay, is right here. Sure, yes, I'll extend your holiday wishes to Mr. McKay. Of course, yes, to you too."

Brenner closed the door and held Sam by the shoulders. "No matter what, don't open this door, until you hear my voice. I'm going to catch them before they drive off. The Sloans mustn't know Paul is alive."

He was gone in a flash and Sam locked the door again.

Across the room our gaze met. The blue was intense and for a moment I floated. She'd aged, matured, looked like a real woman now. There were new curves, still gentle, but oh so womanly. My throat constricted. Even in my weakened state, half dead just an hour ago, I realized how her presence was all I needed.

Downstairs, Sloan shouted something and Brenner calmly answered that he had to report Paul's death to the police. A door slammed.

For a moment there was silence. Then came Colene's shrill cries. "Why didn't you tell them, Father? What are we going to say when they hear about Paul's death?"

"Leave it to me," the old Sloan said as the doorbell rang anew.

More talking followed, several voices mixing, then footsteps. "I'm sorry, we're just in shock," Sloan said outside the door. "He's been ill for a while, just didn't want people to know. Probably had one of those dreadful diseases. All that time on the road with no decent food. A shame."

"I'll never celebrate another Christmas," Colene whined. "Oh, my poor Paul."

The doorknob turned. Sam and I looked at each other,

watched the doorknob wiggle and still again.

"Why is it bolted?" A forceful voice asked. "You have the key?"

"Eh, no," Sloan said.

"I instructed the person inside to keep the door bolted." Dr. Brenner's voice was unmistaken and I sighed with relief. "It's all right, Sam, open up."

Sam unlocked and threw the door wide open.

Two men in uniform, Dr. Brenner, Colene and the old Sloan spilled into the room.

"We were hoping to spare you the sight—" Sloan stared at me and I couldn't help but wink at him with a half smile.

"Not dead yet," I said dryly. "Despite your best efforts."

"Paul, you're alive," Colene cried, throwing herself on the bed.

"Spare your theatrics." I lifted my arms, palms out, not wanting to make contact with the black widow.

"Detective Anderson," the larger of the two uniformed men said. He was heavy-set and looked to be near sixty, though his eyes were sharp and appeared much younger. "Mr. McKay, I presume, please explain."

"I believe my wife and her father tried to poison me."

Sloan's right arm flew to his chest. "Never would I hurt the son of my best friend."

I eyed the man who at one point I'd considered closer than an uncle. "Really?"

"What an outrageous lie," Colene chimed in. "I bet that...that floosy did it."

"She had nothing to gain," I said, my voice sharp and cold. "You, on the other hand, everything."

Sloan shook his head in mock disgust. "Just because you were sick doesn't mean we had anything to do with it."

Detective Anderson raised an arm. "Please gentlemen, let's take this slow." He turned back to me. "Why do you think you were poisoned?"

I opened my mouth and closed it. Sam had told me. Now that I thought about it, it made perfect sense. But I hadn't suspected, not once, that somebody could be so evil.

"I was feeling ill and then today I collapsed. My wife and I don't—"

"Just as I said," Colene cried, "he's been sick." She produced a smile. "I'm so happy you're feeling better."

"With all due respect," Anderson said, "I need more evidence."

"If I may," Dr. Brenner said. "I think I'm partially at fault. I should've known, but then…" He sighed. "The poison used here was Mercury Bichloride, a colorless and odorless medicine. You may remember *Madge Oberholtzer's* sad demise, her terrible rape the KKK man Stephenson and—"

"What does that have to do with—" Sloan thundered.

"Sir, let him speak or I'm going to remove you from the room," Anderson said.

"Well, Miss Oberholtzer took Mercury Chloride to end her own misery before she could be killed. It was all over the news last March."

Colene cackled. "I doubt Paul wanted to commit suicide."

Ignoring her, Brenner went on, "Mercury Chloride is also available as a powder and I prescribed it to a member of this household a couple of months ago." He seemed to struggle with himself. "It is used to treat syphilis, rubbed onto sores to be exact."

I stared and looked at the people in the room, the air stuffy with the number of bodies present. Who in my household was getting treated for syphilis? That's when I noticed Colene's cheeks, which had taken on the color of smashed tomatoes. And I knew. Understood why she'd never undressed in front of me. Understood her craziness, the outbursts and moodiness. She'd contracted it by sleeping around. Before we'd met or maybe….

"I'm sorry." Dr. Brenner's eyes were on me. "I should've said something, but I'm required to maintain confidentiality. When there has been an attempt on somebody's life, though…"

"Who is receiving treatment?" Anderson asked.

Colene's laugh was chilling. "Dr. Brenner isn't even a good doctor. But then, how would you prove such a ridiculous charge?"

"That's where I come in," Sam said quietly. "This morning when Paul collapsed I happened to witness Mrs. McKay removing a carafe of water. The same carafe Paul had drunken from. The same carafe Colene and her father used to try and feed to Paul even after he collapsed. He only drinks water. Even I know this, and I've hardly seen him over the last year."

Colene's eyes squinted suspiciously. "You drank from it and you're fine."

"See, that's where you're wrong," Sam said. "I switched out the carafe when I went upstairs, thinking it may need to be preserved. You saw me drink from the decanter I'd kept in Poppi's room." She smiled. "If you like I can get the carafe, Mrs. McKay tried to pour out earlier."

"Nothing but lies," Colene cried. "Why is she even still here? I want her out of this house."

"She's staying," I said quietly.

"Sam, why don't you fetch the water?" Anderson said, waving at his colleague. "Welsh here will accompany you."

As Sam left the room with the officer, I watched Sloan. "While we're at it, I've got another reason or motive why my wife and Mr. Sloan here want me dead." I watched Sloan's mouth quiver just the slightest bit. Time for the bastard to get nervous.

"I took over my father's company in the spring and noticed that something was amiss. I just didn't understand what until just yesterday. You see, Mr. Sloan's company, Sloan Furniture, got in trouble a few years ago. A lot of the wood they'd purchased to manufacture their pieces had been destroyed by a wood boring beetle.

"They lost their entire inventory, not just the raw wood, but a good portion of their finished product. Sloan kept it private, but he was almost bankrupt. That's about the time my father fell ill and asked his best friend to help. Sloan here was happy to oblige. He funneled moneys meant for gifts and charitable giving into his company. Hundreds of thousands of dollars went to prop up his failed business instead of help the children's ward at Chicago Hospital."

My gaze never wavered as I spoke. Sloan turned red, then pale, rubbing his chin repeatedly. "Just yesterday afternoon I spoke with the hospital and learned that no donations had been made in the past two years. Yet, that money left our company, signed for by Mr. Sloan here."

"You weren't here, son. You were gallivanting the world, accusing your father when it had been your mother who—"

I cringed, yet I couldn't let Sloan see how deeply his words stung. My smile grew wider. "You stole from your best friend. A man who trusted you," I seethed. "And from me."

Anderson looked back and forth between Sloan and me. "I think we better take this to the station. I will call for help to get your statement—"

In a sudden vicious movement Sloan shoved Anderson in the chest. The officer stumbled backwards and hit his head on the post of my bed. Sloan rushed out the door. I jumped up and immediately sank back as dizziness engulfed me. Detective Anderson was out cold and Sloan on the move.

Colene just stood near the window as if she were making up her mind about something.

Sam

I was walking back from Poppi's room, the carafe in one hand, when the old Sloan hurried past me and down the stairs. A cry of disgust came from inside Paul's bedroom.

My heart jumped. Had Sloan hurt Paul?

Detective Welsh, who'd accompanied me to fetch the carafe ran into Paul's room, reappeared and chased after Sloan.

Below, on the first floor, I watched Sloan reach the entrance when Mercer appeared out of the nowhere and tackled him to the floor. Both men grunted, Sloan attempting to rip Mercer's sparse hair from his scalp.

A grim smile settled on my face as Welsh grabbed Sloan from behind and attached handcuffs.

With sudden ferocity, fingernails dug into my throat from behind.

"You tricked me," Colene hissed into my right ear. "You stole him from me."

You were going to kill him, I wanted to cry. But there was no air. Bony hands dug into my throat and squeezed my windpipe. One hand still safeguarding the carafe, I frantically tried to push against the pressure. Colene was still behind me and surprisingly strong, shoving me against the balustrade and back...back until my upper body hovered above the handrail. From the corner of my eye, I watched the tiled entry hall below, a fall of at least twenty feet. I'd either die or break my back.

Stars appeared in my vision, flashes of light. I gurgled.

No air.

"Why don't you just die?" Colene panted at my ear.

My vision blurred. The stars turned black. *She's going to kill you.*

Why was nobody coming? I needed to cry for help, but my throat was no longer able to produce any sounds.

With the glass carafe still in my right hand, my balance was off as Colene slowly lifted me across the railing. *Use it!* It was my evidence, the way we could prove the poisoning. *Too late.*

With a last effort, I swung one arm up and over my head straight into Colene's forehead. The glass burst as water splattered across the painted features. Colene, a surprised look on her face, crumpled to the floor. Blood spurted from a two-inch cut on her forehead, mixed with the water and seeped into the carpet.

I leaned sideways and gulped air. My throat ached as if it were filled with barbed wire. At last I produced a yelp.

"Sam?" came Paul's voice from the bedroom.

"Out here," I squeaked.

Paul appeared in the doorframe and stumbled toward me, his eyes on my neck and then on writhing Colene, the blood. "What happened?"

Colene whined from below, "She tried to kill me. Help."

"She choked me." I pointed at the glass shards. "The poison water...our evidence."

Paul leaned over the railing. "Detective, up here, quick."

"Where is Detective Anderson?" I croaked as I stepped back two feet to put space between me and Colene.

"Sloan hit him hard. Anderson is unconscious and Dr. Brenner is trying to revive him."

"What happened?" Welsh, out of breath, appeared on the landing.

"She wanted to kill me," Colene moaned.

I stared in wonder at the woman who'd cold-bloodedly poisoned her husband and now lied about the attack on me. Welsh's eyes were on her.

"I think the evidence is clear," I said, forcing myself to straighten. "Colene attacked me from behind, choked me and I had to use the carafe to save myself."

Paul bent over me and carefully touched my throat. "Officer, take a look at this. Red and blue splotches—each finger is still visible."

Colene cackled, sitting up and dabbing at the cut on her forehead. Blood ran in rivulets on both sides of her nose and dripped down her chin. "What a joke. I'm injured, Detective. Call for backup. That woman needs to be arrested."

Uncertainty showed in Welsh's face.

"Oh, for goodness sake," Paul cried, leaning heavily against the banister. "She tried to kill me and now she attacked my friend. Who are you going to believe?"

"Use some common sense, Welsh." Detective Anderson stood in the doorframe, holding a towel against his temple.

"Sir, I—"

"Call for backup, then start taking statements," Anderson ordered. "I've got to sit down again." He threw a glance at Paul. "And you should be in bed."

CHAPTER THIRTY-EIGHT

Paul

I sat reading by the fire, though the lines of Edith Wharton's *The Age of Innocence* never made it to my brain.

I felt out of sorts and it wasn't because of the poison. I was feeling stronger and Dr. Brenner had assured me that I'd make a full recovery. Colene was in custody along with her father. Detective Anderson had swiftly organized a team of officers, who'd even managed to rescue a bit of the water from the shards of the carafe. I had turned over my accounting books to the police. Anderson had called earlier to let me know that Colene and Henry would be arraigned.

Yet.

What? What was the matter?

It was Sam. After things calmed down and Mercer had returned with Poppi, Sam had carried her upstairs, avoiding eye contact.

What did you expect, I scolded. Poppi almost died. Then I'd been poisoned. And thanks to Colene, Sam had almost died too. I'd had a wonderful dream, Sam telling me that she loved me. She'd called me 'Bo. A smile flittered across my mouth. Wishful thinking was a great thing.

"I'll be going then." Sam stood in the doorway, dressed in coat and hat. She'd wrapped Poppi in a blanket and carried her on one hip. "I'll return the blanket once I've washed it."

I straightened with difficulty, the book falling on the floor.

"You better rest," Sam said. "I don't know how to thank you enough. You saved Poppi's life." Her eyes glittered brightly, a summer day of blue.

I scoffed, "You saved mine."

"I guess then we're even." There was that brightness again.

"Where are you going?"

"Oh, home. Marina's is supposed to be open already," Sam laughed. "Probably have a bunch of customers complaining."

"You've come a long way," I said. Why couldn't I think of something smart to say, something that would stop Sam from walking through these doors. My forehead ached and I rubbed it furiously.

"You need to rest," Sam said. "Please tell Mercer that I'll miss him."

What about me? Will you miss me, I wanted to cry. Still, I couldn't speak. There were things between us, unspoken things, secrets I'd kept. The space between us grew as the room filled with rigid silence. What was it? Guilt? Regret?

Sam nodded with her shiny eyes and headed for the door. A click and she was gone. The room felt instantly colder. Deserted, almost hostile, despite the crackling fire.

Sam, I thought and despite the roaring fire, the skin on my arms rose into goose bumps.

"Where is she?" Mercer carried a tray with two cups of tea and tiny sandwiches.

I looked up from the book I could not read. "Who?"

"Sam."

"Oh, she sends her regards and left."

"Left?"

I reluctantly faced Mercer. In the short time I'd been back I'd come to appreciate the old man's quiet friendship. "Took Poppi and returned to her restaurant."

Mercer's right eyebrow lifted. "Curious." And after a pause during which he carefully placed the tray on the table and served me a cup, "What did you tell her?"

"What do you mean?"

"You must've sent her away."

"No, no. I didn't. I…she stood there in the doorway and…"

"And…"

Strangely, Mercer sank on a footstool by the fire, sighing. "You're a bigger fool than I thought."

"What—"

Mercer raised an arm. "Listen to me, you stubborn Irish dupe. You love her, right?"

I stared. Had the old butler just insulted me? How did he know…

"You don't have to answer. I know you do." The corners of Mercer's mouth twitched the tiniest bit. "Why didn't you tell her?"

I shrugged. "She's long moved on. Might have a man in her restaurant for all I know."

"Fool!" Mercer jumped from the stool and came to a stop in front of me, a movement much too quick for the old man. To my surprise, Mercer's expression softened. "You didn't do anything wrong, you know."

"What do you mean?"

Mercer's gaze held mine. "Accusing your father when it was really your mother." He looked away for a moment and cleared his throat. "I'm to blame just as much as your father and the other adults around here."

I couldn't speak because there was a lump the size of a baseball in my throat.

"I know you blame yourself for walking out on your family," Mercer continued. "And I blame myself for allowing it to happen." His eyes filled with tears and I realized it was the first time I'd seen Father's butler cry. "You were just a kid. A stubborn one at that." Mercer smiled through his tears.

"I should've known," I said as I felt the lump release into my throat and eyes. "I was stupid."

"Sure you were stupid. Like every teenager—no more, no less." Mercer's bony hand came to rest on my shoulder. "Guilt will eat you alive. It's time you forgive yourself."

I nodded. Mercer was right. I didn't owe Father any longer.

And all of a sudden, a bubble rose from my gut and I began to laugh. Mercer's surprised expression changed to a smile and soon we were both hollering.

When the room grew quiet once more, Mercer asked, "You remember anything from the time you passed out? When you got poisoned?"

"Not much. There seemed to be lots of people milling in the

bedroom."

"You know that Sam saved you or Colene would've fed you more of that poison and you'd be dead now?"

"The detective told me."

"When you were on the verge…" Mercer took a deep breath. "We weren't sure if you'd live, Sam sat on your bed. She talked to you. Called you 'Bo, and you know what she said?"

I remained mute, my gaze glued to Mercer's reddened cheeks.

"She told you she loves you, always did."

Something hot and something cold took hold of me. *Sam loves me!* I was an idiot. Too blind to see. Too stubborn to ask or invite her to stay. And something else registered. Had I not gone away to become a hobo, I would've never met Sam. I'd paid a price, a high price, but the anguish that had ruled me ever since I'd learned the truth about Mother was gone.

"So you see," Mercer went on. "You let her go. She probably thought you'd want to live your rich lonely life in this old mansion by yourself." He chuckled. "Oh, what a daft idiot."

I climbed from my chair faster than I'd moved in days. "I *am* a daft idiot." I patted Mercer on the back. "Mercer, man, you just saved my life."

"That was Sam."

But I was already at the door.

"Sir, I better drive you?" Mercer called after me. "You're supposed to rest."

"Then get your coat," I cried as something wonderful wrapped around my heart.

CHAPTER THIRTY-NINE

Sam

Leaving Paul had been the hardest thing since watching Poppi almost die of pneumonia. In a way, it was harder. My insides ached with every step as I took the streetcar back to Marina's. He'd looked so fragile, not at all like the strong man I remembered. And yet, there was this control, this authority in his shoulders and his expression. And in those green eyes, which always showed his emotions.

He'd acted strange. Probably suffered from shock and the poison, the knowledge he'd been betrayed by his own wife and his father's best friend. For money.

People never changed. It was always like that. The rich took from the poor. The rich took from each other. Who cared about the hurt they caused.

A handful of people lingered in front of Marina's, and I decided to let them in. I needed work and routine, needed to get busy doing what I loved—the comfort of cooking.

"Where've you been, girl?" one of them called.

"We missed you," another cried.

"Merry Christmas," a third said, patting me good-naturedly on the back.

"It'll be a while," I announced, forcing a smile.

"We don't mind," my customers said.

It made me smile even though I felt all soft and weepy inside. I placed Poppi on one of the benches with lemonade and a few cookies leftover from the restaurant party and went to work.

Kneading the dough was comforting, yet despite the calming chat of my regulars, the bubbling tomato sauce, and the rich aroma of olive oil and baking bread, I wanted to cry. For a short time I'd allowed myself to imagine a life I was not going to have. Never. I was a nobody, a cook in a worker's restaurant, a former prostitute and an adoptive mother to the daughter of a prostitute.

I served plates of fresh pasta with heaps of cheese, butter and bread, poured drinks and found absolutely no joy in any of it. It astounded me, this emptiness, this feeling of loss.

I'd always expected to be happy once I'd be able to cook. Not only was I able to do what I loved, thanks to Arthur, I owned a restaurant. The day Al Capone had given me money, I'd found a letter in Arthur's possessions. A letter addressed to me.

Dearest Sam,

I assume that I'll be gone when you read this. I thought it best to be prepared. I loved you like my own daughter and so wished to see you raise Poppi. It is not meant to be. So I'd like to leave you with a bit of advice.

Love, my dear Sam, is the most precious gift, we flawed humans can give and receive. Find it and hold on to it. You're in my heart forever.

Arthur

In the back of the envelope I found a will in which Arthur bequeathed his possessions to me.

And Poppi was mine now, a little girl I could love and raise well. I would help her forget the terrible time at Mary Rose's house, and love her like Arthur had suggested. I'd come far since that day when I'd left Over-the-Rhine with not a penny in my pocket. Mamma would be proud to see me now. Angelo would too.

All this time I'd hoped that Angelo would one day walk through these doors. But he'd never returned to Paul's place. The emptiness I felt about his existence had grown into a huge hole and my memory of his features was fuzzy. What I would've given for one of those photographs.

The sudden loneliness took my breath, and I had to stop and lean against the stove. That's when I heard Poppi's small voice. She'd discovered one of her old toys, a wooden horse and was showing it to one of our regulars.

I scoffed and resolutely grabbed a dishrag. I wasn't alone at all. I had Poppi, and I had my patrons.

Deep in thought, I cleared the tables. I felt the eyes of my customers on me, their curious stares. They tried to joke and make me laugh and I smiled gratefully.

"We're closed," I said when the door jingled open.

"I'm not hungry," Paul announced.

My head jerked up from counting change. What was he doing here?

Paul was serious, not even the hint of a grin on his face as he came to a stop in front of me.

"Sam Bruno, I love you."

The words hit my ears, but it took several seconds for them to reach my brain. I watched incredulously, took in those green eyes, the scent of citrus aftershave.

That's when I took a step back. "I've got to clean up," I whispered as memories of Beatrice's parlor returned. My cheeks burned.

"Sam, what is it?" Paul's eyes drilled into me.

"I...can't," I cried and rushed behind the counter, my safety zone.

"Can't what?" he said, following me. He was much too large for the narrow aisle, cutting off my escape.

Tears choked me as I gripped a cleaning rag. Gentle hands took it away and pulled up my chin until I had to look at the man who'd occupied my thoughts and taken my heart for the past year.

"Tell me," he said.

I swallowed, my mouth dry. At least he'd know and I could move on. "You were right," I said. "As soon as you left me on the roof at Victor's, I got in trouble. I was a prostitute."

Paul's eyes were green pools—fathomless. "Is that where you met Tony?"

I nodded, my throat too thick to speak.

"I can easily top that," he said. To my surprise, he sighed. "I pretty much killed my father because I ran away thinking he'd been unfaithful, causing Mother's suicide." He scoffed, his voice bitter. "Turns out, she'd had a lover all those years and took her life once he died in the war." A lone tear rolled down his cheek. "For seven years I ran around falsely accusing my father."

"But you didn't know," I cried.

And with one step I nestled into his arms. Behind me

applause exploded.

The wedding was small. Just a few people—Dr. Brenner and Mercer, a couple of regulars from Marina's, and a few of Paul's family friends.

Colene had been sentenced to eight years in jail, the advancing illness a mitigating factor. Dr. Brenner seemed to think she wouldn't survive more than a year anyway. Talk of her pregnancy had faded as it became clear she had never been pregnant. Dr. Brenner had confirmed that due to their limited encounters, Paul was free of disease.

The divorce had been quick and final. Sloan was still waiting for his court day because additional evidence of accounting irregularities had come to light. Detective Anderson seemed to think Sloan would go away for a good long time as well.

Tina had been arrested after I told the Detective about Tina's admittance of killing Maggie. Turns out, she was Beatrice's daughter, which explained why she got away with so much. I didn't know what happened to Tony. Not that I cared.

Miss Lola, the Sloan's housekeeper, had moved in, much to the delight of Mercer who had a new spring in his step.

"You happy?" I asked Paul, laying snuggled against his chest. The old fireplace roared and filled the room with comfortable warmth. Above it gleamed the old Winchester. And it occurred to me that for the first time I felt at home. The terrible urge to find a place—my place—to be comfortable had faded. Like Paul, I'd arrived.

All this wandering had led me here. And now I knew it wasn't really about the place, but a feeling of belonging and being with the people we loved. Arthur had been right.

I let out a slow breath and smiled, thinking back to the time when Paul had visited me at Marina's. "You've come a long way," he'd said. He'd been right, too. I *had* come a long way. Against the odds, I'd rebuilt Arthur's restaurant and created independence. Even if I had Paul, Marina's was my treasure, a reminder of my strength and something to cherish in Arthur's memory.

This evening we'd undressed each other and made love unhurriedly with the lights on and our eyes open. Paul's hands on my body ignited fires wherever they landed and I finally discovered what making love really meant.

"Hmm." Fingertips glided along my shoulders and down one arm.

I shivered. "I never knew how good skin on skin feels…your touch."

"Hmm."

I got on one elbow, though I couldn't stop grinning. "Forgot how to talk, Mr. 'Bo? You're awfully quiet this morning."

Paul smiled and pulled me close. "I'd rather do something else.

"Oh, that."

"Hmm."

The End

EPILOGUE

Sam

"Hurry," Paul called from the entrance to the garage. "We don't want to be late."

"Coming," I laughed, placing a wool cap on Poppi's head. Spring had arrived in Chicago, but even this late in April the winds still blew fiercely. "Why do I have to go anyway?"

"I think you'll like it." Paul closed the door behind me and slipped into his seat.

I watched quietly out the window as we weaved down Michigan Ave. This morning I'd stopped by Marina's like I did almost every day. The Italian cook, Dino, was running things. Luckily, he'd discovered a new love for my Italian recipes and was doing a great job.

Outside, the trees were dipped in fresh green. Men and women rushed along, their arms heavy with shopping bags.

A skinny teenage boy was selling newspapers at the corner. "People demand modification of Volstead Act by nine to one," he shouted. "Pony Inn Massacre—Al Capone accused of killing Assistant State Attorney Bill McSwiggin."

Prohibition was a total failure, I mused. The production and sale of alcohol had never stopped—not even close. Instead, the industry had been taken over by bootleggers and gangsters. I thought of my first visit with Mr. Ross, who'd helped save Marina's. Had it not been for the government's failed policies, he'd never have risen to such fame and wealth. Everybody carried a role and a responsibility. The way I saw it, the U.S. government's foolishness had paved the way for the likes of Al Capone and George Remus.

Yet, both had been kind to me, which showed that people with power could still treat every-day people with respect. In the end, it didn't matter how much money a person had as long as they maintained their humanity. I knew Paul would always remember and honor others no matter where they came from. And I loved him for that.

Along the road, handbills announced the second Woman's World Fair. I smiled. This afternoon I'd visit and learn all I could about publishing a book—a cookbook to be precise, a collection of my recipes along with advice on how to make perfect pasta dough. I'd dedicate the book to Angelo.

"You ready?" Paul asked, pulling me from my thoughts. Chicago Hospital loomed as he parked the Chrysler.

"Mr. and Mrs. McKay," Director Fullman cried and opened his arms. "So nice to meet you."

"We thought we'd drop off a belated Christmas gift," Paul said. He pulled an envelope from his jacket and handed it to the man. "I apologize for not honoring my father's plans for the past two years. This, I hope, will make up for it."

Fullman carefully removed the paper from the envelope. "Very generous, Sir, and Mrs. McKay. On behalf of the children's wing we thank you."

I placed an arm around Poppi's shoulders. $150,000 was a fortune, but then it was nothing when one considered the suffering of innocent children. A long time ago, I'd thought that Maggie would save me. And she had. Not with money, but with Poppi, who'd captured my heart as securely as the Federal Reserve kept its stacks of gold.

"If you wouldn't mind, I'd love to show my wife the children's ward," Paul said.

Director Fullman rose. "Of course, yes."

Paul waved. "No need. I'm sure you're plenty busy. We'll find the way."

"As you wish." Fullman bowed and led us to the door.

The children's wing had been painted in yellows and soft pinks. Butterflies and colorful birds hung from the ceiling in the corridor.

"I didn't know you were *that* interested," I whispered as we headed down the corridor.

"Look," Poppi said, pointing at a play area at the end of the hall, filled with low seats and benches, wooden toy trucks, dolls and stuffed bears. She pulled free and took off on stubby legs.

I watched her run, squeezing Paul's hand.

As we neared the play area, I noticed that Poppi was watching a man sitting with a brown-haired boy in a wheelchair, not much older than Poppi. The man was reading from a book.

That's when my knees buckled and Paul's arm kept me from falling. The man had apparently noticed the nearby shadows and looked up from his pages. He had blue eyes just like mine. As recognition flooded them, he jumped from his seat and embraced me.

"Angelo," I cried, leaning against the brother, I'd missed for two years.

"How did you find me?" he said as his gaze moved from my face to Paul's.

"There're ways," Paul smiled. "Though it took longer than I wanted."

I held onto my brother, my fingers clamped into the coarse fabric of his coat. "What happened to you? I thought you were dead."

A shadow ran across Angelo's features, but then he smirked. "I'm here."

"Angelo, the story isn't finished," a small voice said.

Angelo turned to smile at the boy still holding the book. "In a minute, Charles." He kneeled next to the wheelchair and pointed at me. "This is my sister, Sam, and her friend, Paul."

"Husband," I cried.

Angelo rose, his eyes wide. "You're married." He patted Paul on the back and grinned. "I knew it."

His gaze wandered to Poppi who'd discovered a doll wearing a hospital gown and was trying to undress her.

"This is Poppi," I hurried. "Our daughter."

"I didn't know you had a daughter."

I smiled at the tall man, so strange and yet so familiar. "She is now." Paul's hand patted my back.

"You want to play with my dolly," Poppi could be heard. She held out her find to the boy who nodded in return. "You're her daddy and I'm the mommy."

"Already giving orders," Paul chuckled.

But my attention had returned to my brother. I couldn't take it any longer. "What are you doing here, Angelo? I was so worried."

Angelo, throwing a glance at the children and being assured they were entertained, grasped my hands. "I'm so sorry. I wanted to…I couldn't. Not after what happened…I…"

He helplessly looked at Paul.

"Not long after he got here, Angelo had a terrible accident," Paul said. "He was running a load at night. It was raining and his truck lost control. He hit a woman and her child walking home." Paul squeezed Angelo's shoulder. "The mother died and her little boy got gravely injured. Angelo threw his load from the truck and took the boy to the hospital."

"Ever since I've been taking Charles to his treatments," Angelo said quietly, his eyes full of tears. "He's got nobody. Not after I…"

I nodded slowly. Angelo had taken the life of an innocent woman and grown silent. Riddled with guilt, he'd tried to atone for his actions. Not to hurt me, but because he had a soft heart and seen no other way.

Angelo rubbed my hand. "I couldn't return. It was my fault… I'd been drinking." His chin quivered. "The police were investigating and called it vehicular homicide. They were searching for witnesses." He looked at me, his eyes pleading. "I couldn't risk anything. I had to take care of the boy."

I gazed at the two kids playing like old friends, then at my brother. He'd wanted to save Charles just like I'd wanted to save Poppi.

"When we met in jail, Angelo had been caught trespassing at the hospital where Charles was staying," Paul said. "He was never in a brawl like he told me."

"I quit the bootlegging business and I quit drinking. Went to work in the shipyard," Angelo continued. "I didn't care if Remus was furious." He turned to Paul. "How did you know?"

"After we met at *Larry's Diner* and you didn't return, I hired a private investigator." Paul looked at me. "It took a while, but I found out earlier this week that Angelo is at the hospital several times a week." Behind us, Poppi was instructing Charles how to hold the doll to his chest. "I thought we could all go home together," he said. "I need help in the company, a man I can trust. The house is far too large for three anyway. And Poppi could use a playmate."

He grinned at my brother and me—the woman he loved.

Wordlessly, Angelo and I threw our arms around him.

AUTHOR NOTES

Prohibition

The U.S. prohibition (1920-1933) introduced by the Volstead Act is one of the most interesting eras in U.S. history, an example of profound government policy failure. The introduction of the eighteenth amendment forbade the production, transportation, importation and sale of alcoholic beverages. But human beings are creative and resent laws that are overly restrictive. *Drys*, how the non-drinkers were called, had completely underestimated not only the thirst of the masses, but the creative energy these drinkers would expend to wet their throats.

Instead of stopping the consumption of alcohol—except at the very beginning—prohibition allowed the rise of opportunists, namely the likes of Alphonse (Al) Gabriel Capone and George Remus. Both make short appearances in this novel. Without this disastrous law, likely neither man would've attained this level of wealth or fame. Much violence may have been avoided.

There is also the matter of corruption, a widespread problem during prohibition. Corruption reached the highest levels of government, police, city officials and judges and paved the way for nearly unchecked crime by a few wealthy and powerful men. Nobody with any sort of influence was safe from being approached and silenced—one way or another.

Al Capone came to power with the help of his friend and mentor, Johnny Torrio. After Torrio fell victim to a near fatal assassination attempt, Capone assumed Torrio's extensive business interests. Within a short time he took over Cicero, one of Chicago's west side neighborhoods. With the help of Chicago Mayor William Hale Thompson and the city's police departments, Capone ran saloons, clubs, speakeasies, gambling parlors and brothels and supplied them with liquor brought in from Canada and New York.

It made him rich. In 1930 he was worth 100 million dollars, about 1.3 billion dollars in 2018 adjusted for inflation. Al Capone was a ruthless killer, but he also took care of many unfortunates and donated generously to charities. This 'soft' side earned him the respect of many Chicago citizens.

When prohibition hit, George Remus was a pharmacist and a lawyer. He soon watched his criminal clients grow rich and decided to get his share. By selling alcohol for medicinal purposes through pharmacies, he effectively circumvented the law and became the 'King of Bootlegging.' By moving to Cincinnati, he placed himself within reach of eighty percent of the nation's whiskey supplies.

In 1925 he was convicted to two years in federal prison for violating the Volstead Act. After learning that Remus's wife, Imogene, had full control of her husband's money, an undercover agent began an affair with Imogene. Together, the adulterous couple hid Remus's capital and sold his holdings. He was left with one hundred dollars.

When Imogene filed for divorce in 1927, Remus shot her dead and then defended himself in court, pleading temporary insanity. He was acquitted. Like Capone, Remus, who referred to himself in the third person, was generous to his guests and the needy.

As always the limelight of my story does not belong to the mob or the wealthy, it falls on a regular girl experiencing the unjust and harsh life so often reserved for penniless women. The other voice belongs to a young hobo, one of hundreds of thousands traveling the country in search of work. Of course, this particular hobo has a secret past which turns out to be a huge burden. Both must overcome the challenges of their worlds and rise above, finding love in the process.

ABOUT THE AUTHOR

Thank you for reading *Where the Night Never Ends*. My sincere hope is that you derived as much entertainment from reading this story as I enjoyed in creating it. If you have a few moments, please feel free to add your review of the book at your favorite online site for feedback (Amazon, Apple iTunes Store, Barnes & Noble, Kobo, Goodreads, etc.). Also, if you would like to connect with previous or upcoming books, please visit my website www.annetteoppenlander.com for information and to sign up for e-news.

All the best, Annette

Contact Me

I always appreciate hearing from readers. Please contact me via the following social media channels:

Website: www.annetteoppenlander.com
Facebook: www.facebook.com/annetteoppenlanderauthor
Twitter: @aoppenlander
Pinterest: @annoppenlander

Bio

Annette Oppenlander is an award-winning writer, literary coach and educator. As a bestselling historical novelist, Oppenlander is known for her authentic characters and stories based on true events, coming alive in well-researched settings. Having lived in Germany the first half of her life and the second half in various parts of the U.S., Oppenlander inspires readers by illuminating story questions as relevant today as they were in the past. Oppenlander's bestselling true WWII story, Surviving the Fatherland, has received multiple honors, including the 2017 National Indie Excellence Awards, the Indie B.R.A.G. awards and the Readers' Favorite Book Awards. It was also finalist in the 2017 Kindle Book Awards.

Her historical time-travel trilogy, Escape from the Past, takes readers to the German Middle Ages and the Wild West. Uniquely, Oppenlander weaves actual historical figures and events into her plots, giving readers a flavor of true history while enjoying a good story. Oppenlander shares her knowledge through writing workshops at colleges, libraries and schools. She also offers vivid presentations and author visits. The mother of fraternal twins and a son, she recently moved with her husband and old mutt, Mocha, to Solingen, Germany.

"Nearly every place holds some kind of secret, something that makes history come alive. When we scrutinize people and places closely, history is no longer a date or number, it turns into a story."

If you enjoyed *Where the Night Never Ends*, you may also like my #1 bestselling novel, Surviving the Fatherland: A True Coming-of-age Love Story Set in WWII Germany. Winner of multiple Book Awards, this novel took fifteen years to complete and is based on my parents growing up as war children in WWII Germany.

Made in the USA
Columbia, SC
20 May 2019